EXPOSING JUSTICE

JUSTICE TEAM SERIES

MISTY EVANS
ADRIENNE GIORDANO

ALG PUBLISHING

EXPOSING JUSTICE

As a Public Information officer for the US Supreme Court, Hope Denby knows how to spin a story. A journalist at heart, she loves being in the middle of a juicy scoop and has her sights set on future Press Secretary for the White House. When the Supreme Court Chief Justice is accidentally killed in a road rage accident, and a high-profile conspiracy blogger claims it was premeditated murder, Hope has to shut down the paranoid blogger—which should be a slam dunk until she discovers he's not as crazy as she thought and she has more in common with the secretive, hard-hitting investigator then she'd like to admit.

Cyber resistance against government corruption isn't just a theory for Brice Brennan on his blog, The First Amendment Patriot. As a former ATF agent who blew the whistle on his superiors, he's no stranger to government cover-ups and scandals. An anonymous tip on the Chief Justice's death sends him searching for answers. What he finds is a sexy, young idealist about to blow his private, behind-the-scenes world to pieces.

Brice and Hope couldn't be more opposite, but exposing justice makes them partners—and puts them on the track of a ruthless killer. As their investigation takes them into the dark underbelly of Washington politics and murder-for-hire, it also takes them into the bedroom where passion erupts and emotional walls crumble. But when the killer makes an attempt on Hope's life, will Brice be able to keep her safe? Or will blowing the whistle on corruption and greed mean losing the one person he's allowed himself to love?

PROLOGUE

"*I*'m hit."

Chief Justice Raymond Turner lay on the cold cement spanning the Gaynor Bridge and stared up at the late March sky. The brilliant blue, a blue so pure with only a few fluffy clouds destroying its perfection, seemed contrived, painted with an artist's brush.

But, goddammit, his chest hurt.

Someone to his left—Tony—shouted something about a shooter. Then came a scream. A woman this time and Tony demanding she quiet down.

If his chest didn't hurt so damned much, Raymond would have laughed.

He pressed his hand against the wool of his coat where warm blood seeped. Despite the thick material, a slick, oily texture that he'd always hated coated his fingers. Pain ricocheted—*goddamn*—and needing oxygen, he inhaled the coppery smell of his own blood.

I'm dying.

Inside his shoes, those ridiculously expensive shoes Marie insisted on buying, his toes tingled and he wiggled them. Hope-

I

fully wiggled them. All he knew for sure, dictated by the numbness in his extremities, was that his blood was draining fast.

He inhaled again, sparking a string of rapid breaths and as much as he tried, he couldn't even them out, balance the short ones with the long ones. No matter his strength of mind, his body was in charge.

Blue sky. Amazing. Good day to die.

Tony's big head appeared over him, blocking the view and pissing Raymond off. If he was heading to his Maker, he wanted that goddamned blue sky, not Tony's giant head. But his day driver, a member of the Supreme Court Police force, was a good lad, always wanting to please.

How did I get here?

He'd received a number of death threats, no surprise there. But bleeding out on a bridge? This would be his legacy.

"Sir!" Tony said. "Help is on the way."

Too late for that.

Some things were inherent. Sleep. Hunger. Bowel movements. Instinctively one knew when it was time.

Apparently death was no different.

All around voices and car horns blended, the sounds shrill and irritating—crime scene—but that sky?

Spectacular.

Tony disappeared from his view, probably not far off. The boy understood the rigors of a protection detail and wouldn't leave his charge. Under any circumstances. Even for a psycho shooting innocent people.

"Clear that path!" Tony's voiced boomed.

Being a Supreme Court Justice had never put Raymond in the midst of a crime scene. He'd only experienced crime from the bench. Or the prosecutor's table. Something to be thankful for he supposed.

How ironic. Or just plain stupid. All the murderers he'd prosecuted and then, later, sentenced, some to death, and here he was, dying on a gridlocked bridge after a road rage argument.

"Tony? Shooter?"

"Don't worry about it, sir. Help is here. Coming up the bridge now."

Tony's piss-poor attempt to deflect Raymond's thoughts was fairly typical of the man. But if he was dying on this goddamned bridge in this goddamned frigid cold he wanted to know who the son of a bitch was. "Got...away?"

"Sir, please."

An enormous pressure landed on the center of his chest, the pain ruthless and agonizing and the icy numbness in his right foot expanded to his leg. "Hurts."

"You got hit in the chest, sir. My hand is on it."

"Well, don't do that."

At that, Tony laughed. Even dying, Raymond could get the kid to laugh. He joined in, the sound phlegmy and nothing he ever wanted to hear come out of his own body. But hell, he was dying. He glanced down at his chest where Tony continued to hold his hands over the wound as oily blood stained his hands. *My blood.* Raymond's vision blurred and he blinked.

What was I saying?

"Tony, we're going to be late for church."

Is it Sunday?

Raymond closed his eyes, tried to focus his scattered thoughts. He knew what this was. Years of listening to testimony had taught him that when dying, chemical imbalances in the body led to decreased blood flow to the brain. Decreased blood flow equaled confusion.

"Bless me Father, for I have sinned..."

"Sir," Tony said, "knock it off."

"I'm dying."

"No, sir. You are not. It's shock. Help is on the way. Please, sir. Just shut the hell up. Focus on slowing your breathing. Hey! Back away. Unless you're a doctor."

Raymond opened his eyes, saw Tony directing his harshest, most brutal stare off to the right. For five years, Tony had been leveling that stare on anyone who dared to annoy his protectee. Barely thirty, the man had become a second son to Raymond. Maybe more of a son. Considering Raymond the third despised his father. Tony, though, this boy knew loyalty.

And how to give it.

"Thank you, Tony."

"Sir, shut up."

Raymond patted his hand still applying pressure to his chest. "It's okay, son. I'm okay."

A siren wailed. Maybe luck would be with him today. Maybe he'd walk home to his wife, call his son and tell him he loved him. Maybe.

Church today.

"Clear that path!" Tony demanded, his voice shaking but still showing his normal commanding resolve.

The cold spread from Raymond's legs into his torso and he shivered against it. Willed his coat to do it's damned job. Fucking coat cost five hundred dollars and it couldn't do its job?

Or maybe it wasn't the coat. If he was dying, he'd gotten ripped off. No bright lights, no angels waving him home. None of that. Just a paralyzing cold on a sunny March day.

He glanced up at the sky again, took in the puffs of clouds, drew a deep rattling breath. *Our Father, who art in heaven...*

1

*B*rice Brennan sat alone at his computer watching a blinking cursor. He needed a story. A kick-ass story that no one else had.

And time was running out.

It was only three o'clock in the afternoon, yet he sat in the dark, courtesy of his blackout curtains. Today's blog had to be up by nine. Fifty-five thousand and sixty-three fans, and six new advertisers, were waiting for it. After he'd exposed the United States' deputy attorney general and the ATF's collaboration on a gunwalking scandal recently, his readership had exploded.

His readers wanted scandal. Real journalism, not sugarcoated updates running ad nauseam or ratings-whoring gossip passed off as investigative reporting.

Tick-tock.

Brice tapped his thumb against his desktop. Three big news stories had flooded the blogosphere today. Each held potential for him, but none yet had generated any calls from his covert, and oftentimes dissident, sources.

Knowledge was power. Once he hit on a story, he became engrossed in it. He wouldn't let it go until he exposed the truth.

As if summoned by his sheer desperation, his phone rang—the private tip line running through his computer. Brice's pulse jumped. This could be it. The tip he was waiting for.

"'The duty of a true patriot is to protect his country from its government.' This is Hawkeye. Go."

The Thomas Paine quote was his motto and what he founded the blog on. He recorded all his tip calls through the computer, which meant all of them ran through the speakers since he never used headphones. When you were always alone, what did you need headphones for?

"Hawkeye, this is Lodestone."

Lodestone was a government employee who seemed to enjoy being Brice's informant. He'd never said as much, but Brice knew the type. Knew the man had connections Brice could only dream of, and best of all, Lodestone never asked for money. "Go ahead, Lodestone. I'm listening."

"I have information about the death of Chief Justice Raymond Turner."

A spurt of adrenaline shot through Brice's limbs. "The road rage accident?"

"It's no coincidence that he got held up on that bridge." A pause—Lodestone deciding how much he could share? "A sensitive case was on the docket for Turner to decide whether the Supreme Court would hear it or not. Look into it. You never know what you might find."

The line went dead.

Brice disconnected and stared blankly at the screen. If Turner's death wasn't an accident...

The screensaver had appeared on his computer. The Patriot Blog's logo of an eagle. He tapped a key to wake the computer up, ready to start digging, when three loud knocks on his door interrupted him.

The first three were followed by a single knock.

Brice hung his head.

The coded knocks meant only one thing.

The Justice Team had arrived.

Maybe if he didn't respond, they'd go away.

"Open up, Brennan," Justice "Grey" Greystone called from the other side.

Brice swore under his breath. If he played possum, pretended he wasn't even there, Grey would...

"Or I'll have Mitch pick the locks. Either way, we're coming in."

How long was this going to go on?

Jumping up from his office chair, he hustled to the door, unlocked the three deadbolts and doorknob, and cracked the door open two inches.

"I'm not interested, Grey," he told the leader of the Justice Team standing on his front porch looking like the Federal agent he used to be. Dark clothes, fake smile. Batman in his Bruce Wayne persona. "We've already had this discussion. Six times by my count."

The weak smile on Grey's lips struggled to stay in place. The man never smiled unless his fiancé was in spitting distance. He was trying to appear friendly and inviting. Mostly, he looked constipated.

"There are perks." Grey glanced at Mitch, aka, Robin, and nodded.

When all else fails, go to your wingman.

"Like what?" Brice asked, chewing on the side of his thumbnail. "Being shot at? Having to send your girlfriend undercover as a stripper? Oh, yeah, that sounds better than medical insurance and vacation days." He switched his gaze to Robin. "Oh, and how about being framed for your best friend's murder? It's hard to top that as a perk."

Grey's hard eyes turned to pure steel. Although the Justice

MISTY EVANS & ADRIENNE GIORDANO

Team's past operations had all ended successfully, each one had put the members in extreme situations where things could have gone south in a hurry. Brice had been in on one of them in New Mexico with Mitch and his girlfriend, Caroline. Brice was lucky he was still breathing. They were all lucky they weren't in jail.

Mitch grinned and shoved his way inside. His coat was unzipped and it fell open to reveal a T-shirt that read, *I put the Hot in psychotic*. He took up residence in Brice's leather recliner with a big plop and Grey followed. "Jesus it's dark in here. Are you a vampire or something, Brice?" He didn't wait for an answer. "As far as perks, you get to look at my handsome face every day, Brice buddy. Best. Perk. Ever."

Psychotic did not begin to describe Mitch Monroe. Brice left the door ajar and went back to his chair. He didn't like people in his space. Especially not Batman and Robin. "I'm sure Caroline enjoys that, but it takes more than a pretty face to make me want to give up my blog."

"You don't have to give up your blog, right, Grey?" Mitch nodded without waiting for his boss to agree. "Investigating conspiracies is exactly what we want you to continue doing."

Cyber resistance against government corruption wasn't just a theory for Brice. *The First Amendment Patriot* blog was his life. While he valued his privacy and didn't like to call attention to himself, he had a strong internal sense of right and wrong and had no trouble blowing the whistle on corrupt politicians and government agencies. Others appreciated what he did. Donations to the blog paid his bills and he cared little about material wealth or possessions. As long as he kept his lifestyle lean, he'd be fine.

Tick-tock.

Grey didn't look all that happy about Brice keeping his blog. "We have nine open cases right now that involve crooked politicians, lobbyists, and potential cover-ups. Your skills and contacts would help tremendously."

Flattery. Grey was pulling out all the stops this round.

Brice's ego did indeed like it, too. He was damn good at running his blog, and he'd once enjoyed being part of a task-force. Lived for his job as an undercover ATF agent. The commendations in his folder had proven his worth, and the team of men he'd worked with had always had his back. Failure had never entered his mind.

Until his boss—his former partner—and the ATF sent him down in flames. The men he'd been closer to than his three brothers turned on each other.

Those days were over. Lesson learned. *Never trust anyone.*

Facts were more trustworthy than people. Detachment and autonomy were important to doing a good job. Exposing government coverups and bringing dirty cops, politicians, and even heads of the most powerful agencies in the world to heel from the safety of his computer was what he excelled at now.

"I'm no longer a team player." Truer words had never been spoken. Swinging his chair around to emphasize his point, he turned his back on the two men he had let into his personal circle and now regretted. The safety of his computer beckoned. "I just got a lead on a breaking story, and I'm not coming to work for the Justice Team. Show yourselves out, ladies."

Behind him, the leather chair squeaked as Mitch stood. An uncomfortable silence followed, complete with strained murmuring—Batman and Robin trying to figure out their next move.

Let 'em talk.

"What story?" Grey asked.

"Chief Justice Turner. The road rage accident that killed him may not have been an accident at all."

"Murder?" Mitch slapped him on the back. "Make you a deal, Brice, ol' buddy. You join the Justice Team, and I'll help you investigate your lead on Turner."

He was grinning like his offer was an obvious slam-dunk.

Brice stood, grabbed Mitch's arm and hustled him to the door. "I don't need your help, Mitch, *ol' buddy*, and I can investigate Turner's death on my own."

Mostly true. *If* there was anything worth investigating.

Grey stood at the computer, looking at the screen, one hand cupping his chin. "What makes you think Turner's death was murder?"

"I got a tip from a very reliable source." Brice didn't need to prove anything to these men, and yet, the investigator in him liked the credibility. "Claims Turner had a sensitive case on his docket that he was deciding on whether the court would hear it or not. Maybe nothing, but he told me to look into it."

"Sounds far fetched to me. The Chief Justice probably had a long list of possible cases for the Court to hear."

Mitch jerked his arm out of Brice's hand. "Yeah, and every one of the plaintiffs believes their case is sensitive. It's going to take a lot of work to dig into each and every one of them."

A smile—the genuine thing—crept over Grey's face. "How about *I* make you a deal, Brice? We help you get Turner's list and do the digging. Save you a lot of time. If, of course, you help us out with a few of our cases."

He itched to jump on this right away, but he didn't need help. What he needed was for these two to leave him alone. "I'll think about it and let you know my decision in the morning."

Grey seemed unfazed by his delay. "Fair enough."

After Batman and Robin left, Brice dropped back into this chair. A few clicks of his keyboard and he had the phone number for the Public Information Office of the Supreme Court.

He'd do his own investigation, like always. If that lead nowhere, he'd consider Grey's deal.

As the phone rang on the other end, he smiled to himself. Nothing like a good conspiracy to get the adrenaline flowing.

· · ·

"Denby! Get in here!"

Ooh! Hope Denby shot up, sending her rickety government-issued chair sailing against the back of her cubicle. She peeped over the wall in front of her at her cubemate, Rob. "Ohmygod, she's insane today."

Rob didn't bother looking up from whatever he was reading on his computer. "Seriously fucking deranged. You'd better get in there."

Because experience dictated she had thirty-point-two seconds to appear in front of her boss or she'd be bellowed at once again.

"Coming!"

Hope scooped up her legal pad and a pen and hustled to the boss's office just twenty-five feet away. Working at the Public Information Office of the U.S. Supreme Court meant each day brought something new. It could be working with reporters wanting to cover a case, preparing transcripts, or press releases, all of it fascinating and tedious and ripe with possibilities.

Today was no different. Eight hours earlier, the Chief Justice of the U.S. Supreme Court had been accidently gunned down on the Gaynor Bridge while trying to resolve a road rage dispute.

And now, it was all over the news and her boss, Amy Ripling, the Public Information Officer, had been in full-blown crisis mode all day.

"Denby!" Amy screamed again.

Hope kicked off her sky-high heels, left them sitting in the corridor—no time to stop—and picked up her pace. She swung around the doorway, grabbing the frame to slow her down. "I'm here. Sorry."

Amy sat at her desk, random files and papers and notes strewn across the top. Two ringing cell phones sat on top of the mess joined by the incessant beeping of the desk phone. Amy picked up the handset, tapped the hold button and handed

Hope a note. "Call this guy. He's bugging the shit out of me and I'm trying to deal with the networks."

She glanced down at the name. The First Amendment Patriot. Interesting. But, woohoo! Finally, her boss ponied up an assignment on a major case, albeit a tragic one. "Yes, ma'am. Who is he?"

"He's a blogger."

A *blogger.*

The Journalism major in her wailed.

"Damned, bloggers. I am *on* it, Amy."

"I knew you'd love it. You're an animal, Denby."

"Thank you. I think."

Amy waved it away. "Yada, yada. He wants a statement, but be careful. He's one of the those conspiracy theory nutcases. Tell him something that won't hurt us. Until we have more on what happened on that bridge, we're going with what we know."

"Sure. But—"

Amy glanced at the still beeping phone, *beep-beep-beep,* then came back to Hope, her taut skin barely restraining her impatience. "What, Denby? *What?*"

Ignoring Amy's tone, she stood a little straighter. "Yes, ma'am. What is it exactly that we know?"

All day long, Hope, like everyone else in the office, had been monitoring the news channels to see who was saying what. For their part, the Public Information Office had released very few details. Mainly because they'd been given very few details.

The police and the FBI were handling the press on this nightmare.

"What *we* know," Amy said, "is that the Chief Justice and his security detail, consisting of one Supreme Court police officer, were en route to work today and got stuck in a traffic jam on the bridge. The FBI is looking into that. Apparently, there's some confusion as to why that lane was closed. They're talking to DDOT. Anyway, two cars ahead of the Chief Justice some whacko jumped out of a cab and started arguing with the driver of the car next to them. The argument became heated and the judge's officer got out to diffuse the situation. Justice Turner— God rest his soul—defied his security officer's order to stay in the car and got out to see if he could help. While the officer tried to convince the judge to get his ass back in the car, the guy who jumped out of the cab fired a gun; the shot missed and accidentally hit the judge. The shooter ran. That's what we know. But you're not telling our blogger friend that. For him, you're keeping it simple. Road rage, two men arguing, gunshot. D.C. Metro and the SC police are handling it from here."

"Got it. No problem."

"Good. I'm heading into a meeting with the Justices. I'm guessing it'll be a while. Make sure everyone knows they should only disturb me if the building is on fire. Or someone else is dead."

Ew. "I'll handle it."

She spun toward the door.

"Denby?"

"Yes?"

"Where the hell are your shoes?"

Hope pointed over her left shoulder. "In the hallway. They were slowing me down. I didn't want to irritate you."

"Ah. That's what I like about you. You're good on the fly. Now get rid of this goddamned blogger. Bloggers we don't need."

"Yes, ma'am."

She hit the hallway, found her shoes in the exact spot she left them as people stepped over them in a rush to get to wherever they were heading. How insane were the people she worked with that no one questioned a pair of shoes, wickedly pretty shoes, sitting in the middle of the floor?

Craziness.

She slipped her shoes back on and swung into her cubicle. Of all the assignments she could have gotten, a blogger wasn't on her wish list. Bloggers were trouble. They had the freedom to write whatever they wanted. To be careless. To say "oops" when they screwed up. Fact check, people! Second sources, people!

Well, she wouldn't have it.

No pain-in-the-rear blogger would spread unvetted information about a murdered Supreme Court Justice. Not on her watch. She studied journalism for four years and was halfway to earning a Masters and these hacks thought they knew how to report the news?

Forget it. Everything with them was fair game. Off the record didn't exist. At least not in Hope's mind.

She ditched her notepad just as Rob's head appeared over the top of the wall.

"Whatcha got?"

"Blogger." She glanced at the note. "*The First Amendment Patriot.*"

"Shit."

Hope rocked her chair back. "He's that crackpot, isn't he? The one involved with the case against the deputy AG. He's the king of conspiracy theorists."

"That's him. People love him. We're talking cult following." Rob scrunched his face and made a tight fist, squeezing until his veins and knuckles popped. "Balls of steel, this guy. He outs the ATF like they're a bunch of toddlers. I want to be him when I grow up."

Okay. So maybe that fearless thing was impressive, but she didn't trust him or any other blogger. She'd deal with it lickety-split before he sent something viral.

Stabbing the buttons on her desk phone, she dialed the number on the note Amy had given her. "Rob," she said, "do me a favor. Make sure everyone knows Amy is in a meeting with the Justices. She said, and this is a direct quote, not to disturb her unless the building is on fire or someone else is dead."

"Ew," Rob said, echoing Hope's earlier thought. "How incredibly tacky."

Tacky. That was one word for it.

On the other end of the line, the ringing stopped and Hope dropped into her chair, receiving the usual squeak.

"'The duty of a true patriot is to protect his country from its government.' This is Hawkeye. Go."

Hawkeye! Dear God.

"Hello, Mr. Hawkeye." *Mr.* Hawkeye? Whatever. "This is Hope Denby from the Supreme Court Public Information Office."

"Finally," he said. "I've been calling you people for hours."

Hope rolled her eyes. A Supreme Court Justice—the *Chief* Justice—was dead and the blogger had issues because they hadn't returned his call earlier? "Well, guy, kinda busy here. What can I do for you?"

"I received a tip regarding Turner."

That earned him a second award-winning eye roll he couldn't see. "I'm sorry, we're not commenting on it at this time. We've released information and it can be found on our website."

Gotta go. Buh-bye. She shook her mouse to bring her computer out of sleep mode and scanned the latest emails.

"Yeah," he said. "I got that. Didn't help. My source said it's no coincidence that Turner got stuck on that bridge."

Hope stopped scanning. Did he say...? She abandoned the mouse and picked up her pen because crackpot or not, this blogger had just referenced the lane closing the FBI was looking into. "Wait. What?"

"That got your attention. The Chief was about to deliver a ruling on whether or not a landmark case got a hearing."

It sure did get her attention. Particularly when he was insinuating the Chief Justice had been assassinated due to a ruling. "Mr. Hawkeye—"

"Just Hawkeye. No mister."

"Fine. *Hawkeye*. I have no comment on that. It was an unfortunate and tragic road rage incident and the police are doing everything they can to apprehend the shooter. Whatever the judge's ruling would have been, we'll never know. Obviously, you cannot quote me on that."

And now she should shut up. She'd already gone off script and with her luck this Hawkeye character would bury her with it.

"Quote you on what? You didn't give me anything."

"Check the website. We've released everything we have."

"Ms. Denby, you do realize I'm going to run with what I have if you don't give me something."

"Mr.—"

"No mister."

"Hawkeye." *Whatever.* "Who is your source of this information?"

She didn't expect he'd tell her. Any reputable journalist wouldn't. Maybe she was testing him. Maybe not. Either way, trying to identify his source wouldn't hurt.

His chuckle was low and deep. "Ms. Denby, did someone hit you in the head with a two-by-four? I'm not telling you my source."

For a split second, she smiled. That two-by-four line was a good one. She'd maybe use it herself some time. Bonus, he'd passed one test. That got him a rung up on the credibility ladder. The chuckle gave her a couple of goose bumps. Not more than two or three, but still. His voice had a definitely goose-bump-inducing quality.

"One moment please."

She punched the hold button and hopped up to peer over the cubicle wall.

Without a glance up from whatever he was working on, Rob pursed his lips and slowly moved his head back and forth. "You gotta get rid of this guy. He's totally playing you."

Voices from her right closed in and she waited for two of her co-workers to pass. "I know," she said, keeping her voice low. "But he got a tip that Turner might have been assassinated because he was about to rule on a hearing for an important case."

"Shit."

"Amen to that. Still want me to get rid of him?"

"Even more so, but—" Rob flopped his lip out as he considered her question, "what are we categorizing as landmark? This is the Supreme Court. Could be anything."

"Dang it."

"What?"

"I don't know."

Rob laughed. "Okay."

She sat back down, took a deep breath. She could do this. No blogger would bring her down, even one with a sexy voice and dangerous sounding chuckle. She'd get rid of him and quietly poke around about cases the Chief Justice might have been about to grant hearings on. Easy-peasy. If nothing else, she'd blow this crazy conspiracy theory—and Mr. Hawkeye— out of the universe. Just blow them both to bits.

Easy.

Peasy.

Still standing, she punched the button again. "Let me call you back."

"I'm so looking forward to it." The sarcasm in his voice hinted that that was a lie. "When?"

"I guess that depends on when I have information, doesn't it?"

MISTY EVANS & ADRIENNE GIORDANO

"Uh, no."

"No?"

"I'll give you until 8:00 PM. After that, I piece together what I have and run with the story."

Great. Threats. "But you don't have a story. That's why you called me."

Another chuckle, and yep, a couple more goose bumps rose on her skin. This time in the area right under her ear as if his lips had just made a trail there. And hello? They had a situation here and she was fantasizing about a *blogger*?

"I have enough to write a post planting the idea that the Chief Justice was murdered over more than road rage."

Dammit. Eight o'clock. She tapped the mouse again and bent over to check the clock on her computer. Four hours to figure out what case may or may not have gotten a Supreme Court Justice murdered.

"Eight p.m., Ms. Denby. Please don't let me down. I'm out."

She straightened, throwing her shoulders back. "Wait."

The line went dead. Well, the line went dead after the extremely loud click. He hung up on her. *Balls!* She dropped into her chair and sent the usual annoying squeak echoing through the cubicle. Stupid chair. Feet planted on the faux wood mat that allowed her to roll her chair within the cube, she shoved off. Momentum carried her into the corridor where she could see Rob.

"Comin' in hot." Cliff Cody walked by, swerving to avoid a collision.

"Sorry, Cliff."

From inside his cube, Rob spun to face her. "Don't even tell me you're gonna get into this. Company line, Hope. That's it. Until Crazy Pants Amy gives us something else to distribute, it's company line."

Forget that. Sort of. She couldn't get too aggressive on this thing or her butt would wind up with a major spanking and the potential loss of her career. But something told her this Hawkeye wasn't going away. And given his success on the case against the deputy AG a few months back, he had—God save her—credibility on his side. Oh, she could see it now, the *blogger* writing a column about how the now deceased Chief Justice planned on denying a hearing on some big case the same day he was gunned down.

The Internet would explode.

People would tweet and retweet and post and share and within an hour the Public Information Office would be doing major spin control.

She glanced down the hall to Amy's office where just minutes before her boss had told her she wasn't to be disturbed.

Hawkeye had only given her four hours.

She went back to Rob. "I have until eight o'clock or he's running with what he has. So, I can sit around wasting time until Amy is available, then ask permission to pursue this."

Again Rob slowly moved his head left and right in his signature move. "Hope—"

"—or I can start gathering info, just background stuff, and be ready when Amy comes out of her meeting." Hopefully before eight o'clock. With a dead Chief Justice, what were the chances of that? "Rob, you yourself said the guy has a cult-like following. I need to debunk this."

He laughed. One of those sarcastic you-have-lost-your-mind laughs. "Good luck to you then because I'm not touching it. No way, sister." He pulled himself back to his desk. "All I know is I want your desk when you get your ass fired. You've got an end unit."

"Oh, ha-ha."

"Seriously, what are you gonna do?"

She rose from her chair, entered Rob's cube and leaned

close enough so she wouldn't be overheard. "Relax. I'll just chat with one of Turner's clerks."

"Which one?"

"Bigley. He has the loosest lips."

This she knew from rumors and her general snooping and digging around about the court staffers. A little research for her files for emergencies—like now—never hurt.

"Oh. My. *God!*" Rob said, his voice sotto voce but total drama queen. "There is no way a clerk will comment."

"I guess we'll see about that, won't we?"

2

Each year, out of somewhere around one thousand applicants, thirty-six of the country's youngest and brightest legal minds were awarded the coveted position of Supreme Court law clerk. The nine justices typically chose four clerks each. Those clerks were required to prepare the justices for hearings, do research, draft opinions and make recommendations on which cases might be presented.

They were also forbidden to discuss their work. In any way. At least until the justice retired.

Or died.

That dying thing might have been Hope's only chance to break Joel Bigley.

She'd just stepped out of a cab after being stuck in the evening rush on Dupont Circle and thought perhaps it might be a good time in her life to find another city to live in. One devoid of traffic jams and cab drivers that leered at her while stuck in said traffic jams. Montana maybe? There she'd find a hot rancher wearing a cowboy hat and studly boots. If she got really lucky he'd make her holler yee-haw after her fifth orgasm.

Orgasm? What was that? It had been so long since she'd had one, a male generated one anyway, she might need a refresher course.

Cowboy boots and orgasms.

A girl could dream.

Standing in the crisp spring air that was moist with the threat of rain, she double-checked the address on the apartment building. Right place.

A doorman spotted her gazing up at the building and wandered over. "Can I help you?"

"Yes. Hello. I'm here to see Joel Bigley. Apartment 3C."

"Yes, ma'am. Is he expecting you?"

"No, sir. I work with him."

Stretch the truth much? Nah. But she'd just spent hours storming the halls of the Supreme Court trying to find Joel Bigley, all the while leaving voicemail after voicemail. She'd even tried the other three clerks who worked for Justice Turner and managed to run into one of them in the hallway, but he was with another man and the clerk couldn't spare her even a minute. She'd managed to finagle a promise to call from him.

And, yes, she was still waiting.

With the definite lack of ringing phone from any of Turner's clerks, she'd basically hacked—well, called in a favor from—Amy's assistant who had access to all sorts of interesting files and really should work for the CIA. In five minutes Amy had done her magic and supplied Hope with Joel Bigley's home address.

Hope then sat in traffic for forty minutes. Right now, with seventy-five minutes until the Hawkeye deadline, if she knew nothing else, she knew she needed to get through this doorman.

"I'll ring him, but I haven't seen him arrive yet."

"Well, darn." She reached into her purse-slash-briefcase and pulled out one of the files she'd shoved in there to work on when she got home. Right now it would make the perfect prop. "I need to give him this file."

Another lie, but heck, she seemed to be on a roll so why not?

The doorman held his hand out. "You could leave it with me."

"Thank you, but I'm not allowed. It's confidential." She bit her bottom lip, scrunched her face together in her best sad-girl-woe-is-me look. Being a petite blonde and batting her eyes didn't hurt either. "Just shoot." She sighed. "My boss will *kill* me if I don't deliver this."

"Oh, honey." the doorman said.

Yes, my love, come to me.

"Don't get upset. Let me give him a ring. I have his cell number in our files." He winked. "I'd say this is an emergency."

Putty.

In.

Her.

Hands.

She offered up a grateful smile. "It sure is. Thank you *so* much."

Hope pushed through the revolving door of the Corner Tap, a place known to locals for their fancy martinis and young up-and-coming crowd. Singles flocked to the place in hopes of meeting Mr. or Mrs. Right, who also happened to have a Master's or law degree. Yep. This was the place to get hooked up, in whatever fashion necessary, with a future CEO.

Or a Supreme Court Justice law clerk.

The bar was packed, the noise level ear-shatter worthy from all the different voices mingling together. Music played in the background, but for as loud as the place was, the music only served as an annoyance. She focused straight ahead and her skin began to itch at the thought of shoving through the crowd lined four deep at the bar. She glanced left where a single row of tables extended to the back wall of the long, narrow building. At best, those tables were built for three people. Four if they were midgets like Hope. From what she could see, every table had a least five people crammed into it.

Which meant she'd definitely be bumping bodies trying to squeeze through. Chances were, she wouldn't escape without some pig copping a feel, but a girl had to do what a girl had to do.

"I'm going in," she muttered.

Halfway down the bar, she'd managed to not get groped as she reached a group of twenty-something guys about to slam a shot home.

And...hello Joel Bigley. She'd never met him in person, but she'd seen enough photos of him to know, without a doubt, this was him. For one, he had the dark-haired, sexy looks that could have put him on the cover of GQ if his law career went bust.

Given that he was clerking for the Supreme Court, she didn't anticipate he'd need that GQ gig. By the time his one year commitment to the Court was fulfilled, he'd have the nation's top law firms wooing him with six figure jobs and a signing bonus that could top $200,000.

I should have been a brilliant law clerk.

Nah. The money would be great, but she had a taste for something different. Something like the White House. And not as President.

She stopped behind Joel and tapped him on the shoulder. He turned and his dark eyes met hers. A little glassy. Hmmm...she'd have to be careful here. What she didn't want was to take advantage of an inebriated law clerk. Had she been a journalist chasing a story for her next column—or a lawless blogger like Mr. Hawkeye—she'd go for the kill, maybe even buy him a few more cocktails to get him talking a little more.

Not now though. They were, after all, on the same team and part of her wanted to smack him for being fool enough to be out drinking the same day his boss had gotten killed on a bridge. *Dumbass.*

"Hey, gorgeous."

He roamed his gaze over her in an appreciative I-will-give-you-the-orgasm-you-so-desperately-need look. If only he wore a cowboy hat and boots.

"Hi. And I'm not 'Gorgeous', I'm Hope. Your doorman called you about me."

"Oh, right. The *delivery*." Again, he eyeballed her up and down, his eyes dragging over her boobs. "What's this *delivery*?"

And right then she decided that no, she would not let him slide for the 'gorgeous' comment or assaulting her with his eyes. What did he think? She was a stripper sent into a packed bar. For God's sake!

She jerked her head toward the door. "Can we talk a second?"

A sly grin drifted across his face and her last working nerve dropped dead. Bye-bye.

"Relax, sailor. Whatever you're thinking, this is not about me—or you—getting naked and bumping uglies." Joel's friend coughed up part of his beer and Hope gave his back a few good whacks. "Easy there, pal. You okay?"

"Uh, good," the guy choked out. "Thanks. I think I might love you though."

"Excellent. On both counts." She turned back to Joel. "Let me clarify who I am. I'm Hope Denby from the Public Information Office."

"Shit," Joel said.

"Yeah. Let's head outside for a few minutes."

"Don't leave," Joel's friend said. "I'm serious. I might love you."

Men. But heck, it'd been a rough day and a little playful

banter never hurt a girl. While waiting on Joel to ditch his glass, she spun back to his friend, hit him with her flirtiest smile. "Do you own a cowboy hat and boots?"

"If I need to, I can."

"Wrong answer, handsome." She offered up a little finger wave. "Gotta go. Bye."

Once again, Hope pushed through the crowd with Joel on her heels. She'd even glanced over her shoulder to make sure he hadn't bailed on her. He certainly looked spooked enough and she wasn't taking any chances.

Outside the bar she strode to the corner of the building away from the few folks milling around the front door.

"What's this about?" Joel wanted to know.

"Well, if you'd returned any of my calls from the last three hours you'd know it's about Justice Turner."

Joel leaned against the brick and sighed. "I've had reporters calling me all day. I haven't responded. I swear. You guys told us no contact with the press. I'm sticking to it."

"That's good."

"So why are you hunting me down?"

She eyed him, taking stock of his slightly glassy eyes. "Are you drunk?"

"No."

"Liar."

He shrugged. "I'm working a buzz. Rough day at the office."

"And you think it's wise to be in a bar where any reporter might find you? I found you easily enough by flirting with your doorman."

He boosted off the wall, started walking toward the bar entrance again. "I don't need this. Whatever you want, too bad."

Silly, silly boy. As if she'd let him get away that easily. "Joel, I had a call from a blogger today. He had an interesting tip he wanted to confirm. One intriguing enough to get me to leave the office and find you on a night when my co-workers are probably still working the phones."

Joel stopped walking—*yes, now you've got it*—and turned back to her. "What?"

Refusing to move from her spot, she crooked one finger, urging him back to her. He hesitated a moment, which she found amusing since she didn't have a doubt that he'd give in.

He stopped about a foot from her. "What tip?"

"That's the thing. He didn't have details, but this particular blogger is known for his corruption stories. He can sniff it out like a hound dog on a duck. Some bloggers are careless with their facts. I'm not saying he's not, but from what I've learned today his track record is spot-on. Which means his contacts aren't just good, they're solid as hell."

"And?"

"He claims the Chief Justice was about to make an important ruling. One so critical that what happened on the bridge might have been a setup."

Joel's eyebrows shot up. "Ridiculous. It was road rage. The guy went psycho and when Turner tried to calm him down, he got shot for his troubles."

"That may be it. Frankly, I'm praying it is, because then we'd get rid of this nutty conspiracy theorist."

"I don't want to tell you how to do your job, but maybe you should ignore him."

"And risk him writing a blog post that could go viral and create all sorts of havoc? That's asking for trouble. What I need is to steal his thunder, take the air out of his sails and all that other cliché stuff. What I need from *you* is a list of cases the Chief Justice was reviewing to possibly be heard by the Court and might be important enough that they'd risk killing the Chief Justice if he planned on ruling the wrong way. Any ideas?"

A cell phone rang. Joel's apparently because he dug into his suit pocket and silenced it. "I only work some of the cases."

Silly, silly boy.

The justices split their cases between their four clerks, eliminating the risk of four opinions on each case. By splitting the workload, each clerk took ownership of an individual case and did everything from drafting memos on the legal issues to prepping the justice. In some instances, the clerk wrote the first draft of an opinion and the justice did the editing.

Hope knew all this and Joel knew she knew. Only, she wasn't falling for the idea that he wasn't aware of what other clerks might be working on. Maybe they couldn't talk to outsiders about cases, but they also had access to a private dining hall in the Supreme Court cafeteria. In that dining room, Hope had heard, all the good gossip about what went on in the judge's chambers happened.

"Joel?"

"Yes?"

"Don't con me. I'm a journalist at heart. I know you and your fellow clerks discuss cases and I don't believe, not for one second, you haven't discussed the meaty stuff behind the walls of your private dining room. Now, if there's even a chance Justice Turner was murdered on that bridge, I need to know before someone gets ahead of us on it."

Joel squeezed his eyes closed, blew air through his clenched teeth. "I can't talk about it, but we had a heater of a case. We all wanted it. It's career-making stuff."

As if being a clerk for the Supreme Court wasn't? "Was it Justice Turner's case?"

"Yes, but he didn't assign it to me."

"What case is it?"

Again Joel hesitated and for the first time she wondered if Mr. Loose Lips would actually keep those lips shut. Maybe Rob had his info wrong and Joel wasn't the chattiest of the clerks.

She inched closer to him, met his gaze in the dark where only the neon bar sign threw shadows over the sidewalk. "I've got less than thirty minutes until this blogger starts putting together a post that will cause rampant speculation. That speculation may or may not prompt scrutiny over all of Turner's cases. Including ones you assisted with. You ready for that, Joel?"

He gave her a pained look.

"Thought so," she said. "Tell me the case. I promise you I will not reveal who told me. Not even to my boss. All I need is the name and I'll do the rest."

He straightened, adjusted the sleeves on his coat, buttoned it and turned away.

Dammit. She thought she'd had him. He took two steps and stopped.

"Kenton Labs," he said. "Don't contact me again."

Hope stood on the sidewalk, shivering at the dropping temperature because her lightweight coat was so not the apparel for standing outside on a frigid March night. But she needed to speak to her boss and moving inside or into a cab where she'd be overheard wouldn't do. She'd rather take her chances on the street where she could freely move out of earshot.

She'd tried Amy's office line and her two cell phones, but the only answer she'd received was voice mail. Next she dialed Rob. Without a doubt, he'd still be at his desk. When it came to dedication, they were the rock stars.

He answered on the second ring.

"Rob! Are you at the office?"

"The Chief Justice is dead. Where else would I be?"

Right. Whatever. Dumb question. "I need Amy. ASAP. I tried her office and her cells and she's not picking up."

"She's in another meeting. Gave us the fire or death speech again. What's up?"

Ohmygod. She checked her watch for the thousandth time. Fifteen minutes to deadline. "I can't say specifically, but I think I have a lead on this crazy blogger's tip. I need Amy to sign off on me talking to him or he's going to run what he has. Which can't be much. Or accurate."

"Then call him."

"And say what?"

"I don't know. Tell him something that'll keep him from causing rampant speculation that may or may not be true and may or may not make the stock market crash."

The stock market. Yikes.

"Rob!"

"What?"

She gripped the phone, squeezing so tight the screen should have popped off. Her friend was a drama enthusiast, but he could be right. "I don't know." She checked her watch again. Twelve minutes. "I have to call him and stall. I'll tell him I want to meet. That'll buy us time. Sit on Amy's office. If she gets out of that meeting, tackle her and call me before this blogger creates pandemonium."

3

*F*BI SEEKS TO LEGALLY HACK YOU

Brice hit the return key. Denby had never called him back, and while he'd told her he'd run with the Chief Justice story if she didn't contact him by eight, he really had nothing more than a tip. Not enough to create a full-fledged theory that maintained any sort of credibility.

The other breaking news stories had failed to show promise of any conspiracies, and nine o'clock was quickly approaching. This was the best he could do on such short notice.

It was still a damn good story. One his followers would eat up. A recent tip he'd received from an old friend of Grey's still inside the Federal Bureau of Investigation had put him on the trail. The FBI had quietly requested that the Department of Justice make a change in the Federal Rules of Criminal Procedure dictating how law enforcement agencies had to conduct criminal prosecutions from investigation to trial. The specific rule the FBI was targeting outlined the terms for obtaining a search warrant for computers whose location had been hidden through a technical tool like Tor or a virtual private network.

Like Brice's.

Most of his followers were in the same boat, so this would be a hot topic for them as well. Civil rights and privacy, even in one's own home, had been trampled to death by The Patriot Act. The NSA tracked every wire and every airwave, as the Snowden scandal had revealed.

Not that Brice hadn't seen that coming long before Edward Snowden went public. Homeland and the FBI were simply playing catch-up to the NSA's ability to bring Orwell's *1984* into the twenty-first century.

Another reason he didn't trust anyone. Not the government, not the people in authority, not even his next-door neighbor, Mrs. Tilly. Well, maybe Mrs. Tilly. The widow didn't have a devious bone in her body and made him a tuna casserole once a month.

He finished the article, did a spell check, and scheduled the blog to go live at nine o'clock.

Time for a break.

Thank God Grey's fiancee, Sydney, felt sorry for him like Mrs. Tilly and regularly left food on his doorstep. She respected his privacy—something Grey didn't—and never tried to barge inside his home. For whatever reason, she felt indebted to him. Maybe it was his help on the AG case, but Syd had taken a liking to him, and like Mrs. Tilly, she might even be trustworthy. He grabbed a stack of her delicious Toll House chocolate chip cookies and shoved one in his mouth just as his phone rang.

Not his private cell, his computer phone. Another tip on a story?

Dropping the cookies, he answered with his usual quote and ID.

"Um, hello?" A female voice, soft and nervous drifted from his speakers, half-muffled as if she were trying to keep this quiet. "Mr. Hawkeye? It's me, Hope Denby."

Finally. The brat from the Public Information Office.

She didn't sound as fired up this time. He hit the button on his computer to open his recording software anyway. Maybe she would give him something he could run with. If nothing else, he liked listening to her smoky, but oh-so-innocent sounding voice. No wonder they had her on phone duty...she could make any man—even a die-hard man on a mission like him—forget what he'd called for. "Just Hawkeye, Ms. Denby. Like the comic book hero. Do you have a quote for me?"

"Not exactly."

Brice had spent all evening trying to pin down the list of cases Turner had been prepared to review. He gotten through about half of them before he'd had to quit and get the blog written and posted. "Then why are you calling me?"

"I think I know the case your source was referring to. The one Chief Justice Turner was about to rule on."

"And?"

"Can we meet? I'd rather not discuss this over the phone. It's...sensitive." She heaved a breath that sent his mind swirling in lascivious ways. "I know you're on a deadline. I can come to your office."

Oh, no she couldn't. Still, something made him hesitate. Regardless of the sex on a stick intonation in her voice jacking up his thoughts—and teasing his cock—this was definitely not the confident, flippant information officer he'd talked to earlier in the day.

Hope Denby was freaked out. Freaked out meant there might be something to Lodestone's tip. His pulse quickened. He heard himself repeating Mitch's earlier statement. "I imagine every case that comes before the Supreme Court is considered sensitive. Can you give me more than that?"

"Not over the phone."

She was stubborn. *Turn on the heat.* "I'm on a deadline, Ms. Denby. At least give me something so I know how sensitive this case is."

"Sorry, no can do. Just tell me where your office is, and I'll come right over."

She wasn't taking him seriously. "I don't know what game you're playing, but I don't have time for it."

He hung up. Waited.

The phone rang. He smiled as he answered.

As expected, it was the brat. Her tone was assertive again, and highly annoyed. "Did you just hang up on me?"

He couldn't help it. He smiled to himself. "Look, I realize you have no real interest in helping uncover a conspiracy against the Chief Justice, but I don't appreciate you wasting my time so I miss my deadline."

"I'm not blowing smoke, here, Mr. Hawkeye. I really need to meet with you."

Damn it. The itch he'd felt earlier when Lodestone had called flared to life right under his breastbone. He never met his sources face-to-face. Too dangerous. But he had to know what she'd found out.

He grabbed one of his numerous burn phones from the bottom of his desk drawer. "Give me your cell number."

"Why?"

"What part of D.C. are you in right now?"

"I'm at The Corner Tap near my office."

He knew the place. Knew the young crowd that hung out there and often offered up information on their bosses in a state of inebriation. Not that he would ever go fishing there. Some of his sources might, though, one of them being his hacker buddy, Teeg, who just happened to work for Grey...

Sending Teeg would have been an option if the kid wasn't holed up with the Justice Team on some case.

So why did Brice's intuition tell him to tackle this one on his own?

Not intuition. His goddamn cock was doing the thinking on

this one. He wanted to meet Hope Denby face-to-face to see if her body matched her hot-as-hell voice.

The Corner Tap. Fifteen minutes and he could be there.

But if she actually had information that would point to the Chief Justice being intentionally murdered, the bar was not a safe place for this kind of exchange. Too many surveillance cameras in the area. Too many eyes who would know who she was and who she worked for. "Give me your number and I'll text you in ten minutes with the address of a place to meet."

"What's wrong with the bar? It's public."

She was smart, he'd give her that. "If you want me to meet you to discuss this, Ms. Denby, you'll have to play by my rules. We'll still meet someplace public if that puts your fears to rest."

"There's a Starbucks up the street. Would that be better?"

Lots of college kids coming and going. Hackers stealing personal information from the customers using the Wi-Fi. "How will I know you?"

"I'll be wearing a red scarf."

Red. His favorite color. His mind flashed with all sorts of images of Hope Denby wearing nothing but a red scarf.

He shook his head, clearing the Technicolor porn. "Give me your number just in case."

"In case what?"

So much for thinking she was smart. God, she was either an airhead or too fucking naive for her own good. Since you didn't get to the Supreme Court being an airhead, he assumed the later. "Do you want me to show up or not?"

She rattled off her number, all huffy, her voice sexy even when doing a perfunctory task.

He typed the number into the burn phone's contact app. "I'll be there in twenty minutes."

He hung up before she could argue, which seemed to be her normal mode of operation. Arguing. *Great source you got there, Bri.*

For half a second, he sat frozen watching the clock on his screen. Denby's info could be nothing. Controversial cases came up every day for the Supreme Court and it was up the Chief Justice to decide which ones got heard. Didn't mean a man should die to postpone the decision.

Turner could have simply been a good Samaritan in the wrong place at the wrong time like all the papers said.

Or there could be a very real connection between what was on his docket and his sudden, premature death.

Conspiracy theories were just that until they were proven. Brice saw a dozen or so every day, but the ones that niggled his gut, he knew were the real deal.

Right now, his gut was going crazy. Not from Sydney's cookies or from Hope's sexy, yet compelling voice.

Well, maybe from her voice. It wasn't often he had a female caller.

Trusting a complete stranger, even if he was dying to see what she looked like and find out just how much of the Supreme Court's Kool-Aid she'd drunk, was out of the question.

He'd given himself an extra five minutes on top of the travel time. Logging into his background checker, he typed in Hope Denby's name.

What came up thirty seconds later was all kinds of interesting.

Photos filled his screen. Her high school graduation, college, her ID badge for the PIO. In all of them, she looked young and fresh and...full of life. Blond hair, blue eyes, a heart shaped face. Reece Witherspoon's cousin. The all-American girl.

Cheerleader in high school? Check.

Homecoming queen? Check.

Graduation speaker? Check.

Even in college, she'd kept a 4.0 and was in a bevy of clubs, a sorority, and was president of a journalism organization.

She's a journalist at heart. A purist. Most journalists considered bloggers like him to be the scum of the earth. *No wonder she hates me.*

Her Facebook page gave him more insight. She'd traveled extensively in Europe with friends during her freshman break, interned for two different international companies, and each and every day, she posted an inspirational quote on her Facebook page that her one thousand and sixteen friends Liked ad infinitum.

Brice wanted to barf.

Except for the part of him that didn't. She was a young, barely twenty-five, overachieving brat and a part of him admired that fact. He'd once been an overachiever too.

He'd once believed all the bullshit he'd fed himself about making a difference in the world.

Hope Denby screamed idealist. Deep down, he admired her naiveté. Or maybe it was simply that, unlike him, she still took pride in her belief that she could make a difference.

What he really admired was her blue eyes and the way her purple turtleneck hugged her upper body in her employment picture.

Totally fuckable.

What was wrong with him? He didn't have time for relationships, and a relationship required trust. Since he didn't do trust after being blindsided by the ATF, there was no way he could pursue a young, brilliant woman like Hope Denby.

Young being the operative word. She was a damned baby.

Totally *not* fuckable for an old man like him. Yeah, these days, thirty-five felt damn old.

Putting his computer to sleep, Brice found his keys and snagged a cookie for the road.

4

$\mathcal{I}$n the coffee shop, two couples sat in booths and a single guy at a table along the wall typing on his cell phone. Otherwise the place was quiet. The smell of fresh brewed coffee hit Brice's nose as the bell overhead dinged.

"Evening," one of the baristas called.

Brice gave the gal a noncommittal wave. He'd sat in the parking lot long enough to see Hope, with her red scarf wrapped around her neck, enter the Starbucks and meander around. First, she'd sat at a table near the front window, then moved to a leather chair across from a display. Finally, she'd gone to the restroom in the back and had yet to come out.

The perfect place to highjack her.

Not that he would normally corner an unsuspecting woman in a restroom, but a source was a source. He made it a rule never to meet one in public, but if he did, he made sure the exchange of info didn't go down in front of witnesses.

"Can I get you something?" the barista asked as he walked toward the back.

She was twenty at the most, and had a multitude of earrings in her ears and a tiny diamond stud in her nose. Her smile and the message in her eyes said she was bored and hoping he might give her a reason to like her job.

He didn't want coffee, but he also didn't want to stand out from the normal customers who only came in if they did. "Coffee. Black."

"Size?" Her gaze inventoried his dark sweatshirt, ball cap, and worn jeans. "No, wait. Let me guess. Grande."

The little wink she gave him suggested she was no longer talking about the size of the coffee cup.

He gave her his good ol' boy smile and nodded. "You're good."

"It's a little game I like to play when things are slow."

Her gaze said there were other games she'd like to play with him if he were interested. He tossed a five-dollar bill on the counter and kept going. "I'll be back in a minute."

He ducked behind a half-wall that hid the entrances to the restrooms. At the women's wooden door, he heard the sink water running. Good, Miss Denby wouldn't be in a compromising position.

Slipping inside, he had the door shut and locked before she even registered he was there.

Damn, her pictures didn't begin to do her justice. Her eyes were a startling blue. Her nose even perkier than her high school picture revealed. "What are you doing?"

He didn't answer, leaning against the door. Tight skirt, high heels, flawless skin. The shapeliest calves he'd ever seen, probably thanks to her cheerleading days. Yep, everything about her was perfect. Why was she getting involved in this potential dirt?

She eyed him warily, turning off the faucet and holding up her hands. "Look, whoever you are, I have to warn you. I know Krav Maga."

Her gaze was fierce but her body stance said she didn't know jackshit about fighting skills or self-defense.

All bluster. Brice gave her his good ol' boy smile just to see what she would do. "Did they teach you that at the Public Information Office as well? You probably have to defend yourself from all sorts of weirdoes there, don't you? Crazy bloggers and the like. And you know, you really should lock bathroom doors."

She dropped her hands, gave him a puzzled expression. "Mr. Hawkeye? Is that you?"

"You were expecting Santa Claus?" Why did she insist on calling him *mister*? "What do you have for me, Miss Denby?"

"I, uh,..." She grabbed paper towels and dried her hands hurriedly. A faint smile crossed her lips, whether from relief that he wasn't a rapist or murderer, or the fact he'd shown up at all to talk to her, he wasn't sure.

Her coat was unbuttoned, her knit sweater showing off her generous chest and flat stomach. Her heels clicked as she walked toward him and the door, working those sexy calves.

Totally fuckable.

When he didn't move out of her way, her smile faltered. "Shouldn't we go sit down?"

"I'd rather stay here." For more reasons than one.

"In the restroom? Don't you want a coffee, or a cappuccino or something? You can get decaf, you know, and they have really tasty scones. My favorite is the blueberry, but the pumpkin ones are good too. I've been thinking about them ever since you agreed to meet me here. Considering the deadline you gave me and the fact that I *skipped* dinner."

Another wide smile, all teeth. Perfect white teeth.

Brice saw no subterfuge in her blue eyes, yet, something was off. *What is she up to?*

Virgin sources. Always a bucket of nerves. They often stalled in order to make up their minds about spilling what they knew.

His fingers itched to touch her legs. Baby or not, if she hadn't been a potential source, he would have fallen all over himself to buy her a coffee. To joke and flirt and peel back those perfect outer layers and see what lay underneath. To drag his fingers over her calves and up under that tight little skirt.

Except, truth be told, she wasn't his type. He liked them smart but less...bubbly. More serious.

Then again, it had been so long since he'd let himself get interested in a woman, he wasn't sure he had a type anymore.

No woman in her right mind would look at a washed-up ATF agent like him, now a conspiracy theorist, as potential boyfriend material. "I don't have time for blueberry scones and mocha cappuccinos, Miss Denby. I'm on the clock. Do you have information for me or not?"

"Oh, it's Hope." The overhead lights reflected on her pale pink, highly-glossed nails as she held out a hand. "We haven't properly introduced ourselves."

God help him, her perkiness would drive him to drink.

He almost took her hand, then remembered that, after this meeting, he would no doubt never see her again. Which kind of sucked, but his world gave no quarter for young, naive, idealists, and he had enough complications in his life without adding another.

"Is this about money?" he asked her. "If so, I should have been upfront with you. I don't pay sources. Ever. No matter how big the scoop is. I know other, more dubious bloggers will, but I won't. The exchange of money dilutes the validity and legitimacy of the information."

"I don't want money. And I completely agree with you regarding the validity of information." Her cheeks flushed a shade somewhere between the red scarf and the pink nails. "But you could at least buy me a drink."

"This is not a date." A shame, really. The flush in her cheeks only served to heighten her innate beauty. "We are not friends, or even acquaintances. Once we leave this restroom, we never have to see each other again, and even if we do run into each other on the street, we will act like we don't know each other. Got it?"

"For Heaven's sakes! What's with all the covert stuff? We're having a conversation, not exchanging codes."

This was why he preferred his tried and true, experienced sources. "I ruffle people's feathers, and even though I keep the lowest of low public profiles, a determined person could figure out who I am, where I live, who my friends are." *All four of them.* "There are a lot of nut cases in D.C, and quite a few of them are politicians with deep pockets and plenty of minions to do their dirty work. I'd rather not end up in the Potomac, and I certainly don't want you to end up there because you met me face-to-face."

"You make this sound like some CIA undercover operation." Her face was now white. "And your life sounds like a lonely one."

Fuck. The pity clouding her eyes was more than he could stand. "I do what has to be done. A long time ago, I thought the bad guys were fighting *against* our government and the laws in place to keep our citizens safe. Now, I know many of the worst bad guys are *inside* the government breaking those same laws."

"Ah, a cynic. Of course. Well, I hate to burst your bubble Mr. Cynical Hawkeye, but I don't even know if what I found out has anything to do with Chief Justice Turner's death."

"You called me down here at eight o'clock at night so you could get me to buy you a coffee?"

He shook his head, flipped the lock, and opened the door. "Priceless, Miss Denby. Thanks for wasting my time and making me miss my deadline."

He'd only gone two steps when she yelled, "Wait!" and grabbed him by the back of his sweatshirt.

. . .

Now she had problems. As in the text she'd received from Rob two minutes before old Hawkeye scared the you-know-what out of her by ambushing her in the bathroom. According to Rob, their beleaguered boss was still behind closed doors.

Which meant stalling the blogger and not giving him the Kenton Labs case until she got Amy to sign off. How she would manage that with Mr. Persistent here, she hadn't a clue. He was a scrappy one for sure.

And there was only so much flirting she could do with such a crab. But, the challenge he presented, the challenge of *him*, sent every nerve ending on alert. God, she loved it. All that juicy energy and excitement and, well, nervousness over an unusual case? Total rush.

Always.

"Mister...sorry...Hawkeye. Whatever."

"It's not that hard Ms. Denby."

"Well, yes, actually it is. I've been raised to address people formally until they give me permission to use their first name."

And where did *that* come from? Total flyer.

He grinned. "You can call me Hawkeye."

She grinned back. "Ooh, a sense of humor. Careful now, I may actually start to like you. How about Hawk for short?"

"Black, grande coffee!" the barista hollered, her tone screaming impatience.

"Is that yours?"

"Yeah. I didn't want to call attention to myself so I ordered something."

"Excellent!" she chirped. "I'll grab a cup too and one of the scones." She paddled her hands. "Go. Let's chat."

Let's chat? Sounding like a flake hadn't been on her to-do list today, but hey, anything for the job.

Her phone buzzed from her coat pocket and she fished it out. Text from Rob telling her she was still S.O.L. on the boss.

Terrific. Minute by minute updates.

She glanced up at Hawkeye and—ooh, she would totally call him Hawk to rattle him—and smiled at the barista checking him out. If Hope didn't hate him, she'd completely understand the girl's need to do so. After all, he had that whole relaxed, scruffy look going and she imagined, had he not been wearing a baseball cap over his short, honey colored hair that it too would have that messy, but groomed look to it.

Had to love a man who could pull that look off.

"So you like hats," she said. "You don't happen to have a cowboy hat, do you?"

If he had a cowboy hat, she'd be dead meat. From head to toe, blogger and all, this guy might be her worst nightmare.

Or her greatest fantasy.

He scooped his coffee from the counter and headed right out the door.

Rob's dramatics over a blogger bringing down the stock market replayed in her mind. And if Kenton Labs was the case in question, billions could be at risk. Billions that would most definitely impact the economy.

Oh, no sir. Nuh-uh. If she let Hawk walk out, who knew what his next *blog* post would be. If she gave him something, maybe she could leverage it. Keep him in control.

String him along.

At least until she received direction from Amy.

"Stall, sister," she muttered.

Passing the bakery case and the nice little sugar buzz she craved, she hauled butt after Hawk. On the sidewalk, she glanced left, spotted him nearing the corner and started running. Well, as much as the stupid heels would let her. Sometimes it truly sucked to be of diminutive stature.

"Hawk!" she yelled.

That'll get him.

Yep. He spun back, flapped his free arm and stormed back to her. "Are you out of your fucking mind?"

44

Ooh. Rather a harsh reaction. What was that about? "I'm sorry?"

"You just yelled my name on the goddamned street. What do you not get about me wanting to protect my privacy? And it's *Hawkeye*, and no, I don't own a fucking cowboy hat."

What a shame. Although, probably a good thing for her and her little twisted blogger-slash-cowboy fantasy. "I'm sorry for yelling your name. I was trying to get your attention before you left."

"Well, honey, you did that."

And, whew, she sort of liked the way he called her honey. What did that say about her since the man hadn't bothered to hide his derision. *I'm a total flake.* Maybe so. But the flake had a job to do. Lightly, she touched his arm. "Let me make it up to you."

For half a second, she thought she saw something very male and very, well, carnal, flit through his eyes. At least she wasn't the only one feeling a little heat here.

But then he dumped the coffee, she hadn't seen him even sip, in the garbage can and swiped his hands together, staring down at them for a second. Maybe checking for dirt. On top of paranoid, he could be a germaphobe.

"Quit stalling," he said. "I saw you check your phone. Whatever intel you're waiting on, if it doesn't show up in fifteen seconds, I'm gone."

He shoved up his jacket sleeve revealing a shiny silver watch strapped to his wrist. Analog, not digital.

Forget the cowboy hat. The scruffy look, calling her honey *and* a watch. Total panty dropper. He must have vetted her or something and found out she was wickedly turned on by men with watches. God's sakes it was almost a fetish, but there was something so throwback about analog watches, she never could resist. Particularly large, masculine looking ones.

The watch. Not the man. Well, the man too, of course. Yeesh. It was all almost too much.

He stared down at the watch. "I'm timing you. You're down to ten seconds."

Ten seconds? Really? The guy was good. Her phone buzzed again. Rob. Still no Amy. Why did he keep texting her if he didn't have any news?

"Five seconds, Ms. Denby and then I go write a blog saying the Chief Justice of the United States may have been assassinated."

No! PR nightmare.

"Three, two..."

"I'll make you a deal."

"One."

He looked up at her and smiled.

Could the man be any more smug? She should smack him. *Pow.* Just get it over with. He had her all kinds of worked up and she wasn't even sure why. Other than the watch fetish. But that was something altogether different. That could be chalked up to restrained sexual energy because, seriously, she hadn't gotten any lately.

And apparently needed it.

A vibrator could only take a girl so far.

"I'm all ears, Ms. Denby."

All ears. Funny. At the moment, she wasn't thinking about his ears.

She sighed and blew out a breath. She had to give him a lead. Something. Information was what he wanted. This she knew.

Until she talked to Amy, she couldn't necessarily pony up what little she knew. That would mean trusting him. A huge leap for her considering her lack of faith in bloggers.

But, really big but here, he'd stuck to his word so far and hadn't posted anything regarding the Chief Justice. That had to count for something. If nothing else, he'd done what he'd said he would.

Or wouldn't do.

Pow. *Mind-blown.* She'd damned near confused herself there.

"All right," she said, "I'm going to give you the name of a case, but I'm not sure what the relevance is. I haven't had time to vet it yet. So, yes, I was stalling. My boss has been behind closed doors all night and I'm not sure what I have or if I should even be sharing it with you."

"You're nervous."

"No, Hawk. I'm terrified. And worse, I'm going to trust you. Tell me I'm not wrong to do that?"

He inched closer. Typically when men did that it was a power play. A way for them to loom over shrimpy Hope. An intimidation tactic that hadn't worked since grammar school thanks to her three brothers who took turns getting under her skin in order to teach her how to fight back after a mean girl had humiliated her.

She may have been small, but she was most definitely mighty.

Particularly when it came to men.

But, funny thing. When Hawk moved closer, despite the minimum eight inches he had on her, it relaxed her. Made her feel a little taller. Go. Figure.

Relaxed.

Scruff.

Watch.

The man was an orgasm waiting to happen.

And him without a wedding ring. Which didn't always mean he didn't have a wife somewhere, but he seemed like the type who'd wear a ring. Didn't he? She couldn't know that though. Men could be slippery that way.

Why was she even thinking about this when they had a

dead Chief Justice to be concerned with? She shook her head. Crazy-making thoughts after a long, stressful day.

"You're not wrong," he said. "You can trust me. You may have noticed I'm a freak about my privacy. I protect my sources the same way. Whatever you give me, I'll vet it. My readers expect that. And I'm not one of these bullshit bloggers wanting notoriety so they make shit up to start trouble. If you want to compare legit news stories that we've both broken, let's do it. In the last three months, I broke the bribery of that congressman from Idaho, the misuse of power by the Secretary of Housing and Urban Development, and then, Miss Denby, there's the jewel in my crown—"

"—The Attorney General scandal."

"Bingo, babe. I have no problem starting trouble if it fixes a problem, but I won't pull the trigger if I don't have to."

He leaned in a bit more and the overhead street light illuminated his face. Looking into those blue eyes, more grey than blue at the moment, the color of a stormy Atlantic Ocean, she believed him. For whatever reason, and it might be her downfall, but she didn't think he'd lie.

"Here's the deal," she said. "I'll tell you the name of the case, but you cannot do anything with it until I verify it. I know you'll hate that, but I want to give you something. I don't want you posting false information. The Chief Justice is dead and I need to protect his reputation, no matter the reason he died today. If you'll agree to this, I'll give you the name of the case. Obviously, you'll be free to research it as well, but you cannot run even a hint of the name until I look into it."

"And what do I get?"

"Besides the name of the case?"

"Yeah."

Unbelievable. *Think, think, think.* "I'll give you a thirty minute head start on the next big news release. You'll get it first."

Hawk rocked back on his heels, twisted his lips. He didn't trust her. Why should he? She'd tried to stall him. She wouldn't trust her either. She lifted her chin, made direct eye contact. "I promise you, you'll get it first."

"I want a time limit."

Damn. "Oh, come on! You have to trust me on this."

"Hey, who's to say one of the networks won't get something on this and break it first? Meanwhile, I'm sitting here with my thumb up my ass when I had a good scoop. I'll give you twenty-four hours. If the networks haven't picked this up by then, we'll revisit the deadline. Those are my terms."

Considering her only other option was to walk away and let him run some wacky conspiracy theory about the Chief Justice, she didn't have a choice but to accept his deal.

"Fine," she said.

"Deal. Now spill."

She let out a long breath. "Kenton Labs."

"Pharmaceutical company. That's the case about the patent, right?"

Smart man. "Yes. As I said, my source just gave it to me. Literally right before I called you. I know nothing about it other than what has come across my desk."

"Which is?"

"That Kenton is battling with two other drug companies to protect its patent on Donazem. I don't know all of the details, but the clerks believe it's one of the most important cases this term. If the hearing is denied, it could set a precedent for all future hearings on drug patents."

"Okay," he said. "I'll look into it. If I find anything, I'll call you for a comment. Remember our deal, Ms. Denby. I'll hang on to this for twenty-four hours. Stay in touch."

He turned and walked away, shoulders hunched, trying to blend in with the few pedestrians near the corner.

For now, she'd silenced him. Kept him from distributing

some crazy conspiracy theory that had yet to be proven. Whatever that theory might be. Lordy, she had no clue what they were even dealing with.

All that was left was to break it to Amy that a damned blogger would get a jump on their next big release.

5

---

*A*t 9:15 Hope charged into the office, found the place still lit up with people slaving away. A small group of her co-workers hovered around the television mounted on the wall in the corner. Justice Turner's photo adorned the screen as the news anchor spoke. From her vantage point, Hope couldn't quite hear and wandered closer just as the anchor went to a video of a woman who'd been stuck on the bridge, but hadn't witnessed the actual shooting.

"The entire incident is horrifying," the woman said. "We were stuck for over an hour. Total logjam. Then I heard the gunshots and really panicked. I mean, we couldn't move. We *all* could have gotten shot. Then some guy wearing a DDOT vest comes running up and takes the barricades down to get traffic moving. Just like that."

Hope twisted her lips and tried to visualize the scene. If someone from DDOT was able to remove the barricades that easily, there couldn't have been any major construction occurring. If that were the case, why the heck was the lane closed during rush hour traffic?

In D.C.

Way to snarl the morning commute. Flipping DDOT.

The on-site reporter mentioned that police had questioned the cab driver and everyone who'd witnessed the shooting, but so far no leads. Then she tossed it back to the anchor and Hope moved down the aisle leading to her desk, passing cubes where assistants cruised the internet or kept their heads down in an attempt to look busy and basically steer clear of Amy's wrath.

At her cube, she dumped her briefcase just inside the wall and moved the four extra steps to Rob's desk.

"Hey. What's the word?"

Rob leaned back in his chair, stretched his arms and then ran his hands through his neatly cropped dark hair. "Nothing new. The cops haven't found the shooter yet. The networks are all basically repeating what they reported earlier."

"I heard." She gestured to the group huddled around the television. "They've got CNN on. Can you imagine being trapped on that bridge and having some psycho start shooting? Fish in a barrel. Leave it to DDOT to close the lane during rush hour."

"Yeah. All I know is we're all sitting here waiting for some direction. Everyone is afraid to go home." He jerked his head toward Amy's office. "She's back from her meeting. But it ain't pretty. She nearly tore Rosalie's head off ten minutes ago."

Excellent. Truly, excellent.

Sigh.

"How'd it go with the blogger?"

"Fine. I think he's actually legit."

"He brought down the deputy attorney general, Hope. I think that's pretty legit."

"Meaning he's interested in getting the story right. But he's a nudge." She scooted closer to Rob, leaned over his desk, getting right next to him so she wouldn't be overheard. "I had to make a deal with him or he would have floated this crazy conspiracy theory to his readers."

Rob hit her with a look. One that had him scrunching his nose. "What deal? We don't have anything on this yet."

"I know. That was the problem. I had to promise him a thirty-minute lead on our next big press release."

Gagging sounds erupted from Rob. Hardy har. But what was she supposed to do? Just let Hawkeye—Hawk—run with it? She couldn't do that. No way.

Rob opened his desk drawer, whipped out a tape measure.

What the hell was that for? "What are you doing?"

"I need to measure your cube for when I move in there." He dumped the tape measure on the desk, sending it clattering across the top. "Have you lost your fucking mind? The Queen Bitch won't just fire you, she'll skin you, set your body ablaze and listen to you scream while dying."

Didn't that create a stunning visual? Well, as long as she had good shoes on, Hope would accept the punishment. All in a day's work. "I know. I didn't have a choice though. I had to stall him. And Amy wasn't available to help me."

"Denby!"

Hope angled back, arching just beyond the cube wall. Amy stood in her office doorway, her shoulder-length hair an unholy mess and her blouse twelve wrinkles beyond its limit.

Rob picked up the tape measure, slid the ruler out and let it snap back.

Fucker.

But, oh, she wouldn't say that out loud. Good girls didn't say fuck and she'd spent most of her life being a good girl. She pinched him. "Coming!"

Saving her the short trip to her cube, Rob handed her a legal pad and pen. "Let the games begin."

"Shut up. *Ass.*" She swung from the cube, did her run-walk routine toward her boss. "Amy, I was just heading to see you."

"Save it. What happened with the blogger?"

"That's where I was."

"Where?"

"Meeting the blogger."

Amy's head dipped forward. "Oh, Christ. Get in here, Denby."

Following her boss, Hope stepped into the office and closed the door behind her. Amy cornered the desk, sat and glanced at the door.

"I hate closed doors. It's never good when that happens."

"No. It's fine. I just wanted privacy."

So my co-workers don't witness my slaying.

Amy sat back and massaged her scalp. "When I woke up this morning, I was forty-eight. I feel a hundred."

"It's been a horrid day."

She dropped her hands, let them rest on top of a stack of files on her desk. "That it has. What have you got?"

If ever there was a question Hope didn't want to answer, that might be it. Like everything else, she'd find a way to put a positive spin on the experience. Consider it training for her rise to the White House when she'd be required to stand in front of the press corps and answer the really tough questions. Like how a blogger manipulated her into making a deal.

Hope sat a little straighter, shoved her shoulders back. *Positive spin.* "It turns out, the blogger is the guy who ran that series on the deputy AG last fall."

"Shit."

"It's okay though. I stalled him."

"Good girl."

Yay, me. "But only for so long."

"Are you going to piss me off, Denby?"

Boo-me. Hope held up her hand. "No." *Liar.* "We can control him. He got a tip that the Chief Justice's death wasn't—"

"An accident. Sure. Right. These lunatics come out of their dark holes when a politically influential person kicks it. I'm sure this guy has all sorts of theories. Elvis lives. Aliens walk among us. Blah, blah, blah."

"Not really," Hope said. "He's pretty normal."

For a conspiracy theory nutcase.

"Then what's his big tip?"

"His source claims it wasn't a coincidence that the Chief Justice got held up on the bridge. According to the source he was about to deliver a ruling on whether or not a landmark case got a hearing."

Amy angled her head and narrowed her eyes. Thinking. Probably looping the major cases before the court through her brain. "What case?"

"That's what he wanted to know. He gave me until 8:00 PM to give him something that would debunk the tip. Which is why I left you ten voicemails."

"Denby?"

"Yes."

"It's 9:30."

"I know." She held up her hand again. "Even with the blown deadline, he's been contained."

Amy pointed at her and made that clicking noise with her tongue that she always did when someone pleased her. "Good. How?"

"I poked around about what the case might be. I think it's the Kenton Labs hearing."

"The patent?"

"Yes, ma'am. According to my source, the Chief was about to deliver a ruling on whether or not Kenton would get their hearing to extend the patent."

"Who's your source?"

Whoopsie. "I can't say. I'm sorry. It's a credible source though."

"You went to one of the clerks." Amy waved it off. "Forget it.

I know you won't tell me. But if this turns into something, all bets are off and I'll want that source."

Boss or no boss, Hope wouldn't give up Joel's name. If she did, no source would ever trust her. "Hopefully, it won't come to that."

"How'd you'd stall the blogger?"

Tricky question. Admitting she'd gone rogue and made a deal without her boss's permission was new territory. Maybe she could dance her way around it, put it off until morning when Amy wasn't in Bitch mode. But the only thing waiting would accomplish would be keeping Hope up all night anticipating the trouble she'd be in when she finally did come clean. Then that would spin out because Amy would demand to know why she hadn't admitted it when they spoke last and *then* Amy would never trust her again and—splat—her career in D.C. would be over. She'd be lucky if she got a job as a stringer in some podunk newspaper in Idaho.

Not a great idea.

Unless the men wore cowboy hats and boots.

Ugh. Her stomach cinched. She fought off the discomfort and scooted to the end of her chair. "He's kind of a slippery bugger."

"Denby?"

"Yes?"

"Have I mentioned I'm extremely tired?"

Hope furiously waved her hands. "Okayokayokay. I'm just going to tell you and you can crucify me if you must, but he was threatening to unleash this story which would have caused major speculation about the Chief Justice and...and..." Rob's comment about the stock market filled her head. "...think about the stock market! I mean, we don't want to mess with that so I had to stop this guy."

"Jesus, Denby. Are you on something?"

How incredibly offensive. "Of course not! I'm trying to explain why I did what I did."

"Which is fine, except you haven't told me what you did!"

Whew. She'd gotten so churned up about protecting the Chief Justice's reputation she'd forgotten to tell Amy about the deal. "You're right. Sorry. I got a little carried away. Anyway, I had to make him a deal." She scrunched her nose, readied herself for the barrage of hate. "I told him if he didn't run the story I'd give him the name of a case to look into." She pushed her shoulders back. "And I told him we'd give him a heads up on our next big press release."

There. Said it. Done.

Surprisingly, no yelling ensued. Huh. Hope bit the inside of her cheeks and waited, but Amy simply sat staring at her with her tired eyes that were now a little glazed over. Probably that frantic admission Hope unfurled making her punchy.

Four, three, two, one.

Nothing.

I've killed my boss. "Amy?"

Finally, Amy sat forward, rested her elbows on the desk. "Theoretically, I could fire you."

Ouch.

Hope opened her mouth, but Amy waggled a finger at her. "But I'm not going to. I put you in a tough spot here. I thought this blogger was some hack that we could get rid of. Had I known the situation, obviously, I would have handled it or assigned it to a more seasoned person. Not that you're incompetent. You're quite talented and I love your spunk. You're just not ready for something on this level. So, I'm not going to fire you. It's my fault. Now, I need to take control of this. From now on, I'll deal with this blogger. You're to have no more contact with him. Understood?"

Oh, come on! After the night she had, Amy wanted to pull

her off this story. They could have something here. "I understand, ma'am. However—"

"No however. We're done, Denby."

"Please." Hope put her hands together, prayerful and, well, pleading. This is what it had come to. Begging. Pathetic. Eh. So what? "I've met this blogger. He talked to me. And believe me, Amy, he's paranoid. He used to be ATF and he takes his anonymity seriously. He's a tough one and I think, in a twisted way, I connected with him. I won't say he trusts me, but there's something there. If you or anyone else suddenly takes over, it'll make him suspicious. Let me at least be your go-between with him. And I can help with research. Just in case this story might have validity."

Amy flinched. "What makes you say that?"

"That he trusts me?"

"No. The validity part."

"Oh. Well." She thought about it a second, tried to form a persuasive argument, but what it came down to was instinct. Plain and simple. "I don't know. Call it a hunch."

Amy rolled her eyes. "Don't bullshit me, Denby."

"I'm not. Honestly. It's just that talking to him, he doesn't seem like a crackpot. Then I came back to the office and CNN is running that interview with a witness and something doesn't feel right."

"Like what?"

"Like why DDOT closed a lane on that bridge during rush hour and then suddenly opened it again right after Chief Justice Turner was shot and killed."

If that didn't sway her boss, Hope was in the wrong job. No true journalist could walk away from something like this. A true journalist would dig and keep digging until a reasonable explanation could be found.

Amy's cell phone rang and she glanced at it. "Shoot. This is the White House." She picked up the phone. "Okay, Denby. I'll let you stay on this. Don't fuck it up."

Whoot.

"Yes, ma'am. I promise."

"Good. Tell everyone to go home. We'll hit it again tomorrow."

Her twisted state of delirium stayed intact—really, she shouldn't be so happy about being permitted to stay on a story about a dead Chief Justice. Somewhere down deep she was sad for the man and his family. Truly. But she also wanted to know what happened on that bridge. If Hawk's conspiracy theory panned out, Hope could find some satisfaction in helping to blow the story open. In putting a criminal behind bars. Yes, that's what she'd hang on to.

Exposing justice.

Hope wandered back to her desk and on the way found Rob still in his cube cruising the internet.

"Hey," she said. "Amy is sending everyone home. There's nothing left to do tonight and she wants everyone to get some rest. Pack it in."

"Finally. What a rotten day."

"That it was."

"Want to share a cab?"

Typically, unless she needed her car during the day or after work, Hope chose not to brave D.C. traffic and took the bus in. This morning, as if the universe sensed her day would implode, she'd missed the bus by two minutes and rather than wait for the next one, decided to drive in. "I drove today. Missed the bus this morning. Got a question for you though."

"Shoot."

"Do you know anyone at DDOT?"

Rob pulled a face, waggled his head for a second. "I don't think so. Why?"

"This thing about DDOT suddenly opening up that lane

has me curious. The fact that they can just open it up, meaning there were no workers or equipment there tearing up the pavement is a little odd."

"No it isn't. This is DDOT."

Hope scoffed. "Please. Why the heck was that lane closed if no one was working there? I thought if we, meaning you, knew someone there, I could poke around some. If not," she grinned, "I'll do it the old fashioned way."

"Oh, brother. Sorry. I don't have a contact there."

She swung around the corner to her own cube and dug out her phone for Hawk's number.

"Hey," Rob said from his side. "I thought we were leaving."

"We were. Now I'm staying. You go on ahead. I have to call my PITA blogger and see if he knows anyone at DDOT."

Chair tipped back, Brice half dozed in front of his computer. The 31-inch screen flickered with three windows...his blog forum, alive with chatter about the FBI hacking scandal, his Twitter feed of loyal readers spreading the word, and his search engine scanning the web for other potential news stories.

One of his competitors had picked up on the FBI story and spun it into the creative non-fiction zone. They had no credible sources and had lifted direct passages from his original document. Seemed like everyone was a pirate these days, unwilling to do their own work when it was so easy to steal someone else's.

He itched to release something on the Chief Justice's death, even just to let his followers know he'd had a tip, but Hope Denby had tied his hands. He'd given the brat his word and he never went back on that.

In his mind, he'd already framed a brief alert, and made a list of people he wanted to contact tomorrow. The CJ's killer had escaped, but someone had snapped his picture with a cell phone. The picture's quality was good, but the man was difficult for police to identify since he'd covered his face with a hood, sunglasses, and wore a thick beard. Suspicious? Just a little.

An abundance of eye-witness reports had flooded TV, the Internet, and radio, but few accounts matched. The only thing the witnesses seemed to agree on was that Justice Turner and his security detail were trying to help settle an argument.

His computer phone line buzzed with an incoming call. Even though it was nearing midnight, that wasn't unusual in the first few hours after one of his stories went live. Most callers just wanted to let off steam and add their own two cents. Since he'd had a dozen calls already, he let it go to voicemail.

But then he heard Hope Denby's voice.

The chair legs hit the floor and he nearly knocked over his Diet Coke in his haste to hit the connect key on his keyboard. "Denby?"

"Hey, Hawk. Screening your calls?"

The sound of her voice—that mixture of sweetness tinged with confidence—sent his blood flowing to places he'd rather not think about. "What's going on?"

"Do you know anyone at the department of transportation?"

"Should I?"

She told him about a news bulletin she'd seen on CNN and the fact that a DDOT worker had removed the barricade right after the shooting. "Don't you think that's odd? That the lane was closed, but there were no crews there working on it, and then suddenly, it was opened up?"

"This is D.C. Nothing the transportation department does surprises me." He tipped his chair back again. "Although if you wanted to stop traffic long enough to pin someone on that bridge and shoot him, that would do the trick. The timing would have to be just right..."

"I'd really like to know if there's a legit reason why that lane was closed. If there is, it would lend credence that this was just an accidental road rage incident. If there's not, your theory might have more weight."

"Let me make some calls and get back to you."

"If you find anything, call my cell. I'm on my way home."

"You're still at work?"

"Long day. I'm the last one here, closing up shop."

The back of his neck tensed. "Don't you have any common sense, Ms. Denby? A woman leaving the office alone in D.C. at night? You're asking to get kidnapped, raped, or at the very least, mugged."

"I told you, Mr. Paranoid, I know Kro Magna."

"It's Krav Maga, and you don't know the first thing about self-defense. Unless you plan to use the spiked heel on your shoe to take someone's eye out."

She huffed. "I'll be fine. I have acute senses that detect danger a mile away. It's my super power."

Right. He gripped the arms of his chair. "You don't even lock the restroom door in a public place."

"I was nervous about meeting you, *Hawk*! I forgot."

He squeezed his hands into fists, released them. The tension in his neck was another story. "Call me when you get home so I know you're safe."

"So you *do* have a human side. That's sweet."

Another fist squeeze. "Go home, Ms. Denby."

"Hope."

"Hope. Go home, and call me once you're inside with the doors locked."

"Yes, sir!"

She disconnected and Brice rubbed his forehead.

And she thought *he* was a nutcase.

A minute later, he had David Teeg, Grey and Mitch's lackey,

on the phone. Like Brice, he was a night owl. "Teeg, it's Brennan. You have any connections at DDOT?"

A yawn from the other end and the sound of keyboard clicks. "Maybe. Why?"

"Maybe" in Teeg's language meant *yes*. "Why do you think? I need a source who knows about the Gaynor Bridge lane closing."

"Because you're investigating the suspicious death of Chief Justice Turner and want to spin it into a conspiracy theory."

Brice sighed. "Grey told you."

A new voice came over the speaker. "Yes, I told him. I informed him you'd run into a dead end and come to us for help." Grey sounded even more uptight than usual. "Guess what? We have our own highly important investigation going on over here and our services are not free. If you want Teeg's help, or mine, or any other Justice Team member, pony up, Brennan. You help us, we'll help you."

Not this again. Grey was a good guy—for a pain in the ass—but when he wanted something, he went for it. Hard. "I don't have time to work for the Justice Team, nor do I want to."

"Then find your own damn connections and sources. Oh, and don't expect any more of Syd's cookies on your doorstep."

Ouch. "That's hitting below the belt, Grey."

The line went dead.

Balls.

He sat for a few seconds considering his options. On a normal night, no one would be at DDOT this late anyway. Tonight? They were probably still fielding questions from the police, sheriff, and anyone else who had jurisdiction over the bridge, not to mention the Justice Department and FBI. He could take his chances and cold call them tonight or wait until morning.

Regardless, a direct contact, not some public relations

spokesman spouting the party line, would be more efficient. He didn't need another Hope Denby to deal with.

That meant sucking it up and offering to help Grey.

It pained him to do so, but he redialed Teeg's number.

"Yo," the computer hacker answered on the first ring. "Guy's name is Pearson. Brian Pearson. He's in the Bridge Maintenance Department."

Teeg rattled off a phone number. "That's his personal cell. Tell him I sent you and that anything he divulges is strictly confidential. You'll keep his name out of it."

"What about Grey?"

"He said you'd call back in five minutes or less and offer to help us on a contractual basis. Told me to go ahead and spot you this one."

Grey always seemed to know everyone's next move before they did it. Brice hated to admit it, but it was a damn impressive skill. Creepy as hell, too. "How does he do that?"

"Predict the future?" Teeg snorted and lowered his voice. "He was a profiler back in the day. Knows us better than we know ourselves. Scary-ass shit, man."

Scary, indeed. "And what is my first Justice Team assignment?"

"I'll email three files to you tomorrow."

The line went dead.

Brice checked the clock. Ten minutes since he'd spoken to Hope. How long did it take her to drive home? Could be another half hour, even with mostly empty roads at this time of night.

Grabbing a burn phone, he dialed the number Teeg had given him. Brian, the poor bastard, was probably snuggled down in his bed, sleeping off the day's stress. No better time to hit him up for intel.

Six rings before Brian answered. Definitely sleeping. "Hello?" a groggy voice answered.

Brice skipped identifying himself. "Brian, I'm a friend of David Teeg. He gave me your number. I'm sorry to bother you so late, but with everything that happened today, I need some information ASAP." He didn't pause long enough for the man to say anything. "Why was the lane closed on the Gaynor Bridge today?"

A deep sigh. "I went over this with the police. There was a memo that went out late yesterday. The lane was closed for a routine inspection."

So there *was* a valid reason. "How often do these routine inspections happen?"

"Twice a year minimum. If there's been a maintenance issue in the last six months, we do more. That bridge is old and has a lot of issues. We've probably done three or more checks on it in the past two months."

"So the inspection occurred this morning before the traffic jam?"

"Um...who did you say you were again?"

"Whatever you tell me is in confidence. Why was the lane opened up immediately after the shooting?"

"Look, the inspector claims he didn't get the memo. One of the road crews who *did* see the memo set up the barricade, but the inspector hadn't gotten there yet when the incident went down. It happens."

Incompetence. It happened far too often in his book. "Thank you for your time."

Brice punched the disconnect key and rocked in his chair. While the DDOT guys had failed to do an inspection before rush hour traffic, there was no sign of obvious foul play.

Lost in his thoughts, he almost didn't hear his computer line ring a few minutes later. He answered, hoping it was the brat. "Patriot blog."

"What, no Thomas Paine quote?" Her voice was teasing. "Just wanted you to know, I'm home safe and sound. The doors

MISTY EVANS & ADRIENNE GIORDANO

are locked, the windows secure, and the motion sensors activated. The only thing I don't have is the Hulk standing guard outside."

She knew Thomas Paine. He was mildly impressed. With her knowledge and her level of security. "You have motion sensors?"

"If I say yes, will you relax?"

Annoying little shit. Something in him liked her, and not just because she was sexy and a smartass. It was the smell of a scoop. She was a woman who understood his weakness and that made him want to open up, to trust her.

He pushed that feeling down into the deep, dark hole of no-way-in-hell. Trusting Mrs. Tilly was one thing. Trusting a woman like Hope was as scary as having Justice Greystone read his mind. "A source on the Bridge Maintenance Unit says the lane was closed for a routine inspection."

He heard a fridge opening. "Well, that's weird," Hope said. "I listened to a radio talk show on the way home and I swear they said the lane was closed for a pothole repair."

After yet another brutal winter, potholes were as rampant as incompetence. "The guy I spoke with suggested there was a lot of miscommunication within DDOT."

A glass clanked. "Is it miscommunication or is someone lying?"

Brice smiled at his screen. "Now who sounds like a paranoid conspiracy theorist?"

"Oh, please. I'm a journalist at heart. We never stop asking questions. Which is why I'm going to dig a little and see if I can verify what I heard on the radio. I went to school with one of the assistant producers on that show. He owes me a couple of favors. And seeing as his show is on the air right now, I might be able to get to him tonight. I'll call you back. There goes my glass of wine and a long, hot bubble bath."

And, oh, the images that conjured. If only she'd wear those

fuck-me shoes, and nothing else, while she was running that bathwater, his fantasy would be complete. "Call me. Don't forget your deadline."

He could hear the smile in her voice. "Don't worry. If there's a story here, I'm going to find it."

"You wouldn't steal my scoop, would you?"

"Who me?"

He heard tinkling laughter before the connection went dead.

6

$\mathcal{H}$ope dialed Jeremy's cell phone and by the third ring knew she'd get voicemail. That was okay. The man obsessively checked his phone, probably waiting on that next big scoop, and she knew he'd call her back tonight. She'd thrown him a couple of inside tips since she'd gone to work at the Supreme Court and they had a standing agreement to always, always, return phone calls.

Opening the fridge, she bypassed the Chardonnay—almost grieving its loss—and grabbed a bottled water. If Jeremy came back with something interesting, she wanted to be sharp and refused to risk even one glass of alcohol. She'd settle for water and scanning the internet for any late breaking news on the justice.

When she sat, her bones nearly crumbled. Fatigue pressed in on her and a dull throb pulsed behind her eyes. She needed sleep. A few hours to get her mind zipping again. But Jeremy might still call and she couldn't risk missing him.

She tapped her mouse and the computer screen lit up, ready for action.

"Let's see what we've got."

Ten minutes later her phone rang.

Good old Jeremy. She abandoned the internet, checked the caller's ID on her phone and hit the button.

"Hey, Jeremy. Thanks for getting back to me."

"Anything for you, Hopester. What's goin' on? You got something for me on the Chief Justice?"

"Um, no. Hoping *you* might have something for *me*."

"Come again?"

"I listened to the show on the way home tonight. Great work, by the way."

"Thank you."

A little sucking up to an old school chum never hurt. "In the segment on the Chief Justice it was mentioned the bridge lane was closed for a pothole repair."

Jeremy hesitated. "O-kay."

By the tone of his response she surmised his arm hairs were now at full attention anticipating that she'd either debunk the report or possibly say something that would give him some other lead to chase.

"Who told you about the pothole repair?"

"Why?"

Hope slouched back for a second. Jeremy might have been her friend, but he loved a constant state of competition. Friend or not, he was as hungry for a good scoop as she and Hawk combined. If she wanted information, she'd have to give some up. *Go for it.* She sat straight again. "I need this to stay between us. A couple of friends talking. Off the record here, agreed?"

"Sure."

"I have a source that told me the lane was closed for a routine inspection. Then, on my way home, your team says it's a pothole repair. It can't be both. Someone got it wrong."

"Shit. Hang on."

MISTY EVANS & ADRIENNE GIORDANO

Excellent. She'd surprised him. By doing so, she'd alerted him that his team may have screwed the pooch and gave them an opportunity to correct it while still on the air. It might be enough to get him to pony up anything he knew. Hope punched the speaker button on the screen and set the phone on the desk. Shoulders dipping, she rolled her head back and forth to stretch her neck. Part of her, the part that ached to drop into her nice, soft bed that waited for her twenty feet down the hall, wished that Jeremy would come back with a reasonable explanation. That, hey, they'd blown it and it was a routine inspection. That at least would corroborate what the DDOT guy said and she could go to bed, get a solid five hours of sleep before her alarm went off at five AM.

"Hope?"

She snapped to, rested her elbows on the table and stared down at the phone. "I'm here."

"I just confirmed that pothole thing. Obviously, I'm not giving you our source, but it's someone inside DDOT. TOA specifically. We were told the repair was scheduled for this morning."

"TOA?"

"Traffic Operations Administration. Street and bridge maintenance falls under TOA."

Now wasn't this fascinating? Two different sources inside the same department giving two different stories. Someone was a liar, liar with their pants on fire.

"Okay. Thanks, Jeremy. I appreciate it."

"I owed you one."

Hope laughed. "You owed me more than one, pal."

"Yeah, I know. Gotta run. Let's grab lunch one day."

"Yada, yada," she said. "Text me some dates and we'll see if we can pull off a miracle."

"Will do."

She disconnected and sat back again, eyeballed the hallway leading to the bedroom. That damned bed. She'd saved for months to buy it and hadn't spent nearly enough time in it. Sleeping or otherwise.

All because of nights like this when her job kept her curiosity reeling. Something was amiss. And that something could easily be confirmed by a trip out to the bridge. This time of night, traffic would be light and she could hunt down the pothole. From news footage, she knew the general location of where the lane blockage had started. She'd just drive out there and walk it. If she found a giant pothole, the story was credible. If she didn't find a pothole, well, they'd go with this routine maintenance theory, but it wouldn't explain why two sources from inside DDOT gave conflicting stories.

On something this big, DDOT needed to control the spin. And so far they'd done a lousy job.

Hope pushed back from the table, grabbed her phone and her purse and keys from the counter and an energy drink from the fridge and headed out the door. The massive shot of caffeine would keep her up all night, rather than just the couple of hours she needed, but it would be worth it if she eliminated the pothole. On the way she'd call Hawk and tell him what she'd discovered.

Once on the road, she dialed Hawk's number, and given her level of fatigue, put both hands on the wheel while her Bluetooth connected. First ring he picked up—did the man ever sleep?

"Ms. Denby, you have news for me?"

Oh that sound, mmm-mmm-mmm, it held a rough, gravelly edge that hadn't been there earlier and made her think of hearing it only late at night or in the early mornings.

In bed.

With him.

News for him? She had news. And it included revisiting how he felt about cowboy hats and boots. Oooh-wee, something about this man made her feel naughty.

Risking removing one hand from the wheel, she gulped a shot of her energy drink while keeping her eyes on the quiet road ahead. "It's Hope. And, yes, I do."

Through the phone line, she heard the squeak of a chair. Hawk shifting around and she pictured him in front of some high-tech bank of computers and monitors, working them all at once in search of the next big government cover-up. "Do you ever sleep, Hawk?"

"Only when I have to."

"Tough guy, ay?"

"Hardly. What have you got, *Hope*?"

And, oh, the way he said her name. Chalk it up to a lack of male attention over the last few months, but Hawkeye had it going on.

Or maybe she was just lonely.

Which could be the case because most men couldn't handle her blunt demeanor. She never meant to be hurtful, her mouth just moved faster than her brain sometimes. On her last date she'd asked the guy if he minded being short because she liked that he didn't tower over her. Her intended compliment failed miserably and the guy never called her again. Welcome to life as Hope Denby.

So much for giving a damned compliment!

Whatever. *Watch the road.* Just ahead, a car screamed out of a convenience store parking lot and she braked, slowing enough that the car would get well ahead of her. Driving had never been her favorite thing. Driving at night, under normal circumstances, never mind when dead tired, left her a tad jittery. Over-cautious, if there could ever be such a thing.

"Hope?"

"Sorry. Mind travel. I'm heading out to the bridge."

"*Now?*"

"Yes."

"Uh, no. You can't go there by yourself."

Watch me, big boy. "I can when my contact tells me someone inside DDOT confirmed the pothole repair. What we have here, Mr. Hawk, are conflicting stories. I want to see this pothole for myself and I won't be able to do that during rush hour tomorrow."

"I'll meet you there."

"No. I'll be fine. I just want to look."

"I know. But now I'm curious and you shouldn't be out alone this late."

The man took paranoia to a level far beyond anything she'd ever encountered. "This paranoia," she said, "has it always been such an issue for you?"

Hawk laughed. "Honey, go to work at ATF for a few years and then ask me that question. What are you, twenty-five?"

Well, yikes, he didn't have to sound so condescending. "Hey, I'm almost 26!"

"Christ. You're a damned baby."

"Hey! I'll have you know I'm working on a Master's degree."

What that had to do with anything, she didn't know, but falling back on her education to prove her worth didn't seem like a bad idea. At least at the time. Replaying it in her head, she wasn't sure. The replayed version sounded too close to desperation.

Damn, she had to be into hour thirty-five of this day. Fatigue hung on her, begged her mind and body for rest, but she had this one last thing to do. Then she'd go home and sleep for a couple of hours.

On the other end of the line, Hawk stayed quiet. Probably just as well because she was too tired to argue with a damned blogger. "I'm going to the bridge," she said. "I'll call you in the morning and let you know what I found. Goodnight, Hawk."

Stupid men. Always getting her tongue-tied. She should be better at this. Men talked to her all the time. She'd had plenty of opportunities to perfect her social skills. Her *flirting* skills anyway. Mostly though, when they got past the blond-haired-batting-blue-eyes flirting stage, she stunk at it. Men were a puzzle.

She came to a stop at the traffic light just beyond the bridge. In a few minutes, she'd confirm—or eliminate—the pothole theory and go home to bed.

Sleep would make everything clearer. It always did.

While waiting for the light to change, she flipped to her favorite R&B station where Mary J. Blige informed her about not giving up Mr. Wrong.

"Amen, sister," Hope muttered.

The light flipped and she hung a right. Two minutes and she'd be there.

At nearly three-quarters of a mile long, the Gaynor Bridge spanned the Potomac from Virginia to D.C. Not one of the city's most attractive bridges because of its plain old concrete base and steel guardrails, it was low enough to the river that tree branches on the Virginia side smacked against the side rails making the incredibly narrow footbridge an interesting stroll. Add to that the cars zipping by at highway speeds and the lack of pedestrians at any given time wasn't a shock.

After being closed the majority of the day and causing major headaches for commuters, law enforcement had completed their evidence collecting and all lanes were now open. This late, traffic was light and mostly heading out of D.C. where she was on the side heading in. She'd simply pull over, put her hazards on and walk that lane. For safety, she'd grab her flashlight out of her emergency road kit in the trunk and swing it as she walked. Her own walking billboard alerting drivers to her presence. Towering overhead lights scattered every fifteen feet clearly illuminated the roadway, but an extra layer of *here-I-am-don't-run-me-over* wouldn't hurt.

"Just please don't let there be a drunk on the road."

Wouldn't that be a fabulous ending to a career in its infancy? Beyond her windshield the D.C. skyline seemed to rise up and merge with the cloudy sky. A beautiful sight any day, but tonight, she needed to find a pothole and get to bed.

Hope counted down the mile markers posted on the side rail of the bridge and reached the general area where the closure had been at eight a.m.

Pulling as close to the rail as she could, she parked and slapped her hazards on. She scooped up her phone in case she needed to snap a few photos and checked over her shoulder— no cars. Perfect. She'd just walk this lane real quick and be done.

Comfy bed, here I come.

Traffic in the opposite lane moved at a decent clip, all those D.C. power people making the schlep home after a long day or a night of wining and dining. Good thing she wasn't on *that* side of the bridge or she'd be dodging traffic.

Or getting tattooed to the pavement.

Flashlight in hand, she hoofed it along the right lane, her ballet flats infinitely more comfortable than the stilettos from earlier. God, those things were demons. Feet everywhere should form a massive protest.

Twenty yards in and still no pothole. Thirty-four degrees worth of cold air sent a chill straight up the sleeves of her trench. *Should have worn gloves.*

"Where the hell is this pothole?"

If she had to walk the length of this bridge, she wouldn't be happy. She'd also have to break the trip up by heading back to her car, moving it to the farthest point she'd reached on foot and walk from there to the end. Which meant, she might be here awhile.

A car flew by her on the left and she sucked a breath. Oohh. That was fast. Her skin puckered and not from the cold. Seriously, this may not have been her best idea ever.

Another car, a pickup truck this time, drove by moving much slower. It also pulled over thirty yards ahead of her and —uh, oh—what was this now? Could be the shooter coming back. Assuming the Chief Justice hadn't been targeted.

Hope stopped walking. Just froze in her spot until she figured out what was happening with this truck. A slow whooshing sounded in her ears and her chest thumped. If she needed to, she could run and would have a nice jump.

The driver's side door flew open, a jean clad leg giving it a kick. A man—Hawk—hopped out and stormed toward her.

Silly, Hope.

"Hey!" he yelled. "Lunatic! Are you fucking trying to get killed?"

Oh, terrific. After the day she'd had, he wanted to get nasty? *Not happening, pal.* "Of course not!"

Then he started running. Toward her. Waving his arm as he ran and she froze again, that soft whooshing in her head turning to straight-up white noise. She shook it off, focused on Hawk charging straight at her, both arms now arcing through the air, urging her sideways. *Why is he running?* Even in the dark she saw his mouth moving.

The white noise drifted off, bringing a sharp, almost painful focus. *Car.*

"Car! Move!"

And then the sound of an engine with an odd tick. Tick, tick, tick, like a loose belt or something. She didn't know. She turned, squinted against the headlights and the grill of a car. Not a truck. Or SUV.

"Move!" Hawk yelled, his voice to her back, but getting closer.

The ticking engine grew louder, those headlights shining right in her eyes, somehow pinning her from twenty yards away.

Move.

Tick, tick, tick.

A jarring weight hit her—Hawk—and sent the flashlight soaring before knocking her sideways onto the narrow footbridge. "Ooff!"

Over and over they rolled as his arms came around her, stayed tight even after they stopped moving. Hers had encircled him as well. They were both breathing heavily, and even through her trench coat, she could feel his hands against her, pressing into her flesh.

Her shoulder took the major hit, slamming against the cement as Hawk's bigger body crushed her half against the rail and half against the roadway. *God, that will hurt tomorrow.* She sucked huge gulps of air, fought the agonizing pain shooting across her shoulders into her back.

"You okay? Are you *okay*?"

Hawk's voice. Above her. She opened her eyes, found him staring down at her, his nose close to hers, his eyes wild. He pushed himself up, angling the upper part of his body away, but keeping both hands on either side of her. With each gulping breath, his smell—laundry soap—filled her nose and she focused on it. Took it in, let the clean purity of it drift inside as she readied herself to face the fact she'd almost gotten herself killed.

Adrenaline was his friend. Always had been. It honed his instincts, sharpened his responses. Hid his emotions.

Fucking ATF had made sure he never exposed those.

Already juicing from the adrenaline fix when he climbed out of his truck, Brice had been fuming over Hope Denby's obvious lack of self-preservation. What was it with this woman? She was damned determined to leave herself open to all sorts of trouble.

And that's when trouble flipped its lights on and gunned its engine. The car had been moving onto the bridge with only its running lights. He'd seen it when he climbed out of the truck but absentmindedly figured it was some drunk bastard who'd forgotten to turn on his regular lights. Brice had been too high on irritation over Hope standing on the bridge looking for that damn pothole to realize the car was heading right for her.

Two open lanes but the car was in hers.

The hot rush of fresh adrenaline shut down his brain and sent his body running. The asshole wasn't stopping, wasn't even slowing. He was speeding up. And then ran her down.

Or at least tried to.

"What...just...happened?" she gasped.

Her hair tickled his nose. He turned his head to get the license plate number of the car, but it was long gone. *Not a drunk driver*, the voice inside his head said. "Someone tried to run you over."

"Oh." The streetlight overhead cast her face in a pale gold that emphasized her freckles. "Can...you...let me go?" Her eyes were wide as saucers. "I can't...breathe."

He immediately released her. "Sorry."

He helped her stand and she righted her coat. Her fingers trembled as she brushed dirt from her hip. "No, it's okay."

She was still wearing a skirt but she'd switched out the heels for flat shoes. One of them had come off in the roll and her foot and calf were speckled with tiny rocks and dirt. A trickle of blood ran down the inside of her knee.

Instinctively, he reached down and gently started wiping off her calf. "So much for your acute senses that detect danger a mile away. Looks like you're going to need some cleaning up."

At his touch, she froze, then stepped back. "I'm okay, really."

Her eyes wouldn't meet his when he glanced up. Was she blushing?

Brice, you idiot. You may have just saved her from being the second death on this bridge in the past twenty-four hours but you're practically a stranger. Strangers don't touch strangers.

He rose, keeping his hands to himself. It wasn't the first time his need to protect had been more hindrance than help. Double-checking that there was no other traffic coming, he jogged over and picked up Hope's shoe from where it had fallen. He returned it to her.

"Guess this wasn't the best idea in the middle of the night, huh?" Her fingers seemed to deliberately touch his as she took the shoe from his hand.

He held on to the shoe a few seconds longer than necessary, willing her to look at him. When she finally lifted her gaze, he saw that she wasn't scared or even all that shook up. If anything, she looked excited.

Exhilarated.

The same way he was feeling. *Alive.*

A brush with death could do that to you.

Or maybe the weird light and the adrenaline still coursing through his veins were playing tricks on him. "It was damn stupid."

Indignation flashed in her eyes. Her hair was sticking out on the left side. "Guess what?"

He released the shoe. "What?"

She braced herself against him for balance as she tugged the shoe back on. "I didn't find a pothole."

His fingers itched to fix her hair. *Strangers don't touch strangers.* "Good for you."

"Conflicting stories." She stood upright again, but swayed a

MISTY EVANS & ADRIENNE GIORDANO

little as if dizzy. The hand on his arm gripped him a little tighter. "You know what that means."

"Yeah, no one in the department of transportation actually knows what's going on."

"At least on this bridge, they didn't today. The day the Chief Justice of the Supreme Court was *accidentally* killed." Her hand intentionally squeezed his arm. "Suspicious, don't you think?"

More blood ran down her leg. He glanced away from her excited eyes and listened to the soft *swoosh* of traffic on the other side of the divider.

There was a lot that didn't add up, and a nagging voice in the back of his head kept insisting that tonight's drive-by might not be an accident. *Not a drunk driver.*

But he still didn't have anything more concrete than Lodestone's original tip. His journalist here wanted a story. A story they didn't have yet. "What I think," he said, peeling her hand from his arm and guiding her to his truck, "is that we should get you patched up."

"I'm fine." Against her protests, he hauled her up into the truck cab. "What are you doing?"

His better judgment said he should take her to her place and let her clean up her wounds on her own. *When do I ever listen to my better judgment?*

He shut the door without answering, jogged to her car, moved it off the bridge to the emergency parking area on the D.C. side, locked it up and hauled ass back to his truck. They'd come back for the car tomorrow, when he could check the bridge, and the lack of potholes, in the light of day.

On his way back to the truck, he passed the busted flashlight. Bending down, he ran his fingers through the broken plastic. What if he hadn't shown up when he did? What if Hope was now lying injured or dead on this bridge?

He looked up and saw her watching him through the wind-

80

shield of the truck. From her expression, he could see she was thinking the same thing.

When he climbed into the cab and started the truck, she was still staring at him. "That was very Bruce Willis of you back there. Thank you. But I can drive myself home."

She smiled and it was genuine, but he could see her hands were still shaking in her lap. *So damn naïve.*

For a moment, he wanted to share everything with her. All the stuff he'd learned through the years. All the wrongs he had yet to right.

But she was a cheerleader. A believer. A hopeless idealist who thought the world was just and fair.

This time, he gave in, reaching over to smooth down her tousled hair. She didn't move away, but he could see the uneasiness in her eyes.

The aftermath of what she'd just been through would catch up with her in short order. As an adrenaline junkie himself, he knew from experience, the rush would drain off and she'd be depleted, totally wiped. She might even go into shock.

"You shouldn't drive. We'll pick up the car tomorrow."

"I'm fine, Mr. Hawkeye," she said again.

He had to tread lightly. Forcing her to come home with him —what was he thinking?—would only push her away.

"Of course you are." He started the truck and put it in gear. "I have something I'd like to show you, though. Something I think you'll find interesting."

As he pulled onto the road, he sensed her hesitation in the tense silence filling the space between them. "The car will be fine until morning. I have some new info to share with you. Unless you're too tired, Miss Denby. It has been a rough day for a Public Information Officer."

Throwing down a challenge did the trick. The indignation inserted itself in her voice again. "I could go all night, Mr. Hawkeye, and for your information, it's not an issue."

Bingo. He had her.

"So where is this thing you want to show me?" Hope asked.

Taking the off ramp, he kept an eye on the rearview. No cars on his tail. "My office."

Which was stupid beyond stupid, but he had no other choice if he was going to keep an eye on her.

"You have an office?"

Sort of. "Why is that hard to believe? You think all lowlife bloggers blog from their mother's basements?"

Sarcasm laced her voice. "Don't they?"

At least she wasn't freaking out about the car gunning for her. No tears, no rehashing of what happened or endless chatter. Hope seemed to live in the moment. Something he wished he could do.

He changed lanes, taking a roundabout way to his house. "Hackers, yes. Maybe a few bloggers here and there, but the majority of us are upstanding citizens. We own property, pay our taxes, and—"

"Quote Thomas Paine?" she interrupted.

"I was going to say, vote."

"Ah."

They drove the rest of the way in silence. His neighborhood was dark, his house as well. His gaze automatically scanned the vehicles parked in driveways and on the street. Nothing out of place.

He parked and they both got out. Hope stopped on the sidewalk. "Your office looks suspiciously like a house."

"I hide in plain sight."

"Good to know."

Once inside, he flipped on lights and armed his security system. Hope stood unmoving, her gaze sweeping over his shabby, but comfortable furnishings. "Let me guess, your office is in the basement and your mother lives in the attic."

"Not a hacker, remember?" He took her coat and motioned for her to sit on the recliner. "Would you like a drink?"

"I don't suppose you have a decent chardonnay?"

He went to the fridge, grabbed a bottle of water. On his way back, he ducked into the bathroom to snag a washcloth and some bandages.

Returning to the living room, he set up his collection on the coffee table, handing her the water. "Any dizziness?"

She turned up a lip at the water, but took a swig. "What is this thing you're going to show me?"

Dizziness confirmed. He covertly checked her pupils as she tipped her head up for another drink. He thought he'd protected her head on the roll, but everything had happened so fast, she might have smacked it at some point.

Pupils normal. A bit dilated, but they were equal in size.

Handing her the washcloth, he sat on the coffee table facing her. "Your office isn't above scandal."

"Meaning?"

"The woman who had your job before you. Did you ever meet her?"

"Sally Hernandez?" She washed the blood off of her leg. "She was gone before I started."

"Do you know why?"

Hope tilted her head and sized him up. "She got another job in Minnesota or some place."

He took the washcloth from her and wiped at some dried blood near her ankle. "She was sleeping with Justice Robinson."

"What?" Her outrage seemed to override her nervousness about his touch. "You're kidding."

"She was sleeping with a lobbyist with the NRA at the same time."

"No."

Tossing the washcloth aside, he peeled the paper off the

bandage and handed it to her. Nosy journalist types always loved a good scoop. "I have evidence if you want to see it. One of my sources is inside the FBI. She showed me phone records and a transcript of some pillow talk. They believe Hernandez fed court information to the lobbyist for nearly two years before the Feds caught on."

She held the bandage, her eyes alight with excitement again. Her body practically vibrated. "And you didn't break the story?"

He knew that feeling. God help him, she was turned on because of a scoop. *Welcome to my world.* "When they confirmed her involvement, they made her quit. She was shipped off to Minnesota."

"Why didn't the Justice Department make a stink?"

"Think about it. This was going on for two years. Every ruling Justice Robinson made during that timeframe could be called into question. The scandal would have been embarrassing, but any of the rulings he sat on could have been overturned. The fallout would have been catastrophic."

She still held the bandage, totally ignoring her wound. "So they cut a deal. Her silence for a new job and a new life."

"All Robinson got was a slap on the hand. And a divorce."

"What happened to the lobbyist?"

"Committed suicide."

She scooted to the edge of the seat. "Seriously?"

"There was a note saying he was depressed and couldn't go on, but it was typed."

"It wasn't a suicide, was it?"

Her assumption was accurate in his book. He took the bandage from her hand and carefully positioned it over the cut on the outside of her knee. "What do you think?"

She leaned forward, resting her elbows on her knees and tapped her chin with a finger. "Who would have killed him?"

Brice shrugged indifference even though he was anything

but. He'd kept a lid on this story for a host of reasons, and now he finally had someone to talk it out with, keeping Hope around at the same time.

And *whoa*, why did his lower body get inordinately happy at that thought? He was only making sure she was alright and didn't go into shock.

Right, and Elvis was alive and the Pope was his father.

He ran a thumb over the bandage edges to make sure they adhered properly to her skin. Her calf flexed. Nice skin. Smooth, soft...

She cleared her throat and he snatched his hand back. Got busy crunching up the paper. "Who killed the lobbyist? I don't know, but it would be fun to look into."

"I don't think Ms. Hernandez, or this killer, if there is one, should get away with what they did." Her face was still close to his. Too close. She smelled like fresh air and some kind of floral perfume.

He shrugged. "I agree. But there's not enough evidence to risk the fallout that would occur if I released the story. That's why I'm telling you this." He met her gaze. "I want you to know I take this seriously. I understand the responsibility and I'm sure as hell not going to release a story until it's ready to be told."

"Wow."

"Wow?"

Her face split into an all-teeth smile. "That totally just turned me on."

Holy shit. Keeping his distance, he held up his hands. "Great. Good to know."

She snorted. "I'm a freak. A good scoop makes me giddy. And I love that you have a sense of integrity about it. A lot of people don't. They want the drama and the scandal, no matter the cost. The Hernandez story? Plenty of bloggers and reporters would have let that baby fly."

"I couldn't do it."

"Maybe after we clear up Turner's investigation, we should, you know, look into it. Together."

She wanted to work with him to expose a scandal that could rock her employer?

Her big, blue eyes swallowed him up; the offer of help nearly undid him. "Um, sure." He stood and headed for his computer. Safe harbor from the onslaught of Hope Denby. "If you want. We can look into it."

He prayed she'd want.

"Cool. I'd have to stay the silent partner though." The recliner creaked and Hope came to stand behind him as he checked his website's hit counter. Her hand brushed his shoulder. "Thank you for taking care of me even though I didn't need it."

Sweat trickled down the back of his neck. Forty-eight hundred hits on his FBI hacker story. Not bad. The story was being spread around social media as well. "Yeah, no problem."

She leaned over his shoulder, reading the blog post. "So what do your blogger instincts tell you about today?"

Her breath tickled his ear, messing with his thought processes. "Today?"

"You still think Chief Justice Turner was murdered over the Kenton Labs deal?"

"Where there's smoke, there's fire."

"We have a lot of smoke."

At that moment, he had some fire, too, a few inches below his belt.

Fidgeting, he checked his Twitter feed. Lots of retweets and comments. His eyes scanned them, but his brain wouldn't engage. All he kept seeing was that car's lights coming on, hearing the engine gun, that funny tick-tick-tick. Hope standing frozen like a petrified deer. "Did you notice anyone following you today? Any suspicious cars or people

Exposing Justice

Exposing Justice

hanging around? Any unusual activity around your house tonight?"

She straightened. "No, why?"

"When you went to the bridge, did you notice any cars following you, staying close? Maybe too close?"

She hesitated for a second. "You don't really believe it was a drunk driver on the bridge, do you?"

Swiveling in his chair, he faced her. He hated the guarded look in her eyes, but he gave it to her straight. "No, Hope, I don't. My blogger instincts and every other instinct honed by the military and ATF tells me that was no drunk driver. I think someone was purposely trying to run you down."

Hope flopped back onto the couch, stared right at Hawk whose gaze was on her, steady and unsettling. He had a way of not just looking, but dissecting—analyzing—a person. Almost as if he were digging for the underlying truth. As a journalist, she understood. But this? This was something else. Something deep and intense and probing. He must have been awesome at questioning suspects.

Particularly female ones because he had those panty-dropper eyes that totally made her hormones come alive.

Which was saying something since he'd just told her someone had tried to kill her, or at the very least maim her—wasn't that just oodles of fun—and all she could think about was her hormones.

Eight hours ago all she'd wanted was to keep Hawk from releasing an unconfirmed story and now suddenly she was a target?

"You don't believe me." Hawk said, obviously referring to his assertion that someone intentionally tried to make her road kill.

"It's not that."

87

"Then what?"

She rested her head back against the soft cushion, closed her eyes a second and fought the fatigue slowing her brain functions. "I guess I don't see it yet."

"That someone tried to run your ass over? What's not to see?"

Great. Combative. Perfect. She could tangle with the best of them. Fast-talking wasn't a problem. At least when she wasn't bone tired. In her current state, after the day she'd had and well, the whole almost-road-kill incident, the words circling her brain wouldn't string together into a rational argument.

"No," she said. "I mean, obviously I get that. What I don't see is how the fact that someone almost hit me equals someone coming after me because I'm asking questions about the Chief Justice. It's late and like you said, maybe I was careless to be walking on the bridge like that. It could have been a drunk driver. Or someone messing with their phone because traffic was so light. Maybe they just flat out didn't see me."

"Hope! Are you kidding me right now? Jeez."

She tossed her hands up, not really frustrated but feeling a bit of drama might be necessary to back this boy off. Paranoid or not, concerned or not, he didn't get to yell at her. *Find the upshot.* "Hey. I just want to make sure we're on the right track here. That's all. I'm not dismissing it. I just want to be sure." She curled her legs up under her, fiddled with the bandage on her leg. "We're a funny pair. You're Mr. Paranoid and I'm..."

"Miss Rah-Rah."

She stretched her mouth wide. The nerve! "You did *not* just say that to me."

"Yeah, I did. You want everything nice and tidy. My guess is you see the world as a beautiful place. All flowers and sunshine. You're young and idealistic. You can overcome any issues." He swung a fist in the air. "If we all stick together, we can make a difference. Rah, rah. Go, team!"

Seriously. The blogger was mocking her? She liked to stay positive and upbeat. So what? It was a whole lot better than living life his way. Miserable and paranoid. "Listen, old man— that's what I'm going to call you from now on because you keep reminding me that I'm young and you're too darned crabby for a man your age. Well fine. Whatever. Are you done making fun of me? Because if you are, I will tell you that yes, I like to see the world a certain way. When I wake up in the morning, I expect it to be a good day. In this crazy, sadistic world, what's wrong with wanting to feel happy instead of...instead of..."

"Cynical?"

"Yes! Cynical. I mean you walk around telling people your name is Hawkeye for God's sake."

"I'm dealing with crackpots. One of them could come to my door and blow my ass away."

"And you enjoy your life like that?" She waved her hand around the living room where thick, heavy drapes covered every window. By the dust on the top, she guessed those suckers hadn't budged in months. The entire place felt like a cave. One he obviously hid in all day long. "You like living with your blinds and drapes closed like this?"

His lips rolled in and pressed into a thin line before he tilted his head back and stared at the ceiling a minute. Thinking about it.

Some life you got there, sport. "I can't believe it takes you this long to decide if you like your life."

"It doesn't. I do like my life. I like it better now than when I was an agent with ATF. Now, I at least feel like I'm doing some good."

"Careful there, you're starting to sound like an idealist. Before we know it you'll be opening these drapes and letting the sun in while shouting 'Go team!' and toasting me with the Hope Denby happy juice."

Mr. Crabby didn't just smile, he cracked up, a good, hearty

laugh that made his face explode into sharp, sexy angles. *Hey there, fella.*

"Happy juice. You are a total pisser, Hope."

She grinned back at him. Couldn't help it. Being able to make this oh-so-serious man laugh gave her a rush. A warm, syrupy flood that took over her body. The fact that he looked the way he did, didn't hurt. Mr. Crabby was hot.

Capital H.

Capital O.

Capital T.

Rah-rah.

"I like when you laugh," she said. "You should try it more often."

"I like when I laugh too. And you're right, it doesn't happen a lot."

"That sounds like a challenge." She threw her shoulders back, stuck out her chest and dropped her voice. "Hope Denby, your mission, if you choose to accept it, is to make Mr. Hawkeye laugh."

The gravelly voice came out a little too creepy for her liking, but she'd try again some other time. Try to get it right.

"And?" he said.

"And what?" Normal voice this time.

He leaned forward, rested his elbows on his knees and gave her a massive dose of eye contact and...we meet again warm, syrupy feeling. She held her hand up palm out then whipped it around and fanned herself.

Hawk laughed again, shook his head. "Are you accepting the mission?"

"Oh, Hawk. I am most definitely accepting that mission. Bring it, big boy. First, you have to tell me your name. Although, I do sort of like Hawk, but since I'm sitting in your living room, maybe I should know what your mother calls you."

"Jeez, you talk a lot." He shook his head hard. "I think it scrambles my brain."

"I listen a lot too. Makes me a good journalist."

"Why?"

"Why am I a good journalist?"

"No. Why do you talk a lot?"

Easy question. "Middle child of seven. My mother likes to say I talk so much because I had to fight to the death for attention when growing up."

He rose from his desk chair, walked over to the couch and dropped at the opposite end, his back against the armrest and his feet on the cushion. "See now that's interesting. I'm a middle child too. Three older brothers and two younger sisters."

Huh. He didn't act like a middle child. Well, at least in her mind, but who made her the expert on middles? There had to be a study somewhere on classic behaviors of middle children. She'd look that up and see which one of them was more of a traditional middle.

"And yet," she said. "we are so different."

"I was an army brat. We moved a lot. Between the moving and all the kids, I got lost in the commotion. Fine with me. I learned how to fly under the radar and it made me a great undercover agent."

"Probably why you like the anonymity of running a blog. No one needs to know who you are, but you still get to run around chasing scoops."

He touched a finger to his nose. "Bingo."

"On the scoops, we agree. I love it. I love that flutter I get every time I think I'm on to something. Unfortunately, I don't get to do a lot of that in my job and I miss it."

So, okay, she just said *that*. She'd blame it on fatigue because who told near strangers their job didn't quite satisfy them.

"Then why not work as a reporter?"

"Because I have the White House in my life plan."

He drew his eyebrows together, let out a long sigh. "Jesus. A *life* plan? Are you kidding me right now?"

She snorted. "Nope. Got it all figured out. Eventually, if all goes well, I'd like to be the White House Press Secretary. Who knows if I'll ever get there, but," she leaned over, tugged on the loose fabric that bunched at the knee of his jeans, "a girl can dream, right?"

He stared down at her hand, now moving away from his knee, then met her gaze with those panty-dropper eyes again. Whew. *Mr. Crabby had a way.*

"Hope, I think you can pretty much accomplish whatever you'd like. I think you're enough of a pain in the ass to make it happen."

"Well, look at you throwing around the compliments." She fanned herself again. "I'm not sure I can take too much of this."

"Damn, you're cute."

A heavy dose of steamy eye contact followed and the silence in the room, that weighty awkwardness that fell somewhere between what was good for her and what was catastrophically bad, forced her to look down and fiddle with an imaginary string on her blouse.

Eventually, she gave up on the not-there string and nudged him with her foot. "You're not so bad yourself there, tiger. At least when you're not being crabby."

From the desk, his computer dinged and he glanced over at it. "I need to get that." He got up, gave her foot a gentle pat and she studied his fingers, long, beautiful fingers with well-kept nails and suddenly she had a vision of those fingers doing things.

To her.

Naughty things.

Oooh-weee.

"Sure," she said. "Let me know if it's something good. Then we can make a plan about tomorrow and the next steps in our little investigation here."

"A plan. Yep, you bet."

Apparently, from the sound of his voice, he didn't like plans. "Hawk?"

He turned back. "What's up?"

"You never told me your name."

"Caught that did you?"

"I'm a good listener, remember?"

"If you say so." The computer dinged again and he hustled over and shook the mouse to clear the screensaver. Without looking at her, he said, "My name is Brice. Brice Brennan."

Brice wanted to flog himself. He'd told Hope his name. His *real* name.

The urge to bash his head into his keyboard was strong. Too bad they didn't make an emoticon for that. Complete self-destruction. A little smiley face that suddenly frowned and blew himself to pieces.

Speaking of smiley faces...

"Brice Brennan," Hope said from behind him. "That's a solid byline. I can see it in *The Post*...or think if you were on the news!" Her voice took on a serious, newscaster quality. "This is Brice Brennan, reporting from the killing fields of injustice and treachery in our nation's capital. Watch your back out there, Patriots!"

The tension in his shoulders slacked a bit. He almost smiled. Her sarcasm was better than acting like he'd opened his soul and handed it to her. Which it most certainly felt like.

First, he'd brought her to his home. Now, he'd told her his name. What was next? He'd sign over his first born and let her run his blog?

Paranoia will destroy you. Brice focused on his screen, bringing up his personally designed search engine. The Kinks, Ozzy, and so many more angst-y bands had it right. What was the harm in telling goodie-two-shoes, Hope Denby, high school cheerleader and Girl Scout Extraordinaire what his real name was?

He typed the name of the bridge into the search engine and hit enter. Too many undercover ops and false identities had left their marks under his skin. Too many nights of sitting in the dark with his computer online with a bunch of conspiracy theorists with wacky ideas. All of them leaving their marks as well.

The ATF had made him suppress his name for years, becoming other men, other personas. And in the end, the government itself had branded him a traitor and tried to ruin him. They'd taken everything from him—his good standing as an agent, his reputation in the real world. His very life outside these walls.

He'd lost friends. His best friend, in fact.

Most of all, he'd lost faith.

That happened when your partner betrayed you, and the very essence of everything you stood for, in favor of drugs and money.

And the guns. Let's not forget Wes and the guns...

All the criminal activities Wes—a man Brice had been closer to than his own brothers—had done and ATF had turned a blind eye to.

So yeah, Brice was paranoid about his identity for a good reason. It was the only thing he had left.

The sound of shifting on the couch brought him out of the muck in his brain. "That would be your worst nightmare, wouldn't it?" Hope asked around a yawn. "Revealing yourself to the world. Standing in front of God and country and telling everyone your name."

Her scenario was right up there, but his worst nightmare at the moment was wrapped in a five-foot-four-inch package of happiness and denial of all things bad.

His search engine came up with nothing pertinent on the day's events. He typed in Chief Justice Raymond Turner and hit enter again.

And then from behind him, he heard a noise that sounded like the bleat of a dying sheep. Panicked that Hope had actually gone into shock, Brice whirled around, ready to jump into action.

But the brat wasn't in shock. Another bleat issued from her half-opened mouth as she snored loud enough to rattle the window panes.

Snoring. She was snoring.

Falling back into his chair, he rolled his eyes and laughed softly, watching her for a moment. He considered grabbing his phone and videotaping her. After all, he might need blackmail material down the road if she ever threatened to expose him.

Seeing her sleep, though, after their long-ass day from hell, did something to him. This goofy twenty-five-year old who thought she was going to save the world with her cheery, upbeat attitude made him feel...*well, damn.*

Feeling anything but tense and paranoid was a minor miracle. He rubbed his head and let his hand fall back. *How did this happen?* He felt...happy.

Maybe he was a nutcase after all.

Another modicum of the day's tension drained out of his muscles. He rose, snatched a blanket from the closet and gently laid it over her.

Her ponytail was a mess, hair falling everywhere. Kneeling beside her, he gently coaxed a strand away from her cheek where her snoring lips kept sucking it into her mouth. She was so out of it, her snoring never broke stride.

Watching her, being so close to her, eased that last smidgen of anxiety from his body. Like a switch flipped to off, it all rushed out of him in a wave. Leaning on the edge of the couch for support, he let one of his fingers caress her smooth skin.

He didn't have this. Didn't have a woman to be close to, to laugh with and tease. Hadn't missed it either.

Enter Hope Denby.

The brat didn't know all his secrets yet, but she knew the most important ones. And he didn't mind.

For the first time since leaving the ATF, Brice relaxed.

7

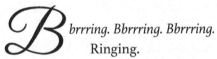*brrring. Bbrrring. Bbrrring.*
Ringing.

Somewhere, her phone was ringing. Hope shifted and a pain shot down her neck into her shoulders. *Holy cannoli.*

Her phone rang again and she fought to open her eyes, the lids so heavy she wondered if her attempts would fail. Finally, she stared at a stark white ceiling that wasn't hers. What the?

My name is Brice.

Hawk's house. He'd brought her here after the bridge incident. She must have passed out on his couch. She shot to a sitting position. "Oh, no."

Time. What time was it? She glanced at the window. No help there. The man had every visible window cloaked in heavy drapes. From inside, it would be impossible to tell whether it was dark or light outside.

How did he live like this?

She ran her hand through her tangled hair, snagging on a knot. "Ow."

Had to be morning. Had to be. She glanced down where a blanket covered her lower half. Had she done that? She didn't remember a blanket. All she remembered was something about a byline and then...nothing. But exhaustion had kicked in long before that so it shouldn't have surprised her she'd gone comatose.

Her phone still sat on the coffee table and she checked the number in her missed calls log. A D.C. number, but one she didn't recognize. No surprise there either. The generic ringtone —that classic *bbrrring*—that had ripped her from sleep was her default tone. Had it been one of her frequent callers, the person would have had an assigned ringtone.

No voicemail. Wrong number maybe.

At the top of the screen, she checked the time. 7:30.

She leaped up. "Crud. Seven-thirty!"

An hour to get home, shower, primp and get to work. No chance.

Terrific. Her office was in chaos over the tragic death of the Chief Justice and she'd overslept. Way to impress the boss. *Woohoo! Yay, Hope.*

She folded the blanket and draped it over the back of the couch, giving it one last fluff before she faced the dilemma of how to get home.

Her car, hopefully, would still be parked in the emergency area at the edge of the bridge. Assuming it hadn't been towed. Which she hoped hadn't happened. That fine wasn't in her already struggling budget. She sighed. What a day that had been.

She glanced down the hall that led to the darkened kitchen. A clunking noise that could have been a furnace kicking on or an ice maker dumping fresh cubes came from that direction.

"Hawk?"

No answer. And given the darkness, she assumed any windows back there were covered as well. Did he ever let light into this place? Ever?

She understood safety measures, but this bordered on prison. Emotional and physical.

She glanced over at the staircase, considered wandering up there. Two steps in she halted. This was his house. One he'd invited her to, but really? She shouldn't be making herself at home by wandering around.

She'd call a cab to take her to the bridge where she'd retrieve her car. Then she wouldn't have to disturb him.

Excellent plan.

On her phone, she searched for the cab company's number only to have the damned phone ring again—*bbrrring!*—the annoying blare shattering the quiet and making her flinch.

Fatigue did that to her. Made her a little jumpy.

Same number as before. Someone was looking for her. She tapped the screen.

"Hello?"

"Hope Denby?"

"Yes. Who is this?"

"My name is Anthony Gerard."

"Okay."

"I'm an officer with the Supreme Court Police."

Oh. This didn't happen every day. "Good morning. How can I help you?"

Above her the floor creaked. Footsteps. Hawk must have woken up. She tracked his footsteps to the right.

"Do you know who I am?"

"Should I, Officer Gerard?"

"I'm part of Chief Justice Turner's protection detail."

Kapow. Why was this man calling her? She wouldn't bother wondering how he got her contact information. He worked for the United States Supreme Court. Somehow she didn't think tracking a phone number would be a problem.

The steps creaked and Hawk's feet came into view through the spindles as he descended. He wore track pants and a T-shirt

99

and when his head finally dipped below where the ceiling opened for the stairway she furiously waved her hand. He tilted his head and listened.

"Oh," she said to the officer. "I'm so sorry."

"He was a good man."

"I've heard that, yes. I never met him."

"Which is why I'm wondering what your car is doing parked at the bridge. You've got thirty minutes to get here, Ms. Denby, and then I have this car impounded as evidence."

The line went dead. *Yowzer.* Did he really think...? No time to ponder that, she cleared the screen and rushed back to the couch to grab her purse and shoes.

Hawk hit the base of the stairs. "What's up?"

"That was one of the officers on Chief Turner's protection detail."

"Why's he calling you?"

"He wants to know why my car is at the bridge. He gave me thirty minutes to get there and explain or he's seizing it as evidence."

"Shit."

"Yuh."

Hawk sprinted back up the stairs. "Give me two minutes. Quick shower and we're gone. Get ready!"

A shower! No time! She stared down at herself, fully dressed in yesterday's clothes, no toothbrush, no clean underwear. Nothing. She'd have to meet with Anthony Gerard in this condition.

And Hawk wanted her to get ready? With what? All she had toiletry wise was a breath mint and hairbrush. Might as well put them to work and wash up as much as she could while she waited on Hawk.

Three minutes later, he knocked on the bathroom door. "Let's roll," he said.

She'd always known men were freakish, but how he showered that fast was nothing short of a miracle.

Totally impressive.

She swung the door open and there he stood, his short, damp hair slicked back, water droplets still darkening his shirt and a soapy clean smell sending the girls trapped in her uterus a wakeup call.

I need a man.

Maybe this one. At least that's what one of the girls—from here on out known as Hormona—hollered.

Damned, Hormona.

Hawk swooped his hand toward the back door. "Are you going to stand there and stare at me all day. Get your sweet ass moving."

"Sorry. I was...distracted."

"I see that."

"I'm jealous of your shower."

"If we had time, I'd let you jump in."

With you! This from Hormona. What a tramp.

"After I get my car and we talk to this guy, I'll go home and get cleaned up. I need to call my boss. There's no way I'm getting to work on time."

He grabbed her arm, dragged her to the back door. "Do it in the car. We're down to twenty-five minutes and who knows what kind of traffic we'll hit."

Twenty-eight minutes and a text to Officer Gerard later, Hawk parked next to Hope's car in the emergency parking area, large enough for a few vehicles, at the base of the bridge.

A tall man wearing a black suit leaned against the back quarter panel of a black SUV. Dark seemed the operative word to describe him. Dark hair, dark sunglasses, dark expression.

He was also, according to every major network in the country, the man who'd tried to keep Justice Turner from bleeding out. The photos and video of him trying to smother the Chief's chest wound, his face tense and focused and...agonized...would stay with her forever.

"He's the one who was on the bridge with the Chief."

Not bothering to wait for Hawk's response, she kicked the passenger door of the truck open and hopped out. Thank goodness for flat shoes. She scooted around the front, pushing a wayward hair out of her face. "Hi. I'm Hope. Sorry we're a few minutes late. Traffic was *rough*. I hate D.C. rush hour."

Officer Gerard jerked his chin at Hawk. "Who's this?"

"This is..." Whoa. How should she introduce him? Based on the fact that she was sitting in his house before Hawk admitted his real name, she guessed he didn't want her advertising it. She turned to him, held her hand out. "Your call."

Hawk held his hand to the officer. "Hawkeye."

"Code names. Great." He offered a brief handshake that bordered on rude and turned to Hope. "You want to tell me why a car belonging to an employee of the Public Information Office of the Supreme Court is parked near where the Chief Justice was killed?"

The man was running on pure emotion. Hope sensed it in the tightness of his stance, the way he pointed at her car. The harsh tone.

Refusing to be intimidated—they were on the same team here—Hope threw her shoulders back. "I don't know what the big deal is, but you need to know I received a tip last night." She glanced at Hawk but he stayed mum. "A tip that led me to think perhaps Justice Turner's death might have extenuating circumstances. I spent all last night chasing it down."

"What are you, an investigator now? The police are handling it."

"The police are handling what they think is a road rage incident," Hope said. "I think it may be more based on the tip I received."

Even with his eyes hidden behind sunglasses, she felt the death glare. "What's this tip?"

Hawk finally stepped forward. "It came from me. I run the First Amendment Patriot blog. I have a reliable source who has me looking into a few inconsistencies."

By the sudden scowl on Anthony Gerard's face, this didn't seem like welcome news.

"Shit," he said. "You're the one who broke the story about the deputy AG?"

Lookie here. Hawk was *famous.* She held up her hand. "Don't panic. Hawk and I have made a deal and my boss signed off on it. He won't print anything regarding the Chief Justice's death until we vet it."

Officer Gerard shifted the death glare to Hawk. "And what do you get out of it?"

Hawk didn't seem to realize he was about to be incinerated. He glared back. "I get a thirty minute jump on the next big story coming out of the Supreme Court."

"Right. And you're gonna stick to this deal?" Gerard waved that away, let out a huff while doing so. "I don't believe it."

"I don't care what you believe. If this tip pans out, this big story is about to get bigger."

"He's right," Hope said. "The tip was about the Chief Justice delivering a ruling on a big case. I started digging last night. I can't tell you my source, but it's a good one. We think the Justice was about to rule on whether or not Kenton Labs would get a hearing on extending their Donazem patent."

Officer Gerard's jaw locked and a muscle jumped and how about *that*! If his body language were any indication, she'd hit a nerve. A giant one. Whether he was grieving, shaken up from a traumatic experience, or her Kenton Labs theory might be solid —all of the above maybe—she couldn't know. But this partic-

MISTY EVANS & ADRIENNE GIORDANO

ular member of the Chief Justice's security detail was not unaffected.

Hawk seemed to realize it too. "What the hell happened up here, yesterday, man?"

Officer Gerard's jaw muscle jumped again. "I can't talk about it. Ongoing investigation."

Driving by the spot twenty-four hours later had a chilling effect on Hope. She hadn't noticed the blood stains last night in the dark. This morning, they seemed to stand out like beacons. "I'm so sorry, Officer Gerard. I know this must be hard on you as well as Justice Turner's family and friends."

"Just tell me why your car is parked here."

What was the deal with the car? *Whatever.* "I came back to the bridge last night because Hawk and I both checked with DDOT,"—she nodded toward Hawk—"and we were given different reasons from two different sources for the lane being blocked yesterday. That, in conjunction with some of the other information we've discovered, is suspicious to me."

"Routine maintenance," Gerard said. "The cops already cleared that detail."

Hawk waved a hand. "That's what my source confirmed, but Hope's source said a pothole needed repairing. Seems they don't have their shit together."

"So," Hope said, "out of curiosity, I came back to the bridge around midnight last night to look for this supposed pothole."

"And?"

"No pothole."

"Instead," Hawk said, "someone tried to plow her over."

The officer's head jerked back. "As in, tried to *hit* you? On this bridge?"

"Yes. I was walking in the right lane, swinging a flashlight. I'd parked my car behind me with the hazards on."

"So they saw you."

"They had to," Hawk said. "She was shook up so I parked her car here and we left."

Hope nodded. "And that's where we are. Hawk here has promised me he will not print anything to damage the Chief Justice's reputation."

"Uh, correction. You had twenty-four hours and you've used most of them already. You now have another forty-eight, but that's it."

Gerard's body posture screamed defiance. "Don't fuck with me. He was a good man. An honest one. Make sure you've got it straight before you print one goddamn thing. I'll come after you with everything I've got."

"I'm not interested in wrecking the reputation of a Supreme Court Justice. The story about the deputy AG? That needed to be told. A dedicated agent is dead because of that man's greedy ambition. The son of a bitch didn't care who he sacrificed to put himself in power, and I know what that feels like. I lived through a similar experience with a man I trusted at one time with my life. Right now, I think the Chief Justice might have been murdered and I'm trying to figure out why and by whom."

"Officer Gerard," Hope said, "you spent a lot of time with the Chief Justice, does any of this make sense to you?"

He ran a hand down his face, let it drop to his side like it weighed too much for him to hold up any longer. The sun peeped from behind a cloud, illuminating the telltale dark circles under his eyes. Obviously he hadn't slept.

Exhaustion would only fuel his distrust of them. Probably should. She wouldn't trust them either. Not yet.

Hope stepped forward but stopped when he folded his arms across his chest, closing himself off. "I can see you cared about Justice Turner. You have no reason to trust us. I know that. But someone tried to run me down last night. I'd like to believe it was a drunk driver. Hawk is convinced I'm wrong. That scares the hell out of me. It also tells me someone doesn't like me chasing down leads on this story. And honestly, we want to control this. Since Hawk called me yesterday, I've done nothing but try to control it and protect the Chief Justice's name. Soon enough, though, something about this will break and we won't be able to stop it. Let's get ahead of it. Let's control the flow of information. If you can help us with that, great." She stepped back, held up her hands. "That's all I can say."

The officer turned away and took long, purposeful strides to his car. What? After that speech he was leaving? "Are you leaving?"

He hesitated for a moment, looked up at the now beaming sun. "You're right. I have no reason to trust you. But I'll vet you. Both of you. If I like what I hear, I'll be in touch. For now, sit tight."

"Understandable," she said. "But trust me when I say, we don't have time to sit tight."

8

When Brice's doorbell rang at three-twenty that afternoon, he almost didn't answer. He didn't want to buy Girl Scout cookies or magazines to support the local youth group. Not that he hated Girl Scouts or youth groups, he just didn't need the distractions. Or the cookies.

But then it rang again. Either it was a persistent Girl Scout, or it was Mitch Monroe, stopping by to be his annoying self and "hang out."

"I do not want to hang out, Mitch," Brice said as he threw open the door and found Hope standing there. She looked like she was two parts her normal cheerleader self, and one part wrung-out public information officer. "Oh, hi."

She pushed passed him, not waiting for him to invite her in. "Hi Hawk. How was your day?"

He simply stared at her, soaking her up. No matter which part was which, they all looked good. Really good.

She raised her brows. "This is where you say, 'Hi, Hope. My day was awesome. How was yours?'"

Normal conversation. Right. *Jeez, Bri, get it together.* "By the

107

look on your face, I don't need to ask how your day was. It was a repeat of yesterday. Brutal."

"Ding, ding, ding, give the blogger a cookie."

At least her usual sarcasm was there. "Why are you here and not at work?"

"Officer Gerard called. He wants to meet at the Washington Monument at four o'clock."

"Does he?" Brice had spent the day researching Kenton Labs and trying to get someone there to answer questions. So far, they'd shut him out. He'd started researching the board and upper management and had turned up zip. "You really think he can help us?"

"He was close to Turner. Had been his security detail for almost five years. He probably saw and heard a lot. Plus, maybe he can give us a more accurate accounting of what happened on that bridge yesterday. Can't beat going directly to the source."

True. He reached out and jabbed her in the bicep. "You didn't go on your own this time and leave me behind?"

She jabbed him back. "I thought about it."

"That a girl."

She smiled. "Officer Gerard said he only wants to meet with me—he didn't like what he discovered about you, I guess—so I probably shouldn't be here, but after last night..."

Her voice trailed off and big, blue eyes begged him not to judge.

"It would be irresponsible for you to go alone to meet a source you don't know."

"I did what you told me." She paced to his curtains, peeked between the panels and looked out at the street. "I've been watching to make sure no one's following me and I've been extra paranoid at home and at work. I haven't seen anyone unusual around. Maybe what happened last night really was just a fluke."

And the three files Grey had sent him to work on contained nothing but fictional crimes by people leading the good ol' U.S. of A. "If we're going to meet Gerard, we better get going."

When Brice helped her into his truck a minute later, she shook her head. "You're setting feminism back fifty years."

"By opening a door for you?"

She only smiled at him, and he tried to ignore the hot flush under his collar as he went around to his side and slid in.

"I didn't have time to do much research on Kenton Labs," she said around a yawn as she slid down in the seat and closed her eyes. "Amy, my boss, had me sending out memos and press releases all day."

"I read through about six hundred pieces on them posted on the internet."

"Did you find anything interesting?"

"Most of the articles were the usual propaganda about their amazing drug and the studies Dr. Martin Block has done with it. He's their leading R&D scientist. Quite the star in the drug development world. There were a few facts that could be damning if you look hard, but won't hold much weight unless we can find a smoking gun."

They hit the highway, merging into traffic. Brice kept an eye out for anyone following them. When Hope didn't ask any more questions, he glanced over.

Was she sleeping?

A loud snore ripped through the cab. Yep, Miss Brat needed more beauty sleep.

He longed for ear plugs, but didn't disturb her until he'd parked as close as he could get to the National Mall. They were a few blocks away, but the day was clear. A walk wouldn't be so bad.

The thought stopped midway out of the truck. Not only had he broken almost every rule he had about sources, he was about to take a walk with one who didn't exactly have his best interests at heart.

And then there was the fact that they were meeting a guy who didn't want Brice around.

Good thing he never ran from trouble, 'cuz he was about to put his foot in some, he could just feel it.

Hope emerged from her side of the truck, stretching. The paranoid side of him said he should have found her a hat and made her wear sunglasses.

Too late for that.

He would have to be her camouflage. Locking up the truck, he grabbed her hand. "Follow my lead. We're just a couple of tourists out sightseeing, okay?"

Her eyes lit up. "Ooh, cloak and dagger, here we come."

"It's simply a security measure. Especially after last night, we can't be too careful."

She squeezed his hand with hers and swung them together like a kid as they started walking. The next thing he knew, she leaned into him, playing the part of his girlfriend with an ease he found slightly terrifying.

And yet, his traitorous body enjoyed it.

"You should probably tell me more about yourself." Hope hugged his arm against her side. "If we're a couple and all. Like who is your favorite journalist of all time?"

"Can't we start with something easier, like 'what's your favorite color?'"

"Your favorite color is red, you like Bruce Willis movies, and you're addicted to chocolate chip cookies, if the stack of home-made ones sitting in a jar on your kitchen counter is any indication. You don't strike me as the type who bakes, so I'm assuming your girlfriend made them? Won't she get jealous if she finds out you were meeting me at Starbucks and holding my hand in front of the Washington Monument?"

For a journalist, she had the eyes and nose of an investigative reporter. And she was on a fishing expedition into his love life. Interesting. "The cookies were made by my mother who lives in the attic, remember?"

"I checked your attic. There were no women up there, so you're a closet cookie baker, aren't you? I bet you even wear an apron."

They were near the reflecting pool. Brice scanned the area, keeping his eyes peeled for Gerard, and trying not to sweat with Hope's body so nicely pressed against his side. "You found me out. No secrets are safe with you."

"Actually," she said, gazing up at him and smiling, "I'm very good with secrets and confidences."

Sunlight reflected off the water, making little stars appear in her eyes. "I'll keep that in mind."

She stopped, forcing him to as well. "Brice?"

"Hope?"

"What are you grinning at?"

"You used my real name."

"And that makes you grin like a geek in Game Stop?"

"Coming from you, the woman who kept calling me Mr. Hawkeye, yes."

She shook her head and grinned back. "Thanks for coming with me. Hawk."

Before he could respond, she went up on her toes and kissed him on the cheek. She stayed there for half a second, then slowly slid her face around so it was lined up with his. "Are we still pretending to be lovers?" she whispered, her breath soft and warm against his lips.

Something came over him—a silence in his head he hadn't experienced in a long time.

Kiss her.

He was no longer looking for Gerard, no longer watching out for suspicious characters who might be stalking Hope.

Kiss her.

All he could see, all he could think about, were those luscious lips of hers right in front of him.

Kiss. Her.

Her gaze dropped from his and landed lower, watching his mouth, as if she were waiting for exactly that.

He swallowed hard. "I, uh..."

He didn't get anything else out. Hope grabbed him by the cheeks, closed her eyes, and planted a full-frontal right on him.

Soft, warm, sexy as hell.

Damn if his legs didn't go weak.

She stopped abruptly and broke away, but he was just warming up. He grabbed her around the waist and hauled her back. *Don't think.*

It was his turn to kiss *her.*

He teased her lips gently, and when she responded, he deepened the kiss. Her hands went into his short hair and she stroked the back of his head, pulling him in even closer.

Hope, Hope, Hope...it was all his useless, empty brain could focus on.

He parted her lips ever so slightly with his tongue and she responded, a wild cat, giving him full access and demanding the same from him. She arched her supple, little body into his and he held her tight as he explored her mouth with his tongue.

They stayed like that for long seconds, maybe a minute or more—Brice lost track of time—until he felt the solid presence of a large man standing off to his right.

The man cleared his throat with an annoyed-as-hell edge to it. "Miss Denby? Can we get down to business sometime this century?"

Hope jumped like Gerard had prodded her with a branding iron. She leapt back, touched her lips, and ran her hands down her trench coat. What he wouldn't give for her to show up naked under that trench someday...

"Hawkeye!"

She was talking to him.

He snapped out of his vacant mind, and straightened his shoulders, giving Gerard the evil eye. "You called us down here. What do you want?"

He pointed a finger at Hope. "I called *her* down here. Not you."

"Didn't like what you found out about me, huh?"

"Not particularly." He jerked his head. "Beat it."

The adrenaline coursing through his system from Hope's kiss egged him on as much as Gerard's pissy attitude. "No can do. Miss Denby asked me to accompany her."

Hope, a flush on her cheeks, was looking back and forth between them. She wanted to know what Gerard had to say, but she also knew Brice wasn't about to leave her alone with him. "Play nice, boys. We all want the same thing. Either Justice Turner was killed by a random person on that bridge, or there's more to it." She spoke to Gerard. "Hawkeye and I are a package deal. If you have something to say to me, you can say it in front of him."

Gerard crossed his arms over his chest and returned Brice's glare. "Heard you were kicked out of the ATF."

"You heard right. Read my blog on the subject and you'll know why."

He rubbed a hand over his face, the creases around his mouth softening. A hint of respect laced his voice. "I read every post back to the first one. You did what needed to be done to protect agents, but I can't say I approve of your methods."

"Fair enough."

With somewhat of a truce between them, Hope chose that moment to go into journalist mode. "Can you walk us through what happened yesterday, Officer Gerard?"

"Off the record?"

"No," Brice said at the same time Hope said, "Of course."

Gerard starting walking. Hope looked at Brice and he nodded for her to follow. Brice stayed behind a few feet, hoping Gerard would feel more comfortable and that way Brice could watch Hope's back just in case the guy—or woman, who the hell knew?—in the car last night made another appearance.

And what could he say? Her backside was worth watching.

As Gerard walked in the direction of the Washington Monument, he removed his sunglasses and rubbed his eyes. Then, miracle of miracles, he took a deep breath and started speaking. "I drive—drove—the justice to work each morning. Yesterday morning, we were on our way in and got stuck in a traffic jam on the bridge. We're trapped in traffic and a couple of cars ahead of us, two guys start having an argument. They get out of their vehicles. One starts yelling. Here I am, a friggin' police officer, and I'm stuck. I can't leave Turner. He's my responsibility. Whatever is going on around me, I can't leave my man. It's been drilled into me. But the judge wants to know what's going on. Then the angry one starts pushing the other guy around. Other people get out of their cars. Judge Turner tells me to diffuse the situation before anything gets crazy. My first responsibility is to the judge, but he insisted. I could see his point. We were landlocked on that bridge and shit could get out of hand real quick."

"So you got out? That's why you were outside your car."

"Yeah. I told him to stay put, and against my better judgment, I got out. Of course, the judge, who is notorious for being a good Samaritan, follows. I have no idea why he thought he could help, but he was the Chief Justice. He was used to people listening to him."

Gerard stopped, faced Hope. The slightest smile passed over his face, then faded just as quickly. "I was in the middle of ordering—and I mean ordering—the judge back in the car and —boom—shots fired."

His gaze dropped to his feet. "The judge went down. The

guy who fired the shot ran to the opposite end of the bridge, pushing through people, waving the gun, the whole nine yards. Most of the crowd dropped when the shooting started. Luckily, no one was hit except Turner."

"Not the other guy involved in the argument?" Brice asked.

Gerard shook his head.

"You don't find that odd?"

Gerard gave him a heavy look. "Not until now."

"What happened then?" Hope asked.

"My boss was bleeding out at my feet and the bad guy was running away. I grabbed a packet of clotting agent from my break-out bag for the judge's wound. Didn't matter. He was dead a few minutes later."

"You did everything you could," Hope said.

Brice felt for the guy, he did. In the field, he too had seen death up close. "Do you remember a DDOT employee taking down the barricade while you were still on the bridge with Turner?"

"I wasn't paying attention to anything but the Chief Justice. The shooter got too good of a jump on me and he was hauling ass, waving that damned weapon. I couldn't get a clear shot even if I wanted to. And I damn sure wasn't about to risk blowing away a civilian."

"Do you know anything about the Kenton Labs case he was about to rule on?" Hope asked.

Gerard waited for an elderly couple to walk past them before he answered. "He never shared information about cases. It would have been a breach of ethics. He was under a lot of pressure from various lobbyists about most all of the cases that passed his desk."

"I can tell you a few things about Kenton Labs," Brice interjected. Hope and Gerard faced him. "I was researching them just before Hope showed up. They filed a suit to extend their patent on Donazem, the top heart drug in the world. It's fifty percent of Kenton's profits and they don't want other companies releasing generics, since it has global implications. There are three other companies developing generic forms of the drug, the biggest being PriceCo Pharmaceutical. As soon as Kenton's patent expires, PriceCo will flood the market with their generics. It could be millions of dollars, maybe more, a year that Kenton will lose if they don't get to keep that patent. Turner was vocal in the past about pharmaceutical companies tying up patents in favor of profits over availability to consumers. What are the odds he was going to deny Kenton their hearing?"

Gerard watched a couple of tourists stroll by. "I don't know. Could go either way, even with his past comments. But I heard him on the phone with one of his clerks a few nights ago. They were reviewing cases. The clerk must have given him something new to think about, but if I had to guess, I'd say he was leaning toward denying the hearing."

"That was three nights ago?" Hawk asked.

"Yeah."

"Interesting timing."

"You're insinuating the company killed him over it?" Gerard sounded incredulous. "What if the next Chief Justice feels the same way? Are they going to off him too?"

"The next candidate in line is Justice Harper," Hope said. "He's on the president's short list. I updated his bio for my boss to take to her boss this morning. He's voted in favor of pharmaceutical patents three out of four times in the past."

"The scientist who developed the drug, Martin Block, spent nearly fifteen years on R&D and claims his patented formula works on a molecular level," Brice added. "I don't know anything about drugs, but Block claims in all of his papers and symposiums that the generics won't work the same way. He's lauded as a genius and had quite a track record in biogenetics research before being wooed by Kenton and going into drug development. There are a million more articles on him, on the Internet, than Kenton Labs itself. The guy has traveled the world and written about sixty papers alone on the amazing properties of his drug."

"So this drug was practically his life's work," Hope said. Her forehead was creased in thought. "The hearing no doubt as important to him as it was to Kenton."

Brice scanned the area, checking out a group of tourists heading in their direction. He turned to Gerard. "Did the justice have any enemies?"

The cop had his eyes on the tourists too, automatically checking them out. "He was Chief Justice. He had plenty of people who didn't agree with his decisions, and sometimes he didn't care for a clerk or had a run-in with another judge. But true enemies? None that I know of."

The group of tourists passed by them. Hope shielded her eyes from the sun. "He always seemed to get along with everyone."

Gerard nodded. "From what I know, he and his son weren't getting along, but most people at the court liked him. He did have this clerk who was pissed because Turner wouldn't give him any big cases. Turner thought the clerk was greedy and cared more about his career as a future justice than about the law. The little prick does seem to think highly of himself, and I could tell Turner didn't trust him. You probably know him, Ms. Denby. Joel Bigley?"

Brice saw Hope's face go slack. She darted a look at him. A look that said, *oh, shit.* "I do know him, although I've only spoken to him once or twice. The word around my office is he has loose lips."

"That was one of Turner's complaints as well. He couldn't prove anything, but he had a feeling that kid was breaking the unwritten rule of not sharing court info with anyone."

Gerard checked his watch. "I've got to get back to work. Do

you two have any actual evidence that yesterday's shooting was premeditated? That Chief Justice Turner was set up?"

Brice blew out a heavy sigh. "No, but we have a lot of circumstantial evidence to look at."

A woman with a bunch of kids wearing lanyards stepped around them and Gerard eased to the side, letting the group pass. After the last kid marched by, Gerard glanced around again, checking their surroundings.

Satisfied by what he saw, he came back to them. "Witnesses on the other side of the bridge saw a man hop into a car that was parked in the emergency area." He pointed at Hope. "Right where I found your car."

Well, shee-it. Didn't that make Brice's conspiracy-hungry self howl. It would also explain why Gerard got a bug up his ass about Hope's car being parked in that emergency turn-off.

"Ah," she said. "That explains your reaction."

"Yeah. He got in and drove off. When I saw your car there this morning, I needed answers."

"Getaway car," Brice surmised. "The shooter got out of a cab right before the argument started. And then there's a car waiting for him on the other side of the bridge."

Hope shrugged. "What if the car were disabled or he caught a ride with someone because he was sick—or loaded—and he took a cab in the morning to retrieve his car?"

Brice scoffed. "Listen, Mary Sunshine, play devil's advocate all you want, but that car is way too convenient." He turned back to Gerard. "What do we know about the cab driver?"

"He was questioned and released. Claims he picked the guy up on the street, doesn't know him, never saw him before, blah, blah."

"You don't believe him?" This from Little Mary Sunshine.

Gerard gave her a bored look. "I'm suspicious. Particularly when someone I care about is dead. But the FBI took over the investigation and I'm boxed out. My office, aside from any assistance the FBI might request, is out of it. Total bullshit."

"I'm sorry," Hope said.

He shrugged. "They can do what they want, but I'm gonna look into this cabbie. See what I can find. If he's lying, I'll nail his ass."

The FBI. With all the crap Grey and Mitch shoveled on Brice, he'd tap into them, see if they had any useful intel. "I have a couple of contacts at the FBI. Not your typical agents. Black ops type shit, but a possible assassination of a Supreme Court justice is in their wheelhouse. I'll see if they have anything on this taxi driver."

For the first time since this conversation started, Gerard focused on Brice and held his gaze in a steady non-threatening manner. No posturing. No venom. No condescension. "I'd appreciate that," he said. "Thanks."

Progress with the pissy cop. Excellent. "I know what it's like to lose a friend. Let me see what I can find."

"Hope has my cell number. Call me if you find anything. I'll see what I can find on my end." With that, Gerard walked off toward the east.

Once he was out of earshot, Brice said to Hope, "Who's this Joel Bigley?"

"He's the clerk who put me on to Kenton Labs. Why?"

He took her hand and laced his fingers through it, trying to keep up the ruse of lovers. "He's our next target."

Hope stared up at Hawk wondering if he'd been hitting the crack pipe. "You think Turner's clerk had him killed? Because he wouldn't feed him cases?"

"Say it a little louder, Hope."

She rolled her lips together. "Sorry. That just floored me. I don't know. It seems like a stretch for a guy Gerard just told us wants to be a justice one day. Why risk it?"

Hawk shrugged. "Money. Imagine what some big corporation, one like Kenton would pay to make sure they got a favorable ruling on something that could make them billions. Billions, Hope."

She squeezed her eyes closed, fought the pounding in her head. She'd skipped lunch and her sugar was far beyond crashed. What a day.

"You okay?"

She opened her eyes again. "Headache. And I'm starving. I need food. Once I have that, I'll be able to focus. Can we grab something and then revisit this?"

"Sure. I'll even buy."

"Wowie. Do I get to choose the place?"

"Depends."

"On what?"

"The place."

Ha. A comedian. Mr. Paranoid who never opened his drapes needed to get out a little. "Since you think someone tried to run me down last night I think we should find someplace busy. A place where we could get lost in plain sight."

"Have I mentioned how much I hate busy places?" he said with a grimace.

"In fact, you did not. I'm not shocked by this admission. You live like a hermit."

"Don't start."

She grinned up at him and bumped his arm. "My goal is to get you out amongst the living. Be a man of the people."

"Isn't that what we're doing now?" He waved his free arm. "I see a lot of people out here."

"Yeah, but the only reason you're out here is because you can't resist the lure of a scoop. That, I understand all too well.

But since you're already out, you should humor me and let me lead you astray."

Oh, how she wanted to lead him astray. Whoop-de-do, it had been quite the male-drought because she hadn't been quite so...um...*lusting* in months. With all the men she worked with or interacted with, none of them gave Hormona this kind of excitement.

"Careful, Miss Rah-Rah. If that kiss a few minutes ago was any indication, I'd have no problem with you leading me astray."

Immediately, her cheeks grew warm. *Whew.* The hotness. *Easy, Hormona.* "We might have to discuss that further. In private. For now, I want you to trust me and let me take you to Barney's."

Hawk burst out laughing. "Barney's? The adult version of Chuck-E-Cheese?"

"Yep. The food is good."

He groaned. "Please, Hope."

"It is! Plus, I'm addicted to video games. They give me a rush. And believe me, right now I could use it. A little fun wouldn't kill us." she tugged on his arm. "Come on. We won't stay long. We'll only play while we're waiting for our food. Then we'll eat and map out a plan for your infiltration of Joel Bigley's life."

"Listen, as much as a place like that makes me itch, I'd do it for you. You've had a crappy couple of days and the break would probably do you some good."

"But?"

"It's too dangerous."

Hope's shoulders dropped. *So close.* "Have you ever been there?"

"No."

"Then how do you know it's dangerous?"

"The place itself isn't dangerous. You being there is dangerous. Christ sakes, someone tried to run you down last night. No."

As much as Hawk thought he'd take charge of this, as much as he wanted to play the stubborn alpha, it wouldn't work. And her slumped, mopey shoulders had to go. Where was the fierce Hope Denby? Huh? *Come on, girlfriend, buck up.* She shoved those shoulders back and got right in Hawk's space.

Right.

In.

His.

Space.

"Listen up, Hawk. Focus on the fact that we'll be lost in plain sight. It's not even 4:30. Way too early for dinner crowds. How would you feel if we went to some quiet restaurant with no people in it and something happened to me? You'd have to explain it to my parents. All because you wouldn't go to Barney's. Barney's is *always* busy. It's the logical choice."

He looked down at her, a sarcastic half grin on his face. If he was buying any of this, it would be a miracle. But she was starving, stressed, and needed a good twenty minutes of distraction to recharge her battery.

"Or," he said, "we'll go back to my house, order food and get cracking A.S.A.P. on Operation Joel Bigley. But if you want to screw around playing video games while your three day deadline is winding down, by all means, let's do that."

Ooh, the rotten scoundrel throwing the deadline in her face. "You're holding me to that deadline?"

"Bet your sweet ass I am. We made a deal. I'm living up to my end, but if three days passes, I *will* release the story if it means beating the networks to it."

"The networks are too busy repeating the company line."

He reached up, tugged on the end of her hair. "Trust me on dinner. Please. Let's keep you safe and get to work on Bigley. I think there's something there. Call it my blogger Spidey sense. I also want to look further into the CEO and board of Kenton. See if any of them have skeletons in their closets."

Doggone it. He had a point. The journalist in her would do the same thing in trusting her instincts. *Get the story first.* At the expense of everything else, including fun, she'd chase the story too.

"Fine. But when this is over, you owe me a trip to Barney's."

He smiled in that smug way men do when they get their way. So annoying that.

"Deal," he said.

"What are we doing about Joel Bigley? We need to find some dirt on him."

Hawk ran his hand over his mouth. Once, twice, and a third time. "If he's talkative, we gotta get into his emails. I'll get Teeg on that."

Hope gagged. "Without a warrant? That's illegal."

Still walking, Hawk grabbed her elbow, pulling her to his other side as two men approached. "What's your point?"

The two men strode by without incident. Hawk might make her insane with his hyper-vigilance. "Even if we find something, it'll be inadmissible."

"Yes, but it'll give us a start. And if we find something, it might lead us to something else that'll get us a warrant. And then we'll have the emails. Done deal."

"And it doesn't disturb you that you're okay with your friend hacking into a United States' citizen's emails?"

"Ha! You don't think the government does it any time they want? Besides, if he's not up to anything illegal, the emails don't come out. No harm no foul."

For a second, Hope paused. What happened to this man that made him this way? That emotionally broke him down to such an extreme that he had an answer—and justification—for everything. Hope shook her head. "I don't like it."

"You're the idealist. Not me. So, if you want to hang back

and wait for probable cause to appear out of nowhere that's fine. It's your deadline. Not mine."

Bastard. But good girls, perky, cheery girls, didn't say things like that.

"Jerk!" she said.

The idiot gave her another of his infectious and highly irritating grins. "This is the world we live in, Hope. If it were different, I wouldn't be doing what I'm doing. I'd still be at ATF chasing down gunrunners." He held his hands wide. "As they say, it is what it is. Now, am I calling Teeg and telling him to hack into Bigley's emails or are we going to sit around with our thumbs up our asses?"

Cornered. If she said no, that deadline he'd given her might expire with them making no progress and Hawk would run a blog post asserting that the Chief Justice had been murdered. It would, no doubt, set off a wave of speculation and put every one of Turner's opinions under scrutiny.

Or, she could agree to hack into Joel's emails, possibly keep the story contained, and protect a good man's body of work.

At least for a little while.

Ugh.

"Fine," she said. "But I want copies of everything."

Thirty minutes later, Hope sat on Hawk's sofa mournfully scrolling through emails on her phone while he dealt with something on his computer. Her stomach howled and she checked the time. Twenty minutes until the food arrived. She could hold out for another twenty minutes. She simply needed a distraction.

Trivia Crack.

The world's most accomplished distraction. That's what she needed. Her mother had introduced her to the extremely addictive game and she'd just about burned through her phone playing. On the mornings she took public transportation it made the ride go so much faster. And even better, she got to play with other people. Some random, some not.

She tapped out of her emails and went to her apps. *There's my baby.*

"Come on," Hawk said, still staring at his computer screen, his voice a cross between this-is-unbelievable and don't-mess-with-me.

He needed a break as much as she did. Yes indeed. Trivia Crack coming right up. A few taps later, she'd sent him an invite. *Come on, fella, let's play.*

Being an obedient, lead-chasing guy, the minute the alert sounded he leaned sideways and tapped the screen.

"Hope," he said, "are you fucking kidding me? A Chief Justice is dead and you want me to play a game? Focus here, woman."

"That's the problem. I'm starving, my sugar crashed and I can't focus. Trivia Crack is therapy. If I play, it'll distract me until the food arrives. Come on. We've been at it all day. One game won't kill us. I can play alone, but it's more fun with someone. Please."

"No."

She held her phone up, waggled it, then ran the tips of her fingers over the screen. "I think you're afraid I'll kick your butt."

"Pfft. I was a History major. Honey, I'll take you out in three seconds."

"If you say so, Hawk. I doubt it though. I'm good, baby."

Again she moved her fingers over the phone, up, down, up, down, up, down. Hormona let out a quiet whoop and as expected, Hawk's gaze zoomed in on the motion of Hope's hand.

Men.

So easy.

He laughed and swiveled to face her. "Two things here. One,

I know what you're doing and I won't be manipulated. Two, you might be good, but I'm better. I have no doubt. If I agree to this half-assed challenge, it's because I want to and not because you played me."

Got him. Did the man honestly believe his own nonsense? She'd totally played him. Whether he wanted to admit it or not. Because, at his core, he was as red blooded as any man and with that, she assumed, came an inherent level of competitiveness no man could resist. Plus, men were horn dogs and she knew exactly where his mind had gone when he watched her fondle her phone. Easy. Peasy.

"Okay, Hawk. If you don't want to, I'll understand."

For emphasis, she opened her eyes wide, blinked a couple of times and waited. Brice Brennan, a.k.a. Hawkeye, a.k.a. Hawk, was getting the full-on Hope Denby I'm-a-sweet-girl-and-am-totally-hornswoggling-you treatment.

If her luck held, he'd be a goner—destroyed—and give her anything she wanted.

He rolled his eyes at her and snorted. "Okay. Since you're working so hard at this, I'll take pity on you. Just don't pout when I pound you into the ground."

She punched her hands in the air. "Ha! Hold onto to your buns, big boy. You are going down."

At that, he burst out laughing and like every other time she'd made him smile or laugh, it came like a lightning strike. Fast and dangerous and one that gave her a sick sense of satisfaction because she'd made this man, the one who was so serious and brooding, chill out.

He scooped his phone off the desk and moved to the sofa where they squared off at opposite ends.

"I'm assuming you know how to play," she said.

"I'm familiar."

"Wonderful. No learning curve. You're up first."

He leaned back against the cushion, stretched his jean-clad

legs—nice, long legs, *whoop!*—out in front of him on the sofa and swiped at his screen. Nice fingers too. Almost graceful for a man who'd been in law enforcement. Hawk had a vibe to him. Alpha but not chest bumpy and...well...yummy.

He glanced up and grinned, slowly, fully understanding she liked what she saw and the girls in her uterus purred.

"Hope?"

Locking eyes with her, he blew a kiss that sent Hormona wailing. "Yes?"

He held the phone up. "U.S. History. You're about to get screwed, sweetheart."

If that announcement didn't kill the mood... Hope narrowed her eyes going for her best venomous look. "Seriously? You got U.S. History?"

Taking way too much enjoyment in it, he laughed. "I did. I'll make quick work of this and then we can get back to it."

Suddenly, there was no woohooing from the girls.

Dammit.

Still facing him, she collapsed back into the cushion to wait her turn. And wait she did. Wait, wait, wait. When her turn finally arrived, she blew it on the second question. But hey, she never said she was an expert on Greek mythology. From there, it only took five minutes for him to leave her bloody, pulverized carcass sprawled across the battlefield known as his sofa.

"Too bad," he said. "I'd hoped you'd have been a better competitor."

And, oh, no he didn't.

Wham. She kicked his foot.

"Ow."

"Please. That didn't hurt."

"Don't be a sore loser, Mary Sunshine."

Oh, no, he didn't again. "Two out of three hotshot. Let's go."

"No. You said one game. It's not my fault I dominated and the food isn't here."

Bastard. He was just so good at throwing her words back at her. Something to remember about him. Reaching behind her, she grabbed the worn throw pillow and whipped it at him.

He caught it and whipped it right back nailing her on the side of the head. Not only did he decimate her at Trivia Crack, he had better reflexes.

"Just give up, Hope."

"Ha! *Never*."

She leaned over, scooped up the pillow and spotted his arms already twitching to deflect it. *He thinks he's brilliant.* She set the pillow against her chest, folded her arms over it and waited. *One, two, three.* As soon as his hands settled back to his sides—*now*—she launched herself at him and started swinging. Just battering him with that pillow. Over and over, from the right, from the left, above him, she walloped him.

"I never give up," she hollered. "*Never.* I'd sooner beat you unconscious with a shovel than give up."

But, oh, boy. He clamped onto her wrists and—*whoopsie*—off balance her body started to bow backward and she couldn't have that. If he managed to bend her completely back, her body weight would take her down and he'd have the power position. Nuh-uh.

Pushing back, she maneuvered her legs, wound up with one on each side of him, giving her a solid base. Even still, he was stronger and had the leverage, but...hello...something—rather large—bulged against her inner thigh.

"Shit," he said.

But the grin on his face was anything but shit-worthy.

Men.

Pigs.

But, she'd play. Why not? She'd utilize any advantage. "Well, well, well." She rocked her hips against him. "What do we have here?"

Keeping a straight face had suddenly become a challenge for him and he gritted his teeth. "Jeez, Hope, knock it off."

"I think not." She met his challenging glare. "That's quite the monster you got there, fella."

"You are such a witch."

His tone, though, was soft, playful, and he still hung on to her wrists and the whole episode brought another round of woohooing from the girls. And, God, she suddenly wanted sex. Fast, hard sex. Totally unusual for her, the good girl, who never rushed such things. No. The good girl wanted to make love to a man, this man, and feel something more than the physical act of it.

As usual, she wanted the fairy tale. Casual sex didn't exist for her. It always had to mean something and just once, this one time, she wanted to not demand that of herself. Wanted to not crave the fairy tale. For once, she wanted a quickie for the sake of a quickie. Nothing more, nothing less.

But good girls didn't do that.

She didn't do that.

Finally, he let go and no... The connection was so fierce and...well...*hot* she didn't want to lose it.

She kissed him. Just unleashed on him, stretching her body on top of his, letting her much smaller frame mold against the hard angles of his and devouring his mouth as his erection bulged against her lower belly and a good, swarming burn stormed her. He locked his arms around her, clamped his hand over her rear and pulled her tighter against him and...oh my...he felt...*big*.

Yikes. What a thought.

Woohoo!

Too long. It had been way too long since she'd felt this way. So, so, good. She shifted one leg, rubbed it along the inner curve of his thigh and—yes, indeed—they were a nice fit.

At least until the doorbell rang.

Say what?

"Son of a bitch," Hawk muttered against her mouth.

She backed away. "Food."

"Yep."

The doorbell rang again, this time three successive chimes. Apparently the driver was in a hurry. He wasn't the only one.

Dammit!

Hawk wiggled out from under her and pointed. "Don't move. Stay right there. I'm gonna take care of this and we'll get back to business. How hungry are you?"

"Starved! Seriously. I have to eat."

He stalked to the door. "Okay. Okay. Fine. We eat and then..." he waggled his hand.

Ripping the door open, he threw some bills at the driver and snatched the bag. "Keep the change."

The kid glanced down at the wad of cash in his hand. "Twenty dollar tip? Dude...thanks!"

"Yeah, yeah," Hawk said. "Merry Christmas."

He shut the door on the kid still standing on the porch. Mr. Charming.

"Well, that was kind of rude," Hope said.

With his free hand, Hawk pointed at his crotch. "And what? I'm gonna stand there and *chat* with this guy raging?"

Before Hope could answer, Hawk's phone went off. The theme from Batman echoing in the room.

He shoved the bag at her then adjusted himself. "Can you deal with the food? This is Teeg. I can't believe I need to talk to him in this condition. Kill me now."

9

*W*hat a difference forty-eight hours could make.

Secrets could be exposed. Careers ruined. Leaders toppled. Sometimes killed.

Brice's neat, orderly, safe world could turn upside down.

Not because the Chief Justice of the Supreme Court had been murdered on a bridge or the possible conspiracy behind it was looking more and more like the truth, but because of one short, scrawny, female who thought she could beat him at a trivia game.

And get him to lose control on his own goddamn couch in his own goddamn house.

Timing was everything. In the world of scandals and scoops but also in a world of Hope Denby on his couch, ready to do more than kiss.

Thanks a lot, Teeg, for ruining my night.

The food bag rattled behind him as Hope dropped it on table next to the couch, her starving stomach apparently forgotten in the face of new information.

Brice checked his watch. An hour and twenty since he'd put Teeg on Bigley's case. Teeg was fast, but when hacking the

Supreme Court's internal communications, Brice had figured it would take the black hat a little longer. He clicked on and glanced back at Hope, putting Teeg on speaker phone. "What'cha got, man?"

Hope's hair was disheveled, her cheeks flushed, her shirt slightly askew, giving him a wicked view of the sweet mound of her left breast.

"Grey wants to know if you even looked at the files I sent you," Teeg said.

"Huh?" Brice snapped his attention back to the phone. "Been a little busy. Did you find anything interesting on Bigley?"

"Grey said I can't give you any more info until you give him something."

Goddammit. Brice dropped into his office chair and quickly called up the first file. He'd already scanned through all three and made a few notes. It had taken him five minutes. "Case 901-A, check the ballistics report on the senator's gun, cross match with his wife's. Something doesn't add up and I'm guessing either the reports were fudged or she swapped out the guns. Case 68-XT, the snitch has to be CIA or Homeland. Need to track him or her down. They're throwing suspicion off themselves and onto the FBI. Again, something stinks in Denmark. And the third case is a non-case. There's nothing there except a bunch of random facts that don't add up to anything concrete. I can't even make up a conspiracy on that one." He paused. "For the record, I'm not helping with any more cases. Period. Now, tell me about Joel Bigley."

Teeg chuckled, then got down to business. "Big shot with a silver spoon in his mouth, which you've already guessed, no doubt. Lawyers and politicians—my two least favorite forms of humanity, if you consider either group human—and he's from both. Long line of politicians on his father's side, lawyers on his mother's. A few dabbled in both professions. Joel graduated from law school with all the accolades, although I did break into Harvard's data bank and read through his profile. He had a sealed file that had to do with cheating on a term paper. Harvard slapped him on the wrist and buried the episode thanks to a large cash donation from the guy's grandfather. Other than that, the kid is clean. I checked his emails like you wanted. His Supreme Court account email was pretty boring stuff, although I flagged one I thought you might look into. Seemed a bit *suspicioso*, if you know what I mean. I'm still working on all of his personal accounts. He has like ten of those."

"Ten?" Hope was suddenly by Brice's shoulder and munching on an eggroll.

A long pause from Teeg. "Do you have a cold? For a second, I thought you sounded like a woman."

"Hope Denby," she volunteered before Brice could answer. "I'm with the Public Information Office of the Supreme Court. I'm investigating Chief Justice Turner's death with Hawk. Nice to meet you, Teeg."

"*Ho*-kay, then." Another seemingly confused pause. "Are you actually *inside* Brice's house?"

"Yeah, I know. Crazy, right? Mr. Paranoid Conspiracy Theorist allowed another human to step into his cave."

"Wow, forgive me. I have to wrap my brain around this. The earth is suddenly turning backward on its axis."

"Ha, ha." Brice cleared his throat. "Can we stop discussing me and get back to Bigley?"

"Right." Keyboard clicking sounded from Teeg's end. "Bigley likes the ladies. He belongs to at least eight hookup sites, some on the Deep Web, and he has a corresponding email for each site to keep them straight, I guess."

"Dating sites?" Hope asked. "Like Match.com?"

"Not exactly..." Teeg's voice trailed off as though he were reluctant to explain.

Brice came to his rescue. "Hookup sites, Hope. One-nighters. One hour, even."

Her eyes widened and her brows shot up to her hairline. "He's paying for sex? Eww!"

"Not paying," Teeg said. "These are adult sites where people find a consenting sexual partner for an encounter. Most of his are straight, run-of-the-mill hookups. Others, like those on the Deep Web are...a little outside the box."

Hope scrunched her brows. "Deep Web?"

The Deep Web or Dark Web is what lays under the surface web of what normal people call the Internet. It's a vast network said to be up to five hundred times larger than the normally defined World Wide Web. Certain subgroups, like hackers and whistleblowers like Brice, used it for its enormous stores of information and its highly prized anonymity.

But certain other subgroups also loved the anonymity.

Child pornographers, drug dealers, human traffickers—the illegal activities are endless. A source for anything you want can be found in certain segments of this lawless, shady, and dangerous Wild, Wild West version of the Internet.

"I'll explain later," Brice said to her. To Teeg, he said, "So kinky stuff?"

Hope repeated her "*eww!*"

Teeg chuckled again, the sound a little strained as if covering for his uncomfortableness. "The worst I've seen so far is LARPing."

"Role-play?" Hope asked.

She knew LARPing. Interesting. At least his erection thought so.

"Live action roleplaying." Brice went back to Teeg. If Joel showed a violent tendency in the bedroom... "So kinky roleplaying? BDSM stuff?"

Hope made a face and paced away from the computer, half-covering her ears. "So don't want that image in my head. I have to see him in the halls!"

"Nah," Teeg answered. "More like *Lord of the Rings* and *Twilight* shit with...you know, married women, probably a few senators' wives who don't want anyone to know what they do in their spare time, etc. That's why these sites are on the Deep Web. They're not easy accessible or widely known."

Now Brice felt like uttering an *eww*. "So no violence of any kind in his past?"

"None. I'm sending you a file containing the emails I snagged. As soon as I have the rest, I'll send those."

Brice's computer dinged with an incoming email dump. "Thanks, man."

Teeg disconnected and Brice waited for the information to finish downloading. Then he pulled up the file. There were hundreds of emails, some short, others pages-long. Didn't the guy ever clean out his inbox? Brice sent the files to his printer and faced Hope. "You ready for another long night?"

Her face was a mix of emotions, some of which were a cinch to read. Her inner government worker bee, who believed in privacy and the American way, was at war with the journalist who wanted the scoop on Joel, regardless of his sexual adventures, and wasn't about to give Brice a leg up on her by letting him do the dirty work in order to keep her perky nose clean. He hated to burst her bubble or put her in an awkward position, but he wasn't about to sit up all night reading Mr. I Love Glittery Vampires' emails alone. And the faster they got this leg of the investigation over, the faster they could get back to his couch.

"Of course. Should we start with the one Teeg flagged?"

"Teeg is a hacker, not an investigator. We'll start with the flagged email, but we're going to read them all."

He snagged the bag of food and Hope followed him into the kitchen. He set it on the table, grabbed plates from the cabinet, and they dug in. "Besides," he continued, "a background check isn't enough. We need to get to know Joel, and if we start asking his friends about him, they'll tip him off. There may not be anything in those emails, but we might get lucky. The guy may just be a regular Joe with no direct tie to the accident or the bridge or this lobbyist, but we need to check them to be sure."

He returned to the living room and snatched up the first batch of emails the printer had spit out. They could read while they ate.

The flagged one was on top, so he divided the stack in half, handing Hope the bottom.

As he stuffed his face with an eggroll, his eyes skimmed the email.

He stopped chewing.

Scanned it again.

Holy shit.

He swallowed half the eggroll, took a gulp of water. "Ah, Hope? You're gonna want to see this."

"It's not Joel in an Edward Cullen costume, is it?" She grinned, proud of her joke.

"No, no costume."

He spun the paper around and tapped a finger next to the email's recipient and then to the body of the text. "Something much more damning."

Hope dropped her fork, quickly wiped her hands and snatched the email from his grasp. She scanned the recipients address. *CWinslow@WinslowSkirka.com.*

Oh, boy.

Winslow and Skirka, being one of the top lobbying firms in D.C., should not be communicating with the clerk of a U.S. Supreme Court Justice, particularly via his Supreme Court email.

Unless there was some mundane, ethically acceptable, reason for it.

Which, given Hawk's reaction to the document, she didn't believe.

Could have been a mistake. Maybe Joel utilized an email organizing system that dumped all of his emails, personal and professional, into one location and when he responded he forgot to click the pull down to change the address. She did that all the time.

Either way, a Supreme Court clerk was communicating with a lobbyist and that, in most cases, wouldn't fly. In the world of Supreme Court Justice clerks, talking any sort of court business with outsiders, particularly a lobbyist, could get a clerk ostracized. Careers were made during a clerkship and navigating the waters could be tricky. Back in the day, lobbyists spent millions wooing politicians and judges with expensive gifts, dinners and yes, *trips,* in an attempt to win favors.

After a lobbying scandal in the 1990's where a lobbyist bribed public officials, laws were enacted to govern just how far lobbyists could go in terms of their gifting. Lobbyists themselves were barred from buying gifts for legislators, something easily manipulated by having a third party purchase the gifts, but how far the laws extended in terms of judges, Hope wasn't sure. What she did know was that if it went on, it went on behind closed doors.

She perused the rest of the email and...whoopsie. Her gaze shot to Hawk's. "Did you read this?"

"I did."

"What do you think?"

He gave her the you're-such-an-infant look. "Hope, seriously? He's telling him the trip to Barbados was excellent. Why would a clerk tell a lobbyist that?"

"Maybe they're friends? They vacationed together?"

"Have you seen Charley Winslow? He's got at least twenty years on Bigley. Somehow I don't see them as frat buddies."

As much as Hope wanted to argue, to find the positive spin, even she had to admit this looked, as Teeg had said, *suspicioso.*

She dropped the email and eyed Hawk. "Let's roll with this for a second. Joel is communicating with Winslow about a trip that maybe Winslow, via one of his clients, sent him on. I'm not a lawyer, but I think companies, not their lobbyists, can still pony up gifts."

Hawk made a note on a scrap of paper. "I don't know the specifics on the rules. I can look into that."

"A few years back, there was a clerk who wrote a book about his experiences after he'd left the court and he was lambasted by the legal community. And that was *after* he left the court. Joel has to know speaking with a lobbyist can wreck his career."

"Of course he does."

"Which makes me wonder if his boss—Justice Turner—knew he was talking to Winslow."

And, wow, did she just imply—to a *blogger*—that the Chief Justice of the Supreme Court might have been not-so-squeaky clean on the bribery front. She'd always been a chatty one, but this? Even for her this was risky. In her own defense, so far, Hawk hadn't let her down. He'd delivered on whatever he agreed to. Something that made it awfully easy to be open and honest with him.

To trust him.

A blogger.

Who'd have thunk it?

"You're assuming," Hawk said, "they had a plan and maybe they were leaking information?"

"I'm not assuming anything. Spitballing here, Hawk. That's all. None of this leaves this room, got it?"

Way too late for that warning, girlfriend.

His head jerked back and he opened his mouth. Closed it

again and frowned. "I'm...yeah...of course. We're in this, Hope. You and me. You don't screw me and I won't screw you. Right? Or did I misunderstand this quasi-partnership thing we have going?"

"No. You didn't misunderstand. I just wanted..." she shook her head. "Never mind."

He shot out of his chair, leaving the dishes scattered on the table and headed to the other room. "I know what you wanted. You were going on record that I can't put any of this in a blog post. Fine. You're on record."

Darn it. In her attempt to protect herself, she'd insulted him. *Great work, Denby.*

"Hawk?" She caught up to him, grabbed his elbow and spun him back. "This is new territory for me. I'm not sure where the boundaries are."

He looked down at her hand on his arm, pressed his lips together, then slowly eased out of her grasp. Not a jerking tug. More of a subtle message—subtle as in a sledge hammer to the head—that he might be the teensiest bit angry with her and didn't necessarily want her hands on him.

Understood. Message most definitely received. "I'm sorry," she said.

"Fine. Whatever. Let's just agree right now that everything, no matter what, is on the table. We share all information and then discuss what can be 'on the record'"

"No boundaries?"

"No boundaries."

Eeeshh. For him, that no boundaries thing might not be an issue. He was a freelancer, so to speak. He didn't report to a woman appointed by the President of the United States. But, if this was going to work, this working together to find out if the Chief Justice was murdered, she'd have to roll with it.

"Okay. No boundaries. With the caveat that if something

comes up and I'm not fully able to discuss it, I will tell you. I'll be as honest as I can."

"Agreed. Now, back to this thing about Joel possibly leaking info. I don't know if I'm buying that. If all they wanted was to leak a tip, there were a hundred different ways to do that."

"And none of them included accepting a trip to Barbados."

"Good point."

Brice's computer dinged with an incoming email. He held up a finger. "It's from Grey. Maybe he found something on our cabbie."

A couple of clicks and he read in silence.

Killing me here. "What does it say?"

"The cabbie is a dead end." Brice let out a deep sigh. "Grey got hold of the police report. Cab driver's name is Lamar Kostas. He claims he never saw the guy before and the man hailed him from a street downtown, so there's no link to his home address or job. The description Kostas gave is so vague, the FBI's sketch artist couldn't do much with it."

He clicked out of the email and just sat there for a moment not moving.

Hope knew the feeling. *Numb.* She dropped her head back and closed her eyes. Even with food in her system, her brain wasn't fully engaging and she breathed in, concentrated on the link between Joel and Charley Winslow. What they needed was someone close to the justice.

Lucky for them, they might have that person.

She held up a finger. "We need to call Anthony Gerard. He was probably as close to Turner as anyone. He might know something about Winslow. At the very least, he could debunk this theory about Turner talking to lobbyists. If he can do that, we know Joel has gone rogue."

10

*B*rice pulled up outside the Corner Tap, the bar Joel was known to hang out at.

"I can't believe we're doing this," Hope said. "Are you sure this is the best way to approach him?"

Hope had volunteered to call Bigley. Brice had said no, he wanted to look the kid in the eyes when he started asking the hard questions. Instead, Hope contacted another clerk who'd volunteered that Joel was out drinking, like usual, at the Corner Tap.

Oh, the life of a spoiled Supreme Court clerk who thinks he has the world by the tail.

After acquiring the kid's location, they'd called Gerard and asked if Turner had been cozy with anyone from Winslow and Skirka, particularly the famous, or infamous, depending on your viewpoint, Charley Winslow.

Gerard had ranted for ten minutes over the phone about the annoying lobbyist and how he'd dogged Chief Justice Turner so much, the judge had threatened to bring stalking charges against him. When Hope had told the cop that Joel Bigley may have accepted a vacation to Barbados from

Winslow, Gerard had nearly stroked out. "That little weasel," he'd said. "No telling what information he offered up in exchange for that. Winslow-Skirka was the group hired by Kenton to push for the hearing."

Winslow, Bigley, and the hearing on the Kenton drug that could cost the company billions—what a conspiracy this could add up to be. Brice knew they needed to put heat on the kid and fast. Even if he was innocent of any wrongdoing in Turner's death, he might point them to whoever *was* involved.

And Gerard had insisted on coming with them for the interrogation.

Now they sat a block from the bar in Brice's truck. Gerard could barely fold himself into the extended cab.

"I'll go in and get him," Gerard said, reaching for the door handle. "He knows me."

Probably the big guy just wanted to stretch his legs.

"He knows me, too," Hope said. "I'll come with you."

"No," both Brice and Gerard said in unison. Brice grabbed her arm before she could jump out. "Let Gerard handle it."

She gave Brice an annoyed look and reluctantly said over her shoulder. "Be careful."

Gerard climbed out and they watched him cross the street. Night had fallen and the streetlights gave off a yellowish glow. The air was heavy with unspent rain.

A group of young women burst from the doorway as Gerard reached for the handle. They'd obviously tipped a few beers or shots or whatever the drink of the night was, their raucous laughter reaching across the street to Brice's ears. Two of the women tangled feet when they nearly ran into Gerard, sending one of them smack-dab into his chest.

More laughter and apologies as Gerard righted the gal and made his way into the bar. Brice climbed out of the driver's seat and into the back.

Hope looked at him over the seat. "What are you doing?"

He shifted to see the door of the bar again. "Ever interrogated anyone?"

"I've interviewed plenty of people."

"Not the same. Interrogating takes it up a notch. I gained a lot of experience working for Uncle Sam. You gotta put pressure on your suspect if you want them to break. Gerard and I sandwich Bigley between us back here and go after him, he'll be more likely to tell us what we want to know."

"Is waterboarding next?"

Funny. "Thumb screws."

"Ha, ha. You're assuming he's guilty before you even talk to him."

"I know you want to see the best in everyone, Hope, but Bigley may have accepted a vacation from a lobbyist who was trying to get his boss, the Chief Justice of the Supreme Court, to hear a decision. It very well may have been a bribe of some sort, and where there's smoke, there's fire."

Her face mirrored the incredulity in her voice. "But you don't seriously believe *Joel* shot Justice Turner, do you?"

The kid had no connections to anyone with a violent past or a criminal record. There was no record he owned a gun, nor did he have a violent history himself. "It's improbable, but like any other story, you follow every lead. That's all we're doing here. If you're uncomfortable with this, go inside the Corner Tap and wait for me to come get you when it's over."

She huffed as if dealing with a spoiled three-year-old. "Don't be ridiculous. I'm staying, numbskull. I just want to make sure you're not going overboard."

Gerard emerged from the bar with the man of the hour. Brice winked at her. "Guess we're about to find out."

The cop led Bigley to Brice's truck. Brice scooted over and motioned for him to get in.

"What's going on here?" Bigley said. His gaze darted between Brice, Gerard, and then locked on Hope when he saw her through the window. "Hey, I know you. You're that happy chick."

Hope rolled her eyes. "Hope, not Happy."

Bigley's speech had the slightest slur to it. His gaze returned to Gerard. "I thought you said you had my briefcase."

"Dumb kid." Gerard hustled Bigley into the backseat, taking up residence on one side as he pinned Bigley in.

Well, wasn't this cozy? Two guys over six foot and one just under, all crammed onto the bench seat built for children under ten.

Gerard managed to mash himself against Bigley and slam his door. Bigley flinched. "I don't understand." He shot a confused look to Hope as she turned and looked at him over the front seat. "Hope? What's going on?"

She was smiling, all sweet and flirty, at Bigley, and Brice's hackles rose. But then he saw the killer journalist reflected in her eyes. "It's okay, Joel. Just tell my friends why you accepted a trip from a lobbying firm here in D.C. The same firm pushing hard for the Kenton Labs court case that Turner was set to give an opinion on."

Bigley's lips moved but nothing came out for a second. "Wha... What?"

Fumes of alcohol emanated from the kid's pores. Brice leaned in—didn't take much since they were practically sitting on top of each other anyway—and got in his face. "Let me make this easy for you, Joel." Taking a move from Hope's playbook, he smiled at the guy. "Charley Winslow, Barbados. You accepted a bribe from him. What we want to know is, what did you offer in return?"

Bigley hesitated a second too long. Brice felt him tense. "I don't know what you're talking about."

Gerard leaned in from his side, creating a tighter sandwich. Bigley had about an inch of personal space left. "I could arrest you right now."

"For what?" the kid practically yelled. He looked at Hope again, pleading. "I don't know what they're talking about."

Her smile kicked up a notch. "Sure you do. The vacation that Winslow-Skirka provided for you back in December. Maybe you've graduated from leaking info to conspiracy to commit murder?"

Bigley's face fell. "Murder! What the hell? The trip was..."

Yep, guilty. Brice wiggled so he could grasp the back of Bigley's neck, putting a little pressure on it. "Answer my question. What did you give Charley Winslow in return? Was it information on Turner? Or did you do a little dirty work for him and shoot the Chief Justice yourself?"

The clerk reared back. His speech suddenly improved. "Oh, my God. Are you serious right now? Turner was shot in a road rage accident, and I was nowhere near that bridge Monday morning. What does that have to do with Winslow?"

"Show him, Hope," Brice said.

Hope pulled the printed copy of the damning email from her pocket, flipped on the overhead light, and held it up for Bigley to read. "Ring any bells?" She let him skim it. "Were you feeding classified information to Winslow-Skirka? All we have to do to get you fired is take this email to..."

"You hacked into my emails?"

Gerard smacked the side of Bigley's leg. "Hey, dumbass, you're in deep shit. I'm a cop. You think I'd do something illegal and put my ass on the line for a pipsqueak like you?"

Bigley was silent, his gaze now focused on the mid-distance outside. Then he turned his stoic gaze on Hope. "Why would I tell you about Kenton Labs if I was accepting bribes from their lobbyist?"

"To deflect suspicion from yourself?" Brice shook him by the back of the neck. "Were you feeding information to Charley Winslow?"

Bigley blew out his lips. "It's not what you think."

Gerard gestured for him to go on. "Explain."

The clerk went silent again, but not for long. Gerard angled sideways, grabbed him by the front of his collar. "I'm done fucking with you. You've got thirty seconds to convince me you're not a criminal or I'm hauling your ass down to D.C. Central and telling them you have information on the Chief Justice's murder. Hell, I'll call the FBI too."

Nice. Brice grinned behind Bigley's shoulder.

"Okay, okay." Bigley shoved Gerard's hand away. "Winslow had tickets for a trip to Barbados. A Christmas gift for his wife, he said. Their youngest got sick, the tickets were nonrefundable, so he offered them to Turner. I overheard them talking in the hallway. Turner turned him down, said he wasn't interested. Winslow insisted it wasn't anything but one friend doing another a solid. Turner told him they weren't friends and walked off."

"And?" Hope insisted from the front seat. "Those tickets just happened to mysteriously fall into your lap?"

"It was December in D.C. I figured if no one was going to use them, what harm could there be if I took them off Winslow's hands?" He shrugged. "I had a lady to impress and a trip to a warm island was just the thing. He was happy someone could use them."

"Bullshit," Tony muttered. "You had to know there'd be a price for them. You didn't become a Court clerk because you're stupid. You rolled the dice that you wouldn't get caught."

"And what did you offer Winslow in return?" Brice asked.

"Nothing!" Bigley looked shocked. Sweat beaded along his hairline. "There were no strings attached, and it was only that once. I swear."

Brice squeezed his neck again. "I don't believe you."

"Neither do I," Gerard added.

Bigley shot Hope another pleading look. "It's the truth!"

"I believe him," Hope said. Her mouth thinned for a

second, then she nodded. "He may have loose lips around the office, but I don't think he'd risk his future career as a politician or a Supreme Court Justice by taking bribes from a lobbyist in exchange for insider information. Especially about a case he'd know probably wasn't going anywhere with Turner."

Brice's gut said differently. "Has Winslow given you anything else? Gifts of any kind? Fancy dinners? Hard to get tickets?"

"No, man. Nothing." He shook his head. "Look, I may have made an error in judgment over that trip, but it was just that. A trip. Cut me some slack. Like you guys wouldn't have done the same thing to impress a woman."

Did you dress up as a vampire to impress her too? Brice kept that thought to himself. "So you haven't had any further contact with Charley Winslow?"

"None."

Hope stuck the email copy back in her pocket and switched off the overhead light. "Let him go. He can't help us."

Brice and Gerard exchanged a look. Brice could see the other man had doubts like he did, but getting anything else from Bigley tonight would be impossible.

"You better hope we don't find out differently," Brice said low and dangerous, close to the guy's ear. "'Cuz if we do, your ass is mine."

Gerard shoved open the door. "Not if I get him first."

When they let the kid out of the truck, he took off so fast, he nearly tripped over his own shoes.

Brice stood next to Gerard, both men staring after the kid. "You think he's taken bribes from anyone else?" Gerard asked.

"I'd bet money on it. We should keep an eye on him."

"Roger that." Gerard turned as Hope rolled down the window. "I'll do a little digging," he said under his breath as he walked a few feet away out of Hope's hearing range.

Brice followed nonchalantly, kicking at a rock with his shoe. "I will too."

"Did you find anything on the cab driver?"

One of the bar's waitresses emerged from the noise, digging car keys from her purse. "My friend, let's call him Batman, got his hands on the police report. Lamar Kostas has no criminal record and has a clean work record. He claims he didn't know the guy, never saw him before. Says the man told him he'd had too much to drink the night before on his way home from a bar and called a friend to pick him up. He'd left his vehicle in the emergency pull-off spot on the other side of the bridge. Kostas said the guy wanted to get to it before the cops ticketed it and towed it off. He gave a vague description, and it conflicts with some of the other witnesses, but none of their descriptions are solid either. If anyone took a picture or video, they're too scared to post it."

Gerard rocked back on his heels. "After our little discussion with junior here, tonight, I'm thinking we should pay Kostas a visit. Just to make sure he's clean."

"Count me in, man."

Gerard eyed him for a moment, then nodded. "I'll be in touch."

"Are you two going to stand there all night?" Hope called, eyeing them suspiciously.

"Nope," Brice answered, heading back to the truck. "We're going to drop Officer Gerard off at his place, and then..." he gave her a covert grin as he jumped into the driver's seat. "You and I have some business to take care of."

Gerard stayed where he was. "Actually, I'm feeling the need for some libations. You two go ahead. I'll call a cab."

He took off jogging across the street and entered the bar.

"Please tell me he isn't going to hassle Joel more," Hope said. "I have to work with the guy. I'd rather he didn't hate me."

Brice reached across the cab, about to stroke her cheek, when he drew his hand back. "No one could hate you, Hope."

A grin flashed across her face. "What were you saying about taking care of business?"

It was nearing midnight, and she looked tired despite the grin. "I better take you home. You have to work tomorrow. What kind of security do you have at your place? For real? I know there are no motion sensors."

"Is it really me you're worried about?" She tilted her head, studying him closely. "Or is it you?"

He started the truck. "I'm used to staying up all night chasing a story. I don't have to be at the office bright and early tomorrow morning. Security?"

She pursed her lips for a second. "You're just scared of what happened on your couch."

"Scared?" He chuckled, shifting the truck into drive. "You don't scare me, Hope. I'm...cautious. You're young and idealistic. I'm old and jaded. A relationship could be—*would* be—challenging for us."

A twitch started under her left eye. "Opposites attract."

She was beautiful in the half-light of the dashboard. And he was a fool for what he was about to say.

"I'm not opposed to trying, Hope. Hell, I've got nothing to lose. You, on the other hand," he checked his rearview and pulled away from the curb, "better think long and hard about what you're getting into. Now tell me about your security."

Refusing to admit how far beyond—epically beyond—exhausted she was, Hope rested her head back and closed her eyes.

Fatigue dragged at her thoughts leaving the words circling each other in her mind but not quite forming a sentence. And if she couldn't form a sentence she wasn't about to say anything.

Not to the sharp-minded blogger and definitely not when she might wind up looking like a fool.

A tired fool, of course, but still a fool.

"Security," she said. "It's a coded building. Everyone has a unique code to the outside door. It doesn't stop people from giving their own code out though so I'm not sure what the point of a unique code is." She waved it off. "Anyway, we've never had a break-in or criminal activity so I think I'm safe."

"You think?"

He never gave up. She squeezed her eyes tighter, forced herself to focus, took a breath and faced him. "Hawk, I'll be fine. It's late and I need to be up in five hours. Nothing will happen—aside from me crashing into the sleep of the dead. Just take me home. Please. I need my own bed tonight."

No response. Terrific. But he turned right at the corner going the opposite direction from his place so maybe, if he chose, for once, to be reasonable, in twenty minutes she'd be home. In her own bed.

"Okay," he said. "I get that needing your own bed thing. I'll just stay with you tonight."

Ha. As if she'd sleep at all with him around, in her space, near her bed. After what had happened earlier and his...um...*arousal*, if he came anywhere near her bed there wouldn't be much sleep happening.

Woohoo! Hormona sent up a shout.

At least *she* had energy. *Too bad, Hormona.* Rushing into a sexual relationship simply to...uh...fulfill a physical need would be emotional suicide for a girl like Hope. One who managed to convince herself she loved every man she slept with.

Nope. Not happening this time. She had a career to protect. A broken heart she could deal with. The loss of her career would decimate her.

She shifted sideways and set her hand on his shoulder to

break the news that she wouldn't be letting him within a hundred yards of her home.

He glanced at her, but quickly went back to the road. "I'm staying, Hope."

So stubborn. "Let's chat a second, shall we?"

"No chatting. I'm a man. Men don't chat."

"Then you can listen and I'll talk. I love this protective streak in you. Even if it's a borderline psychotic form of paranoia, I think it's admirable."

"A backhanded compliment. My favorite."

She smiled. "It *was* a compliment. Trust me. The thing is, regardless of you telling me to think long and hard about getting involved with you, I'm okay with that. With trying. But I'm not about to rush into something. Not when we have this crazy deal between us. I don't want my emotions confusing things. I know myself well enough to know that won't be good."

"I'm not sure I follow."

"If our little deal goes bad, I don't want to be in love with you when it happens."

"Love?" He nearly ran off the road.

Yikes. *Stalker, stalker, stalker.* Blame it on the fatigue. Wasn't this just like her though? To mistake kindness and friendship for love? She wanted her happily-ever-after as much as the next girl. Nothing wrong with that. Unless that girl was silly enough to see every man who befriended her as a possible candidate. Which, as hard as it was to admit, she often did.

This time she wouldn't. This time she would see this as it was. A business arrangement. He needed her as much as she needed him. Maybe more. She was his link to the Supreme Court. And she wouldn't forget that. That knowledge would keep her focused.

On her job.

Even if she did want to sleep with him.

Woohoo!

"Forget it, Hawk. I'm tired and rambling. I'm not sure I have it in me to argue."

Anticipating the left turn that would lead them to her neighborhood, he switched lanes. "I won't *forget it*. Don't be so flip with me. I'm a guy, but jeez, I get it, Hope. I'm not going to use you. No more than you would me." He held up a hand. "Wait. That sounded bad and not at all like I meant it."

"Thank God for that. For the record, I don't think either of us is using the other. We're definitely attracted to each other. I'm not sure now is the time for us to be acting on that. Let's just try to avoid incidents like what happened on your couch earlier. Okay?"

He nodded. "Yeah. Okay. But I'm still sleeping on *your* couch tonight."

11

After Hope left for work, Brice took off for home. A text from Anthony Gerard interrupted him.

Going to talk to our friend.

In the world of law enforcement, that was probably the best invitation Brice was going to get from the cop to go see Kostas, the cab driver.

Maybe if they leaned on the guy a little, like they had with Joel, he'd conveniently remember more than he had told the cops about the shooter.

He typed back, *meet you there.*

Thirty minutes later, he'd fought his way through morning traffic and found the house in a rundown area that wasn't quite the hood but close enough. Rundown houses, yards populated by weeds instead of grass, chainlink fences, and broken windows greeted his eyes everywhere he looked.

Gerard leaned against his black SUV parked a block down. Brice pulled in behind him and rolled down his window.

Gerard sauntered over. "Guy left for work already," he said, eyeing the block. "Something's off. Kostas has been with the Prime Time Cab Company for ten years, no wife, no kids.

Makes a decent income, doesn't gamble or drink. Why does he live here, in this rat hole?"

"Is this where he grew up? Does he have family here?"

Gerard shook his head. "Grew up about forty miles north. His parents are still alive and living in the same town. I checked and the guy has a nice fat savings account, sends some cash home to Mom and Dad from every paycheck."

Apparently, Brice wasn't the only one with connections.

"I don't like it," Gerard said. "I'm going to take a look around."

Brice wanted in on that. He had nothing better to do than read boring bios of Kenton Lab employees while Hope was at work. "Want some company?"

"If you're up for it."

He was up for it. Bailing from the truck, he locked up and followed Gerard.

The gate at the front was locked. Weeds and random bushes grew helter-skelter along the fence line. They followed it around to the back, out of sight from the street.

A line of trees on one side blocked the neighbor's view. In this area, Brice doubted the neighbors paid much attention anyway. Most, he imagined, were still in bed nursing hangovers or camped out in front of their TVs.

The back gate was locked. The yard was littered with garbage, an old grill, plastic lawn chairs.

Gerard eyed the house through the chainlinks. "I'd like to see inside those windows."

The fence was less than eight feet tall. So far, they hadn't seen or heard any guard dog. Brice held up a hand. "After you."

The cop hopped up, sticking a foot in the fence, then boosted himself up and over. For a big guy, he was almost graceful.

Brice followed, not quite as graceful, but still got the job done.

The yard debris was a challenge to walk through. A better security measure than the fence any old day.

Once he and Gerard made it to the back porch, they had to fight through more crap. Plastic tables, chairs, potted plants, an old porch swing that long ago had fallen from its chains.

Gerard took the window on the south side of the door, Brice took the north.

A low whistle emanated from Gerard. "And I thought the yard was bad."

Kostas was a hoarder.

From his vantage point, all Brice could see was shit, shit, and more shit in what appeared to be a mudroom. Front to back, there were piles everywhere. One pile of garbage bags and broken appliances rose nearly the height of the wall. Another pile of junk came half way up the window Brice was peering through. Broken toys, stacks of newspapers, plastic clothes detergent bottles, random appliances, furniture...it made him want to haul out his antibacterial soap.

"None of this is new or in good shape," Gerard said. "I think Lamar needs to lay off the garage sales and invest in better home décor."

Brice had seen this type of thing before when working undercover with mafia boys and gunrunners. "He could be a legit hoarder, but few of them this bad hold down long term jobs."

"Is he hiding something?"

"That would be my guess."

Gerard blew air through pursed lips. "Related to our case, you think?"

"Doubtful, but we're here."

"You saying you want to take a look inside?"

"Only a crazy man would want to go inside this place."

"You strike me as the crazy type."

"Not crazy." Brice grinned. "But I don't back down from

risky shit. If you're not comfortable going any further, no problem. Head back to your vehicle and I'll handle it from here."

"You really think I'd let you have all the fun?"

Gerard was growing on him. "Let's peek in a couple of other rooms from outside," he said, making his way back off the porch. "Then decide if we want to drop in for a more exhaustive search."

The two of them edged around the house, looking in all the windows. Most had some kind of blind or flimsy curtain, but they could still see through them.

The living room and kitchen were filled to capacity. But on the other side of the house, where a bedroom and bathroom rounded out the living space, they discovered both to be clean.

Spotless, in fact.

Definitely hiding something.

"How hard would it be to break in?" Gerard said.

The cop would have made a good undercover operative.

"Depends on the entry point." Bathroom windows were usually smaller and harder to get through since they swelled with humidity. Brice latched onto the bedroom window and gave it a shove. No dice. "Let's go back to the door."

As expected, it was locked.

The nice thing was, the lock was probably the original. "Got a credit card?"

"For what?"

Gerard was a cop, but he was a bodyguard, not a street cop. "To unlock the door."

"Use your own."

"I don't have credit cards."

"None? You're kidding me."

"Too easy to track."

Gerard made a grumbling sound in the back of his throat. "You're weird, man. How do you survive without a credit card?"

It wasn't easy. He took the card Gerard handed him and

slipped it between the door and the frame, right above the locking mechanism. Then he wiggled and pushed and wiggled some more, bending the card until he felt the lock slip backward. He grabbed the knob with his other hand, and voila. "We're in."

Brice handed the bent card back to its owner. "You cracked it," Gerard groaned.

"Sorry. Hazard of the job."

Carefully, the two of them made their way through the mountains of debris until they got to the bedroom and bathroom. "I'll take the bathroom." Brice said.

Gerard took the bedroom.

Brice was careful not to touch anything he didn't need to. He wished he had gloves on. But the fact was, even up close, the bathroom was clean. Cleaner than his.

There was nothing in the medicine cabinet or vanity cabinet that seemed out of place. No hidden cubby holes in the walls or floors. Nothing taped underneath drawers.

He made his way to the bedroom. "Bathroom is clean."

Gerard was in the closet, kneeling on the floor. "Bedroom isn't."

Brice closed the distance and looked over the cop's shoulder. "Well, what do we have here?"

Just then, he heard the sound of a large truck pulling up out front. The reverb from the engine was so low, it rattled the windows. "Company," he said, motioning for Gerard to stay quiet.

The truck shut off, footsteps pounded at a fast pace along the sidewalk, stopping at the front of the fence. "Mr. Kostas?" a man called. "It's Denny. You home?"

Gerard frowned at Brice. Brice held up a hand, signaling him to stay immobile and quiet.

"Mr. Kostas? I need you to sign for this one!"

Silence stretched. Nothing happened. Through the window,

Brice thought he heard the guy mumbling, then the footsteps retreated.

"Friend or foe?" Gerard whispered.

Brice put a finger to his lips, listening. Sure enough he heard the truck rumble to life. "UPS," he said, once again peering over Gerard's shoulder. "Kostas must have been getting a special delivery."

Neat stacks of wrapped bills were tightly packed into a hollowed out section of flooring. "Pension fund?" Gerard asked. "Some people don't trust banks."

"He has a savings account," Brice reminded him.

"Maybe he's a gambler."

"How much do you think is there?" Brice asked.

"Mmm...twenty stacks of hundred dollar bills. Twenty grand?"

"Call me a conspiracy nut, but this looks like drug money."

"As in pharmaceutical drugs? From Kenton Labs? Was that what he had to sign for from UPS?"

Brice considered it, trying to make the threads surrounding Kenton Labs, their drug, and a cab driver fit together. "Possible. This money might be a payoff of some sort."

"For driving the shooter onto the bridge?"

"In my mind, yes. Can we prove it? No."

Gerard replaced the money and the floorboard and Brice moved out of the way so he could back out of the closet. "I'll do some more digging. Maybe keep an eye on this place and get a feel for Kostas's comings and goings. See if anyone suspicious shows up."

They headed back out the way they had come. Being a good citizen, Brice locked the door behind him.

. . .

After a measly four-point-five hours of sleep, Hope painted on a perky smile and marched into her office, breezing by the receptionist with her usual peppy "Good morning!".

It certainly wasn't the receptionist's fault Hope's sleep patterns had been disrupted the last two nights and she wouldn't inflict her crabbiness on her co-workers.

Never.

At her cubicle, she slipped off her blazer and hung it on the hook she'd installed on the wall. Rob's head popped up from his side of the cube and she noted the shadows under his eyes. Everyone in the office was running on limited rest.

"Good morning!" she chirped. "How's things?"

"Hey," he said. "You're perky."

"You know me. Happy, happy, happy." She hid a yawn behind her hand. "Do we have a meeting at nine?"

"Yeah. Amy wants updates on everything. Guessing she's gonna want to hear from you on this blogger guy."

"Ha!"

Rob's eyebrows shot up. "What's *that* about?"

Four and a half hours of sleep. That's what. That darned Hawk had her all churned up. What with that sleeping on the couch thing. Any other man would have tried to worm his way into her bed. Not him. Mr. Honorable. He stayed on the couch. Like she'd told him to.

Shouldn't that have been a plus? Yes. Completely. A true gentleman. And, yet...

She dropped into her chair, threw her head down on the desk. "I'm a mess."

"Hold on. I'm coming over."

As if it were a long way or maybe he'd vault over the top. At that Hope laughed. She raised her head just as Rob swung into her cube.

He sat on the edge of her desk and folded his arms. "What's going on with you? You tore out of here yesterday saying you had a"—he made air quotes—"*meeting* and that was the last we saw of you. Are you okay?"

"I'm fine. This thing with the Chief Justice though is perplexing."

"Tell me."

She held her hands up. "Honestly, I don't know where to begin. Other than I'm confused."

"About?"

"The blogger." She sat back, thought about Hawk on her sofa and shook her head. "He's a good guy."

"Hope, don't start."

She held up her hands. "I know. Same old Hope, thinking she's in love when she's not. It gets repetitive."

Even Rob knew this about her. How pathetic. "At least," she said, "this time I'm aware of it."

"Good. Because as much as you want to see the bright side, find all warm fuzzies in people, this guy is trouble. He won't just inconvenience your career, he'll make sure you never work in this town again."

"He wouldn't do that."

"He's a whistleblower. Those guys are walking targets." Rob studied her for a few seconds, his eyes squinty. "Hold up here. Did you sleep with him?"

Hope flinched. Whether from her friend's mind-reading abilities or the fact that he'd just spewed that statement where anyone, including their boss, could hear it, she wasn't sure.

"Yikes, Rob. Maybe the whole floor didn't hear you. And, for your information, no, I didn't sleep with him."

Rob, the human lie detector, continued to stare at her and finally nodded. "Okay. I believe you."

Gee, thanks. "Your undeterred faith in me makes me feel so much better."

He laughed. "I do have faith in you. Your judgment with men sucks though."

Even her perky, perky, perky self was way too tired for this. And, he was right. No argument. Not a one. "Believe me, I know."

At least she thought she knew. Hearing it from Rob brought a whole new level of awareness. As much as she'd convinced herself she wouldn't allow her emotions to get in the way of her chasing this story, the honorable Hawk-not-slithering-into-her-bed had softened her. If only a little.

And that had to stop.

She sat up, waved Rob off of her desk. "Thank you."

"For what?"

"For being my friend. For not letting me ruin my future."

"Denby!" Amy hollered from her office.

"Here we go," Rob said. "Day three of Amy in psycho mode." He jerked his head. "Get in there. Take the bullet for the rest of us."

Hope grabbed her notepad and pen and hustled to Amy's office. No doubt her boss wanted to know where she'd disappeared to the day before. Amy had been in yet another meeting so Hope had left her a voicemail that she'd had to follow another lead on the Chief Justice story.

And now, Hope had no doubt, her boss wanted answers.

She did her quasi run-walk and swung into the office to find Amy at her desk. A neat stack of folders sat to her left, another to her right, that one not as orderly. In front of her were three newspapers and two cell phones. Another day in paradise. Amy scrolled through one of the phones and waved Hope forward with her free hand.

"Sit," she said.

Doing as ordered, Hope took the seat right in front of her, set her pad and pen on her lap and shoved her shoulders back. Confidence, confidence, confidence.

She had this. No problem. Whatever Amy wanted to know,

she'd tell her. Minus a few key details. Like the hacking into a federal employee' email. Noooooo, not telling her that.

Or the interrogation of said federal employee. Noooooo, not telling her that either.

So, okay. What was left?

Not a lot.

Amy tossed her phone aside, sat back, folded her hands in front of her and fastened her eyes on Hope. "Start talking, Denby."

Hmmm. Rather than risk speaking on the wrong subject, Hope decided clarification might be needed. "About?"

"About a certain law clerk who claims you, the Chief Justice's security officer, and a blogger restrained and questioned him against his will."

Woof! Way to come out of the gate hard. Hope opened her mouth but trapped air in her throat wouldn't let the words out. That little turd Joel had filed a complaint? The balls! Considering Hawk suspected he was in bed with a damned lobbyist.

Relax. She could do this. She was an ace under pressure.

Before she managed a word, Amy shot forward, craning over her desk, her cheeks sucked in and her eyes on fire. "Jesus, Denby! For once you're silent. That alone scares the hell out of me. What the *fuck* did you do?"

And, oh, wow. Amy dropping f-bombs. Nothing altogether new, but she'd definitely never dropped the f-word directly at Hope.

"I...uh..."

What? What could she possibly say? She took a breath, ran her bottom teeth over her lip and held up a hand. "Let me explain."

"Ah, shit!"

"No. It's not bad." Ach. Not bad? It was totally bad. "You know I've been working this tip about the Chief Justice's death.

I spoke to Joel, his law clerk, the other night. That conversation got me thinking about this Kenton Labs thing."

Patience obviously waning, Amy rolled her hand.

"Right. I'll get to the point."

Which was what? That they hacked his emails. *Bad.* Or that they'd interrogated said clerk. *Even worse.* She cleared her throat and sat a little taller. "Anyway, while doing research we came across some additional information we felt we needed to discuss with Joel."

"How did the Chief's security detail get involved?" Amy glanced at a note on her desk. "Anthony Gerard?"

"Yes. He was the one on the bridge with the Chief Justice. We called him."

"You and the blogger?"

"Yes. We called him to ask some questions. Since he spent so much time with the Chief, he had the most interaction with Joel and we thought Joel might be more chatty with him."

Amy closed her eyes, shook her head and blew out a breath before opening her eyes again. "At what point did you decide the prudent thing was to force this kid into a car and ambush him?"

Now that was a little over-the-top. "I wouldn't say we *ambushed* him."

"But you did get him into that car between a Supreme Court Policeman, one I've been told resembles a gladiator, and a former ATF agent. Any reasonable person would find that unsettling. On top of that, he requested to leave and wasn't permitted to."

When put that way, it did sort of sound like an ambush. "Uh..."

Amy held up one long finger. "Be very careful here, Denby."

"Yes, ma'am."

"Now tell me what was discussed in that vehicle."

Here's where it got dicey. The entire conversation

stemmed from the email. An email illegally obtained. By two Supreme Court employees and a blogger. *Damned bloggers!* Admitting it would not only take her down, she'd take Tony with her. And Hawk. Even if he wasn't a Court employee, he could probably still go to jail. She'd have to research the penalties on hacking.

That thought produced a slightly hysterical giggle, but they both knew there was nothing even remotely funny. "Amy, I'm sorry. I can't tell you."

Her boss cocked her head. "You can't...what?"

"I'm sorry."

"I don't give a shit that you're sorry, Denby. I've got this law clerk making all kinds of noise. Give me something, anything, to defend you with."

The emails would do it. All she'd have to do is say they'd uncovered evidence that Joel was accepting gifts from D.C.'s top lobbyist—a lobbyist who, by the way, had a client with a major case about to be ruled on—and she could spin this whole thing. Take the heat off of her and Hawk and Tony and put it square on Joel.

But she was no lawyer and didn't have a clue about the ramifications of hacking into someone's work email. Particularly a government email account.

"I want to, Amy. Believe me. I'm not sure I can though. It wouldn't be—" What? In her best legal interest? "I don't think I should say anything more until I speak to a lawyer."

"Mother of God. Denby, what the hell have you done?"

"Honestly, I'm not sure. It could be no big deal."

"But you're not sure?"

"Correct."

Amy sat back again, dug the three middle fingers of her right hand into her forehead and muttered something about boxes. Boxes? Whatever.

A long minute passed and Hope sat silently, her stomach

flip-flopping, her skin on fire while she waited for her boss to speak.

Finally, Amy dropped her hand, grabbed the edge of her desk and scooted forward. She let go, loosely clasped her hands. "Well, then, Denby, here's what I need to do. Until you tell me what the hell you're into, I'm putting you on suspension."

"Amy!"

"Don't say anything, Denby. Not one word. Whatever this cluster is, you've had a hand in it. Frankly, you're lucky I don't fire you after that stunt with the Chief's clerk. The entire thing is under investigation. So, if you can't help yourself here, neither can I. Now go home, Denby. And stay the hell away from that law clerk."

The Bat Cave, an old, abandoned army base, was a dreary site. The main building, probably thirty thousand square feet with a couple of stories, all covered in brick. A few of the windows were smashed and the drive in front was littered with weeds and gravel.

A handful of squat barracks and equipment sheds dotted the landscape behind it. Left to its own devices, nature was encroaching through the fences. In the distance, Brice heard gunfire. No doubt Caroline was keeping her sharpshooter skills up to snuff.

No fancy headquarters for the Justice Team, but then they didn't exist on paper.

Brice stopped at the gate, keeping his face turned away from the camera. He knew it was still live thanks to Teeg.

The hacker had called him shortly after he'd gotten to his house. Teeg had sounded agitated and insisted Brice come to the team's headquarters so he could show him something even though Brice needed a shower and some breakfast.

He didn't want to talk about it on the phone, nor would he send an email. "It may be nothing," he had said, but Brice could tell by the way Teeg's voice raised the hair on the back of his neck that the hacker had found something Brice wasn't going to like. Teeg being so secretive compounded that feeling.

The speaker at the gate crackled to life and the sound of Mitch Monroe's voice grated on his nerves. "Welcome to the jungle, Brice, ol' buddy. Figured you'd end up here eventually."

Brice stuck up his middle finger in response and a buzzer sounded, releasing the locked gate.

He drove through and parked near the east end where Teeg had instructed. As Brice swung out of the cab of the truck, the door opened and Mitch stood there grinning.

"I'm not joining the team," Brice said, brushing past him.

Mitch wore a T-shirt that read, *Sarcasm is my Superpower!* He locked the door behind them. "Of course you're not."

Mitch led him down a long hallway with concrete walls, linoleum floors, and poor overhead lighting. They went through a set of double doors and ended up in a large, open conference room.

Grey stood in front of a smart board on wheels, studying a handful of photos and bulleted information. Teeg sat behind command central, three oversized computer screens in front of him, two keyboards on his desk, and an impressive array of speakers and other peripherals rounding things out.

Grey took one look at Brice and motioned toward a makeshift counter on the far wall. A brightly colored box of donuts sat next to a coffee pot. "Help yourself."

Coffee. Nothing he wanted more at the moment. Too many long nights and no sleep. All he'd done at Hope's house was think about her sleeping, warm and drowsy in her bed. His dick had wanted badly to go wake her up.

But he'd given her his word. And while he was determined to keep her safe from any outside forces who might not like her snooping around Turner's death, he'd been more worried about keeping her safe from him.

"Caroline made the coffee, so you're safe," Mitch said. A banged up banquet table was piled with stacks of manila folders, sticky notes, and colored highlighters.

Next to all that crap was a model airplane about a foot long. Black with wings and a bloated looking cockpit it was the ugliest damned plane he'd ever seen. He angled his head. Wait. That wasn't a model airplane.

"Holy shit," Brice said already reaching for it. "You guys have a *drone?*"

"Test model," Teeg said. "Mitch and I search for girls in bikinis with it. Don't tell Caroline. It's pretty slick, but we have some bugs to work out."

"Yeah. Like the facial recognition," Mitch said. "That's a problem."

"Hey," Teeg shot. "Working on it."

Grey cleared his throat. "No more stalking half-naked females. It's for work purposes only."

Mitch rolled his eyes, sat at the table, and opened a file. "Caroline said to tell you hi and welcome to the team."

Brice gritted his teeth. "I'm not joining the team."

Batman and Robin exchanged a look that said they knew differently. The smallest of grins passed over Grey's lips before he turned back to his board.

Whatever.

Teeg motioned him over. His eyes were bloodshot, probably due to no sleep.

Made two of them.

"What's up, man?" Brice asked, pulling up a chair next to the command desk.

Teeg's nails were bitten down to the quick like Brice's. His fingers darted over the keys. "I was digging into those dating sites last night. The ones Bigley is in? I came across a private forum, with kind of an odd name for a dating site. I took a screenshot to show you."

He hit return and the middle screen in front of him changed. A typical forum layout, where a user asked a question and members of the forum replied. The users in this particular forum had odd names, but not the kind Brice expected on a dating site. No TeddyBearForYou or MissGrins&Giggles. The names weren't made up of letters at all. They were all numbers.

"What am I looking at?" Brice asked.

"This site is called Assassin's Creed."

Brice's mind immediately went to roleplaying and Joel. "Like the computer game?"

"No, man." Teeg shook his head. "This is on the Deep Web."

"A dating site for assassins?"

"Guess they need love too." The joke fell flat and Teeg cleared his throat. "We're definitely talking murder for hire."

"On a dating site?"

Teeg nodded. "Paid assassins who specialize in risky targets are most likely using it for a cover. Homeland and the FBI are too familiar with the Deep Web these days, so the bad guys are digging down a little further, looking for unusual places to hide."

A cold, hard lump formed in Brice's lower stomach. At the same time, his pulse raced the way it always did when he smelled a scoop. "What does this have to do with Turner?"

"Read the post."

He did, and it made no sense to him, so he read it again. "Is this some kind of code?"

The kid looked slightly surprised Brice didn't understand it. "Uh, yeah." He pointed to some random words about a shark. "This refers to a judge, someone high in the food chain. This," he moved to another set of words about being eaten alive, "means he needs to disappear. As in die. Those numbers under the code are longitude and latitude coordinates."

"Let me guess. Washington D.C."

Teeg nodded. "And the set of numbers at the bottom is a day and time," he finished. "The exact day and time of Turner's death."

"Was the poster looking for bids on who would do it?"

"Nah, he only corresponded with one guy. Offered him what amounts to $65,000 in cash."

Brice's mind flashed to the store of cash in Kostas's closet. But the cabbie hadn't been the shooter. "And did the assassin respond?"

Teeg moved the cursor down, bringing up a message. "The proof of the hit was posted in a private chat room thirty minutes after Turner died. It took me a while, but I was able to hack into that room."

He clicked on a second screenshot and Brice's entire body went cold. The proof of death on the screen was definitely a picture of Chief Justice Turner lying on the bridge, bleeding out. Gerard was in the shot, leaning over him, trying to stop the bleeding.

"Shit."

Lodestone was never wrong.

Brice's gut was never wrong either. "I need to know who this killer is, and more importantly, who took out the hit."

"Like everyone in the Deep Web, these guys are invisible, Brice. You know that. I can hack into these chat rooms and forums and find stuff, but there's no way I can track down the people behind the scenes. And, dude, I don't want to. You don't mess with these guys."

Not if you want to live. Brice scrubbed his face. "There has to be away to bring this to light. We can't let them get away with it."

"There's something else you need to see." Teeg tapped the keyboard and moved his mouse around, pulling up a new file.

Grey came up behind them. "You need to back down, Brice."

"Why? I'm not scared of going head to head with whoever's behind this."

"Because of this," Teeg hit the return key. "It was posted an hour ago in the same forum."

A new image appeared on the main screen and Brice sucked in his breath.

The eagle logo Brice used for his blog stared back at him. Superimposed over the top was a large, red bulls-eye.

"It's open season on the Patriot Blog," Grey said. "You've just become a target."

Brice's mind went back to the picture of Turner bleeding out on the bridge. On the heels of that came the memory of the car bearing down on Hope. "Goddamn it," he said, jumping up.

Hope, Hope, Hope. Get to her!

He ran for the door.

12

*H*ope sat in her car rhythmically banging her head against the steering wheel. Bump, bump, bump. In the last twenty minutes, the future she'd imagined for herself, the rise in the ranks, the ultimate goal of reaching the White House, had just slipped from her grasp.

Not that she ever had it in the first place. But she'd been working toward it and succeeding—at least she'd thought so—until Hawk and his tip showed up.

Damned bloggers.

Always creating chaos. Well, he'd better damn well hope this conspiracy theory panned out or he'd owe her a career.

From the middle of her forehead an ache spread to her temples and she stopped pounding, just let her head rest on the steering wheel. Just one little second to wrap her mind around the fact that she might be on her way to being unemployed.

Somewhere in this mess she's have to find the upshot. She sat up, set her shoulders back, breathed in. *I can do this.*

Of course she could. Since the third grade when that mean girl, Jennifer Jacobs, had told her she was boring in front of the entire class and everyone laughed at her, she'd been finding the upshot.

Back then she'd figured out that if she put on her happy Hope face and acted upbeat and positive everyone would love her. Flock to her, wanting her to share all that good, never-ending energy.

From that day on, no one had ever called her boring again.

And Jennifer Jacobs? By the eighth grade, she was regularly giving blow jobs in the boys' bathroom and being labeled a slut. A fact that shouldn't have made Hope feel some sort of satisfaction, but most certainly did. Because Hope, by transforming herself into sunshine on a rainy day, had survived the trials of adolescence while Jennifer Jacobs, her tormentor, hadn't.

Find the upshot.

That's all she needed to do.

Her phone blared.

"Not now," she muttered.

Whoever it was would have to wait. Rob probably. She'd barely had time to talk to him on her way out. She'd been standing in her cube, scooping up her purse and briefcase and he'd—as usual—peeked over the wall. Then she'd hit him with it. Suspended.

Adios.

Vomit backed up in her throat. She gagged once, tasted the nastiness in her mouth, that acidic, foul taste of puke that people never forgot. *Don't.*

She wouldn't do it. Wouldn't sit in this car feeling sorry for herself, wallowing in her misfortune. Allowing herself to become physically ill over a job.

A job.

No one was dead. And she hadn't been fired. Yet. Only a suspension pending an investigation into her actions. She'd have to hang on to that.

Her phone rang again and again she ignored it. A few

seconds later, her voicemail chimed followed by three staccato knocks. The knocks were a text.

Then the phone rang again.

Three calls, a voicemail and a text in the last ninety seconds.

Someone wanted to talk to her. Quite badly.

She dug the phone out, hit the button and Hawk's name filled the screen.

"Ha! Of course. The troublemaker himself."

She clicked on the envelope and his message popped up. *WHERE ARE YOU??? CALL ME ASAP. URGENT!!!!*

And, oh. My. God, the man was a total drama queen. King. Whatever. She tossed the phone down and the minute it hit the passenger seat, it rang again.

Hawk.

"Are you insane?" she shouted at his name on the screen.

As desperate as she was to ignore him, she knew, sure as she was sitting in this damned car anticipating her career being sucked into oblivion, he'd keep calling. Like her, he had that dogged personality. Whether chasing a story or a person, he'd keep bugging her.

Just as she'd do.

Without picking the phone up, she tapped the speaker button. "What!"

His response to that was nothing but a few seconds of dead air.

"Hope?" he finally said, his voice clipped and questioning.

As if she didn't have a right to be crabby. *As if* for just a few minutes she didn't have the right to not be an optimist, to not be the sickening mixture of Perky Patti and Little Miss Mary Sunshine and be *upset*, no, be flat-out *pissed* that she was on the verge of losing a career she dreamed of.

I'm pissed. Huh. So, that's what it felt like?

"Yes," she said. "What is it?"

"Where are you?"

"In my car."

Again, dead air. "Your car? Why? You need to be in your office. Your thoroughly secure office."

"I'd love to. It's not happening today."

"Why?"

She let out a loud and more than a little sarcastic snort. "Well, Hawk, here's the thing. That little stunt with Joel last night, the one I didn't want you and Tony to pull?"

"What about it?"

Oh, he'd love this. And she'd make him wait a few seconds. Let him sit there and stew while she lined up the money shot. *Four, three, two, one.*

"Joel squealed," she said.

Money.

Shot.

Apparently, she'd made her point because more dead air filled her car. Then again, she was in a parking garage. She could have lost the signal. Wouldn't that be just perfect? The one time she wanted to be scathing and the call drops.

She finally picked up the phone, checked the signal.

"He did what?" Hawk's voice boomed.

Still there. "He filed a complaint against Tony and I. My boss called me into her office the minute I arrived."

"And?"

"She suspended me. I'm betting Officer Gerard suffered the same fate. He's a cop for crying out loud."

"Um, yeah. I can't believe she suspended you. Wait. What am I saying? Of course they suspended you. Because that's politics and bureaucratic bullshit. This kid files a complaint and they want to save their asses—never mind asking why we'd go to those lengths. Same shit, different year. Pricks."

Great. Him and his anti-government rhetoric. Just what she needed right now. She half agreed with him because—come to think of it—Amy sure jumped to that suspension thing pretty quick. No thought, no warning, no consideration.

Just bam.

Which meant, Amy knew before Hope stepped into her office how that meeting would end. No matter what Hope had said, a complaint had been filed. Period. No back up. No protecting her employee. No loyalty.

Damn that Hawk. Now he had *her* preaching his message.

She stared straight ahead at the dull, gray cement support beam of the parking garage. Beyond that, a cloudy day only reinforced her mood. What she needed now was to leave here. Sitting here stewing did her no good. All it did was churn the acid inside her and one thing she never wanted was to give into the negativity.

She started the car, shifted and backed out of the parking space. "Hawk, I've gotta go."

"Where?"

"I don't know. Home I guess."

"No!" he hollered.

His harsh tone made her pulse jump and she hit the brake hard enough that her head snapped forward. Having lived in D.C. for years, she'd gotten used to public transportation. Something that dulled her driving skills, made her reflexes a little less sharp. Meaning, she'd become a crappy driver. And Hawk screaming at her while performing said crappy driving might get her killed.

"Dammit! Don't scream at me. I'm driving!"

"Hope, I'm on my way to you."

"What? Why?"

"Check around you. Is anyone following you?"

The man's paranoia had reached an all-time high. Still sitting in the middle of the full garage, she glanced around, then checked her mirror. Nothing. She lifted her foot off the brake and swung the turn for the first floor of the garage.

Parking garages were creepy anyway and Hawk was only making it worse.

"No. I don't see anyone. Why?"

"Okay. Good. Just drive Hope. Blend into traffic, but keep moving. I'm three minutes from your office. Just stay on the line with me and tell me what streets you're on. I'll find you and then we'll go someplace safe."

What in hell was he talking about? "Hawk, seriously, it's barely nine in the morning and I'm already exhausted. I don't have a safety drill in me today."

"Honey, this isn't a drill. Teeg found something and it's bad."

At the garage exit, she braked again. "What do you mean?"

"I'll explain later. Just keep moving."

The garage gate lifted and she pulled forward, checking her mirrors and glancing around again. No cars following. A nerve in her jaw throbbed and she bit down. *Don't let him spook you.*

"No. You'll tell me now. What's going on?"

"Are you still driving?"

"Yes! I'm driving," she hollered. "I just pulled out of the garage. Now spill."

"Someone is after me. And probably you too."

At the sight of Hope's car half a block ahead of him, relief flooded his body and Brice let go of the mental breath he been holding. "I see you," he said into his phone. "I'm three cars back."

"Now what do we do?" She came to a stop at a stoplight.

His phone dinged with an incoming text. Grey.

Safe house, it said. Ask for Ling-Ling. Tell her I sent you. Attached were GPS coordinates.

How does he do that?

Brice drummed his fingers on the steering wheel, anxious

for traffic to start moving again. "Let me pass you in the next block and then follow me."

"Where we going?"

"Somewhere safe." *I hope.*

The light changed and traffic began to flow. Hope did as instructed, and soon Brice was in the lead. He followed the GPS coordinates, all the while listening to Hope ream him out.

"I knew I shouldn't have let you and Tony hammer on Joel like that," she said. "He didn't do anything except make a stupid mistake accepting a vacation from a lobbyist to impress his girlfriend. And now I'm paying for it instead of him because I can't tell my boss how you had Teeg illegally hack into the Supreme Court email system. Even if I don't lose my job over this, it will be a blot on my record forever. I'll never make it to the White House now. In fact, I might as well kiss any job in our nation's capital buh-bye."

Had she even heard what he'd said about someone being after them? At least she was still alive to complain. Thank God.

Probably not the best time to tell her about his little B&E earlier with Gerard.

But when I catch up to that pompous little ass, Joel, he won't know what hit him. "Our lives could be in danger, Hope. Can you stop bitching me out long enough for me to get us to a safe place?"

Silence from the phone met his ears.

He'd take that as agreement.

The arch welcoming them to Chinatown loomed ahead. The place they were heading to was on I Street. Where the hell was Grey taking them? Brice turned north on 7th Street before the arch. Several American businesses lined the street, their names in Chinese as well as English.

"If you think Kung Pao Chicken with a side of fried rice is going to make me feel better," Hope said through the phone, "you're sadly mistaken."

Brice followed the GPS around the corner to an alley. Should he go down it? The coordinates indicated the place was in the middle of the block.

He took the plunge, driving into the alley. In his rearview, he saw Hope hesitate at the entrance.

"Are you sure about this?" Her voice sounded small and unsure. A trick of the speakerphone, he assured himself. She was going to beat his ass as soon as she had the opportunity.

Although he wasn't sure about anything at the moment, he lied. "Of course."

A section of parking opened up just past a line of dumpsters. As he wheeled into one of the open spots, he was facing the back of a nail salon. A glance up showed the entrance to a second-story apartment.

A set of wooden stairs went from the ground up to the apartment's covered doorway. A clothesline ran between the support beams and a bunch of pots with dead plants lined the railing.

Hope pulled in next to him. "What are we doing here?" She was still speaking via her phone.

Brice turned off his car, snagged his phone and got out, cutting the connection and motioning for her to stay put. He hopped the single concrete step to the back door of the salon and buzzed the doorbell.

A short, dark-haired woman answered a minute later. Her nails were impeccable; her hair as shiny as the hood of his truck.

She looked him over but didn't say anything, so he spoke first. "Ling-Ling?"

"Who is asking?"

Her accent was so faint, he wasn't sure it even existed. "Grey sent me."

She stepped back and shut the door in his face.

What the hell? All the adrenaline coursing through his

system needed an outlet and he punched the wall. The ragged brick cut his knuckles and sent a sharp pain up his arm.

He was texting Grey when the woman reappeared, a key in hand. She shoved it at him, pointed up the outside stairs, and disappeared back inside.

Stepping off the concrete, he peered up at the apartment. This was the safe house?

Hope was peering at him through her windshield. A quick scan of the area showed they were definitely alone in the alley and few of the buildings had windows. Even those that did couldn't get a clear view of this alcove.

Brice took the steps two at a time. The key fit in the lock and a second later, the door opened.

"Hello?" He leaned in slightly. The place was small but immaculate—the complete opposite of the outside appearance. "Anyone here?"

When nothing but silence met his question, he deleted the less than nice text he'd been about to send Grey and went to get Hope.

"Here we are," he said, guiding her out of the car and up the steps before she had time to even look around. "We'll be safe here for now."

She hesitated before stepping across the threshold. "Safe from whom?"

Jostling her into the apartment, he gave the area one more scan before shutting the door and locking it. When he turned, he found her arms crossed over her chest and her gaze boring into him.

"If this is another of your paranoid delusions...," she started.

Delusions? "I may be paranoid but I'm not schizophrenic." He moved around her, tossing the key on a side table. The entry was in the middle of a brightly colored kitchen and a comfortable looking living room. "Teeg found evidence that Turner was indeed murdered on that bridge, and not over a road rage incident."

Her forehead creased in a frown. "What kind of evidence?"

"You might want to sit down."

"I'm fine standing."

"A hit was put out on Turner on a murder-for-hire forum on the Deep Web. A forum hidden behind the pretense of a dating site. One linked to Joel, by the way. We don't know who put out the hit, but there was a follow-up photo for proof of death."

Teeg had yelled at him on his way out of the armory about what happened next. "Teeg took screen shots, but the postings disappeared the minute someone realized he was doing so. Wiped clean out. There's no way to trace who posted the hit or who responded."

"I don't understand the Deep Web."

He rubbed his forehead. How quickly he'd forgotten he was dealing with an innocent. "The part of the internet the general public doesn't know about and never accesses. It's a haven for criminal activity."

At her blank look, he searched his mind for something she would recognize. "Blue Silk trial? Ever see that story in the news?"

Recognition sparked in her eyes. She smacked her forehead with her hand. "Of course. Sorry, it's been another long, flippin' day. I do remember that trial. Had something to do with a criminal kingpin brokering deals and laundering bitcoins into real money. The FBI wanted to charge him with being an accessory to murder-for-hire killings, as well, but the judge threw those out."

Bitcoins were the commerce used on the Deep Web. "That's the one."

"Damn." She ran her hands through her hair, pulling it tight at her temples. "So we don't really have evidence to prove anything."

"Except those screenshots. And the posting is in code. There's no direct mention of Turner. Or Kenton Labs. It's all circumstantial. Even the post-death shot. Any decent attorney could claim it was taken by a bystander on the bridge."

She walked slowly over to a gray suede loveseat and sank down on it. Her eyes were big in her face as she peered up at him. "And now someone's after you? Like as in one of these paid assassins?"

"Looks like they want to take down my blog, and the only way to do that is take me out."

Her body gave a slight tremble as if she were cold. "Because you're digging into this Turner thing?"

"*We're* digging into this Turner thing. You and me. If I'm a target, so are you. We've both been poking the hornet's nest and this is the fallout."

She bent forward, elbows on knees, and hung her head in her hands. "I think I'm going to be sick."

He rushed into the kitchen, throwing open cabinets until he found a bowl. Hauling ass back to Hope, he handed it to her.

"Thanks," she said, her face too pale. "That car that nearly ran over me on the bridge? You were right." Her voice hitched as reality drove home exactly how deep the shit had gotten. "Someone tried to kill me!"

He eased down onto the love seat next to her and drew her against his chest. Filtered sunlight shone through the blinds, reflecting off dust particles floating in the air. "You're safe here, Hope, with me."

13

The bowl hit the floor as Hope brought her hands up to cover her eyes. Craziness. Turner, the Deep Web, an assassin. All of it. She drew in a long breath, squeezed her eyes tighter willing the sickness rolling in her stomach to beat it. Just hit the road. *Vamoose.*

Somewhere along the way, her life had whirled from her organized plan, spinning faster and faster with her trailing behind, chasing it like a frantic parent, desperate to grab hold and reel it back to safety.

Her life.

Her control.

She could do this.

But she needed Hawk's hands off of her. When he touched her something short-circuited in her brain and she turned into a horny teenager. For the love of God, she hadn't been with a man in months and the ones she *had* been with barely got her temperature above freezing. But Hawk? That man could melt an iceberg. Where was he when the Titanic needed him?

And worse, he made her feel weak.

At least that's what it felt like right now. Like she needed coddling. Comforting. And that wouldn't do. Not one bit. All the men before were just...there. With them there was none of this weakness. This vulnerability. Hawk was different. Extremely so.

And they were in a pickle here. She glanced around the safe house, took in the sagging window sheers littered with snags and pulls.

The pickle had crappy curtains.

Where is my brain?

She dug her fingers into her forehead. *Think.* "How long will we be here?"

He shrugged. "As long as it takes. And before you start bitching about not having your stuff, we'll send someone to your place—a woman—to grab you some things."

"I can't even go home to get clothes?"

"No. Someone could be watching. But I have a friend, Caroline, she works with Teeg. She can go to your place."

With all this subterfuge Hope might as well be a criminal on the run. And how the hell did *she* wind up the bad guy?

No. No good. These negative thoughts. Nuh-uh. All she needed was to corral her emotions, get this wild sense of chaos under control and organize it into pieces. When she'd been an intern chasing stories she'd mindmap all of her leads, drawing circles around them and connecting them with arrows until it all started to form some order. Until a story developed.

That's what she'd do now. Pulling out of Hawk's arms she popped off the love seat and paced the room to rid herself of the negative energy tearing her up.

"Hope? You okay?"

She spun back on him and pointed. "I'm fine. And I'm not an infant. So, as much as I appreciate this whole Tarzan thing you've got working, I don't want to be babied."

His eyes narrowed and his face took on a hard look she so

far hadn't come close to seeing. "Babied?" he repeated. "That's what you think this is?"

"I don't want to fight."

"Jesus, Hope, you're tough."

Exactly what she wanted to be.

Wasn't it?

Perhaps not with the way he looked at her, that steel gaze and...disappointment...yes, that's what it was, all over him.

She held her hands up. "Wait. I'm sorry. I didn't—"

"What?"

She shook her head. "I don't know. I could say I didn't mean it, but that would be a lie and I won't lie to you. I don't want to be coddled. Am I scared? Yes. Do I want to give into that? No? That's all I meant. If I give into it, it'll destroy me. It'll prove I'm weak and you can bet your life that's not something I ever want to be. So, please, let's just do something here. Let's figure out how we got into this mess and get the heck out of it. *That's* what I need. Please."

He studied her for a long minute and she imagined all the descriptors—whackjob, lunatic, psycho—roaming inside his brain.

Finally, he jerked his head. "Okay."

"Okay?"

"I get it." He grabbed his messenger bag off the floor and flopped it onto the crummy, about-to-fall-down coffee table. "You need to get some form of control back."

Yes. Exactly. She nodded, thankful for the understanding. "What are we doing?"

"We're going through all the screenshots Teeg gave me. We've got emails, copies of Joel's phone bills, texts. It's a lot of tedious crap, but hey, you wanted to do something. Gerard is looking deeper into the cab driver, by the way, and I'm still looking at Kenton's board and the scientist—Dr. Block—for possibilities. For now, let's hit Joel. He's the one that led us to the dating site." He handed over a stack about an inch thick. "Here you go, sweetness. Start reading."

This is what she needed. Tedious or not, it was work. And progress. Even if nothing came of it, she wouldn't be sitting here crying over her rotten situation.

She wouldn't be collapsing under pressure.

She snatched the papers away from him. "You're on, Hawk. What am I looking for?"

"I have no idea. Just start reading and flag anything suspicious."

Two hours later, after a rather delicious lunch delivered from the Chinese restaurant three doors down, Hope had read through at least three hundred emails, texts and memos. Nothing suspicious. Not one darned thing.

"Hawk, I've got nothing here."

He held up a finger. "Hang on."

"Hang on what?"

He scooted to the edge of the sofa, set the sheets he held in his hand aside and rifled through the stack on the coffee table.

"What are you looking for?"

"Texts. From—" he glanced at the sheets he'd set aside "last month. Do you have anything dated last month?"

That would be easy to know because she'd sorted her stack into chronological order by item type. She perused the three piles in front of her, found the one marked TEXTS/JAN-FEB. " Sure. It would be in here. What do you need?"

"February twenty-second. 3:07 PM. I have the first part of the exchange. I need the last bit."

She fired through the stack. "Why? What is it?"

"Not sure. It's Joel having a conversation with Charley and Charley talking about someone else. 'My guy', he's calling him. Let's see who his 'guy' might be."

Hope located the pages marked the twenty-second and dragged her finger down the list of time-stamped texts. Did this kid do any work? Who had time to send this many texts in a day? His data rates must have been outrageous.

"Got it!" She held up the page and pointed. "Right here. Charley says 'I'll talk to my guy. Thanks for the info'."

Hawk slouched back. "That's it?"

"Yep. Why?"

"Damn. I thought maybe it was something. I got a weird feeling about it."

Hope stood, stretched her back and rolled one hand. "Not so fast there, big guy. Let's go with that. What are you thinking?"

"I don't know what I'm thinking. It's a weird conversation. Almost like it's in code. Joel is telling Charley about a restaurant opening next month and Charley is saying he'll talk to his guy about it. I mean. Who cares? Google it. Right?"

"Right. Unless it is code for something else."

Hawk waggled his finger at her. "Yep."

"We need to see Charley's emails or texts or whatever for the time period right after this. Maybe he contacted whoever 'his guy' is. Can Teeg get us that?"

A wicked grin slipped across Hawk's face. "Well, look at you coming to the dark side."

"Listen, baby, my career is going down in flames. I might as well."

14

---

a storm was moving in, darkening the skies as dusk approached. Brice had gone back and forth with Teeg, spelling out what he wanted and pushing the kid to do whatever it took to hack into Charley's accounts.

Illegal? Hell, yeah. So was bribing Supreme Court clerks and possibly being tied into a judge's murder.

Thunder sounded overhead. A soft rain pelted the windows. Hope had disappeared a few minutes ago down the hall while Brice paced the floor with Teeg on the line.

"This Charley guy has a bunch of email accounts, all personal, each labeled by the company or industry he's pushing legislation for," Teeg said.

"Any associated with Kenton?"

"They're listed under an umbrella account called Pharmaceutical. Want me to look into that folder and get the emails?"

"Absolutely. In his texts with Joel, he referred to 'my guy'. I want to know who that is." A sound in the back of the apartment caught Brice's attention. Was it coming from the bedroom? He glanced down the hallway, saw the bedroom door was closed. "So I need Charley's texts too."

A heavy sigh. "That will take longer, but yeah, I can do it. The phone companies aren't as easy to hack into as Outlook."

Microsoft made hackers very happy on most occasions.

Brice heard another sound...a squeak? A hiccup? Maybe it was the noise of the salon downstairs or the storm outside. "Thanks, man. I owe you."

"I'm sure Grey has plans for you to pay him back for my time."

I'm sure he does. "Forget it. I'm not working for the Justice Team. Any more on the Deep Web stuff?"

"Nada. Maybe that bulls-eye thing was just a bluff."

A bluff. Right. And moonbeams would shoot out his ass later. "When Caroline has a chance, I need her to pick up some stuff from Hope's place."

"Grey already sent her to grab clothes for you and for Hope. She should be by to see you after dark."

"She doesn't need a key for our places?"

"Would you?" Teeg snorted. "She's a Fed, man, and she's *Caroline*. She can look at a lock and it cowers in fear."

For the first time that day, Brice smiled. "Roger that. Is she going to make me sign a contract with Grey before she releases our clothes?"

"In blood if Grey has any say in it."

Brice owed the man for this, but he was not selling his soul. "Call me as soon as you get those emails and texts."

They disconnected and Brice stood looking at the pile of papers on the coffee table. He needed a conspiracy board to lay everything out and...*damn it*. There was that muffled noise again.

"Hope?"

He started down the narrow hallway. The walls were covered with cheap paneling. He wasn't too sure there was anything but a few studs underneath. He could probably punch the wall and go right through to the other side.

He heard a sniff as he stopped next to the bedroom door. "Everything okay?"

"What?" Another sniff and the sound of her blowing her nose. "You bet," she said in a falsely cheery voice. "Peachy keen. Now go away."

There was a hiccup in that cheery voice that kept him planted where he was. "Are you trying to sleep?"

"Haha. Yeah, sleep." He heard another catch in her voice. "Like I could sleep right now."

The doorknob was a brass number straight out of the 1980s. He tried it, found it locked. A niggle of worry set up shop in his gut. "Why is the door locked?"

"Because I need...I don't know...space."

For all her bluff and swagger, she was freaking out. He understood the feeling. When Wes and the ATF had pulled the rug out from under his feet, he'd been in the same situation.

"A part of me just wants to run, you know? To get out of town and clear my head. Two days ago, I woke up and everything was perfectly normal. Now, everything is spinning out of control and I don't know what to do to stop it."

There was no way to stop it and that was the true crux of the matter for Hope. The young, naive girl she'd been two days ago had been bombarded with the ugly and unforgiving side of life in D.C. "We're going to get through this," Brice told her through the door. "I'll get to the bottom of this, Hope, and if it's the last thing I do, I'll find the bastard that tried to run you down and I'll hang him by his balls. I'll also do everything in my power to clear your name and get you your job back."

Silence. He snugged an ear against the door and listened. Sure enough, he heard a muffled crying, as if she were trying to silence it by shoving her face in a pillow.

That sound. Her trying to hide that she was scared, and angry, and devastated. He wanted to punch the wall.

Damn it all to hell. He jiggled the doorknob. "Unlock the door, Hope."

"No. I'm...fine."

Right. That's why she was crying even harder now.

He rattled the doorknob harder. He wasn't Caroline. Locks did not cower for him and he had no credit card this time. "Hope..."

"Go away! I don't want you to see me like this."

"I'm not going away. Open the damn door."

"My life was normal." Her breath hitched. "I had the White House in my sights, and then...and then...this happened. Now it's ruined. Everything I believed in is...gone."

"Nothing is gone. You're just on suspension." He jammed his shoulder into the door and felt it budge a little. "I told you, I'll figure out how to clear your name."

"But that won't change the fact that Chief Justice Turner was assassinated and that certain people in my office are more worried about covering up a scandal than seeing justice done." Another sob ripped from her throat. "Isn't that the exact thing the Supreme Court stands for? Justice? Truth? Fair and equal treatment?"

He couldn't stand the disappointment and sheer anguish in her voice. It wasn't just her life being turned upside down that was killing her. It was the fact that all her pie-in-the-sky, Mary Sunshine ideals were being shredded.

He'd had enough. Stepping back from the door, he lifted his leg and kicked right above the doorknob.

The hollow core door exploded in a spray of splinters, the lock buckling and ripping pieces of the frame off with it.

Hope was on the bed as suspected, curled around a pillow. At the noise, her head jerked up and her tear-wet eyes went big as saucers.

Brice went to her side, sat down next to her, and pulled her into his arms.

For half a second, she was stiff. "What are you doing?" And then she didn't wait for his response before her shoulders started to shake and she melted into him.

Crying women had always made him nervous. Usually, he did whatever it took to get away from them. This time, though, the woman crying in his arms made him want to rail against the world. Nothing and no one could peel him away from her. *Protect.*

Yeah, the alpha male in him had hit Code Red the moment he'd seen that car on the bridge gunning for her. Now, he could finally let that side have its way.

"Let it out, Hope." He stroked her back and held her close, her tears soaking through his shirt. "And just so you know, the Supreme Court does stand for truth and justice and I think Justice Turner would have admired your determination to uncover his murder and see justice is done."

She lifted her head and sniffed. "You do?"

Digging out a white hanky from his back pocket, he handed it to her. "Hell, yes. I certainly admire you. So don't give up on the White House just yet, okay? A journalist with your grit and resolve can do anything she puts her mind to."

She wiped her eyes and blew her nose. Her eyes were red and puffy but she still looked beautiful to him. "You're only saying that to get me to stop crying."

He put a hand to his heart. "I'm wounded you would say that. I love bawling women."

She smacked his arm. "Smart ass."

They both laughed and she blew her lips out in a heavy sigh. Then she snuggled up to him again, her arms circling his waist. She laid her head on his shoulder, her warm breath caressing his skin. "First, I'm nearly run over, then I'm suspended, now my boyfriend has a hit put out on him. Could this flippin' week get any worse?"

Boyfriend? "Boyfriend?"

She tensed. "Well, I meant, um...you're my friend, right? And you're a boy, right? So that's...yeah...forget it. That's not at all what I meant. I meant boyfriend. There, I said it."

Ho-kay, then. He patted the back of her head somewhat awkwardly, although he was totally digging the teenage-sounding term. "I warned you getting involved with me was dangerous."

She sighed against his neck. "And yet, here I am, in an apartment in Chinatown, on the brink of being fired and watching my future go up in flames, and instead of running for the hills and pleading temporary insanity to my boss, I'm snuggling up to you." One of her hands slowly rubbed over his chest. "What the hell is wrong with me, because this is the most alive I've felt in...oh, I don't know...forever maybe."

She had totally lost her mind. He was sure of it. Stopping her hand when it started to descend lower, Brice scooted a couple inches back and looked her in the face. Her eyes were clear again, her cheeks pink from crying.

Or maybe from lust.

Was this what normally happened after a woman had a good cry?

He couldn't make a case for delayed shock. Temporary insanity, like she'd said, however, might just fit the bill. "I'm going to hide you away and keep you safe until I can expose who put the hit on Turner and bring him, and the actual killer, to justice."

"Hide?" She looked appalled. "I'm not hiding."

"Hope, this isn't an ice cream social for the glee club. This is life-and-death."

Her fingers touched his cheek. "You would risk your life to keep me safe?"

"Of course I would. You don't belong in his world. I dragged you into it. Protecting you is my highest priority at this point."

"And it's not at all because you might, sort of, kind of want to be my boyfriend?"

Was she kidding? He took her chin between his fingers and tilted her face up. "I want to take you in every position imaginable and then do it again. I want to take you to restaurants and movies and all the normal things people do as a couple. But I'm not normal. My life isn't normal. You deserve better than that."

She took one of his hands and brought it to her breast. "I know I've been thinking nonstop about it. The other night, I mean. Even in the midst of everything else—being irritated with you, being put on suspension, finding out I could be in real danger—I keep wondering, if my world really did come to an end today, what would I regret?" Raising her head, she brushed her lips against his. "The only thing I'd truly regret is not being with you." Her lips spread into a wide, mischievous smile. "I want to *seduce* you, Hawk."

Seduction. She'd been seducing him since he'd first heard her sexy voice on the phone.

He started to protest—he would not take advantage of her in this state—and then she leaned forward and nipped his bottom lip.

There weren't many times in his life when Brice admitted defeat. *This might be one of them.* "Bad idea, brat."

She grabbed a handful of his hair and tugged none too gently. His cock twitched. "Did you just call me a brat?"

His answer was to kiss her and shut her the fuck up.

Her mouth was warm and Brice tasted the salt from her tears on her lips. He parted those lips and dipped his tongue inside, a rush of satisfaction raced through him when she moaned and arched into him.

This is wrong.

But could something this wrong feel so damn right?

The invitation to sex was so obvious, he'd be stupid to confirm it. He did so anyway.

"Hope," he said, pulling back. She was inexperienced with the dark side of life and he'd dragged her into that without thought. Now she was paying the price. He wouldn't drag her into a sexual affair without making damn sure she understood the consequences. "Are you sure this is what you want?"

The storm outside had intensified, a dull thunder rattling the windows. She clung to him, trying to catch her breath. "Yes. It's what I want. I mean, that was my tongue making its way down your throat."

There *was* that. "I know you want sex, but...you know I'm not relationship material."

This time she took both of his hands and put them on her breasts. "Can we talk about this later? Maybe you can just shut up and kiss me again. I love it when you kiss me. I forget about everything else."

And there was the rub. The invitation to sex had morphed into the promise of sex without commitment.

She was using him to forget.

As she leaned forward and teased his lips with her tongue, Brice's moral fiber was sorely tested.

"You kicked the door down," she said, her breath soft on his mouth. "God, that's sexy."

Oh, hell. He was no saint and she knew it. He'd shown her his hand and been totally honest and upfront.

She wanted him anyway.

To forget.

Technicality. Once he made love to her, she'd never forget *him*. The alpha male in him rose once again to the surface.

He took her mouth with force; she gasped at the contact, opening on the quick inhale and allowing him deeper access. With his tongue down her throat this round, he forced her onto her back, pressing her into the bed and hearing the springs groan in protest.

She rocked under him, her fingers digging into his back,

nails scratching him right through his shirt. He rode her through their clothes for a moment, then created enough space between their bodies to undo the buttons on her shirt, one at a time. He kissed his way down the curve of her neck and into the hollow of her shoulder as he revealed her luscious skin, inch by creamy inch.

He didn't stop kissing her as he undressed her from the top down. His lips teased her clavicle and the dip between her breasts as his hands massaged those glorious mounds through her lacy bra. Once he had the bra off, his fingers went to work on the clasp of her slacks, his mouth moving to her stomach.

She sucked in a breath when he flicked his tongue out and edged the top of her underwear with it. He felt her muscles tense for a panicked moment as he thumbed her through the silk, but then she ran her fingers through his hair and said, "More, please."

It sounded so funny, so like her—that please—he nearly laughed. "My pleasure, girlfriend."

She raised her head and arched a brow.

He kissed her stomach. "Well, you are a girl and my friend, right?"

That earned him a smack on the head.

He stroked her and her head fell back against the pillow again. "Bodyguard with benefits," she said and her voice was barely above a husky whisper. "My BWB. I like it."

Would she ever stop talking? He deepened his stroke, over and over, until he was sure from the way her body squirmed, she was mindless again. And then he slid one finger under the lace edge of her panties and found her clitoris.

"Oh, my God," she said, but she moved hard against his hand, wanting more, so he kept going.

She was beautiful, her head thrown back, her lips parted, eyes closed. The picture of happiness. Satisfaction.

I did that, he thought, seeing the new flush to her skin, the way she was half-smiling as he worked her toward orgasm.

Legs splayed around him, her body moved in rhythm with his hand, hot and needy as the rain fell outside. He couldn't help it, he needed to taste her. Shifting his fingers, he slipped one inside her. She moaned and he slipped in another, bending to taste her at the same time.

She cried out, shuddering against his mouth as the orgasm hit, and Brice smiled to himself. There would be no more tears tonight.

Orgasms, Hope decided, should be right up there with chocolate cake and milk shakes and her Aunt Lulu's famous meatloaf. No joke. That meatloaf was spectacular.

Right along with the mind-blowing climax she'd just experienced from Hawk the master of the big O.

She let out a little sigh when he trailed kisses up her belly, up, up, up to her wildly sensitized breasts and she grabbed hold of his hair, dragged him up until they were face to face.

"Amazing," she said.

"Plenty more where that came from," he said.

Instinctively, she spread her legs, like they'd done this a hundred—a thousand—times before. Taking his cue, he settled in between them, his erection most definitely pressing against her and then he did it. He smiled at her and the girls in her uterus howled.

She wanted him.

Fast.

Wanted to feel that oneness, that connection that came with a man—this man—being inside of her.

She stared up at him, met his gaze as a streetlight threw shadows across the upper part of the wall and darkened ceiling. Someone had tilted the blinds up, instead of down, giving the room an eerie, wicked glow that only added to the exquisite night.

Already she was gone.

Because this is what happened with men she chose to become intimate with. She got attached. Too quickly. And she knew it and somehow could never stop the landslide of emotions that fooled her into believing she'd found *the* one.

Not this time. He'd been clear about it. Making sure she understood he was a lone wolf. A free spirit who didn't do relationships.

So she'd made up that crap about being fuck buddies. The term was so distasteful she couldn't bring herself to say it aloud.

But they were consenting adults. Even if her emotions tried to whack her out, she'd control it this time. She would.

That alone made this time different. Right? Right.

She'd be okay. She could do it.

Hawk slid into her and she gasped, arching against the intrusion, but at the same time widening her legs, wanting more. He stopped—*no, no, no*—looked down at her, his eyebrows drawn.

"You okay?"

Oh, she was better than okay. And she'd prove it. She clamped her hands over his rear, pulling him closer, needing him deeper because, *holy moly*, that felt good. Older guys. Who knew?

He dipped his head low, nuzzled her neck. "I guess that's a yes."

"It's definitely a yes."

"Good." He pushed deeper and groaned. "Damn, Hope, you're amazing."

She pulled her legs up, needing him deeper still because she couldn't get enough. Not nearly. She wanted...she wanted...him.

All of him.

Hawk picked up his pace, rocking his hips, each thrust bringing her already over-sensitized body closer to that fantastic edge he'd already pushed her over. She reached up, cupped his cheeks and brought him down to kiss her, a gentle melding of their lips while each thrust nearly split her in two. More.

More.

More.

And a beautiful explosion of light swirled inside her head and she closed her eyes. Let it happen. Let that moment build and come to her again. *Please*. Her core tightened and she breathed through it as her breasts tingled and...her body grew more taught, a vicious coil—*don't stop*. Layer upon layer, the tension mounted and she gripped the edges of the sheet—hold on, hold on, hold on.

Yes...her body gave in, handed over control, and simply exploded into more swirling lights. She drew a long breath, desperately trying to cling to the warm buzz shooting through her. She sank deeper into the creaking bed, focused on Hawk, above her, still moving inside her.

"Fantastic," she said.

But then he arched away, throwing his head back, squeezing his eyes closed and she knew. So close. She wanted to see it. Wanted to give him what he'd given her.

She smacked her hands over his rear again, drove him deeper and pumped her hips, waiting, waiting, waiting to see him come apart.

"Hope, I'm..."

He drove into her one last time and cried out, holding himself up as his body stiffened and then his face, those granite features that were so tense just seconds ago, eased.

She touched his face, ran her thumbs over his cheeks, smoothing the lines that reminded her he had eleven years on her.

He liked to gently remind her of those things. That he'd experienced more, understood the world more, sacrificed more.

And apparently had way more sex because the man had some *skillz*.

But she'd concede his greater experience. On all fronts. Simple math. He could still learn from her though. Learn about faith in humankind. He needed that.

Needed her.

And here we go...

The falling in love was complete. What the hell had she just done?

15

---

ope lay on the lumpy bed staring straight up at the ceiling and those slashes of light washing over it.

Beside her, Hawk shifted to his side and without bothering to look at him she knew he was studying her. Could feel it in the sudden change in the atmosphere, the awkward *we-did-that* silence morphing the energy from passion and heat and laughter to a death zone. But she wouldn't give up on her fascination of the ceiling. Nope. Not right now.

Because looking at Hawk, after he'd just rocked her already-quaking world would be a mistake. Oh, she'd been in the death zone before. She was Hope Denby, senseless romantic searching for Mr. Right in every flipping man that took her on two-point-five dates. Yes, she'd averaged them all.

That's how pathetic she could be.

Each time she started dating someone, if there was even a little, bitty spark, her heart got ahead of her brain and—bam—she started buying wedding magazines. Well, maybe the magazines were a stretch. But out of the last four men she'd dated, she'd convinced herself she loved three of them.

Hawk might up her average to four out of five. But something with him was different. With him, she felt calm and safe and alive. Settled. And that had never happened before.

She sighed.

Not doing this. *Not this time.*

"Hope? Are you ever going to look at me?"

For another few seconds she kept her gaze fixed, unwavering, as her thoughts stormed and railed against her because she was a fraud. A fake. A conniver. A woman who'd lied about being able to keep things casual simply to get this man to screw her.

Enough.

She turned her head, and even through the darkness, met his gaze. "Hawk, I lied."

And what a horrible lie it was. As if she, the girl who'd been a virgin until her twenty-first birthday could really buy into the friends with benefits thing? She simply didn't have the emotional fortitude for it. Sex, for her, couldn't be casual. When she slept with a man, it was intense and all-consuming. Deliriously so. She loved that about sex. That attachment. That melding of two people. *The connection.*

Fuck buddies didn't get that. They skipped all that and went straight to the orgasm. The big bang. Which she could get from her trusty vibrator.

"You lied? About?"

"Well, call it a lie by omission. I'm notorious for falling in love. Every time I like a guy I convince myself I'm in love."

"Uh...okay."

"I don't want to do it this time. I mean, I like you. A whole lot. For that reason, I don't want to get ahead of things."

He shook his head, lifted his free hand and rubbed his eyes.

Confused. Who could blame him?

"Look, Hope—"

"I've never been a casual sex girl. Being with you, I could

feel that emotional pull. That yearning to be part of your life. To be your other half. And that's not fair. I unintentionally tricked you and I don't want to be that person."

For once, she cared too much, about him, about herself and what little self-esteem she had left after this horrendous day, to mislead him. To let him think this could be casual for her.

Propping himself up on one elbow, he shook his head. "So, you want a relationship?"

"No."

"Christ, Hope. You're totally screwing with me here."

When he rolled sideways and sat up, she hooked her arm around his waist. "Wait. Please. I want to explain."

Her request was met with silence, but he hadn't moved either so she took that as his willingness to listen. "This isn't a big deal," she said, loosening her hold, but moving closer as she sat up and focused on the back of his shoulder and the lean curve of sloping muscle. Yeah, that's it. Focus on the shoulder. *Distract yourself.* If she faced him, met his gaze, even in the dark, she'd chicken out. "I'm letting you off the hook. That's all. We had fun and blew off some major steam, but I want you to know, I don't expect anything else from you. We'll just chalk it up to a fun night and let it go. Call it a freebie. No emotional cost involved."

"Meaning?"

"Meaning, this can't happen again. If it does, I'll fall a little bit more in love with you and I'll scare you off. I don't want that. If nothing else, I want us to walk away from this as friends. So, I think we should just not sleep together anymore. I'm sorry. I know I sound like..."

"Hope, do you ever shut up?"

What now? Here she was trying to be honest and admit her shortcomings, something she'd never—as in *ever*—done before and he was being...well...mean. "I don't think there's any call for that."

She snatched her arm away. Before she could get far, he latched onto her arm.

"Just...give me a second, will you? I'm processing everything you said and you were jabbering and I couldn't think."

She did that. Jabbered. Her mother told her that all the time and insisted it was some sort of nervous tick. For all Hope knew, it could have been. She did tend to babble when anxiety set in.

"I'm sorry."

"And quit fucking apologizing."

"Hey!"

He held up his hand. "I don't like the idea of not doing this again." He let go of her, turned to her and cradled her cheeks in his hands, the touch so gentle that part of her, the sane, rational part that had convinced her not to fall in love, sent up a protest. How did he expect her to stay distant when he touched her like that?

Slowly, she pulled back, but he held on. "No," he said.

"No?"

"I don't like that idea."

"Now I'm confused. You said no relationship."

"I know. I'm a worse liar than you. A fucking disaster of a liar."

"You are?"

"I am. Let's see where this goes. Who knows, we're both so screwed up we might make a great couple. You the hopeless romantic and me the hopeless non-romantic. Wouldn't that be a pisser?"

"Sure would."

He laughed. "Yeah. What do you say? Wanna give it a try? See if we can keep from killing each other?"

Her body responded, inching closer to him, seeking that closeness, that connection, they'd had just a few minutes ago. Hormona wanted a replay.

And it appeared she'd get it.

"I'd like that," Hope said. "Now screw me blind again."

Hope was snoring softly as Brice slid out from under her arm. He eased out of the bed, careful not to wake her. While she seemed to be satisfied and content after their lovemaking, he felt like his nerves were on fire. He needed to get up. He had to move.

Darkness had bathed the bedroom in shadows. Hope's blond hair stood out against the blue sheets like a soft, warm light guiding him home. Her tussled locks fanned out on the pillow, a few strands falling across her face, the ends blowing out on air puffs from her snores.

Gently, he took one of the strands and rubbed the silkiness between his thumb and index finger. *She's falling for me.*

He'd heard it in her voice, seen it in her eyes. She claimed she wanted to go slow and make sure the feelings she had for him were real, but he'd known they were real—at least for her —before the words even left her mouth.

You're in a pickle now, Brennan.

Except, he'd been in pickles before, and they felt nothing like this. He should have been happy that Hope wanted to take things slow. He should have been forcing her to stop things, in fact, before they went further. Instead, he wanted to climb back into bed and wake her up in the most lascivious way possible.

Dropping the strand of her hair, he moved back. He hadn't been lying when he told her he wanted a real relationship. Dinners out, movies, the kind of relationship normal couples had. How long had it been since he'd had that type of relationship with a woman?

Too long.

He and Hope we're completely incompatible, and yet, here he was, acting like a horny teenager who had the whole world by the tail. Adrenaline pumping in his veins, his pulse skipping around like a chipmunk on crack. He wanted to hunt down every single threat to Hope's happiness and kill it. At the same time, he wanted to prove to her that he wasn't a schizo paranoid freak, jumping at every possible threat out there. He wanted to be the man he saw in Hope's eyes when she looked at him.

Normal.

Not some washed up former ATF agent who spent his days and nights in a cave trying to prove the government was out to screw all of them.

It was an amazing feeling, normal. One he hadn't felt in a long time, maybe had never felt.

Yet, their current situation was anything but. Picking up his jeans, he quietly tiptoed out of the bedroom and drew the door with its broken lock closed behind him.

After slipping on his jeans, he grabbed up the stacks of emails and other papers in the living room and took them to the kitchen.

He'd seen a dry erase calendar on the side of the refrigerator. His mom had had three of those when he was growing up, as she tried to keep six kids and all of their extracurriculars organized.

A marker dangled from a string on the side of the calendar. Brice set the stacks of info he had on the cheap kitchen table and rummaged around in the cabinet drawers until he found some tape and a pen.

Then he went to work.

Up went the names of all the men involved, who they worked for, where they lived. Every scrap of information he had went on the board, including a bubble with the twenty grand he and Gerard had found in Kostas's house. He was absorbed with creating a timeline when his phone dinged with the text from Teeg.

Incoming was all it said.

Thirty seconds later, there was a knock at the door. Three knocks, actually, with a pause, and then another series of three knocks.

Caroline.

Ever vigilant, Brice still pulled back one corner of the drapes and glanced out the window to double check. When he saw who was with Caroline, he let go of an inward grown.

Mitch, a.k.a. Robin, was standing on the porch with her.

Against his better judgment, he opened the door. Mitch took one look at him and lifted an eyebrow. "Are we going shirtless these days?"

Caroline pushed inside and set a soft-sided pink suitcase and a drab black garbage bag on the floor. A briefcase with a long strap hung across her body. She gave Brice an exaggerated once over. "I bet Miss Denby enjoys it."

Mitch scowled. He, of course, was wearing one of his usual smart ass T-shirts. This one read, *I have a black belt in sarcasm and a degree in smartass.*

Caroline glanced around. "Where *is* Hope? I want to meet her."

Brice, still holding the door, rubbed his eyes with his hand. "She's sleeping. Rough couple of days, you know." He motioned for them to leave. "Thanks for the clothes. I'll be in touch if I need anything else."

No surprise, Mitch ignored the blatant hint. He scanned the living room, then poked his head into the kitchen. "Not bad." He caught sight of Brice's work in progress on the fridge. "Hey, what's this?"

Brice rolled his eyes and gave Caroline an irritated look. "You had to bring him, didn't you?"

She shrugged. "I know he's a pain in the ass, but sometimes he's also a damn good person to have on your side."

Shutting the door, Brice locked it and shook his head.

"Is this a conspiracy board?" Mitch said from the kitchen. "I love a good conspiracy board."

Brice followed Caroline. It appeared that, whether he liked it or not, Mitch was staying. He'd taken off his jean jacket and hung it on a kitchen chair, and now stood staring at the dry erase board with his feet planted and his arms crossed. He'd already grabbed a marker and was drawing lines between people, places, and events such as the DDOT unblocking the bridge right after the justice was killed.

Brice had taped Dr. Block's, Joel's, and Charlie's pictures to the top of the board and started his timeline leading up to Chief Justice Turner's death. A paper with a question mark for a picture hung next to Charley and Joel, representing the anonymous "my guy" referenced in one of the emails. Could it be Kostas? Or was it the killer?

Along with tape, Brice had found some colored sticky notes in the kitchen junk drawer. The dry erase board contained a bunch of shorthand memos on the sticky notes at every junction of the timeline and around the border. He kept moving them around in different configurations based on the emails and texts he and Hope had organized, trying to find a link or some kind of pattern. Anything that could give them their next clue.

So far, he didn't have a solid theory that involved Joel, but the nagging feeling at the base of his neck wouldn't let up.

"Got coffee?" Mitch asked, glancing at the kitchen counter. "Looks like it might be a long night."

Going through the material with Mitch was the last thing Brice wanted to do. However, he was out of theories and his concentration was terrible because all he kept thinking about was crawling back in bed with the sexy, young thing in the other room. Having a new set of eyes on the board might not be terrible.

"Make your own coffee," he said.

Robin grinned, knowing that was the equivalent to Brice letting him stay and help.

"I'll make it." Caroline lifted the briefcase strap over her head and hung it on a chair. She went to the cabinets, pulling them open one by one. "Unless you like straight mud, you don't want Mitch in charge of the coffee."

As she pulled a can of Folgers from a top shelf and loaded the coffee pot, Brice stood next to the fridge and began to walk her and Mitch through his timeline.

Pointing at a blue sticky note at the top of the board, he gave them the background. "Kenton Labs is an American pharmaceutical company whose biggest drug is Donazem. Dr. Martin Block is the lead scientist. He's been working for years on this drug. His career was made when Donazem succeeded. Now, Kenton is battling to protect their patent on Donazem in order to block other companies from releasing generics."

He explained the details of the drug and the ramifications if the patent ran out. "Chief Justice Turner was prepared, from all accounts, to deny a hearing on extending the patent. Six months ago, he ruled on a similar case in favor of other companies wanting to market generics of a drug. If Turner denied the hearing, that was it. Within thirty days, Kenton stood to eventually lose billions. It would cripple the company, possibly forcing it into bankruptcy."

He pointed to Charley's picture and a yellow sticky note. "Charlie Winslow is a lobbyist for Winslow-Skirka. Kenton is one of their largest accounts and he's done them proud before. If Kenton goes bankrupt, Winslow-Skirka also stands to lose revenue big time. He might even be ousted from his own company. From a credible source, we know that Charley spoke to Chief Justice Turner on multiple occasions and may have even tried bribing him in order to get Turner to hear the case."

Next was Joel's picture and a pink sticky note. "Joel Bigley is a clerk with the Supreme Court. At one time, he worked exclusively for Turner, but Turner didn't like him, and apparently didn't trust him, so he passed Joel onto another judge. An entitled little prick, Joel is known for having loose lips, but he's never received more than a wrist slap because his parents are influential in D.C. By his own testimony, he accepted a vacation package to Barbados from Charley in December and we believe strongly that he may have been feeding confidential information to Charley about court proceedings and plans, including the fact Turner was going to deny the hearing for Kenton."

At the bottom of the board, Brice tapped a green sticky note. "Finally, there's the fact that Teeg found this information on the Deep Web about a hit being put out on Turner. The bridge closure is probably bogus, a way for the assassin to trap Turner on his way to work and make it look like a road rage incident. While Hope and I were on that bridge the other night investigating a supposed pothole repair, she was nearly run over by a car. I don't think it was an accident. She'd questioned Joel about the cases on Turner's docket earlier that day, and then called the DDOT asking about the reason the bridge lane was closed. I think she stirred the pot and someone came after her. I still have to look into the DDOT and see if I can find a link between anyone there and Charley."

"What's that?" Caroline pointed to a yellow note.

"Turner's security detail. Guy's name is Tony Gerard. He and I did some snooping at the taxi driver's house. We found a large cache of cash, wrapped neatly and hidden in his closet."

Caroline *hmm*-ed under her breath. "Bribe."

"Or payoff," Brice said.

"Who's 'my guy'?" Mitch asked, referring to the paper with the question mark.

The smell of coffee filled the kitchen. "Not sure, but I feel like he's the missing link in all of this. Could be the cabbie, the DDOT link, or it could be the assassin himself."

Caroline found a set of mugs and lined them up next to the

pot. "So you think this Joel guy is involved with the hit or just Winslow?"

"I'm waiting for Teeg to get me Charley's emails and texts since November." Brice rubbed his eyes again. He was running low on sleep, but the edgy buzz under his skin would never allow him to relax. His sixth sense about cases told him he was close to busting this thing wide open. "Charley references this 'my guy' in a response to Joel, but I need the original email to figure out who he was talking about."

"Oh." Caroline scooted over to her briefcase and took out a handful of papers. "These are from Teeg. Maybe what you need is in here."

A shot of hope ricocheted around inside Brice's chest. The hum under his skin intensified. He snatched the papers from Caroline. "Thank you, but lead with that next time, huh?" He started thumbing through them, scanning dates and names.

"You've obviously got this under control," Caroline said, pouring a cup of coffee and handing it to Mitch. "But we could stick around and help."

Brice dropped into a kitchen chair, never taking his eyes off what he was reading. "Not necessary."

Mitch pulled out the chair with his jean jacket on it and sat down, making himself at home. He grabbed a stack of Joel's texts from the center of the table.

Brice pause in his reading and looked up. "What are you doing?"

Mitch cocked his chin at Caroline. "Have a seat, babe." He handed her a second stack of papers and glanced at Brice. His shoulders lifted and fell in an off-handed, totally Mitch Monroe, shrug. "I'm curious. So sue me."

Caroline took the papers and the third and final chair. "Besides, you're part of the team, now, Brice. We've got your back."

The last team that had claimed to have his back was gone.

Some dead, others disappearing into the stratosphere.

The old paranoia flared low and sharp in his gut. His automatic response was to tell Caroline and Mitch to get lost or they could end up as good as dead over helping him. He had too much red in his ledger as it was; he didn't need to add more.

Especially since there was now a Deep Web target on his back.

Dropping his gaze back to the papers in his hand, Brice continued to scan them as his mind circled ways to get Mitch and Caroline to leave without having to be downright rude. He liked Caroline and knew how stubborn she could be. She wouldn't be easy to get out of the house, but he could do it. Mitch on the other hand...

One thing he learned about Mitch was that the guy was a bulldog. The more you resisted his help, the more he pushed his way into your business.

And then Brice's gaze fell on a series of emails going back and forth between Charley and a person with a weird, coded name from December regarding a trip to Barbados. "Well, I'll be damned."

"What is it?" Caroline asked.

Brice zeroed in on his board. "It seems Charley was in Barbados *with* Joel, and there was another man they met there."

"So?" Mitch said. "All three of them went to Barbados. Big deal."

It was a big deal if the buzz under Brice's skin was to be believed. "Joel claimed that Charley couldn't use the tickets he'd bought for the vacation package and they were nonrefundable. He said that's why Charley offered them to Justice Turner, and when he refused to accept them, Charley offered them to Joel."

His pulse was jumping around again. He went to the board and tapped the timeline, holding the paper up with the other.

"According to this email, that's not true. Joel and Charley met in Barbados that weekend, and they met with another guy."

"They enjoyed some fun in the sun with each other." Mitch leaned back in his chair. "It's not a crime."

"No," Brice said, tapping the board again. "But planning the murder of a Supreme Court justice is."

"Big assumption." Caroline stood, coming over to face the board as she scanned Brice's notes. "You need more than a lying court clerk and a coincidental trip by these three men at the same time to the Caribbean."

Brice held out the paper to her. "It was no coincidence, I'm sure of it from reading these."

Before Caroline could take the copy of the damning emails, the bedroom door squeaked open—*Jesus, I hope she has clothes on*—and Hope stepped into the hallway wearing Brice's T-shirt and sleep tousled hair. Damn, she was cute.

Oblivious to Mitch and Caroline, she stared straight ahead at the wall and rubbed at her eyes. "Hawk?"

"Uh, Hope? We've got company."

After a second, she turned her head, spotted Mitch and Caroline, and her mouth stretched open. Brice had to laugh. Had to.

She tugged on the hem of his shirt, doing a terrible job of covering her shapely thighs as she shifted her weight from one bare foot to the other. "Oh, I uh...."

Mitch's gaze scanned her bare legs and the oversized shirt and then he eyed Brice's naked chest. He gave Brice a cheeky grin.

Hope turned her big eyes to Brice. "Are these your friends?"

If Mitch kept looking at her that way, he was going to be an ex-friend before he'd finished his coffee. Brice forced a smile. "Hope, this is Caroline Foster and Mitch Monroe." He shifted his gaze to the two ex-Feds. "Caroline and Mitch, meet Hope Denby."

16

There were certain things in her life Hope had never asked for. The floor opening up and swallowing her would be one of them.

She glanced down at her bare legs and Hawk's shirt that she'd haphazardly thrown on for a trip to the bathroom. Her first inclination had been to forego the shirt and just walk naked to the bathroom across the hall before returning to bed.

That would have been the true disaster. At least now she wasn't standing naked as a jay in front of complete strangers.

Upshot.

As usual, she'd found a way to ignore the looming disaster and humiliation.

Always an upshot in Hope Denby's world.

"Um." She gestured behind her with both hands. "I'm just gonna..." What? Put pants on after Hawk just proved what a manly man he was? *Several times.* She cleared her throat, thankful for the low-lit hallway because thinking about Hawk, on top of her, under her—everywhere—released a storm of hot flashes women should only get from menopause.

Whew. That man.

Get out of the flipping hallway, Hope.

She whipped backward, faced the open bedroom door and the rumpled sheets and another hot flash flooded her. God, that bed. Talk about it being the stuff of dreams. "Be right out," she called.

Two minutes later, she entered the kitchen, this time in her slacks and blouse from work, her hair brushed and her face washed. The man Hawk introduced as Mitch kept his steady gaze on her and his mouth lifted into a crooked half-smile. An I-know-what-you-did smile if she ever saw one. Well, whoopdee-doo, she and the Hawkster had sex.

Darn good sex, too. *Deal with it, bucko.*

She reached her hand to him. "Hello."

"Hi."

He clasped her hand, gave it a good solid pump and released it. No prolonged squeeze, no brushing of the fingers, no innuendo of any sort. Just that stupid grin that should have made her want to vaporize herself, but instead, left her smiling. Almost laughing in fact, which immediately diffused any tension she'd felt just minutes ago.

Hope repeated the routine with Caroline, who was quite possibly the most beautiful woman she'd ever met. Her perfect cheekbones sloped into an arresting, natural curve that made her a little more girl-next-door rather than striking super-model. She stepped around the table to shake Hope's hand and her long pony tail swayed with the movement, the silky brunette strands glistening against the overhead light. Her brown eyes were the killer though. A deep chocolate that despite their dark intensity somehow twinkled.

"I'm Caroline. I brought you some clothes from your apartment." She smiled. "I didn't snoop."

"Thank you. That's very nice of you. But how did you get in?"

"Uh..."

"She picked the lock," Mitch said. "You really need better locks."

Oh, my. "Alrighty then. I guess I'll work on that. Anyway, thank you, Caroline."

Caroline looked over at Hawk, still shirtless, but with his arms folded across that manly-man chest Hope had thoroughly explored an hour ago. "Anything for Brice. He saved our asses on our last case."

"Blah, blah, Caroline," Hawk said. "Can we get back to it here?"

She grinned at Hope. "He's modest. I think he's been in that cave of his for so long he's forgotten how to let himself take credit for things."

"Hey," Mitch said. "I helped."

"Oh, God," Hawk muttered. "Please, can we not get him started? I'm not up for the Mitch Monroe Show tonight."

Apparently, Mitch took offense to that because he shifted in his seat. "Dude, that's your problem. You need more of the Mitch Show."

"In case you were wondering," Caroline said, "Mitch is modest as well."

At that, Hawk laughed. "Yeah. She keeps threatening to shoot him and throw his body in the Reflecting Pool."

Mitch popped out of his chair, wrapped an arm around Caroline from behind and nibbled her shoulder. The sweet gesture was cute, but the look on Caroline's face, a cross between eye-rolling indulgence and affection, said it all. These two were in love and the easy banter and flat out heat between them could ignite the building.

Immediately, Hope glanced at Hawk who met her gaze, but too quickly pulled away, staring down, studying his feet. Whatever was happening down there must have been pretty darned interesting.

MISTY EVANS & ADRIENNE GIORDANO

Interesting enough to prove whatever Mitch and Caroline had didn't compare to Hope and her silly girl dreams of love.

"You know what," Mitch said, dragging his arm from around Caroline. "We're gonna get out of your way." He smacked her on the rear. "We have things to do."

"Great idea," Hawk said. "Get out."

Caroline laughed and turned those amazing brown eyes of hers on Hope. "It was nice to meet you. Let me know if you need anything else."

"I will. Thank you."

Hawk and Mitch exchanged what Rob liked to call the *shug* —a combination shoulder pat and hug that was a staple in the male arsenal when saying goodbye to friends.

"Later, dude," Hawk said. "Thanks for everything."

"No, sweat. Watch the B&Es though. Grey will stroke out if he has to bail you out of jail."

"When isn't Grey stroking out?" Caroline added.

The second the door closed, Hawk shook his head and ran his hands over his face. "Jeez, I'm sorry about that. I should have warned you they were here. I figured you'd be out awhile."

Hope waved it off. "It's all right. Let's just be glad I didn't go with my first choice of strolling to the bathroom naked."

Taking that in, Hawk grunted. "That wouldn't have been good. Interesting, but not good."

"What B&E was Mitch talking about?"

Hawk got busy pouring her some coffee. "Gerard and I checked up on the cab driver, Kostas. He's hiding at least twenty grand in his house."

"You broke into his house?"

He handed her the cup. "Don't get self-righteous on me, Hope. You know this is what I do, and sometimes the way I do things isn't pretty, but I follow my leads wherever I have to. I don't know that Kostas is dirty, or that the money he's hiding is, but it is interesting, don't you think?"

Accepting the cup, she decided not to argue. "But we know he's not the killer."

"He could have been paid off and that's why he can't give the Feds or police a decent description of the man they're after."

On the refrigerator hung a white board with photos. Earlier, it had been blank. Hawk and his friends had been busy while she snoozed.

She slid into the chair Mitch had vacated and pointed. "What's this?"

Hawk stepped over to her, setting his hands on her shoulders, which, in a purely I-refuse-to-fall-in-love-with-him-way was kinda nice.

His thumb worked a knot in her right shoulder and Hope closed her eyes, let herself enjoy the pampering.

"My conspiracy board," he said. "We've figured out Charley was actually in Barbados with Joel in December. The question mark is a third guy we have to find, the 'my guy' from Joel's texts. I think it may be the same person Charley exchanged emails with about the Barbados trip, but nowhere is an actual name or mention of the trip."

"Expense reports," Hope said, tilting her head to give him better access. "He probably submits detailed expense reports. If we can find any from around the time of the trip, we can look through them."

"Excellent idea."

And then his fingers—oh, that magic thumb—were gone. Pity that.

She opened her eyes in time to see him leaning over the table and grabbing the stack of papers from the other side. His bare skin was just inches from her. So touchably close. *Don't.* But it would be so easy to just reach up, run her hand over his trim waist to the dark swirling hair that ran right up the middle of his chest and fanned out over his pecs. Not too much to be off-putting, but definitely enough to let a girl know he didn't manscape and didn't need to. Call her twisted but she had a thing for men with chest hair.

And watches.

Oh, look, Hawk had his watch on.

Rowrrrr. If this kept up, she'd shove him on the table and have her way with him. For a good long time. *Don't.* She set her hands in her lap and looped her fingers together.

"I saw some stuff in one of these files," he said.

Yes. Let's focus on the files.

He shuffled through the stack until he found one marked with a B. Taking half, he handed her the other half. "Teeg pulled anything that mentioned Barbados. Let's see what we've got."

Five pages in, Hope found an email between Charley and someone named Marly. Subject line: Barbados Flight. "Do we know who Marly is?"

"His assistant. I think. She takes care of scheduling meetings and whatnot. Why?"

She perused the email. "He's requesting a bottle of MacCallan whiskey for the flight."

"Charter."

"Pardon?"

He snatched the email from her. "On private flights you can request special items. He must have chartered a plane."

"Which could mean all three of them flew to Barbados together."

"Keep looking. Anything that mentions a charter company, pull it."

"Well, look at you going all Carl Bernstein on me. I love a man with investigative reporting skills."

He grinned at the reference to the famous journalist duo who reported on the 1970's Watergate scandal that drove President Richard Nixon from office.

And darn, that was hot. Game over. She needed to touch him. Just for a second. Feel that same spark from earlier that sent them straight to making each other moan. She shifted sideways, bumping his leg with her knee and ran her hand along his rock solid abs. The warmth traveled through her palm right up her arm and oh, yes, before the night was over, she wanted to hit replay.

He met her gaze and held it as a slow, knowing smile tugged at his lips. "Hope, we're busy here."

"We certainly are."

He set his hand on top of hers and held it. "Honey, I promise you, as soon as we find the name of this charter company, I will take you back to bed and do wicked things to you. But now we have work to do."

"How wicked?"

He laughed. "Really wicked."

She smacked her hand on the table. "Then let's get to work here. What else were you and your friends talking about?"

"I was bringing them up to speed on the Charley-Joel connection. We've got to figure out who that third guy is or we're nowhere."

"And the DDOT connection." She walked to the board, uncapped the marker and added a line extending from Charley's name and the word DDOT followed by a question mark. "We need to figure out how DDOT ties into this."

"Yeah. We're dead in the water on that one."

Dead over water was more like it if they didn't uncover who closed that bridge lane and why. But so far, there'd been no proof the lane had purposely been blocked.

Not yet anyway.

What they needed here were drastic measures.

Wanting to protect the office she worked for had propelled her to make a deal with Hawk. A deal that would keep the

Chief Justice's name from becoming fodder for the conspiracy nuts.

Hawk, at the time, being one of them.

But he'd kept his word and hadn't run one blog post about the Chief's death. He'd proven himself. Plus, he possessed the sharp mind and tactical prowess of a legitimate journalist. The *blogger* had won her over.

In more ways than one.

But in a matter of days they'd gone from living normal lives —at least her life was normal—to hiding in some rundown safe house from a killer. Add to that Hope on suspension and just short of being fired and they were at Defcon One, journalism style. At Defcon One, the military's most severe state of alert, war was imminent.

Up to this point, Hope had done everything she'd known to do, followed every lead and yes, maybe they'd made some progress, but not enough. Not enough to blow this story open and determine who killed the Chief Justice of the United States.

Not enough to save their own butts.

Don't let them get away with it.

Being a person who thrived on staying positive while working a problem, she was about filled up on feeling helpless. She knew she shouldn't feel that way, but being evicted from her life tended to jade her.

The motor on the refrigerator clunked and wheezed— ancient, that thing—and she glanced around the kitchen, halting at a water stain on the ceiling that three days ago would have skeeved her. Three days ago this entire set-up would have skeeved her. She wouldn't have sat in one of the chairs much less sleep—naked—in that lumpy bed.

Don't let them get away with it.

Defcon One.

Now.

Recapping the marker, Hope set it in the holder, let her fingers linger there a second as her thoughts aligned. *Do it.*

"Hawk, it's time to make a move. Shake things up a bit."

At that, he grinned. "That's my specialty. What do you have in mind?"

She turned from the board, met his gaze and held it. "You need to run a blog post questioning why DDOT closed that lane."

17

The DDOT lane closure wasn't exactly the hard-hitting expose he had in mind for his blog. "While there are plenty of people out there who think the DDOT exists solely to ruin their morning drive to work, closing that lane isn't much of a conspiracy unless we show how it could be the key to figuring out if Chief Justice Turner was murdered for a reason other than road rage."

"That's what I'm saying. You need to question why that lane was closed until he was shot dead and then reopened as if nothing were amiss. And how convenient the killer had a car waiting for him on the other side."

A strong lead for a story, but... "You didn't want me to say anything about the judge until we had proof."

"I'm changing my mind."

His pulse double-timed it. "What we have is circumstantial, and not a credible story unless I can point fingers at those we suspect are tied into this."

She bit her bottom lip, chewed on it for a moment as if it might help her sort through the conflicting emotions playing over her face. "Leave their names out of it, so Joel and his parents don't sue you, but...you have to do this, Hawk. It's time to play hardball."

His fingers itched to start typing, yet, he had to put something—someone—before the story this time. Hope's safety was paramount.

She looked like she might jump out of her skin if he so much as touched her, so he didn't. He did, however, move closer. Not too close, but close enough that she knew he was there and wasn't about to let anyone do her harm. "I know I've already mentioned this, but I'm saying it again. We're dealing with some very dangerous people, here. People who will do anything—including kill—to protect their futures, their companies, their positions."

Her chin rose and she stopped chewing on her bottom lip. "I'm not afraid of them."

"Hope, *I'm* afraid of them."

She snorted, as if she thought he were joking.

He wasn't. "Are you sure you want this? For me to expose this? We could be wrong."

Her gaze dropped to his shoulders and she reached out and touched his chest. "Do you think we're wrong?"

"Hell, no, but once we put this blog out there, there's no taking it back. You sure you're ready for that? For the blowback that might land on you?"

"Yes." She dropped her hands from his chest. "I...dammit."

This back and forth flip-flopping would drive him insane. Except, this was her process. It was growing on him. *She* was growing on him.

He brushed a finger across her cheek. "It's okay. Let's take a minute and think this through."

Her eyes hardened. Her hands went to her hips. "I'm as sure as you are that we're not wrong."

She was *so* not sure. He could see it in the nervous fidget of her toes, the faint twitch under her eye. "You know, as an ATF undercover agent, I was trained to spot liars."

Her eyes went wide. "I'm not lying. I'm—" she flapped her arms. "I don't know what I am."

Gullible. Another thing he found charming about her. "You'll lose your job, I guarantee it. No matter how I write the blog post, your boss will know you were involved in this investigation."

"I'll find a new job."

"What about the White House?"

"Screw the White House."

This was definitely a new Hope Denby. One he had a sudden surge of fresh admiration for.

He couldn't help the grin that spread across his face. "Things are going to get messy. Are you sure?"

"Honestly, I don't know if I'm sure, but bring it on. Everything we've done so far isn't working. Not as much as I'd hoped. And we still have a dead Chief Justice. One we think was murdered and that's just wrong. So, if it means finding out who killed this man, I can handle messy just fine."

He almost believed her. His admiration, that subtle warmth low in his stomach, turned to pride. "You are some woman, Ms. Denby."

Her chin inched up again. "Don't you forget it."

"Want to help me write it, Bernstein?"

"I'm Woodward. You're Bernstein."

Brice held up his hands in surrender. "Whatever makes you happy."

She tapped the end of his nose with one slim finger. "Another thing you should never forget. Keep me happy and you can have your way with me anytime, anyplace."

He smacked her bottom playfully and went for his laptop. "That's a deal I can't refuse."

Two hours later, Brice read the blog post, read it again. It was the third one he'd written and it still wasn't right.

He hit delete.

"Hey!" Hope punched his arm. "I liked that one."

He rubbed a hand through his hair for the hundredth time. "We can't use names but using all these random sources makes the piece come off sounding like...like..."

"Amateur hour?" she supplied.

"Yeah." He slammed his hands on the table. "And using 'texts' and 'emails' without actually printing what they say is bogus. It sounds like we're making it all up. We need a legitimate sounding source."

"Like Deep Throat."

He tore his eyes from the screen. "What did you say?"

"Deep Throat. You know, Watergate? The source Woodward used?"

A wave of excitement rolled over him. "Sources," Brice corrected. "Woodward claimed later that Deep Throat was the FBI Director, but some other investigative reporters figured out it had to be multiple sources Woodward combined into one to make it easier and more...marketable, let's say, to the general public."

"Yeah, cuz being nicknamed a porn movie title like Deep Throat is much easier to remember and a whole lot racier than saying 'my source'."

"Exactly. People ate it up."

"You never told me who your original source was," Hope said. "Does he have a sexy undercover name? Or is it a she?"

"Lodestone is male."

"Lodestone? Really? Not exactly a sexy code name."

"He's been my confidential informant on a few cases. I don't know his real name or how he gets these leads and tips, but I suspect he's inside the government at a high level with access to a lot of shit. His use of code names suggests NSA, and he'd kill me if I used his in my blogs. He seems to be one of the few people around this town with a conscience."

"And he works for the NSA. Go figure. Is there any way you could talk to him about what we've found out? See if he knows anything else?"

"He contacts me. I don't have a number for him. I've tried tracing the numbers he calls from but they're dead in the water as soon as he uses one. Most likely he has a pile of burn phones."

"Sounds like your kind of guy."

"I've wondered about that—if he was burned by the NSA or CIA like I was at ATF, or if he's just a good guy trying to make sure the scum in Washington don't take over."

"You never told me about what happened, back when you were in the ATF. What made you quit them and become what you are now?"

It was a long story and not one he relished rehashing. He hadn't talked about it to anyone. Not all the sordid details, anyway.

"It's okay if you don't want to tell me," Hope said. "I know it must be very personal."

This woman. She accepted him for who, and what, he was. No pressing, no pushing to lay his past out on the table. Getting to the bottom of this case had pulled her into the hazardous and ugly depths of his world. She was certainly going to lose her job—a job that meant everything to her—because of him.

Seemed like the least he owed her was an explanation for his often odd and irritating behavior.

His skin itched. His eyes burned. He rubbed them and took a steadying breath. "I met Wes Colton in the Army. We were both intelligence officers. After we got out, we both joined ATF. He was my partner, like a brother to me, for seven years. We were inseparable."

The blank computer screen of his laptop stared back at

him, the cursor blinking, waiting for him to type. "His brother was a rapper and actor who went by the moniker, Nasty Playa, living the life in Hollywood. Behind the scenes, he was running cocaine and heroin from L.A. to Chicago. The drugs were originating south of the border. A DEA agent contacted me on the down low, asked me about Wes and his brother. Were they close? Did Wes have any idea about his brother's involvement in the drug ring?"

He shook his head. Even after everything that had happened, he still couldn't believe Wes's deception. "I blew up in the guy's face, told him there was no way, he had the wrong guy. If Wes suspected his brother was a criminal, he'd be all over it. Later, I found out I was wrong."

Hope's voice was soft. "What happened?"

"Wes not only knew his famous brother was running a drug ring, Wes was setting up contacts for him. I only found out after Wes received a promotion to unit chief of our team. The whole time, even in the army, he was working with his brother. Once he was in good at ATF, Wes expanded the business to include guns. Wes had the gun cartel contacts and his brother had the drug contacts."

She was quiet for a second, then said, "He betrayed you. That had to be horrible."

Brice's fingers twitched. "He didn't just betray me, he used me and the rest of our team to cover his ass." Slowly, he turned his head to look at her. "I tried to talk to him, tried to get him to turn himself in. He refused... And then, he came after me."

Her brows scrunched. "Was this part of the gunwalking scandal?"

Those days were far behind him now, but the sting of Wes's betrayal burned like acid on the back of his neck. "The beginnings of it, and because Wes's brother was famous and had plenty of high-priced lawyers, his role in the initial operation was never revealed. He walked, as did Wes—after he destroyed our unit."

Brice looked down at his hands. At one point, when everything had gone to hell, and Wes had threatened Brice's life, Brice had considered taking him out. In the end, however, he'd held the gun to Wes's head, but couldn't pull the trigger. "Some of the men in my unit died mysterious deaths while undercover. Others, like me, had their careers destroyed for trying to blow the whistle on Wes, and in turn, on the ATF."

"What happened to him?"

"The only concrete evidence I had I gave to that DEA agent. My mistake that I didn't make backups. He and the evidence disappeared shortly afterwards. His body was found in an alley in Mexico. An undercover op gone wrong, they claimed. So in the end, I had nothing, the DEA had no hard evidence either. Wes hid behind his brother and his fleet of lawyers. Last I heard, Wes is living in Palm Springs. He changed his name, grew a beard, and works for his brother, who won a Grammy last year, I believe."

"Bastard." Hope rose and went to the kitchen. He heard her moving around, slamming cupboards and clanking cups. She returned a moment later, setting a steaming cup of coffee in front of him. "Sorry I don't have something stronger, but the safe house isn't stocked with hard liquor. You should talk to your friend, tell him to pony up the good stuff."

Brice almost smiled. Thank God, she didn't reach for him or give him *the look*. The one filled with emotions like pity and sympathy. He couldn't stand anyone feeling sorry for him.

His hand shook as he wrapped it around the warm mug, so he didn't lift it just yet. He preferred Hope didn't see that he was still a basket case over what the fucking ATF, and a man he'd considered his friend, had done to him.

Not just to me.

The DEA agent, Henry Eno. ATF agents, Jeff Bekker and Cal Koch.

And eventually Tommy Nusco, who had no idea that Wes and the deputy attorney general were the two biggest players behind the gunwalking scandal.

"So this Lodestone guy called you and told you to look into Justice Turner's death?"

Back to business. "He suspected foul play and it looks like he was right on the money."

Her lips kissed the edge of her own mug as she blew gently on the liquid to cool it. "Even if we can't call him, there is a way we can contact him."

"How?"

She pointed at the blank screen. "Write the blog and ask him to contact you."

Brice smiled for real this time and saluted her with his coffee mug. The shakes were gone and a new confidence steadied his hands. "You're pretty smart, Woodward."

"What can I say, Bernstein?" She turned one hand palm up and gave him a smile back. "I didn't land a prestigious position with the Public Information Office of the Supreme Court on my good looks and sunny disposition alone."

He sipped his coffee. *God, I love her.*

The thought caught him right in the gut. He nearly spewed coffee across his keyboard.

Coughing, he set the mug down and beat on his chest.

"You okay?" Hope asked.

"Couldn't be better." He placed his hands on the keyboard and started typing. "And just for the record, your sunny disposition is growing on me."

His hands flew over the keyboard, this version of the blog post taking him only minutes to write. Hope came over, leaning against his back as she draped her arms around his neck and down his chest, reading the column as he typed.

Which was distracting as hell. She smelled like sex and coffee and that hint of flowery perfume she always wore. Her fingers teased his rib cage, strands of her hair tickled his cheek.

He wouldn't have had it any other way. Shifting his head, he kissed the inside of her elbow, and finishing the blog with a subtle invitation for Lodestone to call him, he hit Save.

"Last chance to back out," he told Hope, the cursor hovering over the Publish button.

"I told you." She nibbled at his earlobe. "I'm all in."

A sexy woman who knew his story, telling him she was all in when it came to exposing a cover-up. What was a whistle-blower like him supposed to do?

He hit Publish.

"Now what?" Her breath was warm on his ear. "I guess all we can do is wait?"

Normally, that was exactly what he did.

Tonight wasn't normal.

He grabbed her, lifting her off the floor and settling her in his lap, facing him. As if reading his mind, she parted her lips and kissed him, raking her hands through his hair and grinding her pelvis into his lap.

Ah, yes, that sunny disposition was definitely growing on him.

They were heavy into the makeout session, the blouse she'd been wearing now lay on the living room floor, and one of her luscious breasts was in his mouth, when a phone rang from somewhere deep inside the house.

His burn phone. Damn it. Where had he left it?

Bedroom.

Releasing Hope's breast and hating himself for it, he tried to disengage her from his lap. She didn't comply.

Brrrring.

"Hope, I have to get that. It could be Lodestone."

He stood and she wrapped her legs around his waist, kissing his neck.

And...oh, yeah. That felt good.

Too good.

So he carried her...past the couch, down the hall, into the bedroom.

Brrrring.

Hurry.

There. On the nightstand.

Brice sat on the bed, Hope still in his lap, fumbling for the phone. She nipped at the top of his shoulder and he accidently sent the phone rocketing off the nightstand. "Shit."

He should join Cirque de Soleil with all the maneuvering he had to do to keep hold of Hope as he went for the phone on the floor.

Dropping back to a sitting position on the bed, he huffed out, "Patriot Blog. This is Hawkeye. Go."

"What the hell are you doing?"

Lodestone. Good thing he'd answered.

Brice put him on speakerphone. "I'm at a dead end with this. I need more."

"You've ran with less and still nailed the bad guys."

At the sound of the man's voice, Hope stopped undulating on top of him and met Brice's eyes. "Lodestone?" she mouthed.

He nodded and put a finger to his lips to signal her to stay quiet. "If you read my latest article, you know that since the murder was ruled road rage, and I have nothing on the real killer, the circumstantial evidence means shit in this case."

There was a long pause. So long, Brice wondered if he'd hung up.

"Aunt Minnie."

The line went dead.

Hope blew air out her lips, lifting the hair hanging over her forehead. "What does that mean? Who's Aunt Minnie?"

Brice tossed the phone aside, his mind whirling. "It's spy talk. An Aunt Minnie is a photograph, taken by an amateur in most cases, of a place of interest. The photographer includes a relative or a friend to make it look like an innocent picture, but to a spy or government scoping out a target, it's invaluable ground-level intelligence."

"I saw that once on a cop show." She ran her hands through her hair, creating a ponytail but had nothing to hold it with and let it fall again. "Some sleeper cell terrorist gal was taking pictures of a D.C. monument her fellow terrorists were going to blow up. She posted the pics on Facebook so the head of the terrorist group back in the Middle East could see the security setup."

Brice was still trying to make sense of how a picture could help them when Hope jumped off his lap. "Barbados. That's it! Joel's girlfriend. Maybe she took pictures."

"We don't know her name."

Hope snatched his shirt off the bedroom floor and yanked it on over her head. "Trust me, no girl goes to Barbados with a hottie Supreme Court clerk and doesn't have an entire photo album somewhere on the internet. Snapchat. Instagram. I bet she has accounts with both, and by golly, Miss Molly, I will find them with a more detailed Google search of our friend Joel. Charley and this anonymous "my guy" might be in one of those pictures."

"You think Joel's a hottie?"

"Really?" She had her slacks in her hand and swatted his leg with them. "Don't be ridiculous. I know he's an asshat, but that girl sees Mr. Trust Fund and future Washington power player. That makes a lot of girls look past the truth."

"But not you," he said, trying not to sound jealous.

She crawled into his lap again and kissed him. Just bam, a solid, quick kiss on his lips. "Maybe once upon a time I might have been suckered into believing a guy with a future in politics was my cup of tea, but not anymore. I like my men a little more..." She nipped his bottom lip and looked at him with her big blue eyes and he melted right there. "Dangerous."

Then she kissed him deeply, her tongue doing all sorts of amazing things in his mouth. She shoved him backward on the bed, one hand undoing his zipper. Apparently, Hope Denby had a healthy sexual appetite.

He grabbed her butt cheeks and squeezed, kissing her back. She was solid in his hands, her presence a balm to his heart.

Her hand went inside his underwear and he broke the kiss. "You keep doing that and we aren't leaving this room for a while. We have a lot of research to do. You on Instagram and me locating the charter company Charley used to fly him and Joel to Barbados."

"True," she said, licking her lips. "Could be a very long night. But first..."

Her hand hit pay dirt and she gave him a little squeeze. "Oh, my. Seems to me we can make this fast."

All thoughts of Joel, Kenton Labs, Charley, charter companies, and pictures went right out of his head.

18

"Instagram is a bust," Hope said.

Still wearing Hawk's shirt, she set her laptop on the couch next to her and slouched back, propping her feet on the crappy coffee table.

From his spot across from her, Hawk glanced up from his own laptop. "Nothing? At all?"

"Well, there are photos from Barbados, but it's just him. No bimbo in sight."

"What bimbo?"

"The woman Joel took to Barbados."

Hawk waggled his head as if trying to clear it. "Oh. It sounded like you knew her. The way you called her a bimbo."

"No. I...hmmm...I guess that was rude of me. She could be a highly intelligent woman. I'd just think if she were, she would have questioned why a Supreme Court law clerk was flying to Barbados with a lobbyist. I mean, she has to know that's not copacetic. And if she knew that and didn't show some outrage, in my mind, that makes her a bimbo."

"Jesus. You got all that from a photo?"

She shrugged. "Sure. Well, not really the photo itself, but the Barbados thing as a whole."

"All right. I'll roll with this. We've checked Facebook and Instagram. What about Twitter?"

"I'm heading there now." She picked up her laptop again. "How'd you do on the charter company? I'm still going through his emails. So far, no mention of the company."

"Did you check the expense reports?"

"Yeah. But I can't find one for the Barbados trip. Not yet anyway. I still have an entire folder to go through though."

Hope yawned and let out a little sigh. At some point, she'd need a nap. Being a girl who couldn't function on less than six hours of sleep, she'd given up late nights after graduating from college. And now, it was nearing midnight and she was most definitely about to turn into a pumpkin.

"You're getting tired."

"I am," she said. "I want to check Twitter first though."

At the Twitter home screen, she did a search on Joel's name and the list of his most recent tweets filled her screen. Mainly retweets of funny quotes and pictures. Nothing even remotely scandalous. At least he'd remained politically correct on social media. Still, she scrolled through the list, backtracking to December where she slowed her skimming. A trip to the zoo, dinner at the Capitol Grill, a visit to the Crime & Punishment Museum—how appropriate.

Nothing on Barbados. Except, of course, the giant hole in the timeline of tweets that just so happened to match the dates of the Barbados trip.

"Anything?" Hawk asked.

"No. Just generic stuff and there are no tweets the week he was in Barbados. At least he was discreet."

She scrolled down further.

"Whoa."

Hawk looked up from his computer. "What?"

"Joel and the bimbo."

She zeroed in on the photo of what might be the world's best looking couple. People magazine should seriously be calling these people and putting them on the cover. That's how beautiful they were. In contrast to Joel's dark features, the woman was a platinum blond. Her straight hair fell below her shoulders and the teeny-tiny black dress she wore showed off long legs and the tall, thin frame Hope had always dreamed of having. The tweet accompanying the photo said "Happy anniversary to the sexiest girl I know."

How sweet.

Hawk hopped up from his seat and joined Hope on the couch. "Whatcha got?"

"Just a photo. But he tagged her on it. Let's see if she's a little more generous with her information."

Hope clicked on the girlfriend's Twitter link and up popped her photo. Yet another perfect photo displaying the female half of the world's most beautiful couple.

She scanned the brief bio on Daisy Tilmann who loved to travel, eat greasy French Fries and do hot yoga. Yadda, yadda. But wait. The last line of the bio stopped her. No way.

Hope snorted. Sometimes life was just amazing. "Oh. Oh. Oh. Ohhhhh."

"What?"

She swung her head to Hawk, smiling the whole time because, yes, she was tired and maybe taking way too much pleasure in her little find.

"Guess what?"

Hawk drew his eyebrows together and stared at her with a quasi-laughing-slash-confused face. "What?"

"She has a blog. Daisy's Delights."

"Get the fuck outta here."

Hope went back to her laptop screen, tapped the last line of

Daisy's bio. "Right here, big guy. I mean, this is rich. Not only does she have a blog, it sounds like a porn site."

She clicked on the link and watched the little icon spin for a few seconds until a home page popped up. Pink with swirling white letters shouting the name of the blog and in smaller type a brief description.

"What is it? Like a diary or something?"

"No. Apparently Daisy feels that the world needs to be in the know on her favorite things. Maybe she thinks she can top Oprah's list."

She scrolled through the posts, spotted various photos of Daisy's favorite foods and places in the city. Two weekends ago, she'd been in New York and did several posts from different locations. And, yep, there was Joel, right along with her, smiling for a selfie.

Could these two be any more full of themselves?

But what were the chances Daisy had gone to Barbados with her man? "Let's see if the happy couple vacationed in Barbados together."

"Scroll down."

She quickly bounced down the page until she reached the older posts from December. Three posts in, she stumbled on one entitled *Paradise Found.* She clicked. A new screen displayed a photo of a sunset view of a beach complete with Adirondack chairs. How romantic. Just below the photo Daisy proclaimed the spot her new all-time favorite.

Barbados.

Hope perused the post and came across a link to a photo album.

She looked over at Hawk. "Remember when I said I hated bloggers?"

Hawk rolled his eyes. "Yeah."

"I've come a long way in a few days. First there's you, who, you may have noticed, I'm incredibly fond of."

"Gee, thanks. Blinded by the orgasms."

"Then there's Daisy. The wannabe Oprah who might just make my night perfection by posting photos of her fellow vacationers. I'm almost afraid to look."

Hawk reached over, dragged his finger across the mouse pad and clicked the link. "I'm not," he said.

A second later, a slew of thumbnail sized photos filled the screen. "God bless her. Looks like she uploaded everything. Now I *really* love bloggers."

"Okay, Hope. Ease up."

"This is an absolute gold mine. And she didn't think twice about what she might be causing by posting them. And, hello? Does her boyfriend even know? If so, he deserves to go to jail just for being stupid." She let out a heavy breath. "People. They frustrate me."

Attempting to lock down her nerves, she hummed to herself while clicking through the photos.

"Oh, and look at this."

"What?"

She puckered her lips and angled her laptop so Hawk could take in the full screen. "The happy couple flew private. Laughlin Charters."

Hawk snatched the laptop and took in the photo of Daisy and Joel standing in front of a sleek private plane with the name of the charter company emblazoned on it.

"Son of a bitch," he said. "She is stupid. That's fantastic."

"I'll download the photo. While I'm going through the rest of these shots, you find that charter company."

He reached over, grabbed his laptop from where he left it on the coffee table, then sat in the chair next to Hope. Kinda snuggly that.

She continued scanning the photos. Mostly location shots and selfies with Joel. At least until photo twenty-two.

"Whoa. Look at this."

Hawk glanced over, studied the screen a second. "Yep. I see it."

In the photo, Joel stood on a patio in front of a table holding up a rocks glass while he smiled at his apparent beloved. Behind him, thick green foliage blew in the wind and a man sat at the table in what looked like a Tommy Bahama button-down shirt. Very tropical. He must have just started to turn away from the camera because he appeared to be staring off in the distance.

But, yes indeed, the lovely Daisy had gotten his full face. If only by accident.

"It could be some random person. Not necessarily with them."

"Could be. I'm downloading that shot though."

After downloading, she moved through the next series of photos and the very last one nearly made Hope giddy.

I totally love bloggers.

In the last photo, darling Daisy snapped a photo of a colorful bird perched on the back of an empty chair at one of the tables. At that same table she'd caught half of Joel and right next to him a portion of someone else's sleeve. A sleeve with the same print as the man in the Tommy Bahama shirt.

She looked over at Hawk. "Still think it's some random person?"

"Nope," he said. "I think we just found the third guy."

19

*L*aughlin Charters had a closed computer network.

"I can't hack in from here," Teeg told Brice. "You might be able to piggyback their mainframe, however, if you can get close enough to their Wi-Fi and bypass their encryption. The actual database has a backdoor once you're inside the network."

Not what he wanted to hear. "How close do I need to be?"

"From what I can tell, the Wi-Fi setup is pretty weak. It's only meant for their office use and their clients who are waiting to board planes or take off."

Leaving the safe house was a bad idea. Leaving Hope at the safe house alone was also a bad idea. But everyone on the Justice Team except Teeg was out working cases, and Brice was getting stir crazy.

Not that Hope hadn't kept him busy. They'd slept, ate, had sex three times, and slept some more. It was now late evening. A whole day playing house with Hope was pretty damn fun.

But if he didn't do something—*anything*—other than sort through papers and twiddle his thumbs, he was going to lose it.

"There's no way Grey will okay you leaving the safe house," Teeg said.

A quick drive to the airstrip, a minute or two tops to hack into Laughlin Charters' mainframe and copy the manifests, and a quick drive back to Chinatown, all under cover of darkness— it was doable.

If he had accurate intel. "Let me worry about Grey. Ballpark it. How close?"

"Ten yards? Ten feet? I can't tell from here. The closer the better."

Brice thanked Captain Obvious and hung up.

"Well?" Hope asked.

She'd showered and changed into fresh clothes, put on makeup and secured her hair in a ponytail. She looked like she could be heading to the office.

He secretly liked her the other way better. He wanted to kiss off the sticky gloss on her lips, mess up her hair, and take her back to bed.

What was wrong with him? He was acting like a sex-starved maniac.

Oh, right, he was. At least until last night.

"Road trip," he told her. "We're going to the charter company."

Her eyes lit up. "Oh goodie. What are we doing there?"

"Hacking their mainframe to see who's listed on the plane manifest for December 14th."

"Is it safe?"

"To illegally hack into a business and steal files or to leave the safe house?"

"Either. Both."

"No and no. You live for danger now, remember?"

She balled a fist and swiped it through the air in a gung-ho motion. "Right. Absolutely. Let's go."

Brice grabbed his laptop. He had illegal software on it that would help him bypass the charter company's encryption and piggyback their software. He'd never used it before, but there was a first time for everything. After making sure the coast was clear, he hustled Hope downstairs to his truck.

The drive wasn't quite as quick as he'd anticipated, traffic thick due to an accident on the interstate. Once clear of that, however, they flew down the road, Hope finding a pop station to listen to and singing along with every song that played. She was in awfully good spirits for someone on the verge of losing her job and possibly being on an assassin's hit list.

Brice put down his window, letting the cool night air blow over him as he drove. He felt the same way—like he could break out in song.

Again, he had the errant thought, *what is wrong with me?*

He didn't sing along with the radio and he certainly didn't sing pop songs, but there was something so normal about driving down the interstate on a spring evening with a pretty girl in the cab next to him that made him want to forget his troubles and pretend he was a normal guy.

Pretending wasn't his game, however. As the sign for the airport came into view, he reminded himself that he was a realist. A pessimist. He and Hope were not out for a casual drive. Someone had painted a target on his back and she could very well be caught in the crossfire.

He took the exit ramp and rolled up his window.

The office of Laughlin Charters sat at the end of the airstrip, a small parking lot to the east. Everything was thoroughly lit by streetlamps. Cameras were everywhere.

"Shit." He slowed, driving around the outer perimeter fence. He'd known from their website that Laughlin catered to the power players in Washington. Power players who took their security, and oftentimes anonymity, quite seriously. "Pull up my laptop, would you?"

She did, and he slowed even more as he got closer to the

back end of the grounds where the office sat. One story brick façade. The front of the building was floor to ceiling glass windows so those waiting could see their planes. In the back, there was a single window and a door.

And a broken camera.

The small black box was cocked at an odd angle, possibly due to the recent storm. It was probably still recording, just not the area around the door.

For half a second, he toyed with the idea of breaking in, but with this much security, the company no doubt had more cameras inside.

He parked the truck and took the laptop from Hope.

She scooted across the bench seat to sit next to him. "What are you doing?"

He scrolled through his apps. "This will pick up the Wi-Fi connection and decrypt the security so I can log in to their network."

"Don't you need a password?"

"I have a different app for that."

She snuggled against him. "There really is an app for everything, isn't there?"

There was when you knew the right people. He opened the software, scrolled through the available networks, and hit the one he wanted. "Come to papa, baby."

"Are you talking to me or the laptop?" Hope watched the screen, laying her head on his shoulder. "I have issues with being called 'baby.'"

The software sped along, latching onto the network and spinning through a decryption algorithm. "That's because you're young and I've thrown it in your face time after time."

"I know. It's one of your defense mechanisms."

He had defense mechanisms she didn't have a clue about. "Well, just so you know, I was talking to the laptop, not you, so don't throw a hissy."

"A hissy? You haven't seen me throw a hissy. Trust me."

She pinched his leg and he jerked it away, chuckling as he nearly bobbled the laptop. "Hope...trying to work here."

She shifted her face to plant light kisses along his neckline. Her right hand latched onto his thigh and stroked down and in. "I'm just trying to help," she said in that innocent voice that wasn't innocent at all. It was the sexy voice he'd learned meant only one thing.

Hope Denby wanted to be fucked.

Again.

She was nympho. A total freakin' nymphomaniac.

How had he gotten so lucky?

His screen flashed with a window confirming the software had decrypted the security code. He was now able to see the Laughlin network. "We're in."

"Good, because the sooner you get that manifest, the sooner we can get back to the safe house and you can get in *me*."

If she didn't stop in the next two seconds, he was going to toss the laptop in the back and take her right there.

He clicked a couple of keys, finding the folder for manifests, then searching for December's. A couple more clicks and the database was downloading all the manifests for the month.

"Hey!" A voice came from somewhere behind them. "You there!"

"Ah, shit," he said, catching a figure dressed in a uniform bearing down on them. "Security guard."

Brice hurriedly shut the laptop and jammed it under the seat as Hope reared back to look. They could make a break for it, or...

Brice grabbed Hope and kissed her.

She broke the kiss. "What are you doing?"

"Play along," he murmured against her lips. "The computer needs another minute or so to finish downloading."

She did and by the time the guard knocked his flashlight

against the window, she had her tongue down Brice's throat and her hands clawing at his back.

"This is private property." Mall Cop tapped again. "What are you doing back here?"

Brice shifted to look at the man, plastering a goofy grin on his face as he rolled down his window. "Um, seems kind of obvious, doesn't it?"

The guard narrowed his eyes, doing a full body scan of Hope with the flashlight. Her hair was now falling out of its ponytail, her lipstick smeared. She gave the guard a smile that matched Brice's goofy one. "Sorry, sir. We couldn't help ourselves and this looked like a safe place to park."

She winked at him and the guard switched his gaze back to Brice. "She legal?"

Ho-boy. Look out.

"I am twenty-four freakin' years old," she said, her voice too loud in Brice's ear.

Mall Cop didn't look convinced. He pinned Brice with his light. "How about you step out of that truck and show me some ID, boy."

Boy? Granted, Brice gauged the guard to be twenty-years his senior, but he was no boy. Maybe Hope's youthful look was wearing off on him. "We didn't mean any harm. I assure you, my friend here is of legal age, and we'll be going now."

Swiping back his jacket, the guard made sure Brice saw his sidearm. "I said, get out of the vehicle."

Like the crack about Hope's age sent her into rage mode, threatening Brice, a former ATF agent, with a gun the guy probably couldn't hit the broadside of a barn with, was the wrong move.

The goofy grin slid off Brice's face. He leaned out the window, knocked the flashlight away from his face, and pinned Mall Cop with a deadly look. "I don't think you want to do that, old man. Now take a step back and my friend and I will be on our way."

Something in the tone of Brice's voice, or maybe in his eyes, made the guard do exactly that. The guard stepped back.

And then he raised a two-way radio to his mouth. "Code 44. We have an intruder on the premises."

Stupid laptop better be done downloading.

"Hang on," Brice said to Hope.

Putting the truck in gear, he started to step on the gas when *crack!* Brice's forearm, the one still on the window ledge, exploded in pain.

Brice jerked back, his fingers tingling, his arm throbbing. "What the hell?"

Mall cop had hammered him with a baton.

"You fucking prick," Brice said, ready to throw the truck back into park and teach the man a lesson.

And then he saw the baton coming through the air again.

Anger, hot and fierce, roared through him. He shoved the guy back and hit the automatic button to raise his window.

Mall Cop didn't know how to take no for an answer. The man was a bulldog. A second before the baton swung at them again, Brice yelled, "Get down!" at Hope, his hand already on the back of her head, shoving her toward the floor of the truck, even as he stepped on the gas for real this time.

Too late, the fucker managed to slam the baton into his back window.

In the split second Hope's head went down, the rear window shattered in a hail of glass. White-hot pain sliced through the back of Brice's neck.

He rounded the corner, pushing the truck faster. As soon they hit the main road and were well enough away, he looked over. Even with the extended cab behind him, plenty of glass had found its way to the front seat.

The bastard damaged my truck.

Hope covered her head with her hands. "Go, go, go!" she yelled to Brice without looking up.

The back of his neck was already slick with blood and he could barely move his left arm. A dark rose bloomed on his skin. *Shit. That'll be black in an hour.*

Hope was curled into the passenger foot well, arms over her head. Light from the streetlamps they whizzed under reflected off bits of glass stuck in her hair.

"Talk to me," he said over the motor noise. "Are you okay?"

She looked up at the broken back window from between her arms. "Is it over?"

He nodded. "We're clear."

Slowly she unfolded herself, brushed glass off the seat, and sat, never taking her eyes off the road behind them. "Are you sure?"

"I'm sure." He needed to put pressure on his neck, stop the bleeding, but there was no way he could turn loose of the wheel with his right hand. He had no feeling in his left. "Can you find the first aid kit behind your seat?"

"First aid...?" Her gaze finally swung to his and she sucked in a breath as she caught sight of his neck. "You're bleeding!"

"Just a scratch. A little gauze and a bandage and I'll be good to go."

Without warning, she flopped over, putting her head between her knees. "Ohgod, ohgod, ohgod."

Apparently she didn't do blood.

But, in true Hope Denby style, she rallied a moment later, hyperventilating now under control. "Shouldn't we get you to the hospital? You might need stitches."

"Nah, like I said, it's just a scratch." Or a gash with glass still embedded in it. "It's not the first time I've been hurt. I'll be fine."

"What about your arm?" Her eyes jackknifed between his swelling forearm and his bleeding neck. "Is it broken?"

"It hurts like hell, but it's just bruised," he reassured her.

Averting her eyes, she found the kit behind her seat, opened it and started cracking open packages of gauze and antiseptic wipes like a woman on fire. "I can't believe he did that!"

Brice drove toward Chinatown using an awkward combination of his good hand and his knees as he tried to bandage his injury. Finally, Hope sucked up the last of her queasiness and took over cleaning up his neck.

"I'm *so* going to sue his ass," she said, making little gagging noises as she wiped away Brice's blood. "I got his name and badge number."

"Hope, we were trespassing and performing an illegal hack into the company's mainframe. Probably not in our best interest to sue the guard who was doing his job."

"Oh, right. Still, excessive use of force! Come on. We were making out behind the building. Big deal! He didn't know we were actually hacking into the computer. Overreact much, Mr. Idiot Cop?"

Brice found himself smiling into the night. Thank God for Hope's tirade and the laptop, still safe under his seat. Whatever was on those manifests, he hoped it was worth it.

20

─────

*H*is arm stung like a son of a bitch. Blood and perspiration soaked his back. Goddamn security guard.

He parked in the same spot behind the safe house apartment and killed the lights. From the outside, everything looked the same as they had left it. "Stay here," he told Hope.

"Why?" she asked.

"I want to make sure the safe house is still safe."

Brice hopped out, took the laptop out from under his seat, and snuggled it under his good arm. He closed the truck door and headed for the steps.

The third from the top, he stopped. Cool air drifted over him. The hair on the back of his neck rose.

Someone was there.

A quick glance over his shoulder told him Hope was still in the truck. For once, she'd listened.

But he was unarmed and injured. Not a great combination to meet whoever was inside.

He should turn around, get back in the truck, and drive the hell out of there. Instead he took the last three steps on ninja feet, snugged his body up next to the door, put his ear against it and listened.

Not a sound came from inside. They'd lowered the blinds so he couldn't peek in at the window. Yet he knew from the hair on his neck and the tingle down his spine that there was a definite presence inside.

Setting down the laptop, he heard Hope rolling down the passenger side window of the truck.

"Is everything okay?" she staged whispered.

God help him.

With two fingers, he signaled to her to be quiet. He could almost hear her huff of indignation.

He'd just picked up one of the ceramic plant pots, devoid of anything but hard-packed soil, from the railing to use as a weapon, when the door swung open and the last man on earth Brice wanted to see stood in the doorway.

"Are you coming in any time tonight or do I need to call Sydney and tell her not to hold dinner for me?"

Grey.

Brice lowered the pot. "What the hell are you doing here?"

Grey's gaze dropped to Brice's bloody neck and slid down to his already black and blue forearm. "Checking up on you, and for good reason, it appears." He glanced over Brice's shoulder. "Where is Miss Denby?"

"Right here," she said from the bottom of the stairs.

So much for staying put.

She took the stairs two at a time, eyes taking in Grey. "Who are you?"

Grey stepped back. "Let's take this inside, shall we?"

Brice nodded at Hope and motioned her to follow. He grabbed the laptop.

In the living room, Grey held out a hand to Hope. "Nice to meet you, Miss Denby."

She glanced at Brice. "Friend or foe? Friend, I assume."

"This is Justice Greystone," he told her, not identifying him as either since he wasn't always sure himself. He wasn't as much of a pain in the ass as Mitch, but he still had his moments.

Brice handed her the laptop. "See if we got what we went for."

"Sure." She seemed to understand that Brice wanted to talk to Grey alone. "I'll be in the kitchen."

Like she wouldn't still hear them, but whatever.

Grey crossed his arms over his chest. "You left the safe house."

"Teeg told you."

"He also told me why. Risky."

The gash on the back of his neck was still dripping blood. It ran down his arm and now dripped on the floor at Brice's feet. "Rewards don't come without risk."

Grey's gaze once again slipped to Brice's bruised arm. Being of the male species, he didn't make a big deal over it. "So did you find out the identity of 'my guy'? Why is that so important?"

So not only had Teeg told him about Brice heading to the charter company, Mitch and Caroline must have filled him in on the conspiracy board. "Gut feeling."

From the frown on his face, Grey didn't put much stock in gut feelings. "Cops going to be looking for you?"

The guard had no doubt gotten Brice's license plate number. "Probably."

"I'll take care of it."

"Not necessary."

"Consider it one of the benees of working for me."

Staying out of jail was a nice perk. "Who said I'm working for you?"

"The moment you involved Teeg in this case, your ass become my property. Like it or not, you're working for me."

The adrenaline was wearing off. His vision swam slightly from blood loss and the throbbing pain that had migrated all up and down his arm. All he wanted to do was sit down and have a stiff drink. "You might consider stocking hard liquor in this place."

"Amen to that!" Hope called from the kitchen.

A slim smile touched Grey's lips. He gave a chin cock at Brice's arm and the blood dripping on the floor. "You need someone to look at that?"

"I'm good."

"All right then." Another chin cock at the kitchen. "Read your latest blog post. You've kicked the hornet's nest. Don't be surprised at what comes for you."

"Been there a few times. I'm prepared."

Another glance at Brice's injuries told him Grey wasn't so sure. "I'd recommend staying inside the safe house."

Hope emerged at that moment. "Um, Hawk?"

"Yeah?"

The look on her face said it all. "The manifest? The only people listed on December 14th are Joel and Daisy. No one else."

His gut bombed. He needed to sit down. Now.

"Balls," he said, stumbling into the kitchen and sitting in front of the laptop. His eyes dropped to the file Hope had open. The private flight had three crew members and two passengers listed. That was it.

"Did you check the days around the 14th?" he asked. "Maybe My Guy took a different flight."

"There were no flights to Barbados."

My Guy was a dead end.

"What about the pictures? We have those photos from Daisy's blog," Hope said. "There has to be some way to run his photo or something. Do you have a facial recognition app?"

Her voice was full of hope. He had an app for everything else, why not that?

Brice swung back to Grey, his stare steady, hoping the suit would take the hint. "Well, since you're under the assumption you own my ass, what do you say? Help a guy out, here?"

Grey sighed. "The Justice Team has access to the FBI facial recognition software and database. Send the photo and we'll run it. Teeg will send you the next set of files for you to work on."

Brice felt his adrenaline hangover lift ever so slightly. A deal had to be struck. "One file. I'll work on a case-by-case basis only. Okay? Great. I'll email you the pictures."

Grey started for the door. "Send them to Teeg. Oh, and..." he paused before opening it. "Welcome to the team. You're back on Syd's cookie list."

As he closed the door behind Grey, Brice laughed and flipped him off.

"Well," Hope said. "He's...interesting."

"FBI profilers are unique, that's for sure."

Blood continued to drip down his neck and Hope thought back to the night when he'd doctored her leg. Between them, they were a hot-mess.

She grabbed his arm and hauled him toward the bathroom where she'd wash out the cuts from the glass and make sure he didn't need stitches. "Let's get you cleaned up."

At the bathroom, she gently pushed him inside. Hawk stepped in, moving right up against the tub so they'd both fit in the tiny room.

She grabbed a washcloth from under the sink, turned the hot water on and waited for steam to rise. "You've got blood all over you. Your shirt is trashed. Take it off."

He glanced down at his arm. Dried and fresh blood stained

not only his arm but the front of his shirt. "Shit. This is one of my favorite shirts."

He reached over, shut off the water.

"Hey," she said, "we need to clean you up."

"I know. I'm gonna jump in the shower real quick. It'll be easier to see the damage."

"You might need stitches."

"Doubt it."

Lovely. Mr. Know-It-All strikes again. "Right. I forgot."

"What?"

She pushed around him, whipped the worn shower curtain back and slapped on the faucets, jerking the little lever for the shower while the water warmed up. "You're doing it again. Reminding me you're older and wiser. So, of course, if you say you don't need stitches, I guess you don't need stitches. Whatever, Hawk."

"Whoa, Hope." He touched her arm, gently guiding her so she faced him again. "I didn't mean it that way. I didn't. Honey, it's not bleeding that bad. I've been cut, shot, and beat to a pulp before in my former job. I have experience with these kinds of wounds. I figured I didn't need to get stitched, but if I do, absolutely, we'll get it squared away."

The mirror behind his head fogged up. *Shower is ready.* She reached out, grabbed the hem of his shirt and eased it up. He cooperated. Let her do the work and lift the shirt up over his head. Even if she had to go up on tippy-toes to do it, he let her.

Thank you. For once, she wanted to be in charge and do the comforting. And she needed him to let her do this for him. Even if it meant being pushy about it.

"Get those shoes off," she said.

"Yes, ma'am."

He kicked out of his shoes and made a move for the button on his jeans.

"I've got it," she said.

"Hope, my arm is fine. I think I can—"

"Shut it. I'm doing it."

His eyebrows shot up. "Uh, okay."

A minute later his pants were at his ankles and she bent low, tapped his right foot. "Lift up."

"Hope—"

"Shut it." She smacked at his foot again. Not hard, but enough for him to know she was riding a perilous edge of emotions and if he pushed hard enough, she'd tumble in the wrong direction and light him up.

When he didn't move, she glanced up at him, held his gaze for a few long seconds, keeping those emotions locked in place. Hawk was a lone wolf, he might need a little time to adjust to someone, a woman who actually gave a damn about him, ordering him around. She'd give him that time, but it wouldn't be limitless. She smacked his foot again. "Up."

Finally, he did as he was told.

"Now the other one."

Seconds later his pants were off and she guided his boxer briefs down his legs, her fingers moving over his skin and her mind flashed back to her wrapping her legs around him for the first time, him pushing inside her and the way his body felt against hers. Warm and male and protective. All of it came back to her and she breathed out.

"Damn," he said.

She glanced up and her gaze landed on his crotch where a healthy erection greeted her. Apparently she wasn't the only one with naughty thoughts.

"I can't help it," he said. "You do this to me. I hate it sometimes. The lack of control."

She stood, cupped her hands over his cheeks. "Don't hate it. Please. It's an amazing feeling. Knowing I do that to you. And for you to admit it? That's...a gift."

A small smile lit his face. "You know," he said, "to properly clean this cut you'll have to get into that shower with me."

"Is that so?"

"Yep."

There's a thought. But she wouldn't be that easy. She'd make him work for it. At least a little. "I'm not sure about that. I think you should just hop in there and get cleaned up. Then when you get out, I can look at it."

"I think you're wrong." He leaned down, nuzzled her neck. "My idea is better."

Oh, wow. That neck nuzzling? Total jackpot. Then he upped the pressure by nipping the skin and her body self-combusted. She moaned softly, admitting to herself that maybe he had a point.

"You are older," she said, "And sometimes wiser."

His arm came around her, went straight for the zipper on the back of her skirt while she worked the buttons on her blouse. Three seconds later, they climbed into the tub and the hot spray slammed against her skin, shocking her at first, making her wince.

Hawk went for the faucet to adjust the temperature. "Too hot?"

She slid in front of him. "No. It's perfect."

And it was. Her fatigued muscles immediately relaxed, but this wasn't about her. This was about him and her being in charge and she wanted that. Wanted that moment when she could be the wiser one. She faced him, then slid around him, her back connecting with the tile on the wall as she maneuvered.

"Where you going?"

"First things first. I need to see that cut. Let the water hit it and turn back around."

He angled back, once again facing her, letting the spray soak his back while his hands came up and cupped her breasts.

She should yell at him for it. For not focusing on getting that cut clean, but God, when he touched her, something inside her just broke loose, let her relax.

But then he slid his one hand lower while the other one pressed on her nipple and—no, no, no—he would not distract her.

"Turn around," she said.

His mouth dipped into a pout and she rolled her eyes before dropping a body searing kiss—one of those tongue inclusive, soul skimming ones that she only had nerve enough to initiate with Hawk. Something about him unleashed a sexual beast inside her.

She liked it.

A lot.

He pulled her closer, crushing her against him, but she pushed back, breaking the kiss and earning another boo-boo face. She patted his cheek. "Don't pout. You'll get what you want. Believe me. I need to take care of you first."

He grinned. "This would be taking care of me."

"Shut it. Turn around."

"Yes, ma'am."

He turned to the wall, but kept one hand on her hip, as if he were afraid to let go. As if she'd vanish.

Not a chance.

Slowly, she ran her hand up his back, over the lean muscle of his shoulder and let it rest there as she eyeballed the inch long cut that would need a butterfly bandage. The glass had sliced him good, but it didn't look fleshy enough to require stitches.

She leaned in, kissed him between the shoulder blades. "You'll live, sailor." She held her free hand out. "Give me that soap."

"Lucky me," he said. "Make sure you get the below the waist parts."

Hope burst out laughing. "Lord, you are a pig."

He didn't seem to mind because as she worked the soap up over his back, he set his hands on the wall and leaned into it, groaning a little as her hands moved over his skin. Water rained down on them, bouncing off his back, hitting her breasts where his hands had just been and she bit her lip, thought about all the things he'd already done to make her body come alive.

He'd done this to her. Made her sex-crazed. Before him, with the men she'd dated, the ones she'd thought she loved, she'd enjoyed sex, but didn't feel that ping—that enormous longing—she'd always dreamed she'd have with the man she loved. And she'd craved it, desperately clung to the idea of it, trying to force it. After a while, she'd given up, assuming she'd expected too much. That she'd bought into the whole I've-never-felt-this-way routine because the truth was, she had felt that way before.

And it was nothing special.

So sex became just sex. Nothing too terribly exciting and certainly nothing she couldn't live without.

Until now.

With Hawk, she didn't feel desperate. Or clingy. Or obsessed. Not at all. When near him she was safe and happy.

So easy.

She moved the soap over his back, then grabbed the wash-cloth and dabbed at the cut on his neck and somehow his body pulled her closer until she pressed right up against him and he groaned.

"Hawk?"

"Yep."

"Thank you."

"For what?"

"For making me love sex."

He raised his head, but continued to stare at the wall for a few seconds before turning back to her. "I love how much you love sex. Makes me a lucky man."

"I never did before." She shrugged. "Now? I can't get enough. You did that for me."

He sucked in a breath, backed her against the wall. "Don't move."

Not. A. Chance.

He shoved the curtain halfway open, reached for something on the floor and then waggled a condom at her. "Wanna get crazy in the shower, Ms. Denby?"

Another first. Sex in the shower. How the hell would this work without them slipping?

"Uh," she said while he dealt with the condom. "I've, um, never..."

"What?"

She put one hand over her mouth and giggled. Giggled? Really? "In the shower."

Condom in place, he inched forward, went right to that spot on her neck he'd hit the jackpot with before. "A shower virgin? Again I say, lucky me."

Then his hands were moving over her belly, back around her hips to her rear. She arched away from the wall giving him access.

"Atta, girl. Ready?"

For what? Before she could ask, he gripped the back of her legs and boosted her up. "Eeep." She splayed her arms out, her fingers slipping against the wet tile, desperate for something to hang on to before they both fell over.

"I've got you," he said. "Always."

She believed it. Finally. Closing her eyes, she tilted her head back, let her body go loose and relaxed into the sensation of the slick tile against her back. Hawk dragged kisses up her neck to her face and she lowered her head, met his lips, and brought her arms around him.

He pushed inside her and she gasped, digging her fingers into his back, loving the feeling of him so deep as he anchored her against the wall.

And then she let her hands drop and hang at her sides, giving all control to Hawk as he pumped his hips, at first slow and then faster and faster. His eyebrows drew in—total concentration—and she reached up, ran her fingers over his face, smoothing the hard lines as they worked together, hips moving in rhythm.

He opened his eyes, met her gaze and blew her a kiss and something inside her burst open, just a huge whoosh that stole her breath because finally, finally, finally, she felt it, that connection, that contentment she'd never had before.

"Oh, my," she said.

"Oh, my, indeed."

To avoid his injured forearm, she clamped her hands on his biceps, squeezing because, no, no, no, everything inside her went rigid and she knew it was coming, that huge release. But no, she didn't want it yet. Too good. *Make it last.* The emotional link. *Please, let it last.*

Hawk changed the rhythm and—boom—something behind her eyes exploded. She slammed them closed and moaned, gripping his arms hard as she tumbled over that crazy edge.

"I've got you," he said again.

"I know."

"Can't..."

His words broke off and he leaned in, skin to skin, pinning her against the wall as he worked his hips harder and harder and she hung on, loving the loss of control and then it happened, he reared back, met her gaze and gritted his teeth, fighting for control.

She dragged her hands over his shoulders and as if her simple touch fired something, he cried out, pumped his hips twice more then pinned her against that wall while water poured over them.

Still holding her, his chest heaved against hers and his shoulders shook and she bit him on the ear earning a roar of laughter from him.

"If you drop me, I'll kill you."

He straightened and kissed her. Softly this time. "I've got you, Hope. Always."

21

*T*he ringing of Hope's phone brought her out of a dead sleep. *What the?* She shot up to a sitting position, looked around the room where a sliver of sunlight peeked through the blinds.

Safe house.

She rubbed her eyes, focused on clearing her sleepy fog.

Phone.

Bedside table.

She reached across Hawk who was face down on the bed, his long, lean body on top of the comforter as he slept in only boxers. Apparently, the man was a furnace when he slept.

Not wanting to disturb him, she took the phone into the hallway and checked the screen. Amy.

Hopefully her boss had good news. "Hello?"

"Denby," Amy said, her voice quiet and even.

Too quiet. Way too even and Hope knew whatever it was, she wouldn't like it.

"Yes. Hi, Amy. Good morning. What's up?"

"I just got in and found an interesting link in an email. From the White House."

The White House. "Okay."

Now, the White House sending Amy a link probably wasn't all that astonishing. After all, Amy had been appointed as the head Public Information Officer by the president. The astonishing part was that Amy was telling Hope about this link, particularly after being put on suspension.

"Not okay, Denby. The link took me to the The First Amendment Patriot blog where our blogger friend has declared the Chief Justice of the United States was assassinated. Dammit, Denby!" Amy exploded. "I thought you had this guy under control. You made a deal with him. He trusts you. That's what you told me."

"I did make a deal with him. He does trust me."

"So what the hell happened?"

She could easily throw Hawk under the bus here, tell her boss he went rogue on her and ran the story despite promising not to.

She could.

But she wouldn't.

She glanced back into the bedroom where he hadn't moved from his spot on the bed. His hair stuck out in every direction and in sleep, he was peaceful. Not paranoid or worrying or lecturing her.

She probably loved him.

There. She admitted it. It didn't terrify her this time. Didn't feel like an illusion. It simply was.

"I helped him write the post."

Silence.

"You...Wait. Did you just say you helped him write it?"

"Yes, ma'am. Amy, you have no idea what we've been through. Of course, had you given me the opportunity to tell you what we've discovered before suspending me, maybe you'd have counseled me not to help with the post, but it's done now. We had no choice."

"Oh, you had a choice. You should have called me before he ran that goddamned post!"

"You suspended me. Based on our last conversation, I didn't think calling you was an option."

"Well, congratulations, Denby, you and your blogger friend have caused quite the shit-storm. I have the White House all over me. They want answers and I can't give them any. Now every network wants to know why the White House is covering up the assassination of a Supreme Court justice. The Chief Justice! Dammit, Denby!"

Yes, Turner was dead. And she and Hawk had discovered important information about that death. Information her boss hadn't even asked about. "Amy, I'm sorry the White House is unhappy, but something isn't right here. We think Turner's death revolves around the Kenton Labs case."

"Denby, stop talking."

Hope stopped. When Amy got on a roll like this it was best to let her rage on and get it out of her system. "All right."

"Thank you. I'm so disappointed. You were my rock star. The one I knew I could count on. You're young and aggressive, even if that damned cheeriness gets on my nerves, you were the rock star."

Hope squeezed her fingers closed. Since the third grade she'd been killing herself trying to be the positive one. Always painting on a fucking smile and finding the fucking bright side. For years, she'd survived on the idea that if she stayed perky—happy, happy, happy!—she'd never be called boring.

Never again.

"Amy, it's a solid story."

"I don't want to hear it."

Of course she didn't. She'd proved that when she'd suspended her without letting her mount a defense. Hope sagged back against the wall. "Okay. I'm sorry I've upset you."

She wouldn't apologize for the story. It was a good story with merit and Hawk deserved the credit without her minimizing it by faking an apology.

One of Amy's long sighs came through the phone line. "Denby, you've left me no choice. I'm going to have someone pack up your things and they'll be delivered to your home. You're fired."

Hope shot up straight, her entire body going rigid. "You're *firing* me? Seriously? The Chief Justice was assassinated and you're canning me?"

Unbelievable.

"It has nothing to do with this supposed assassination. You disobeyed me."

"Not true, Amy! You know it. The story is solid and for whatever reason the White House is trying to cover this up. I'm the first sacrificial lamb. You've probably already spoken to the networks letting them know a junior staffer blew it and has been terminated."

Ten long seconds of silence ensued. Who knew ten seconds could take that long?

That meant Hope's assessment was accurate and Amy couldn't insult her by denying it.

"Hope?"

She spun back, found Hawk sitting up in bed, staring straight at her with that Mr. Cynical hesitant look he sometimes wore.

Well, she finally understood, didn't she? He knew all about getting screwed, had even tried to tell her it would happen to her if she stayed with him and chased this story. But she wouldn't listen. Didn't believe him. Didn't *believe* that her boss would use her as the scapegoat. Nope. She just kept on thinking if she could be perky, perky Hope everything would work out.

That she could change the world.

Fool.

She went back to Amy. "Fine. When we prove the Chief Justice was murdered, maybe I won't sue you for wrongful termination. And, Amy, have a wonderful day."

Ha!

To emphasize her point, she stabbed at the screen. "Witch! The nerve."

Hawk stepped into the hallway, hair sticking up every which way and those stormy blue eyes narrowed. "Did you just get *fired*?"

"I sure did."

She latched onto the waistband of his shorts, yanked him forward and kissed him. Disgusting morning breath and all.

He gripped her shoulders and set her back, studying her face. "What's going on with you? Are you mad? Sad? What?"

All of the above.

Somehow, it felt good. Later, she'd realize she was out of a prestigious job most would kill for and that the louse Joel Bigley, after all the wrongs he'd done, got to keep his job, but oh well. Sometimes life sucked and no matter how positive she tried to stay, she couldn't change that.

Obviously.

But right now, she was free. Free from being an eternal optimist who always found the upshot.

No upshot. Not now.

"Hope?"

"I'm...free."

"Huh?"

She paddled her hands in front of her, all the energy from the last few minutes roaring through them. "In the third grade Jennifer Jacobs told me I was boring. Everyone laughed. I was completely humiliated. Do you know—wait, of course you don't know, I never told anyone."

"Okay, now you're whacking out on me."

"Yes, I am." She poked him. "And guess what Mr. Cynical, it feels great." She threw her arms up. "I'm free, Hawk! No more of this Mary Sunshine crap. If I want to be pissy, well, goddammit I'm being pissy. And I will swear like a mother-fucker if I want to because that's what people do when they're *angry*."

Hawk's eyebrows shot up. "Wow."

"I know, right?"

"That swearing thing from you is kinda hot. Never thought I'd say that about the chirpy idealist."

"And you know what else?"

"No idea, but I'm sure you'll tell me."

"Damn straight I will. You and I, we're going to blow this story out of the water. I'm done being the good girl. Forget spin control. Someone is going down for this. And it won't be me."

She was pissed. Deep-down to the roots of her hair angry.

But most of all, Brice knew Hope was hurt. Disappointed.

Been there, done that shit.

Brice had been angry, too, when he'd been forced out of ATF, but mostly, underneath the outrage and disgust, he'd been disappointed. Hurt at the betrayal of his agency and the government of the United States of America.

He'd gotten some satisfaction when he'd helped Mitch and Caroline expose the gunwalking scandal and put the Deputy Attorney General, the man behind the curtain, in jail. It hadn't brought back the dead agents or made up for those who were terminated, like him, for doing their jobs, but it had given him some closure. Vindicated him. Settled some old scores.

That was exactly what Hope needed right now. Vindication.

He took her hand, weaving his fingers in between hers.

"We're going to get to the bottom of this, I promise. Why don't you go get cleaned up, and I'll make us some breakfast?"

"First, I need to do this." She marched into the bedroom, over to the dresser, and picked up a knickknack sitting there. Swiping it up, she reared back and whipped it against the wall. The cheap ceramic dog shattered into half a dozen pieces and landed on the floor.

Hope brushed her hands together, her chest heaving slightly. "There."

"Feel better?"

"Immensely."

"Quite an arm you have there," he teased. "You might have a future in baseball."

She rolled her eyes, grabbed some fresh clothes, and headed for the bathroom.

Brice tamed his hair with one hand. His forearm was now a deep purple with smudges of green. The bandage on the back of his neck was half off. He yanked it the rest of the way, tossed it in the wastebasket, then grabbed his jeans and pulled them on.

Breakfast was going to be light since they hadn't gotten any groceries.

To his surprise, however, when he opened the fridge door, a carton of eggs, a loaf of bread, and a package of bacon waited for him. There was half a gallon of milk and another half of orange juice.

Sydney.

Grey must have brought the groceries the day before, but Brice knew it was Sidney who had told him to do so. She wasn't officially part of the Justice Team, but she worried about all of them equally. To Brice, it seemed she was the best benefit to joining the team.

He found a couple of skillets and started the eggs and

bacon cooking. Then he plunked slices of bread into the toaster and found a jar of grape jelly in the tiny pantry. As everything cooked, he cleared the kitchen table of papers and files and set it with plates and silverware.

A few minutes later, Hope emerged from the bathroom in a cloud of sweet-smelling steam. She eyed his handiwork as he slid two eggs, sunny side up, onto her plate. "Look at you, all domestic and everything."

"I've been on my own a long time," he said. "A guy's gotta eat."

She wiggled a finger at him. "The bare-chest-and-jeans look really works for you. Especially with that watch."

His watch? "Whatever does it for you, babe."

"How's the arm?"

"Sore as hell. I'll live."

She sniffed the air. "Is that bacon I smell?"

"It is indeed."

"I could get used to this."

Helping himself to eggs and piling the bacon on a plate, he returned to the table and plunked down in the seat across from her. "Turnabout's fair play, by the way."

Snatching up two pieces of bacon, she dug in. "What does that mean?" she said around a bite of food.

Brice spread jelly on a piece of toast and handed it to her. "You can serve me breakfast shirtless anytime."

Accepting the toast, she made a snorting noise. "Pig."

"This pig just made you breakfast, and I believe he provided you with multiple orgasms last night."

Pink rose in her cheeks and she grinned. "Yes, he did. He's going to do it again tonight."

"Sounds like you have plans."

"Oh, I have plans. World domination and great sex with you topping the list."

They shared a smile and then ate in comfortable silence. That was the thing about Hope. Sometimes she was a complete chatterbox. Other times she was just as happy in silence. Like when they were working together. Three days ago, he would have laughed at anyone telling him he'd found his match, as an investigator, in Hope Denby. That he'd be screwing her blind every chance he got.

A lot could happen in three days.

"This is so good," she said.

"It's just bacon and eggs."

"No." She waggled her fork in the air. "It's more than that. It's like I'm tasting food for the first time. Every bite is like... good. Really good."

"That's what happens after you've survived a traumatic experience. Food tastes better. Sex is better. You notice little things you never did before."

She was staring at him. "Like the fact you have little gray flecks in the irises of your eyes?"

Weird, but... "Yeah, like that."

"You're squirming. You don't like being under scrutiny."

He was not squirming. "Everything I did in the army, and then in the ATF, was under someone's scrutiny. The Patriot blog is under constant scrutiny. I'd say I'm pretty comfortable with being put under the microscope."

"I'm not talking about the things you've done or the blog. I'm talking about one on one, in person, physical scrutiny. Me sitting here talking about your chest and your watch and the color of your eyes. It makes you uncomfortable. It's an invasion of your personal space, your privacy."

"You've had a field day invading my personal space in the past couple of days, Hope. Have I protested even once?"

"Nope."

He spread his hands. "You've seen pretty much every side to me. You know most of what there is to know. Take it or leave it. I don't have anything to hide from you, and..." He grinned. "You're free to look at my chest all you like."

Her return smile could have lit up Manhattan. "You told me you don't let people get close to you, that you would be bad for me. You were wrong on both counts. I see how you push Grey and the others away, but secretly you like that they want to help you. You pushed me away at first, tried to make me believe you were too damaged. A lost cause. But underneath it all, you're just scared. Of being betrayed again. Of being hurt."

The investigative reporter was back. Brice kept his face straight even though he wanted to suck in air. His chest felt tight. The cut on the back of his neck itched. Couldn't they just continue their semi-quiet breakfast together?

"Yep, there it is," Hope said. She bit off a piece of toast.

"What?"

She chewed and swallowed. "That shuttered expression you get when we talk about emotions."

He didn't respond, and dug into his eggs.

Like usual, she wouldn't let it go. "You just said, and I quote, 'I don't have anything to hide from you', but you're hiding your feelings right now."

Feelings sucked. They led him down dark alleys and ambushed him. "I'm not a touchy-feely kind of guy."

"I don't know about that." He glanced up and she winked. "You're very touchy-feely when I'm naked."

He couldn't help it. Just like Grey had caught him off guard the day before, Hope had done that now. He laughed.

God, it felt good to laugh.

And just like that, the wall around his heart crumbled. Not piece by piece, layer by layer, but all at once, as if Hope had blown a gigantic hole in the center and its structural integrity disintegrated, laying it to waste. "Hope?"

"Yeah?"

"I think I...I..."

His phone rang.

"You what?" she said.

Saved in the nick of time. Before he laid his heart out right there on the table and told her how he felt about her.

Leaning back in the chair, he grabbed his cell off the kitchen counter. "It's Grey. Maybe they found something out about our guy."

Hope didn't look all that excited. As Brice answered, she looked away, snatching up her juice and taking a sip.

"We got a hit," Grey said without preamble. "Name, address, job."

Yes! Brice jumped up, feeling the surge of adrenaline. He put Grey on speaker. "Who is he?"

"Not over the phone. You better come in for this."

Grey had called, not Teeg. He didn't want to share the information over the phone.

Shit, this must be big. "You told me to stay put yesterday, now you want me to come to headquarters?"

"You're going to need to handle this information with kid gloves. I feel it's prudent to discuss your next step in private."

Meaning without Hope. Brice glanced at her. She had that look on her face. The one that said she was already pissed and not about to let him leave her out of this. "Hope can handle it."

"I don't doubt Miss Denby can handle the information. My concern is that she have plausible deniability down the road."

"I've already lost my frickin' job," she said loudly. "I don't need to deny anything."

Grey's pause was so slight, Brice knew he was biting his tongue. "Your involvement could lead to more serious circumstances, Miss Denby. I have concerns about your safety."

A light bulb went on over Brice's head. His gut was going crazy with nerves. Now he felt an extra twinge that Hope could be in more danger. "I'll be there in twenty," he told his new boss and hung up.

Hope stood and took her plate to the sink. "You're not going without me. We're in this together."

He grabbed her arm, held her still. "When Grey says you need deniability, he means it. When he's concerned about your safety, we need to listen."

"You've kept me plenty safe so far."

Even after everything they'd been through, she didn't understand the depths of danger they were swimming in. "This guy, whoever he is and however he's tied to this case, must be someone who's untouchable or has a lot of pull in D.C. Something's got Grey's boxers in a bunch. We need to do what he says for now. I'll be back as soon as I can."

"What am I supposed to do?"

He'd planned to look through the info he'd gathered on the CEO and board of Kenton along with Dr. Block, the scientist. Maybe he and Teeg had both missed something. "On my laptop is all the dirt I could dig up on the Kenton folks. Read through it and see if anything jumps out at you."

"You said they were all dead ends."

"A fresh set of eyes might see something I missed."

She pulled away from his hand. "Fine, but you better not leave me out of any plans you make with Grey. I don't care if my butt is on the line down the road. I lost everything over this, and I'm not backing down now."

He kissed her forehead. "Don't worry, Woodward. I'll make sure you have your day in the sun."

She tagged along behind him as he left the kitchen and went to find a shirt. "And don't think you're off the hook about what you said earlier."

What had he said? "What?"

"You were going to tell me something at the table before we were interrupted."

Right. He tugged a shirt over his head, grabbed his shoes. "It was nothing important."

She followed him to the door where he grabbed his truck keys. "Brice?"

"Yeah, babe?"

Her heart was in her eyes. She chewed on her bottom lip. "Be careful, okay?"

He grabbed her and kissed her, then ducked out the door.

22

_a_fter a quick shower, Hope killed time by cleaning up the breakfast dishes, a chore she suddenly didn't mind so much. Hope Denby, domestic goddess. Most definitely a new concept since she couldn't whip up a grilled cheese sandwich without scorching one side.

But with the kitchen back to sparkling, the silence in the tiny apartment, the bland nothingness that came with Hawk's absence, drove home just how alone she was. Here she was playing house, no job, possibly on the run from a murderer and, God help her, despite her best efforts, falling in love.

With a blogger.

The lack of a job and running from the murderer she might be able to handle. Truly. Because down deep, she liked the drama. Twisted as that was. She didn't like being in danger, not for one second, but knowing that danger stemmed from the work she and Hawk had done in pursuit of an assassin? Total turn-on.

Clearly a big one with the way she and Hawk had been humping like bunnies.

"Girlfriend," she muttered, "you're a sick person."

The baseboard heater, one of those old metal ones let out a little clink and she stared down at it. Any second, a burst of hot air would fly from the thing. They couldn't regulate the heat in the place. If they turned the thermostat down, the living room became a freezer. If they turned it up, where it was now, it quite literally drove them out of the kitchen. *Can't stand the heat, get out of the kitchen.*

Except, she was in the only safe place for her. Nowhere else to go. She glanced left, studied the living room's threadbare rug. *Safe place.*

In a matter of days she'd gone from being the rock star in her office, an up-and-coming young woman with dreams of a future in politics, to living above a nail salon in Chinatown.

All because she wanted to know how a Supreme Court Justice wound up dead on a bridge.

As if on cue, a burst of hot air rose and slid up her right arm. She needed something to do. And not in the kitchen. The kitchen made her think too much and she'd always been way better at doing versus thinking.

Find the upshot.

Files.

Hawk had left files. Basic background stuff on Donazem and the patent case. While she waited, she'd go through it. Fresh set of eyes, Hawk had said. If nothing else, she could provide that. All this feeling sorry for herself wasn't doing a damned bit of good.

The heater hissed and she stepped back before the next burst of air hit her. She needed to get busy and ignore this unsettling aloneness.

From the fridge, she grabbed a bottled water and made her way to the living room where Hawk had left a legal pad and a stack of files. She perused his handwritten block-lettered notes with ease. How she loved a man who wrote legibly. Half the men in her office scribbled to the point where she needed an interpreter.

His thoroughness didn't stop there. Not Hawk, his writing, like the man, was direct, well thought-out and organized, starting with the origins of Donazem and all the players involved. On the side margin, he'd noted the scientist's name—Martin Block—with a question mark.

When they'd met Tony near the Reflecting Pool, he'd given them a summary of Dr. Block's successful career. Obviously, Hawk had questions and wanted to perform further research. Might as well dive into the professional history of one Martin Block PhD. Hope typed the scientist's name into her search engine and—voila—pages and pages of articles popped up. Ah, the Internet. What a wonder.

She scrolled through the list, didn't see anything to get her jumpstarted and refined her search to *Martin Block PhD Donazem*.

Again, pages and pages of articles filled her screen. She perused the subjects and chose the fourth listing that included a bio with all the yada-yada boring facts about the man's rise to head of research and development for Donazem.

Rather than co-mingle her thoughts with Hawk's, she flipped to a fresh sheet of paper and jotted a few notes. Nothing worthy of stopping the proverbial presses—or blog postings—as it were, but she noted several items. The drug had been in development for fourteen years with a manufacturing cost of $359 million. Impressed by the number, Hope whistled.

More interesting was that Donazem, one of over four thousand drugs that Kenton had developed, had actually made it to human trial testing when all the others had failed. Kenton manufactured other drugs of course, but one in four thousand?

Huh.

Hope circled that little tidbit. Was that the industry average? She shook her head. *No idea*. She'd research that next.

Back to Martin Block. She closed the current screen, scanned more links and clicked on one referencing an interview with Dr. Block. She perused the text of the interview, rolling her eyes at some of the man's incredibly pompous answers. Why, of course, he was head of his class. Why, of course, he'd been one of the lead scientists on a cancer fighting drug that saved millions of lives.

Of course.

Of course.

Of course.

Trend here. One that showed this guy had an ego the size of the moon. She drew a picture of the moon in the margin of her notes.

Ego.

Which might not mean anything, but in her short career she'd seen all kinds of wacky things happen when egos were involved.

She scrolled to the bottom of the interview. *And, hello, my darling.* The wondrous Dr. Block, as part of his normal salary package received 'significant bonuses in cash and stock options' based on the performance of Donazem.

Hope read the line again, then a third time before slouching into the cheap sofa. She nibbled her bottom lip.

Ego.

Money.

Years of work.

She popped off the sofa, set her hands on her hips, tapped her fingers as energy poured from her core into her limbs.

"Okay, Hope, don't get crazy here. So, the guy has a stake in the performance of the drug. So what?"

She paced the length of the room, avoiding the front window, and flopped out her right hand.

"If the drug doesn't sell well, he loses a good chunk of his income."

She flopped her other hand out. "Which means, if they don't get to keep their patent and other companies develop generics, all those juicy profits belonging to Donazem will be splintered. And that, Woodward," she said, "means an income reduction for the good doctor."

Which nobody liked. Right? Everyone wanted to make money.

Huh.

She scooped up her phone, hit Hawk's number. Voicemail. Shoot. She needed someone to dig into Martin Block's finances and Grey seemed like the man to get that done. Grey or Teeg. Both of whom she didn't have contact info for.

Tony.

Even on suspension from the Supreme Court Police, he had to have friends who could run a credit check on the scientist.

A minute later he picked up. "What's up, Hope?"

"Hi. I need your help. Hawk is out of touch and I just found something that may or may not be related to Donazem's patent.

"What do you need?"

"Again, this could be nothing."

"Hope, I get it. Now shut up and tell me what you've got."

She grinned. A man after her own heart. "I think I might love you."

"Honey, if that were true, my life would be made. Besides, seems like Brice has dibs. Whatcha got?"

Dibs. Funny.

"I've been doing some research on the scientist behind Donazem. Martin Block, PhD. He's head of R&D on the drug. Fourteen years and a manufacturing cost of $359 million later, the drug brought in $3 billion last year alone."

"*Billion?*"

"You heard right, big boy. It gets better. Our esteemed Dr. Block, as part of his salary package receives bonuses and stock options in the company. If the drug sells well, he gets a gold star by way of a lump of cash."

"How much?"

"No idea. That's where you come in. Know anyone at the IRS? Can we figure out how much he made last year? Maybe even run a credit check and see what his financial profile looks like?"

"As in, does he own a house in Barbados?"

She didn't need to comment. They both knew he'd nailed it.

"This is good work, Hope. Let me get into it."

"Thank you."

"Hey," he said. "I want answers on Turner as much as you do. By the way, sorry you got canned."

If he'd heard, so had a lot of other people. A week ago, the humiliation would have paralyzed her. Now? Not so much. Now, she just wanted answers about Turner's death.

"You got shafted," Tony said.

"Well, so did you. What's the status of your suspension?"

He hesitated. "Not sure. I may not care either."

"Uh."

Hope stopped talking, took a second to align her thoughts. That alone was a switch, but she didn't need to be pissing Tony off with flip comments.

Clarify. That's what she'd do. "What do you mean?"

"Eh. Without Turner I'm not sure this job is for me anymore. For two years I've been bored out of my skull. There's not a whole lot of excitement, which I knew going in. Mostly protection details and threat assessments. I liked Turner though and he kept me from leaving."

And with Turner gone, there was nothing keeping him there.

Not only was Tony grieving the loss of his friend, he might have a job upheaval to deal with. "Are you thinking about resigning?"

"Not yet. But I am thinking about applying for the FBI. Maybe DEA. Something. Anyway, let me look into this scientist. Get back to you."

"Thanks, pal. I'll dig around more on this guy. I may even go old school and ring him up. Tell him I'm a reporter for the Patriot Blog and see if he'll talk to me."

"Pfft, he's an idiot if he does. He'll never talk to you."

The big man would be surprised. "Tony, one thing I've learned in D.C. is that sometimes really smart people do really stupid things."

The abandoned armory was as dark and dreary as ever on the outside. Perfect place to film a post-apocalyptic zombie flick, Brice thought as he pulled his car around the back.

Or the next Batman movie.

Inside, the overhead industrial lights glared harshly, and from the looks on everyone's faces as he walked in, the zombie movie might actually be a possibility. "Long night?" he asked Teeg.

"You ain't kidding," the techy murmured, chin in his hand, eyes barely open.

Brice grabbed a chair from the table Mitch sat at and hauled it over to Teeg's station. Mitch never lifted his eyes from the file he was working on, but grumbled something Brice didn't understand. The circles under his eyes and lack of smart-ass comment told Brice he'd pulled an all-nighter as well.

Caroline sat alone at a table in the back of the open room, cleaning her rifle. She nodded at Brice once, then went back to checking her scope.

"Where's Grey?" Brice asked.

Teeg's lips were becoming misshapen as his chin slid off the shelf of his hand and he leaned over onto his arm. His eyes fluttered shut. "Bagel run."

Great. Grey dropped a mysterious bomb on him and then went out for bagels. He turned the chair around and plunked down in it. "Show me what you found."

Teeg's response was a soft snore.

Brice thought about pinching the kid's arm, then decided he'd get what he wanted faster if he let Teeg sleep.

Reaching past him, Brice grabbed the keyboard and started to type.

"Hey!" Teeg sat bolt upright. "Nobody touches Frodo except me."

"Frodo?" Brice forced himself not to roll his eyes. "You named your computer?"

From behind them, Mitch spoke up. "Each part of the computer. The keyboard is Frodo, the CPU is The Ring, the monitor to your left is Gandalf, and the one to your right is Legolas. It's a Lord of the Rings reunion."

Teeg grabbed the wireless keyboard and hugged it to his chest. "LOTR is the greatest story ever written!"

"And I'm the president," Mitch murmured, going back to work.

The side door opened and Grey strolled in with two white bakery bags. "Breakfast," he said.

Caroline laid the scope on her table. "Thank God. I could eat a horse."

Grey tossed a bag at her and one at Mitch.

"What about me?" Teeg asked.

"Yes! Cinnamon toast bagels," Caroline hooted. "What did you get, Mitch?"

He dug into his bag. "Looks like spinach, honey wheat, and one with everything."

"No bacon parmesan?" Teeg looked like someone stole his puppy.

Another white bag materialized in Grey's hands. He set it on Teeg's desk. "All yours."

"Now that everybody has their favorite bagel," Brice said, "can we get down to business?"

Mitch flipped him the bird. "Give us a frickin' minute, will ya? We were up all night working while you were enjoying hot sex with a pretty, young girl and sleeping in."

A cinnamon toast bagel sailed through the air and—*whack*—hit Mitch in the back of the head. He flinched and echoed Teeg's sentiment. "Hey!"

Caroline went to the counter and poured herself a cup of coffee. "Shut up and eat, Mitch."

He did a silent, exaggerated mimic of Caroline behind her back.

"I saw that," she said.

Mitch got busy with his bagel.

What the hell did I get myself into?

Teeg set down Frodo and went for the bakery bag Grey had given him. The smell of bacon and cheese filled the air. Grey cleared his throat and Teeg stopped with the bagel halfway to his mouth. "Eat later," Grey said. "Show Brennan what we found."

Thank you.

The kid shot Brice a dirty look before making a big deal out of returning the bagel to the bag. He licked his fingers, rubbed his hands on his pants, then clicked a couple of keys. "This is your picture, taken with a high res camera phone. The guy's in profile, but with the Next Gen Identifier software, courtesy of the FBI, it's easy to identify a face from a range of angles, including a profile view."

"I know how facial rec works, man."

"Right. Well, the software came up with a match from an interesting government database."

"Government database?" Brice shook his head. "Why am I not surprised. Who else would a lobbyist take to Barbados on vacation?"

"Yeah, but this is probably not what you think of in the line of conspiracies." Teeg typed in a web address and hit enter. A page came up and asked for a security code. Another couple of keystrokes, and Teeg cleared the login. "Welcome to the D.C. Department of Transportation."

Department of Transportation? "What's Charley doing with a DDOT guy? Are they friends or something?"

"You could say that, but, well, I'll get to that in a minute." A listing of names with corresponding pictures appeared on the middle screen. Teeg scrolled through several pages. "All DDOT employees are photographed and fingerprinted. This is the guy NGI flagged."

Brice read the name. "Felix Warren."

In the photograph, no doubt taken for the guy's employment badge, he seemed younger than the profile picture from Barbados. His dark hair was slicked back, his face clean-shaven. "You're sure this is him?"

"NCI doesn't lie." Teeg brought up one of the Barbados pictures and put it side by side with Felix's employment photo. He zoomed in on a spot just above Felix's colorful shirt in the vacation picture and pointed to what looked like an ink blob. "See that?"

Brice leaned closer. "Yeah, what about it?"

"Tattoo. Just the tip, but NCI matched it to this." He zoomed in on the second photo. Since the employment photo was a head-on shot, almost none of the tattoo showed above Felix's polo collar since it was on the side of his neck. "Scars, tattoos, birthmarks...the system can match all of them."

"It can also match palm prints, voice, even walking stride," Grey added.

"Jesus," Brice muttered. Big Brother had turned into all-seeing, all-knowing Big Brother.

"The interesting thing is,"—Teeg minimized the vacation photo and brought up a video. He clicked play and Brice watched an amateur shot of the bridge the morning of Turner's death. Teeg had the sound off and as the video played, he skipped to a section near the end—"this."

He paused the video at the spot where a DDOT employee in an orange vest started removing the barricade to the closed lane.

"Holy shit," Brice said.

Teeg zoomed in on the face, enlarging it next to the vacation picture. "Yep. Your guy Felix is the one who removed the barricade after Chief Justice Turner was murdered."

What was Felix Warren doing in Barbados with Charley Winslow and Joel Bigley, and then on the bridge after Turner died?

"Hey," Mitch said, now also standing behind Brice. "Didn't you tell us Hope nearly got run over on that bridge the other night?"

Brice gritted his teeth, said to Teeg, "You got an address and phone number for Warren?"

Teeg hit the enter key on Frodo. "Just sent them to your phone."

Brice jumped up and started for the door. Grey stopped him. "You can call Warren and do your research from here."

He pointed to a six-foot long banquet table with peeling, fake wood grain, laminate top and a crooked metal chair next to it.

"What's that?"

"Your new office."

"Wow, you really went all out."

Caroline snorted from her "office" as she chewed her bagel. "We did get Grey to buy you a state-of-the-art laptop."

A shiny, silver laptop did, indeed, sit on the tabletop.

"It's got all the bells and whistles," Mitch said in a you-know-you-want-to-check-it-out voice. He did a Vanna White arm wave. "Teeg approved, even."

Teeg was nodding. "Check it out, man. I customized it myself."

A warm sensation flooded Brice's chest. *I have a team.*

Friends.

A girlfriend.

Damn. Could life get better than this?

"There's something on there you'll want to see," Grey said. "Your cabbie friend, Mr. Kostas, and Mr. Warren have a history together."

Brice didn't need any more reason to throw himself into the metal chair and open the laptop.

It sprang to life instantly, the wallpaper on the screen a big, bold Justice Team logo. A plethora of icons sat in the bottom tray. Kaleidoscope, NCI, and six more official government databases.

All at his fingertips.

Brice rubbed his hands together.

Kid in a candy shop.

Or more like a conspiracy blogger in intelligence heaven.

"I cross-checked all the parties in your investigation," Teeg said. He pulled out his bagel and eyed it lovingly. "If you click on the JT symbol on the lower left, it will bring up the results."

Brice did as instructed. A window opened with a folder containing four files.

Lamar Kostas.

Felix Warren.

Charley Winslow.

And one labeled "Turner Conspiracy."

"Check out the picture in the Conspiracy file," Teeg said around a mouthful of bagel.

Brice opened the file and found himself looking at a newspaper clipping with a black and white photo. The article read, "Warren Leads High School Shooting Team to Regionals." It was dated 2004.

"I'll be damned," Brice said under his breath as he scanned the article. Felix Warren had been an expert marksman back in high school.

Then his eyes went to the picture of the team. A dozen young guys grouped together for a yearbook shot. Brice read the caption under it, looking for Warren's spot in the cluster of teenagers.

That's when he spotted the other names.

Lamar Kostas.

Charley Winslow.

No way.

Not only had all three men attended Jefferson Springs High School, they'd all been part of the Competitive Shooting Team.

"So Warren and Winslow were friends in high school," Brice said. "And Kostas and Warren were both on the bridge two days ago. Kostas had $20,000 hidden in his house. Any chance Kostas was in Barbados at the same time the other two were with Bigley?"

Grey was staring at Teeg's monitor again. "I checked. Kostas was here in D.C. the whole month of December. Busy time for cabbies."

"So who's the shooter?" Caroline asked.

Everyone looked at her.

"What?" She shrugged. "You've got a dead justice and at least two of your three marksmen were on that bridge the day he was shot. Seems logical one of them may have done the deed."

It couldn't be that easy. Brice had to play devil's advocate. "They were marksmen in high school with rifles. Doesn't mean they can shoot worth a damn now, and besides, Turner was shot with a handgun."

She smirked. "Given the right situation, I'm as accurate with a handgun as I am with a rifle. I bet if they loved guns in their teens, they still do. Do any of them have guns registered to them? Any of them belong to a shooting range?"

Grey's gaze slid to Brice. "All three, in fact."

More evidence, but all of it still circumstantial. "I need to talk to Warren." Brice said. He looked for Teeg's text with the number. "Feel him out."

"I'll go with you," Mitch said. "Better to do these things in person."

He had a point.

"Mr. Warren is not at work today." Grey marched to the counter and grabbed a mug, started pouring coffee. "I already checked. He called in sick. Perhaps you can catch him at home."

"We can stake out his house." Mitch clapped his hands together and motioned for Brice to follow him to the door. "Maybe do a sneak and peek if he's not there."

Robin was way too excited to leave the Bat Cave. Brice couldn't blame him.

"I've got it covered." He dialed Tony Gerard's number. "Tuner's bodyguard will want to know what we've found."

Gerard's phone went directly to voicemail.

Balls.

"No luck?" Mitch stood in front of him with pleading, puppy dog eyes. "That's too bad. Guess you're stuck with me."

He grinned from ear to ear.

Bastard.

"I can handle it on my own," Brice insisted, rising from the chair.

"We use the buddy system, here." Grey didn't look at him as he walked over to his dry-erase board and fiddled with a photo, his commanding Batman voice echoing in the room. "Take Mitch. Report in if you find anything." His gaze swung to Brice. "And no stupid shit this time, Brennan, or next time, *I'll* be your partner."

A threat. *Great.*

"Watch your back, Brennan," Caroline called out as Brice gave up and headed for the door. "And keep an eye on Mitch's too. He's a pain in the ass, but I love him."

Defeated, but not all that upset about it, Brice waved over his shoulder as he went out the door and his new partner followed on his heels.

23

_____

*T*wenty minutes after Hope had left a voicemail for Dr. Martin Block, her phone rang. Kenton Laboratories.

Cha.

Ching.

"Hello?"

"Hope Denby?"

Male voice. Deep. Commanding. Somehow she didn't imagine a scientist to sound this way. But, hey, everything else in her life in the past few days had surprised her so why not a male phone sex operator posing as a scientist?

Wow, she was tired. *Fucking* tired. Ha. This swearing thing might be fun.

"Yes. This is Hope Denby."

"Good morning, Ms. Denby. This is Dr. Martin Block. You left me a message."

"Yes, Dr. Block. Thank you for returning my call. I'm on a wicked deadline here."

The deadline lie couldn't hurt. And it wasn't altogether a lie. They were dealing with the murder of a Supreme Court Justice for crying out loud. If that wasn't an urgent matter the world needed an upgrade on crime prioritization.

"Of course. You said something about an article?"

"Yes. I'm doing a follow-up story for the Patriot Blog on the death of Chief Justice Turner. I believe my boss tried to reach you as well."

Her boss. Hawk would love that. If she told him.

If.

"I've received many calls this week."

"I'm sure." But since she had him, she wasn't letting him cut loose. "Since the Court was about to rule on whether Donazem's patent hearing would be granted, I thought you might want to comment. From my research, I see that Donazem is your baby."

And your cash cow.

"It certainly is. I have an entire team responsible for the success—or failure—of the drug. But yes, I call the shots."

"Dr. Block, would you have some time today to meet me for a short interview?"

Another thing Hawk would love. If she could set a meeting with Dr. Block, she'd get Hawk to tag along with her. Maybe she'd go all FBI on this thing and wear a wire so Hawk could listen.

"An interview? Today?"

"Yes, sir. As I said, I'm on deadline. But I'm just fascinated by the work you do. We could get some pictures of you to run with the story." Yada, yada, blah, blah. Stroke, stroke, stroke. "Honestly, sir, I think we could turn this into a feature on how a drug goes from development to getting approved by the FDA. I'm not sure consumers realize the rigors of the process. I know I didn't. Plus, it's certainly topical right now."

The line went quiet, but Hope waited. She'd already thrown a ton of bull at him, and if she layered any more on, he would absolutely get suspicious.

Another three seconds passed. "An interview," Dr. Block repeated. "I could make that work. I'm not in my office though. I'm on my way back from an off-site meeting in Virginia. Are you in D.C.?"

"Yes, sir."

"If you're familiar with Branchbrook Park, I could save you a trip out to the lab and meet you there in thirty minutes."

She knew the place. One of her old boyfriend's used to run there. Two hundred acres of winding paths, a few manmade lakes and various sports fields, the park was a popular attraction year round. And it was public with plenty of places for Hawk to hide while she did the interview.

"Yes. I know it."

"Park at the north entrance. About two-hundred yards in there's a statue with several picnic tables. I'll meet you there."

"I'll be there, sir. And thank you."

She disconnected and immediately dialed Hawk. Whatever he was doing with his nutty friends, he had to put it on hold. They had a doctor to interview.

For the second time in less than a week, Brice was doing a sneak and peek on a stranger's home.

This time, he had the joy of Mitch's presence.

Joy being the operative word, and not one Brice normally used for someone who irritated the hell out of him.

"Good cop or bad cop?" Mitch said.

"What?"

"You're better at bad cop, aren't you?" He rubbed a thumb under his chin, his thumbnail rasping against two-day stubble. "Problem is, that's my specialty."

Annoying cop was more like it.

Brice parked a couple houses down from the townhouse listed as Felix's address and surveyed the place. Not a dump like the cab driver's, thank goodness. "I'm just going to ask the guy a couple of questions."

"What if you don't like his answers?"

He sent Hope a quick text to let her know he'd be home—if the rundown safe house could stand in for such a thing—as soon as he could. He'd forgotten to charge his phone the night before thanks to Hope distracting him, and the battery was down to almost nothing. He turned it off; he didn't want any interruptions right now. "I'll unleash you on him."

Mitch grinned. "Now we're talking."

The two of them exited the truck and made their way up to the front door. The townhouse was brick, a steep front staircase to a door framed with a classic, white trim. Brice was about to ring the doorbell when he overheard a man's raised voice.

"You can't do that...I don't care if it's just an interview about the drug..."

Mitch and Brice exchanged a look. What drug? Donazem?

The voice was coming from his left. A long, narrow window was framed with the same white trim as the door. Brice eased next to the window, then crawled underneath to the other side. Mitch stayed put, head next to the house, listening.

They leaned in, continuing to eavesdrop, both of them scanning the neighborhood for anyone who might raise an alarm or question what they were doing. The street was quiet, most people at work.

Warren talked about screwing things up, but never said what those things were. After a couple of minutes, Brice's ear was growing chilled next to the cool bricks and his feet tired of standing motionless on the spot.

Finally, the man said something that made his ears perk up.

"...they're getting too close...the less we say..." He paused as the person on the other end spoke. "We never should have pulled him into the group. I told Chuck that. Bigley's an idiot."

Brice couldn't disagree there. But what specific Bigley-stupidity was Warren referring to?

"...nah, I told Chuck to leave that to me. I wouldn't have missed."

The cold tone of the man's voice made the hair on the back of Brice's neck rise.

Missed what?

Or was it a *whom*?

Mitch nodded at him to take a peek. Brice carefully angled his head to get a look inside.

A sheer curtain covered the window and it took time for his eyes to adjust to the dim interior, especially since he was trying not to be noticed.

A tall, slender man paced the wooden floor of what looked like the living room. The townhouse was narrow, the stairs to the second floor right inside the front door. An old, stone fireplace was directly across from the stairs with a few pieces of white Ikea furniture grouped around it. Above the mantel hung a forty-inch flatscreen. The typical layout put the kitchen in the back, the bedroom and bath upstairs.

"God, you always were full of yourself, Martin." Warren paused in his pacing, hung a hand on the mantel and shook his head. "Interview or not, you can't talk your way out of this, don't you get it? The more you say, the more likely you are to incriminate yourself, and the rest of us."

Brice's gut did the cha-cha, the feel of a scoop, of a lot of sleepless nights and endless digging, about to produce something credible. A warm shot of energy zipped along his limbs. The hair on the back of his neck wasn't just standing up now. It was positively humming.

Mitch had a knowing look in his eyes. He felt it too. "Who's Martin?" he mouthed.

"Scientist for Kenton," Brice half-mouthed, half-whispered.

And somebody was about to interview him.

Scoop.

Someone could steal his scoop.

If there was one.

He'd planned to dig deeper into the scientist, but hadn't had the time or inclination.

Until now.

From what little Brice had read, the scientist was a god in his own mind. He didn't care about research and development of drugs for the sake of helping people. He cared about creating drugs that made him superior. Drugs that created a financial windfall for Kenton Labs and himself.

"...no, whatever you do, do not meet with anyone. Yes, I know you're better than she is...and smarter." He shook his head and slammed his hand on the mantel. "Dammit, Martin, listen to what you're saying. This isn't all about you."

A long pause. "And if it's not? What if this reporter knows more than she's saying? What if she ties you to me and the bridge? Or to your stupid rantings about The First Amendment Patriot Blog and that guy?"

He seemed to blow out a long breath, his head falling back on his spine as he looked at the ceiling and listened. "Oh, you're going to take care of her? How? We can't have another body turn up right now. Until the investigation is over, we all have to lay low..."

Brice's body stilled completely. The scientist was talking about killing someone. A woman.

"Do not talk to her," Warren demanded. "Give me an hour. I'll talk to Chuck. We'll find another way."

Warren jerked the phone away from his ear as if Block had hung up on him. Then he threw the phone at the couch where it bounced off, hit the floor, and spun in circles.

Mitch made a *let's go* motion with his thumb. Brice, mind whirling, dropped and made his way back under the window. The two of them tip-toed down the steps and out of the yard.

As he and Mitch hit the sidewalk, Mitch said, "Are you thinking what I'm thinking?"

Brice didn't answer. He turned on his phone, picking up his pace on the way to the truck. It flashed a low battery sign at him, then beeped with a missed call and voicemail message.

Hope.

He jabbed at the screen, his fat thumb missing the play button. Twice. "Goddammit."

They were nearly to the truck. The third jab made the connection.

"Hawk, it's me," her sexy voice burst from the phone. "I've got a lead! I'm meeting Dr. Block, you know the scientist guy who developed Donazem? He agreed to talk to me. I know you wanted me to stay at the safe house, but this could be good. I'm being careful and wearing baggy clothes and your hat and sunglasses. Plus, he's meeting me at Branchbrook Park. Totally public like the monument. I'll text you as soon as I get there and if you get this message in time, meet me there. Just don't do that thing like you did when we first met Tony, okay? It's very intimidating. Okay, love ya. Bye."

His brain short-circuited for half a second. He stopped walking and stared at the phone. ...*love ya.*

Love love ya or just a friendly, *we-have-amazing-sex* love ya?

Mitch cleared his throat. He already had his door open and stood on the boost step, looking at Brice over the doorframe. "She okay?"

"What?"

"Hope. Is she okay?"

Brice snapped back to reality, a sense of urgency and fear racing down his spine. The interview. The reporter. Dr. Block.

Her message was time stamped twenty minutes ago. She must have called right after he turned off his phone.

Like Felix Warren, Brice wanted to throw the phone.

He hit the call back number. Hope's phone rang. And rang. And went to voicemail.

Brice climbed into the driver's seat and gunned the motor. "She's meeting Martin Block at Branchbrook Park."

"Fuck," Mitch said. "And let me guess, she's not answering your calls."

Brice stared straight ahead, his limbs and organs—his very cells—seemingly frozen in fear.

And then, miracle of miracles, his phone rang.

The most beautiful sound in the world.

"Babe, where are you? Are you at the park? Whatever you do, don't meet with Martin Block. Turn around right now and go back to the safe house."

"Brennan, it's Gerard." The man's deep voice threw Brice for a loop. "What the hell are you talking about? Where's Hope? Isn't she with you? I've been calling her and all I get is voicemail. She wanted me to look into Dr. Block's financials. He's got a farm north of the city that's about to go into foreclosure."

Cold sweat broke out along Brice's hairline. He threw the truck into drive. "The scientist is in on it, Tony. Hope's meeting him and I think he's going to kill her."

"Go!" Mitch said, tapping the dash.

"Where?" Gerard said in Brice's ear. "Where is she meeting him?"

Too late, too late, too late. The words churned in his head. "Branchbrook Park."

"I'll meet you there."

The connection went dead.

And then so did his phone.

Brice let it slide from his ear and land on the seat. "I can't lose her," he mumbled. "I just found her."

Mitch had his own cell out and was dialing someone. Probably Grey. "You're not going to lose her. Now speed the hell up, Brennan."

Brice gripped the wheel, shoving aside the emotions battering around inside his chest. *I will not lose her,* he told himself, flooring the gas pedal.

Love ya.

Ah, Hope.

I love you.

Hawk's paranoia was rubbing off.

That was the only explanation Hope could accept when she hustled down the apartment's steps, baseball cap, big sunglasses and a change of clothes tucked into her tote bag. She had the whole plan ready. She'd scoot in the back door of the nail salon, hop into their restroom, do a quick change, slap the cap and sunglasses on and stroll out the front door.

If someone watched—the optimist in her wanted to believe that wasn't the case—hopefully her Clark Kent routine would throw them off. Then again, what was the point of a safe house if someone had located them? And, if the killer *had* located them, by now, she'd be dead.

D.E.A.D.

Still, employing relatively easy evasion techniques couldn't hurt.

Quick change complete, to further ensure she didn't raise any suspicion, she stopped at the front desk of the salon, made an appointment for later in the day, slapped her hat and glasses on and sauntered out the front door.

Her car was parked around the corner. The car would be her only weak point. If someone were watching, they'd see her drive off, something she shouldn't risk, but choices were limited and they had a murder to solve.

Wasn't like she could take a cab or a bus to a park. How would she get back?

Plus, hello, *safe house.*

She had to be overthinking this. Being in the safe house—and still being among the living—meant no bad guys had located them and thus, driving her own vehicle would be acceptable to Mr. Paranoid.

Hope kept moving, her pace steady but not fast. Nothing to draw attention. Eyes forward, she zoomed in on her car just half a block away.

She could do this. She'd just slip in and drive off. Hopefully without a tail.

Hands still in her jacket pockets, she wrapped her fingers around her key fob, found the button on the right and gave it a double click.

Mid-morning traffic had slowed enough that only four cars sat stacked at the light. A cabbie honked at another driver as he roared through the intersection. Yelling from the offended driver—thank you, sir—created enough of a distraction that the handful of pedestrians all turned their attention to the clamor. A stream of obscenities flew. Hope kept moving. So close now. Three more strides and another round of swearing and she slipped into her car while the show from the cabbie raged on.

Road rage. Who knew it could occasionally serve a purpose?

Once inside, she hit the lock, fired the engine and edged out of her parking space, checking her mirrors, quickly scanning her surroundings. Nothing unusual. Except for the argument brewing on the opposite side of the street.

Hope kept driving, headed straight down the street away from the safe house, checking her mirrors, making a random left, checking her mirrors again. No cars followed.

At least that she could see.

Safe house.

She squeezed the steering wheel a little tighter, let out a breath and headed for Branchbrook Park.

MISTY EVANS & ADRIENNE GIORDANO

Fifteen minutes later, she parked just inside the North entrance to the park where two minivans and an SUV—probably soccer moms out for a stroll—lined up alongside the grass connecting the walking path. A red Porsche was parked opposite of the mom-mobiles and that thing stuck out like nobody's business. Clearly, someone was making a statement.

Not seeing Hawk's truck amongst the few cars scattered within the two-dozen spaces, she checked her voicemail and texts. She hadn't heard any alerts, but it wouldn't be the first time her cell service had disappointed her.

Voicemail and texts were a bust. No Hawk. Where was he and why wasn't he returning her damned call?

Unless he was on his way. Yes. On his way.

Stowing her phone in her tote, she stepped out of the car, buttoned her trench and inhaled a good dose of the fifty-three degree air. If nothing else, it would be a lovely spring day in D.C.

"Ms. Denby?" Someone called to her from the opposite row of parking spaces.

She turned, spotted the man she'd seen on the internet. Martin Block strode toward her in a black suit, the jacket flapping open as he approached. His sandy blond hair was combed back, gelled into place and if she'd run into him on the street she'd have pegged him as a banker. A scientist? Never.

"Dr. Block?"

An easy smile drifted across his face, the look so kind and effortless she immediately relaxed. This would be an easy task. She'd ask a few leading questions, get him to chatting about the success of Donazem and—wham—she'd ask about Charley Winslow and his efforts to win them a patent extension.

If she did this well, Dr. Block might give her another lead that would help them figure out who played what role in the Chief Justice's death.

That's all she needed. Another lead. She shut her car door,

hit the button on the fob just as Dr. Block reached her and extended his hand.

"Hello." She clasped his hand and the warmth of his palm traveled up her arm.

She pasted on one of her bright and cheery smiles. That's what normal people did when they met people.

They greeted them. Shared a pleasant hello and if they were anything like her, offered the benefit of believing they might in fact be a decent person.

Perky Hope.

Doing her thing.

A light breeze blew the ends of her hair against her cheek and she shoved them back, out of her face still shielded under the baseball cap and glasses. A week ago she wouldn't have believed she'd show up for a business meeting wearing a baseball cap.

How life changed in days.

Dr. Block released her hand and another gust of wind blew, this time harder and whether it was the lack of warmth from Block releasing her hand or her minimal layers, she shivered a little.

She glanced up at the much bigger man, met his gaze and stilled. Now, after all that pleasant hand shaking and smiling and warmth, for the first time, she saw something in his dark eyes. Something cold and...harsh.

Impenetrable.

And—wow—the realization that she stood in the nearly vacant parking lot of a three-hundred acre park with a man she'd never met before most definitely cracked her across the skull.

What had she done?

The better question? Where the hell was Hawk? Thanks to him and his crazy paranoia, she'd suddenly started doubting people based on the color of their eyes? Really?

Another breeze smacked against the branches of the huge Willow Oak above her, drawing her attention up and away from the creepy eyes of Dr. Block. A bird—a Starling maybe—sat on one of the branches and tweeted. At least until shooting off across the pond just beyond the walkway. Maybe the Starling had the right idea.

That, or Hawk's paranoia had rubbed off on her.

What have I done?

From the corner of her eye, she spotted Dr. Block moving and instinctively stepped back.

In his left hand, he held something small and white that resembled one of the breath spray devices she kept in her purse.

A few seconds ago, he hadn't been holding anything. More importantly, if it was breath spray why wouldn't he have dealt with that before getting out of his car?

The bird definitely had the right idea.

Hawk. Should have waited.

"You stupid girl," Block said. "Didn't your mother ever teach you not to meet strange men alone?"

Every nerve inside her sparked and snapped and an explosion of pain erupted inside her head.

Run.

She lurched sideways, about to bolt, but Block raised his arm and a stream of something, light particles floating on the air, hit her, splaying across her cheek in a light, odorless veil of moisture. Her skin tingled and she swiped at it, immediately transferring the tingle to her fingertips.

What the heck? She wiped her hand on her trench. "Hey," she said. "What was that?"

A tickle caught in her throat. She coughed once, then again, but—no good. A wave of dizziness assaulted her and Dr. Block swayed back and forth. She blinked three times, one, two, three, refocused on Dr. Block, on the cars behind him, anything stationary that would anchor her. No good. Spinning, spinning, spinning. Her stomach flip-flopped while her tongue nearly shriveled from thirst. All at once, her senses went to overload and she shook her head, held out her hand, as if to grab on to something, anything that would keep her upright.

A burst of panic shot up her neck and her skin burned, a searing heat that should have melted her flesh, but underneath, a fierce cold penetrated. Mixed signals. Everything haywire.

No. No. No.

"Just relax," Block said. A distorted, creepy grin slid across his face. "In a few seconds this will all be over."

24

*F*ear.

Brice hated fear more than anything in the world.

The sting of it cramped his stomach, the grip of it tightened the muscles in his neck like a vise grip. Oh yeah, he hated it with a passion.

After the shit with the ATF, he'd told himself he would never feel this kind of fear again. Never watch a friend die again. Never believe in the goodness of the world again.

And he certainly would never allow himself to feel anything for anybody again.

Because feeling lead to fear. Fear lead to pain. Pain led to loss.

At that moment, he was feeling all three. What was wrong with him that he was unable to stay focused and unattached during this investigation? Why the hell had he let himself fall in love with Hope?

Her car was parked in a spot under a shade tree, but she wasn't in it.

And Brice's heart was nearly beating through his chest, thanks to his arch nemesis, fear. "Where is she?"

His world was about leads and conspiracies. Government cover-ups. Dry, emotionless facts.

And yet, here he was, nearly blinded with fear, and discovering a deep-seeded loathing for himself.

I didn't protect her. All of this, all the shit I've survived, and I let her walk into a trap.

Hadn't he learned his lesson with the ATF?

Mitch checked, and sure enough, the doors of the car were locked up tight.

Brice cupped his hands around his mouth. "Hope?" he called, praying against the awful rot-gut feeling flooding through him that she was simply out walking in the park. That they had gotten to her before Martin Block did.

Her name, a noun and a verb that hadn't been in his vocabulary until he'd met her, slammed through the trees and faded into silence. Mitch took up the call as well.

"*Hope!*"

"*Hope!*"

"*Hope,*" they kept calling, even after there was no response.

The park was empty, except for a few mothers with young kids and a couple of hikers.

The past few days played out in Brice's head, a damning loop of information that he hadn't tied together until now.

He leaned over the trunk of Hope's car, tried to force air into his lungs. "Tell me she did not go off with Block willingly."

"There was no sign of a struggle," Mitch said.

Brice grabbed Mitch's phone and called her again. The call went directly to voicemail.

A black SUV came roaring into the parking lot. Tony Gerard.

He took off his sunglasses and rolled down his window. "Where is she?

Brice let out a soft curse. How could she be so naive to go off with a stranger? "No idea. We believe she's gone with the scientist, but we don't know where. There's no sign of struggle, but we know Block is up to no good. She's still not answering her phone, and I'm..."

"Worried," Gerard supplied. "You fucking should be. She's gutsy, but naive. No telling what she's gotten herself into."

Fuck. Brice wanted to ram his fist into the bed of his truck, let off some frustrations, but a few broken digits wouldn't do him any good.

A ringing came from Mitch's phone. Not Hope. It was Teeg. Mitch snatched the phone from Brice. "Yo," he said by way of greeting. "What'cha got for me? Is it up and scanning?"

Gerard spoke to Brice. "You think Block would hurt her?"

While Mitch talked to Teeg, Brice filled Gerard in on the latest. "The cab driver, Lamar Kostas, along with Charley Winslow and the DDOT guy, Felix Warren, all went to school together. They were part of a high school competitive shooting team." He pointed at Mitch. "We were just at Felix's house, and overheard him talking to Block. They know we're onto them, me and Hope. Dr. Block set up a fake interview with her, but he wasn't planning on talking, if you know what I mean."

Gerard's grip on the steering wheel tightened. His jaw locked for a second and he scanned the area. "So someone in that group killed Turner and now they've got Hope?"

Brice nodded, the fear once again cramping his stomach. *I failed to keep her safe. This is on me.*

"Block has a horse farm about twelve miles west of here that's up for sale. Has been for a while," Gerard told him. "It looks abandoned from what I saw on Google Maps. Block bought the place for his wife ten years ago but she died last year and he let it go. Ironically, she was on his miracle drug, Donazem. If I wanted to make someone disappear, a place like that would be perfect."

Mitch snapped his fingers at Brice to get his attention. "The drone is half a mile out. Where do you want Teeg to send it?"

"Drone?" Gerard said, at the same time Brice felt a spark of optimism.

Teeg's drone. It could fly over the area and look for Hope. "What's the address of the farm?" he said to Gerard.

Gerard put the SUV in reverse. "It's the only one on 9 Mile Way. Forty acres with two giant horse barns, a carriage house, and a covered round pen. You can't miss it."

Mitch nodded and relayed the info to Teeg. Brice hustled back to his truck. "Do you know what type of vehicle Block drives?"

Gerard flipped on his sunglasses and nodded. "He has three vehicles registered to him. A black Escalade, a red Porsche, a white TT Cruiser."

Overhead, the buzz of a propeller made all three men look up.

The drone zoomed by, tipping its wings before disappearing over the tree line.

"I'll head that way," Gerard said. "Text me if you get a hit."

Mitch and Brice jumped in Brice's truck. Mitch was staring at this phone's screen. "Damn, that thing is fast."

Brice leaned over. "You're getting video feed from the drone?"

"Teeg is streaming it directly to my phone. It's already six miles from here, and lookie there..."

Mitch pointed to the screen. The aerial view from the drone's camera was clear as a bell. A small red car was flying up the highway.

The drone seemed to drop elevation, zeroing in on the vehicle's back end. Brice's stomach contracted. The muscles in his neck tightened another notch. "Red Porsche Carrera."

"Let's go," Mitch said, grabbing his seat belt.

Brice had already put the truck in gear and was wheeling out of the parking lot.

Hope awakened to a wicked case of stomach heaves. She gagged once, fought the rising bile in her throat and swallowed it back.

Arms.

She shifted, but her arms wouldn't move and her hands had fallen asleep. She looked down, waited a few seconds for her blurry vision to clear and hone in on her wrists where gouging pain cut into them. She wiggled her fingers to get some blood moving and reduce the pricklies.

Where?

Zip-tied. Her wrists were zip-tied to the arms of a chair. Wooden chair. Heavy. From a dining set. Where the hell was she?

Head throbbing, she rested her head against the high-backed chair and ticked back to the park, meeting Dr. Block, the creepy feeling, the breath spray.

The spray.

What have I done?

Piercing whacks ripped through her head and she squeezed her eyes closed. Whatever he'd sprayed her with had cold-cocked her. Bam. She'd gone out. And the after-effects? No picnic.

"Help," she said, her voice more of a croak than any kind of demand.

Her tongue was huge and dry in her mouth. At least it felt huge. Swelled. Most definitely. She opened her mouth again, stretched her tongue, testing it. If she could reach up and touch it she would have done so, just to get a sense of whether it was, in fact, giant or whether the extreme parch led her to believe it.

So thirsty.

"Help," she called again. This time louder.

Getting her bearings, she scanned the room. Some sort of study with an oversized, dust-covered desk and empty book shelves lining the walls. In the corner sat a clump of what appeared to be covered furniture. Two narrow windows just beyond had blinds pulled low, blocking her view of the outside. She breathed in, felt the dry dust travel down her throat and coughed. Wherever she was, it hadn't been cleaned in a while.

House.

Block's?

The crushing pain in her head subsided for a few seconds. Brief, but long enough for her to know that yes, she was alone, tied to a chair and most definitely not in the place where she'd told Hawk he could find her.

Whatever this was, she was on her own.

And tied to a chair.

But her legs were free. *Think.* Ignoring the tingling in her hands, she gripped the front of the seat where her hands were bound, tried to wrap her fingers all the way around it for lever- age. Damned tiny hands wouldn't reach that far.

Make it work.

She jerked up, tried to stand, her fingers taking the brunt of the pressure from the weight of the wooden chair. *Slipping.* Only the front legs lifted and she gripped tighter and tighter —*come on, come on.* The back legs scraped against the wood floor and she stretched her fingers apart. Better grip. That's all she needed.

After readjusting her hands, she lifted again. *Won't work.* Her hands were too far forward for her to balance the weight of the heavy chair.

"Don't bother. You're not going anywhere."

Hope found Martin Block leaning casually against the archway leading to a hall. Watching the whole show.

What the hell was he doing?

"This might be a stupid question," she said, "but are you insane? I told people I was meeting you."

Block grinned. "And I will tell them we had our meeting and I left. There are no security cameras at the park and I'm a distinguished scientist. You're a young, stupid girl who chose to wander a city park alone." He swiped his hands together. "None of this comes back to me."

Meaning, Hope wouldn't be leaving. At least not outside of a body bag.

Block boosted off the archway, stuck his hands into his pockets and entered the room. "The plan was near perfect. Except for that idiot Bigley." He waggled one finger. "I knew he'd be a problem. All that moron had to do was get Turner to assign him our case. That's all."

"But," Hope said, "Turner assigned Kenton Labs to someone else."

"Exactly, my point. Quarter of a million dollars should have guaranteed it. He assured me it wouldn't be a problem."

Quarter of a million... Dear God. Hope closed her eyes. Joel Bigley's mistakes obviously didn't end with accepting a trip from Winslow. She opened her eyes again, watched Block wander to the desk just a few feet from her and prop on the edge.

"You paid him to come up with and provide Turner with a sound argument for extending the patent?"

"You bet your ass we did."

"Who?"

He waved that off. "Doesn't matter now, but you could figure it out if you tried."

"Like I figured out that you receive a bonus based on Donazem's total sales. And the lobbyist. Charley Winslow. He stood to make a bundle."

Block waggled his finger again, a twisted grin lighting up his face. "Now you're getting it."

"And then there are the stock options."

Block held his hands in prayer, did a little bow. "I knew you were a smart girl."

She sure was. All that reading she'd done on Dr. Block and Donazem told her the drug had taken fourteen years to come to fruition. A three-billion-dollar cash cow. Dr. Block wouldn't want to give up on that.

Block raised his arms. "Donazem bought me this farm. It bought me a career and a life. It's my baby. And no one gets to take it from me."

The room went quiet, but the wind, that same wind from earlier, had picked up and rattled against the windows. She wiggled her fingers, got some blood moving again.

"Please," she said, "would you untie me? Just for a minute. The plastic is painful."

"Tell me who you told about me."

"About you?"

"You called me for an interview. Something led you to me. Who knows? Who are these people you told about me?"

A piercing blare sounded from the outer hall and Block launched off the desk, snatched his cell phone from his pocket. Block's lips pressed into a tight line.

"Goddammit," he said.

He snatched scissors from the desk drawer, slamming it shut and rushed toward her, his movements hard and jerking as he slid the scissors against her skin. She flinched at the cold metal, but gripped the cushion, forcing herself still.

"What are you doing?"

"Shut up."

The blaring noise continued as he snapped the second zip-tie, grabbed her by the arm just above her elbow and hauled her to her feet.

"Try anything and I'll kill you. Now let's go."

He squeezed her arm tighter, the tips of his fingers ripping into her flesh as she stumbled to keep up.

"What's that noise?"

"Motion detectors. Someone just climbed the east fence. Looks like your boyfriend is here."

Hawk.

He'd found her. Relief mixed with fear. Block was seriously unhinged. Whatever his plan was, she didn't think he intended on her leaving this farm alive. He couldn't risk her going to the police.

And now, Hawk had inserted himself into the middle of it. Block would kill them both. No doubt.

At the hallway, Block turned right, dragging Hope toward the back of the house, through the kitchen to an oversized mudroom with an outside door. He flipped the lock, shoved her through. Ten yards in front of them, a driveway wrapped from the front of the house to a barn and a battered work truck.

Freedom.

"We're getting in that truck. Try anything and I'll hit you hard enough to knock you out for a week. Understood?"

Hope nodded, but her mind reeled. *Freedom. Hawk.*

Block gripped her tighter, hurrying her along and she stumbled, the momentum carrying enough force that she went down, breaking the contact with Block.

Run.

She kicked out, drove the heel of her flat shoe right into his knee. The knee buckled and he howled.

"Goddammit!"

On all fours, Hope scrambled, her shoes sliding against the cold pavers as she got to her feet. Had to get away. The knee wouldn't incapacitate Block. She knew it. Hadn't kicked him hard enough for that.

Weapon. She needed one.

She took off toward the barn. One door was cracked open

and she squeezed through, shutting it behind her. A stream of light shined in a high window illuminating the space enough for her to see. On the wall hung various tools. Scythes, saws, sickles. Exceptional weapons. Sickle. That was the one. Small enough for her to hold in one hand and easy to maneuver.

She just needed to avoid falling again and slicing herself open.

A squeak. Behind her. The door.

She turned.

Block stood in the doorway, one door half open, his body backlit by the outside light. She raised the sickle, jabbed it toward him.

"Ms. Denby, don't be stupid. Put that down before you hurt yourself."

Stupid. Ha. One thing she'd never been was stupid. The brilliant doctor was about to learn that.

"Come near me and I'll gut you."

"Barn. She's in the small barn on the south side." Brice hopped another wooden fence, his breath coming hard as he relayed instructions to Mitch and Tony, who were coming at the place from opposite sides.

With only three of them, it was challenging to keep all the house exits in sight, but he'd been lucky. He'd seen Hope jet out the side door of the house as he approached. She'd hightailed it across the lawn to the nearest barn. "Block is following her."

"Roger that," Gerard said. The three of them were connected via earpieces Mitch had grabbed before leaving the armory. *Never leave home without 'em, he'd claimed.* "Weapons?"

Brice hit the edge of the utility barn, flattened his body against it and lowered his voice. "None that I saw, but we can't be too careful."

"I'm armed." A grunt, as if he, too, had just jumped something. "I'm approaching from the north. I'll wait for your lead."

After all this time, and all the fighting against working with anyone, here he was with a partner. Two to be exact.

"I'm armed as well." He saw a flash of Mitch sneaking around to his right. "I'm in position."

Great. I'm the only one who's not armed. The barn door was two feet away. Brice inched closer, heard the low sound of Block speaking, then Hope's reply and the scientist's laugh.

Another inch. The door was ajar. If he could take Block by surprise, he wouldn't need a weapon.

Wind blew through his hair. Mitch, now appearing at the opposite corner, had a sleek Glock in hand, pointed at the sky.

Brice crept the last few centimeters and peeked into the barn.

The interior was half in shadows, a few rays of sunlight coming through small, square windows, high on the walls. The scientist blocked Brice's view, but he saw a flash of blond hair behind the man and the glint of sunlight off metal.

Hope.

The previous fear was replaced with anger. White-hot and all encompassing, Brice balled his hands into fists and squeezed hard. Martin Block was no longer a person.

He was a target.

Medium height. The coat hid his frame, but Brice guessed his weight at a hundred-and-fifty, maybe a hundred-and-sixty pounds. Non-military.

Easy target.

"I assume these men trespassing on my property know all about Charley's little scheme?" Block was saying.

"*Charley's* scheme?" Hope took a step back. "Donazem was your baby, your cash cow. Seems like you had as much, if not more, to lose as Charley Winslow."

"If you say so."

"Oh, hold on."

"Shut up, Ms. Denby."

"Charley knew the right people to make it happen. So, maybe you suggested something and Charley put the players onto the chessboard. What about the cabbie and the shooter? Did he line them up? Or was that you? After all," Hope said, her tone goading. "You're the brilliant one. And with the money he stood to make, he needed that patent as much as you did."

Block advanced a step and Hope moved back, matching him but shifting to the scientist's left enough that Brice could see her face. She held a sickle in her hands and swung it, although awkwardly, as if she'd never held one before. "Stay away from me! I know Krav Maga!"

When this was over, he was teaching her some actual Krav moves.

Her face was set, but he knew her well enough to see the strain of fear behind her assertive body posture. A renewed fury burned through his veins.

I'll kill him.

"I'm afraid I can't let you go until I know if you have any real proof," Block said, closing the gap between them. "And if this is going to blow up, I need to be far away from here as soon as possible."

"Where are you going?" Hope asked. "Barbados? They have an extradition treaty with the U.S. You won't be safe there."

Her brashness nearly made Brice laugh. She was right, of course.

He still couldn't tell if Block was armed, but if he was, the gun was still under his coat somewhere, not in his hands.

No time like the present.

He nodded at Mitch and signaled he was going in.

Mitch gave him a chin cock. Go.

Brice stepped inside. "We have plenty of proof, you asshole, and I'm taking it straight to the Justice Department when I'm finished with you."

"Brice!" Hope yelled.

Brice. Not Hawk.

As expected, Block whirled in Brice's direction. Only then did Brice see the gun as the man went to pull it from his waistline where it was secured by his belt.

Hope saw it too. As Brice launched himself forward to grab the gun from Block's hand, Hope bought the sickle around.

It was a cacophony of errors.

The sickle blade made contact with Brice's bicep, splitting open his shirt and ripping a long gash of his skin. It then stabbed Block in the ribcage just as Block jerked the gun free.

The man howled, the gun went off, and Brice seized the weapon, all at the same time.

A sharp pain hit the top of his foot as the bullet zinged through bones and tendons. He gasped at the burning sting but held onto the gun, wrestling with Block, and sending the man to the floor.

"Oh, my God!" Hope yelled.

His instincts kicked in. Brice grabbed the man's wrist and landed a sucker punch to his stomach.

Hope yelled again, "What I should I do?"

Blood from Brice's arm and Block's rib was everywhere, making Brice's hands slippery. Block tried to roll his body like an alligator.

From his peripheral vision, Brice saw Hope take another swing. He ducked to the side, barely getting out of the way. "What the hell are you doing?"

The sickle blade landed next to Block's ear. He yelled and the gun went off again, just as Mitch came hauling ass inside. The bullet ricocheted off the door, right above Mitch's head.

Mitch jumped back. "Fuck!"

Hope brought the sickle up again. "I'm helping you!"

Mitch was aiming for Block, except Brice had to shift again, more from the flying sickle in Hope's hand than from the wriggling, fighting scientist, blocking Mitch's shot. "Well, stop," Brice said to Hope. "I've got him."

And he did. He raised the hand with the gun and slammed it into the floor, breaking the scientist's hold. The gun went spinning away, and Mitch jumped forward at the same time Hope dropped the sickle and went for it.

At that moment, Gerard came busting in from the other end, gun raised.

Except it wasn't Gerard.

"Hold it right there," Felix Warren said, looking down the nose of a .40 caliber Smith & Wesson as he stalked toward them.

Mitch's weapon went back into action mode, aiming at Felix. He motioned Hope behind him, and miracle of miracles, she went. "Put your weapon down," Mitch said.

Where the hell was Gerard?

"I don't think so," Felix said to Mitch, and then he motioned for Brice to move. "Get off him."

Brice raised his hands in the air and rose to his knees. Blood ran down his arm and dripped on the floor as Block shuffle-kicked away from him, grabbing at his torn shirt and the blood running from his injury. "I'll need stitches!"

Fucking baby. Brice had a bullet lodged in his foot and a serious gash in his arm. Not that he hadn't been shot before, but seriously?

Felix gave his partner in crime a disgusted look. "You've done it now, moron. You've put us all in a real mess.

"Shut up." Block slowly gained his feet. He was brushing dust and hay off his coat and didn't see Gerard slip in behind Felix, quiet as a cat. "Charley didn't hire you for your brains. He hired you to clean up the messes. So..."

A sharp snap pierced the air. A handgun racking a bullet to

the barrel. Both Felix and Block froze. Block's head whipped around.

Gerard's lips slid into a faint smile. He was holding a semi-automatic H&K a few inches from Felix's head. "I don't really like messes, so I suggest neither of you move or we'll have one big fucking mess."

Felix slowly lowered his weapon. Brice grabbed Block, and when the guy struggled, he punched him in the jaw. Nice. That idiot would not learn.

Block swayed on his feet, his eyes rolling up in his head. A second later, he fell to the floor, lights out.

Mitch moved toward Felix. "Drop it."

Brice half-walked, half-hopped in front of Hope, shielding her from Felix's weapon in case he decided not to cooperate. The guy's lips thinned, but he followed instructions when Gerard tapped the muzzle of the gun against the back of his head.

Inch by inch, Felix lowered the gun to the floor.

"Kick it away," Gerard told him.

He did so, the gun skittering across the floor to Brice. Mitch picked it up, never taking his aim off Felix.

Without warning, Gerard raised his H&K, took his finger off the trigger, and knocked Felix on top of the head. The guy did a good imitation of Block and crumpled to the floor, just like his buddy.

Gerard stared down at Felix. "That was for my friend, Justice Turner, you asshole."

Brice, feeling a blast of relief, turned to Hope. "Are you okay, babe?"

Okay or not, she rushed him, jumping into his arms. "I'm so sorry!"

His bad foot and her sudden weight nearly toppled them. Brice gripped her tight, reveling in the hair that tickled his nose and the smell of her. "It's okay. Everything's okay." He muzzled her ear. "Except my arm where you cut me," he teased. "And my foot where, because of your help, I took a bullet."

She drew back, scanning him from head to toe. "Oh, my God, I am so, so sorry."

"And I am so never letting you live this one down, Woodward."

The feisty Hope, the one he loved so much, rose to the surface. She smacked his good arm. "You're terrible! And I was trying to help."

Mitch was calling Grey, who Brice figured would call the police or the FBI or whoever needed to come pick up the two men. And find Lamar Kostas before he went into the wind. Gerard moved Felix, dragging him across the floor by one arm, next to Block and zip-tying their hands.

Brice felt a little woozy, either from blood loss or relief. He tweaked Hope's chin. "I wasn't bluffing to Block. I've got the proof we need."

She flew into his arms again, hugging him tight. "You're a damn good investigative blogger, Brice Brennan."

He was just glad she was safe. They had to work on her survival instincts.

Block coughed and moaned, blinking himself awake and trying to sit up. "I'm...innocent," he muttered, his eyes not quite focusing yet. "It was all them. I'm a renowned scientist. I want... to cut...a deal."

Well, he hadn't lost his ego, that was for sure. As if being a famous scientist meant he could commit crimes without being held accountable for them.

Hope turned loose of Brice and stood over Block with her hands on her hips. "I've got news for you, buddy. You drugged me and tried to kill me! If nothing else, you're going to jail for that."

Atta girl. Brice pulled her to him. "Let's go home, Woodward."

She looked into his eyes. "Was there something you wanted to say to me, Bernstein? We never finished that talk."

There was something he wanted to say to her all right. "Brat."

She bit her bottom lip and shook her head. "I don't think that was it."

"Really, here? You want me to bare my soul in front of those two?" He jerked a thumb at Mitch and Gerard, both watching intently. Waiting.

"This is better than reality TV," Gerard said to Mitch.

"Ain't it though?" Mitch nodded at Brice. "Go ahead. You certainly eavesdropped enough on my embarrassing moments with Caroline when we were in New Mexico. Seems like my turn, now."

Brice sighed. "I guess everyone knows anyway."

"Yep," Hope said. "Even Block guessed you were my boyfriend. You may be good at undercover ops, but you suck at love."

Love. The word made him do a knee-jerk cringe inside.

But he did love her, and the cringe morphed into a warm, solid feeling in the center of his chest.

He tugged on a lock of hair. "Fine. I care about you."

"You *care*. Come on, Hawk. I'm a journalist at heart. I know there's more to this story."

In the distance, he heard the sound of sirens. Or maybe that was his mind playing tricks on him, warning him away.

He ignored the sirens. Ignored Mitch and Gerard. He even ignored the pain in his arm and foot. Staring into Hope's eyes, he smiled at her. "I love you, Hope Denby."

She grinned from ear to ear, threw her arms around his neck and popped a kiss on him. "I love you, too, Bernstein. Now let's get you to the hospital."

25

wo days later

"What's the password?" Mitch's voice came from the speaker at the closed gate of the Bat Cave.

Brice, window down, held up his middle finger.

"Come on, man. I brought you balloons after your surgery."

Brice's foot had needed microsurgery to remove the bullet and repair some damage. He was supposed to hit physical therapy later that day, which he dreaded, but at least Grey had broken him out of the hospital twenty-four hours after he'd entered. "They were pink and one said 'Happy Sweet 16.'"

"They were the only ones left in the gift shop."

Liar. The hospital gift shop didn't carry birthday balloons.

In the background, Brice heard Caroline yell, "Let him in, Mitch, before I shoot you and finally be done with the whole affair."

The volume of Mitch's voice decreased, as if he'd turned his head away from the mic. "But he doesn't know the password."

"Holy atomic pile, Batman," Brice murmured.

The gate buzzed, then started to swing open. "You want to talk atomic pile," Mitch said, "wait 'til you see the pile on your desk, Brennan."

Brice drove through the gate, glad the bullet had struck his left foot and not his right. He could still drive himself around and not depend on Hope, or worse, Mitch. The bruise from Mall Cop's baton was a lovely shade of mustard yellow and still sore, but his neck was healed. The wound in his arm, courtesy of Hope, had been cleaned and stitched and was on the mend. It didn't bother him like his foot, but he sure enjoyed giving Hope hell about it.

Hope. Just the thought of her made him smile. When he'd awoke from surgery, she'd been curled up in bed with him. Her soft snores had felt normal, familiar, and he'd brushed a strand of hair from her face, thanking the universe she hadn't been hurt. He'd take a dozen more bullets to the foot if it meant keeping her safe.

They'd been pretty much inseparable since he'd left the hospital, but he could tell she was a bit adrift. Without her job or the investigation, she had a lot of pent up energy.

Of course, his injuries had garnered him a lot of sympathy and he'd used that to his advantage, taking her to bed, taking her in the shower, taking her just about anywhere and everywhere in his house to burn off her restlessness. Good thing she'd slipped off to grab a candy bar from the vending machine and hadn't heard the doctor order him not to overexert himself when the guy had released him early from the hospital.

Brice parked and hopped out of the truck, grabbing the stupid crutch he had to use since his foot was bandaged up like a fat, white marshmallow and he wasn't supposed to put weight on it. Hope had insisted on going with him to meet with the physical therapist that afternoon—one of the only reasons he'd go at all.

First, he had to check in with his boss. Aka, Batman.

The side door of the armory creaked open and Robin stood there waiting for him. Brice threw the crutch back in the truck and gritted his teeth as he hobbled over. Showing any kind of weakness to Mitch was a no-no. He'd never live it down.

Mitch raised his voice from its deep baritone to a squeaky high soprano. "Oh, Hawk, look how manly you are walking around on your poor, injured foot!"

His impression of Hope made Brice wish he had the crutch back so he could wop Mitch.

Suddenly a hand shot forward, grabbed Mitch by the front of his shirt and jerked him inside. There was a slight commotion and then Caroline appeared in his place, recomposing herself by pulling on the bottom edges of her dark, business jacket, and giving Brice a bright smile. "Glad you made it. How's the arm?"

Brice moved it around in its socket. "May be a while before I can shoot straight, but the therapy will help."

"I'm happy to work with you, too," she said, ushering him inside. "Anytime you want to do some target practice out back, just holler."

Brice stepped across the threshold and came to a halt.

Grey, Sydney, Teeg, and Mitch were standing around his desk. The laptop was still there, along with the pile of folders Mitch had mentioned.

But there was also a new, black, leather office chair, a 27-inch screen monitor, a vase of flowers, and a big plate of chocolate chip cookies.

Someone had hung a banner from the rafters that read, "Welcome Back!"

As he stood taking it all in, they all started clapping.

Clapping. For him.

Heat rose up the back of his neck. He'd never been appreciated in his last job, and while the blog garnered a lot of fans and he appreciated their loyalty and support, it was a rush to be part of a group, he realized, of people who knew and understood him—paranoia and all—and still respected him.

In fact, they even seemed to *like* him.

The clapping died off and Caroline pinched Mitch in his side. "Apologize."

Mitch flinched and smacked her hand away. "For what? For giving him grief about Hope? That's what guys do, Caroline."

Sydney, on the other side of Mitch, pinched him as well. "Apologize."

"Jesus, fucking A," Mitch said. He rolled his eyes at Brice and opened his mouth to do what the ladies ordered when Brice held up a hand and stopped him.

"Don't. Just don't." He hobbled over to his desk, Sydney's cookies calling to him. He snagged one and took a bite. "As long as he has my back when push comes to shove," he told the group, "we're good. Right, Robin?"

Mitch looked confused. "Robin?"

Brice waved him off, spoke to Grey. "What's the status of Winslow and the others?"

Grey went into Fed mode. "Dr. Martin Block did as he said and cut a plea deal with the Attorney General. He was furious with Justice Turner for his comments regarding the need for cheaper generics all citizens can afford. He didn't believe Turner would allow the Donazem case to make it in front of the Court this spring. He pressured Charley Winslow to find a solution. Winslow bribed Joel Bigley to feed him information about Justice Turner's intentions and when they found out Turner planned to deny the case, Winslow concocted a plan to have the Justice murdered."

Swallowing the bite of cookie, Brice said, "And he hired Felix Warren, the DDOT guy, to do the job?"

Caroline jumped in. "Yep. Turns out, one of the weapons found in Felix's residence was used in another murder. Apparently, he has a side gig doing murders for hire. His DDOT job allowed him to close that lane. He disguised himself and had Lamar Kostas take him to the bridge in Lamar's cab that morning. They'd mapped out Turner's commute to and from home and picked the bridge as the best place for the road rage incident to occur. Felix and Lamar are busy pointing fingers at Winslow and Block, who are pointing fingers back, but they're all facing a long stint in federal prison. We're still not sure which one posted the target on the Patriot Blog logo, but Warren claims it was Doc Block playing with Photoshop."

"And you," Sydney tapped a folded newspaper on Brice's desk, "received recognition in today's *Post*, along with Hope, for uncovering the real crime."

His heart sank to his knees. He hadn't paid attention to the newspapers. He and Hope had drafted a post for the Patriot, and he'd been caught up in the success of the reveal from the moment it went viral fifteen minutes after Hope hit upload.

A new record for him and the blog.

Now he read the section of print Sydney was pointing to, and relief swamped him. He wasn't named except as "Hawkeye", owner of The Patriot Blog. Further down, Hope had also escaped public exposure. She was credited as "an unnamed source, formerly an employee of the United States Supreme Court."

Nowhere was Lodestone mentioned or even hinted at, mostly because Brice never mentioned him, even as a source. Now, Hope had become his Deep Throat.

Still, Brice owed the guy. Maybe someday, he could do something for Lodestone.

Glancing up, Brice shot Grey an inquisitive look. "This investigation was a team effort. You sure you're okay with me and my 'unnamed source' taking all the credit?"

Grey's expression didn't change. "Your blog thrives on notoriety. We want the blog, and you, to continue succeeding. The

MISTY EVANS & ADRIENNE GIORDANO

Justice Team has to operate behind the scenes, but your blog doesn't. It may come in handy for us in the future if we need something to go public."

"For propaganda purposes? I don't know about that."

Grey's answer was a shrug. "Not in the manner you're thinking, but if it helps us solve a case by misleading the higher powers that be...?" He let the idea trail off. "I'm not above using every tool in my toolbox to solve cases."

Justice. Brice needed to remember the purpose of working with this team. A purpose he'd dedicated his life to. "I have some conditions before we make this official."

Grey simply looked at him, not a smidge of emotion on his face or in his straight posture.

But no argument from him either.

"First," Brice continued, "this is a part-time gig for me. My first responsibility is The First Amendment Patriot Blog. The Justice Team comes second."

"We can work with that for now." Grey glanced at Brice's bandaged foot. "You're on light duty anyway."

He had him there. "Second, I prefer to work from my house."

Caroline snorted. "I don't blame you. Those of us working here at the armory should get hazard pay for putting up with Mitch."

"Hey!" Mitch complained.

Brice had been thinking the same thing, hence his request. "Is that a problem?" he said to Grey.

Grey folded his arms and took a moment before answering. Brice felt the Batman stare trying to wear him down.

He held firm.

Teeg raised his hand as if he needed permission to speak. "I have no problem sending cases to Brice via a secure email link like I did this past week. That worked pretty well, actually."

"There's a team meeting every Monday morning," Grey

said, ignoring the computer geek. "I'll expect you to show up in person for those. Otherwise, it will be on a case-by-case basis. Since you're only doing consulting for now, I don't see why that should be an issue."

"All right then."

Caroline and Mitch exchanged a glance. "That's it?" Mitch said. He shook his head. "You should have held out for a bigger salary and paid vacation, man."

Grey had slipped him a salary number while visiting Brice in the hospital. It wasn't much by D.C. standards, but it was enough to buy Hope a sizable ring down the road if things went the way Brice planned.

"Oh." Brice snapped his fingers. "There is one last thing."

Teeg, who'd been rubbing his hands together at the idea of Brice joining them, let out a groan. "Uh, oh. Here it comes. You want access to my play station over there, don't you? I knew it. I knew one big monitor at your desk wasn't enough. You want a setup just like mine."

"I have a setup like yours—better than yours, actually—" Brice informed him. "What I want is an unlimited supply of Sydney's cookies."

He winked at her and she stepped forward and pinched his cheek. "I knew I liked you."

Everyone laughed, except for Mitch, who snagged three of said cookies from the plate and walked over to his desk where he plopped down to go back to work.

The others faded off, Sydney kissing Grey on the cheek and heading for the door. Caroline stole one of Mitch's cookies and walked over to her own desk to make a call.

Teeg returned to his "play station" and started typing on Frodo.

"As long as you're here," Grey said, "we need input on our next case."

Brice sat in his new leather chair, testing it out by rocking it back and forth a couple of times. Comfortable. Maybe even more than his own at home. He propped his foot on the desk, thinking he could actually get used to this. "What's the case involve?"

"An important, high-profile person who needs protection."

"You need a security guard?"

"More like witness protection."

"Since when is the Justice Team in the Wit Sec business?"

"We're not. This is an unusual case, not one for U.S. Marshals. I was hoping you'd do the honors, but since you're on light duty, we need someone else with the right skills. He, or she, needs to know their way around guns, have superior defensive driving skills, and have experience with personal security. Sound like anyone you know?"

Sounded like Tony Gerard's resume in a hat. "I might."

"Good. Reach out to him and see if he's interested, will you?"

Grey retreated to the back. Brice pulled out his cell phone and called Gerard. When the man answered, Brice gave him the latest update on the Turner case.

"I heard," Gerard said. "They've reinstated me, by the way, but I don't know. I'm not sure I want to go back. Turner's murder...still feels like my fault."

Maybe Gerard *wasn't* the right man for the job. "You ever think of doing something else?"

"Besides joining the Secret Service? Nope. Personal protection is what I'm good at, and in general, I like it. It's just...Turner was my friend. I feel like I let him down."

"You wouldn't be a good agent if you didn't feel responsible, Tony."

There was a pause. "Yeah, maybe you're right."

"So it's the Supreme Court or the President? Those the only two security details you're interested in?"

"I'm taking a few weeks off to figure that out. Like I told Hope, maybe I'll apply to the FBI. Why?"

"I have a proposition for you."

Another pause, this one not as long. "I'm listening."

Brice smiled up into the rafters as he rocked back in his chair. Similar to Hope with the promise of a scoop, Gerard liked a challenge. "I don't know all the details, but I'd like to put you in touch with a former FBI agent and his people who do some good work. Behind the scenes, all in the name of justice. They happen to be in need of a protection detail of your caliber and I can vouch for them being stand-up people. You've met one of them already." He let Gerard digest that for a moment. "What do you say? You interested?"

"Will Hope vouch for this group?"

Brice laughed. "She will indeed."

"Good enough for me, then. Give the guy my number. No promises, but I'll talk to him."

They said their goodbyes. As Brice signed off, his phone buzzed with a text. Hope. Was he ready for PT?

Getting back on his feet, Brice grabbed what was left of the cookies and saluted Mitch. "I'm out of here. Tell Grey that Tony Gerard is willing to talk. I'll text him Gerard's number."

Mitch saluted back. "Take care, Hawk!" he said in his imitation of Hope's voice. "Hurry back!"

Brice flipped him the bird once more and hobbled to the door, already planning his revenge. "The next time you take one of my cookies, Robin, Caroline won't have to shoot you. I will."

The sound of Mitch's chuckle followed him out the door.

26

*T*he drapes were gone.

Hope stood on Hawk's—*Brice's*—front walk, her mouth agape, most likely drooling, at the sight of the two front windows, normally cloaked in heavy drapes that had been shoved open. And not just open a little bit. Those bad boys weren't even visible from the street. Access had been granted to streaming sunlight and nosey neighbors.

"Well, good for him," Hope said.

Cliché or not, her heart swelled, just pumped right up in her chest because she knew, without a doubt, he'd done this for her. That he'd made an effort to open his mind to the idea that maybe, just maybe, a little bit of optimism—the bright side—didn't mean naiveté.

Heaven help her she'd fallen for a fucking blogger.

She laughed to herself. Not only the swearing, but the blogger part. So much had changed in a matter of days. The biggest being, for once, she didn't have a plan. Planning, she'd learned, was overrated. Mainly because the life map she'd had a week ago, the White House, falling in love with a man who saw the world as a stunning, exciting place, and yes, the picket fence, had fallen apart in extraordinary fashion.

What she'd wound up with was no job, a paranoid blogger as the man of her dreams and the realization that the world, although beautiful, contained dangers she'd been too stubborn to acknowledge.

Somehow, she liked this new worldview better.

The honest, realistic view that came with Brice. Hopefully naked.

At that, she smiled and decided going inside might be a good idea. Hormona agreed.

Her phone rang, probably Hawk wondering why she was four minutes late because God forbid he should actually look out the windows that were now not completely blocked and let the world see in as easily as he could see out.

He must have recently arrived because he'd phoned her an hour ago, letting her know he was just leaving his meeting with Grey and would meet her at his place so she could drive him to PT. Not that he needed a driver, but she liked the idea of it. The couple-ish part.

Her phone continued to ring and she checked the caller ID. Amy Ripling. Oh, this should be good. She tapped the screen.

"Hello?"

"Hope? It's Amy."

"Hi."

"How are you doing?"

Besides being fired for solving the murder of a Supreme Court Justice, getting kidnapped and almost killed? *Doing just great thanks.* The new Hope, the swearing Hope, begged to let off some sarcasm. No. Some things needed to remain. Her professionalism being one of them. She'd treat Amy respectfully and then she'd go inside and *fuck* her boyfriend blind.

Te-he. Swearing. Who knew?

Giant grin on her face, she glanced up at the window where

Hawk stood peering out at her, head cocked as he obviously tried to ascertain what she found so amusing. He'd better be using that crutch to help him get around. If not, she'd kill him. Men could be so stubborn.

She gestured to the phone at her ear and then held up her finger letting him know she'd be a minute.

"I'm okay, Amy. Thanks."

In the window, Brice nodded, but stayed rooted in his spot. He may have been making strides on Operation Ease Up, the open drapes proved it, but his paranoia would always be part of him and something told her, he'd continue to obsess about her safety.

But this was what men did for women they loved. They watched over them. Kept them safe. Even when standing in front of the house.

I love him.

And this time, it was the real deal, that pure and potent I-will-jump-in-front-of-a-bus-for-him love that she'd always craved and wished for, but somehow seemed just...out...of...her...grasp.

What she'd needed was Hawk. She just hadn't known it. Of course, in true Hope fashion, he proved to be the reverse of what she'd planned. This relationship was actually pretty darned complicated considering their differences. The perky optimist and the brooding pessimist. With that killer combo there'd never be a lack of debating.

But one thing was for sure; this was the real deal. No forcing it or convincing herself that—*yes!*—he was the one. This time, she knew. Down deep, where it counted, she knew.

"I need to talk to you," Amy said in her typical aggressive tone.

At one time, Hope admired Amy's drive and ambition. Her ability to master spin control while manning three phones to keep the networks at bay.

Yep. At one time, Amy had been her hero. Now, after being fired without an opportunity to explain or defend her position, Amy's aggression scraped her skin raw.

Hope glanced back at the window where Brice leaned against the frame, checking his phone. Watching, but not watching and managing to avoid looking like a controlling stalker.

"What is it, Amy?"

"I've spoken to the powers that be. Given all that's gone on, we feel like you should come back to work."

They feel. Fascinating. Once again, no one bothered to ask if she had anything to say or wanted to offer up an opinion.

But they wanted her back.

The road to her dream job would be open again.

If she wanted it.

If she *wanted* it?

A week ago, Hope would have happily waved goodbye to Hawk in that window and high-tailed it back to her office. To her job. The job she once thought made a difference in the world.

She needed to grow up. Pushing press releases wouldn't satisfy her. Sure, it was important work, but she ached for the hunt.

The scoop.

She tilted her head back, warming her face in the morning sunshine. Something she normally wouldn't be able to do this time of day because she'd be at her desk, grinding through a fifteen hour day.

Instead of standing on Hawk's walkway watching him not watch her.

"Amy, I appreciate the call. But I won't be coming back."

"Hope?"

"Yes?"

"Are you okay?"

Hope laughed. "Yes. I'm fine. No head injuries, if that's what you're wondering."

"I guess I'm surprised. I thought you liked it here."

"I did like it there. Until you fired me."

"Oh, hey, Denby, listen—"

"No, Amy. It's okay. I actually understand. It's politics and politics is brutal. I get it."

"I'd really love for you to come back."

Hope tilted her head away from the sun and focused on Brice, still in the window, still fiddling with his phone. After a few seconds, he looked up and pointed at her.

"You okay?" he mouthed.

Baby, I'm great. She gave him a thumbs up and he smiled. Not just any smile though. A fast, ferocious one that transformed him from a brooding, paranoid blogger to the hotness known as Hawk-slash-Brice and Hope's heart swelled again. *I love this man.*

How had she gotten this lucky?

"Amy, I have to go, but thank you for the offer. I do appreciate it. But the truth is, I enjoyed chasing this story. Being out of the office, digging up leads. I'm not meant to be behind a desk writing memos and releases. I'm a journalist. It's what I love. Heck, maybe I'll even be able to finish my grad courses before I'm fifty."

"You're killing me here, Denby."

She continued to watch Brice, who gave up on his phone and shoved it in his back pocket, then leaned against the window frame again. Patiently waiting.

Slowly, she walked toward the door, toward her future.

"Sorry, Amy. It's time for me to move on."

The front door came open just as Hope disconnected. She held up the phone. "That was Amy."

"Your boss Amy?"

"My old boss, yes."

"What did *she* want?"

Loving the protective insolence in his voice, Hope tossed her purse on one of the living room chairs, then dropped onto the sofa. "She offered me my old job back."

He hobbled over to her, nursing the gunshot to his foot. "No shit?"

She nodded. "No shit. I told her I wasn't interested. How's the foot?"

"Huh," he said, as if mildly surprised but not really.

"Are you surprised? I can't tell. And, I will ask again, how's the foot?"

"Please, Hope. You've got the killer instinct of an investigative journalist. You belong writing press releases as much as I belong on reality television. Get a job at one of the networks. You'll be happy doing that. And the foot hurts like a mother fucker. I'm dealing with it."

"I'm sorry you got shot." She waggled a finger at the bandage under the sleeve of his T-shirt. "And that I filleted you."

His mouth tipped up on one side. A wicked sexy half-grin. "Eh. You'll make it up to me, I'm sure."

"That I will. Don't you worry." She rested her head back and sighed. "You're right about my job."

"That had to hurt."

"What?"

"Telling the *blogger* he was right about something."

Ha. Funny man. "Actually, smart ass, it didn't hurt at all. In fact, I'm beginning to wonder if you'll have time for that blog you're so fond of. What with going to work for the Justice Team, you'll be busy."

"Not that busy. Grey said I can do both. But getting back to you, you don't need your old job. You're better than that. There's something else out there for you. You need to find it is all."

Hmmm. Where would she even start? She'd make a list of

contacts at the news outlets. She had plenty of those from her old job. She might have to start as a grunt, but she'd be okay with that. With her skills, she'd move up fast. And after what she and Brice had just accomplished in solving the Chief Justice's murder, something told her she wouldn't be out of a job long.

Heck, she might even wind up working for one of the digital outlets. Wouldn't that be a kick? The woman who hated bloggers basically becoming one.

Becoming one. She opened her mouth, drew a breath. "Oh."

"What?"

She sat forward, raked her hands through her hair, considered her words. Once she said them, they'd be out there. An absolute option. She looked up at him, met his gaze. They worked well together. Very well.

But...

Blogging?

She cleared her throat, prepared for the teasing to come. "I was just thinking it would be a riot—considering my love of bloggers, aside from you, of course—if I went to work for a digital news outlet."

"All the major metro newspapers have digital content now, Hope. There's plenty of opportunities."

Un-huh. "I'm not talking about the metros. I have a proposition for you."

He quirked an eyebrow, blew her a kiss. "Oh, I like the sound of that."

"Later, my love. I'm being serious here."

He casually scanned her body, lingering on her chest. Hawk was a breast man. She'd figured that out early.

Hormona let out a whoop.

"So am I," he said, dropping next to her on the sofa and running his hand over her torso.

She scooted sideways and turned to face him. "Focus here. I have an idea. You may not like it."

"Then why are you ruining a great moment?"

She smiled. "With you being busy with the Justice Team, maybe I could pick up the slack on your blog."

That certainly did the trick. He jerked his head back and drew his eyebrows in tight. "You want to be a *blogger*? You? The Queen of I-Hate-Bloggers."

"We kicked butt on the Turner story. And your blog isn't just any blog. You have credibility. That's what I didn't understand in the beginning. That all bloggers aren't hacks."

"Gee, Hope, thanks."

She tweaked his nose. "You are quite welcome, *Hawk*. Now, what do you say? Want to give me a job?"

"Does it include quickies at lunch?"

She rolled her eyes. Such a man. "Stop it. I think I could be happy working for your blog. It's challenging and energizing. I love the hunt and with the things you report on, I can have that. What do you think?"

He shrugged. "I think if you're motivated, we'd make a great team. And, hey, you could cut your teeth on some big stories. Even if you wind up hating blogging, the Turner thing alone would definitely get you a job at a network."

"Well, look at you all concerned about my future."

"As long as that future includes me, you're damn straight. I want you happy. And not perky, fake happy."

She snorted. "You just like hearing me say mother fucker."

"That's true. It's a twisted turn-on."

She straddled him, ran her hands up the front of his T-shirt and kissed him. Long and slow, enjoying that buzz that came with his hands on her, holding her. Loving her. She pulled back, dropped another quick kiss on him. "Then, my love, you're all mine. In every way. How's that?"

"Sounds like you finally got your plans right, Ms. Denby."

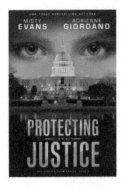

Keep the adventure going!

Thank you for reading *Exposing Justice*. If you'd like more of the Justice Team Series, check out *Protecting Justice*.

As the premier political spin-doctor in the U.S., Fallyn Pasche can fix any problem--except her own. Her twin sister, Heather, a United States Senator, has been murdered, her father is barely speaking to her, and someone is after coded files Heather hid in a private safe. In order to decode the files and figure out what happened to her twin, Fallyn turns to the Justice Team. What she doesn't expect is the sexy bodyguard who shows up needing a little personal fixing of his own.

Tony Gerard sees failure every time he looks in the mirror. The former Supreme Court police officer lives with the knowledge that the Chief Justice—a man who was like a father to him —died on his watch. Now he's sure he can't protect anyone. When his first assignment for the Justice Team lands him in the media spotlight, working side-by-side with the country's foremost political fixer, Tony wants to run the other way. But Fallyn's devil-may-care attitude and tantalizing beauty bring out all of his protective instincts.

As Fallyn and Tony peel back the layers of a government scandal that threatens to bring down the most powerful man in the world, sparks fly along with the intoxicating danger. Desire and passion escalate with their perilous search for the truth as they find relief in each other's arms from their respective demons. When an unexpected enemy puts Fallyn's life on the line, Tony is forced to face his own failures in order to help her conquer hers. But will he once again fail to protect someone he loves?

READY FOR YOUR NEXT JT
ADVENTURE?

o undercover with Tony and Fallyn in *Protecting Justice*

Chapter 1

The place smelled like Heather. Scents of lilac and vanilla. A cheap, but fragrant perfume her sister had loved since high school.

The doorbell rang for the twelfth time mixing with the drone of voices. People, food, a constant barrage of visitors. That's what happened when someone—particularly a United States senator—died. Friends and family gathered.

From her spot at the front window, Fallyn let her father have his moment greeting the newcomers in the foyer. All the while, out on the tiny front lawn, the press fought over a few feet of grass and badgered guests as they approached the front door.

Two hours earlier, Fallyn's plane had landed in DC and she'd gone into fixer mode, giving the press a statement, making sure her father had his meds, dealing with calls from the coroner and finding creative ways to fit the shitstorm of visitors into her sister's 900-squarefoot brownstone.

Jordan Lomax squeezed between Senator Morgan's staffer and a woman Fallyn didn't know. The young woman's Latino features were devoid of makeup, her hair in its normal braid. As Heather's trusted assistant and family friend, Jordan had been the one to find Heather's body. She'd also been the one to organize the casseroles and other food streaming through the door all morning.

"Fallyn," Jordan said, "there's someone who'd like to pay their respects to you personally."

All she wanted was for everyone to leave. To give her a moment to catch her breath and process.

The look on Jordan's face, though, told her it was someone important. Of course it was. Everyone in Washington had known Heather. "I'll be right there."

She took a moment to glance out the window. Damned press. After greeting whoever was looking for her, she'd have to deal with them. Call the cops or figure out some other way to clear them from the lawn. A lot of people in this town owed her favors. She needed to cash in and get rid of the vultures.

Staying close to the wall, she angled around an armchair and spotted a man in a black suit with an earpiece—Secret Service—waiting at the bottom of the steps.

Secret Service meant one thing. The president.

He must have come in the back way.

Taking a steadying breath, Fallyn entered the foyer. President Abraham Nicols was shaking her father's hand, Eric Pasche beaming as the packed house of visitors hovered close, listening in on the president's words.

"She'll be sorely missed," Nicols said to her father. Secret Service formed a circle around them, keeping the visitors at a respectful distance. "Her legacy won't be forgotten."

He'd been one of Heather's biggest fans.

Behind the president stood Ryan, the president's grown son, staring at her over his father's shoulder. His gaze connected with hers and froze for an instant.

She'd been getting looks like that since she'd been here—people struck by her identical appearance to her twin.

Ryan stood tall, broad shoulders filling out his Air Force dress uniform. The medals adorning his chest created an array of colors indicating they had a real-life hero in their presence.

He skirted his father and held out a hand. "You must be Fallyn."

She accepted his handshake and mustered a smile. He didn't know her, but she knew him. His father had asked for a favor concerning him not long ago. "And you're Ryan."

"Home for a few days leave and wanted to pay my respects." His sad smile seemed sincere. "My father thought a lot of your sister. I did too. She was a big supporter of the armed forces and everyone knew it. We're so sorry."

A lump formed in Fallyn's throat, as if she'd swallowed a peach pit, rough, and painful. "Thank you."

A pitiful, useless comment, but what else could he say?

The president moved over to them and reached out to embrace her. She flinched, then realized her faux pas. Abraham Nicols didn't go around offering hugs to just anyone and she'd have to suck it up or risk an embarrassing situation.

Reluctantly, she went into his embrace and gritted her teeth. She hated being touched, and she didn't have *that* kind of relationship with the president. If they'd been out in front of the reporters, she would have known it was nothing but a political move on his part. Knowing him, it still was.

But hugs were part of the process too. Everyone wanted to hug her right now.

"My condolences, Fallyn," Nicols said close to her ear. "Heather was special."

Fallen pushed aside the emotions his words stirred. The guilt. "Yes, she was."

If I'd only come to see her like I promised a hundred times. If I'd only picked up the phone.

The 'if onlys' were pointless, but their hovering presence, like the visitors hanging on every word by President Nicols, was a familiar weight. Fallyn had a lot of 'if onlys' in her past, especially where her identical twin was involved.

She tried to pull back, but Nicols wasn't done. "I'll be at the funeral. Send my office the details."

Jordan saved her, stepping up and offering the president and Ryan a drink. Always the hostess.

The two men begged off, and a moment later, hurried out the front door in a hail of goodbyes, the Secret Service clearing the way through the reporters.

That's what I need. A couple of big, burly guys to clear that lawn.

The media weren't going to be chased off, though. Just like the swamp of people inside Heather's house.

For a moment, Fallyn fought the urge to yell and tell them all to get out. Her heart hurt and her head was pounding. A part of her had been ripped away and she needed a moment—or maybe a billion moments—to figure out where she went from here.

Work the case. Stay focused.

It was her motto when Pasche & Associates' clients went spinning out of control. When you ran an elite consulting firm specializing in crisis management and media relations, every client—from the Bible-thumping politician coming out of the closet to the junkie actor returning to rehab—could make or break you. One wrong move and you could do irreparable damage to their careers, their lives, their families.

Jordan touched her back. "Can I get you something? A soda? Some green tea?"

From the time she was a kid and their mother had left

them, Fallyn had been driven to fix other people's problems. She was good at it, too, the best. Her firm's multi-million dollar net income the past two years and its list of high profile clientele proved that.

Like her sister, power sped through her veins like a steam engine. Fallyn had even taken care of a few private messes the president had gotten caught in, making them disappear.

Talk about being in good with the most powerful man in the world. The paycheck had been sweet, but the fact the prez owed her a favor was even sweeter.

Yes, she was the best fixer in the country. Maybe even the world.

If only I could bring Heather back. "No, thanks, Jordan. I need to make some calls. I'm going upstairs."

Her father's voice cut through the room. "You're working at a time like this?"

Silence fell. All eyes swung her way.

Heather had been his golden child after their mother, Christina, had left him. With Heather gone—Fallyn still couldn't stomach the word *dead*—he'd taken to his bed and dumped all the funeral arrangements and other responsibilities on her. Carl and Jordan had managed to get him up and moving and over to Heather's place by the time Fallyn had arrived, but she hoped she wouldn't have to get him out of bed when the time came to bury his daughter.

"I need to make arrangements with the funeral home, the florist, and the caterer," Fallyn said, giving her father the stink eye. "You're welcome to help."

Dad turned up his nose, brushed past her on his way to the kitchen.

The front door opened—a guest leaving—and Fallyn heard a commotion on the lawn. She strode to the door and peeked out.

A fight had broken out between two of the cameramen.

They traded insults along with fists, falling in a heap on the ground. Fallyn lost sight of them as the crowd closed in, ringside seats.

Oh my God. This is frickin' ridiculous.

Hustling upstairs to Heather's bedroom, she placed a call to an old college friend, Caroline Foster. Recently, Caroline had left her position with the FBI and now worked for Justice "Grey" Greystone.

Greystone ran a secret agency specializing in bringing certain criminals to justice. Specifically to people who thought they were above the law. One of Fallyn's clients had run afoul of Greystone's team last year, and after seeing the evidence on her client—and the confidence in the former FBI profiler's eyes—Fallyn had advised her client to get a lawyer rather than a spin doctor.

"Fallyn," Caroline said after she answered, "I'm so sorry about Heather. What can I do?"

This is what friends—real friends—did. They dropped everything to help. "The press is creating chaos on the lawn. Where do I get decent security guys in this town? Mean ones who aren't afraid to get their feathers ruffled?"

"Give me a few minutes and I'll have the best in the biz on your doorstep."

Had she been in New York, on her home turf, she'd have the situation rectified already. Here in DC things took longer. "Thank you. One more favor."

"Anything."

"Can I borrow your hacker? There are files on my sister's tablet I need help with."

"I'll see what I can do."

"Thank you. I owe you."

Fallyn disconnected, tossed her cell phone on the bed. Heather's bed. The one she'd died in.

Her breath became ragged, her vision tunneling to the intricate pattern of the comforter.

Five hours. It had only been five hours since Heather's body had been discovered.

The thought, mixed with the sensory overload, brought a flood of memories. Some good, a whole lot bad. She glanced around the bedroom. Small, conservatively decorated like the rest of the place, it drew Fallyn in. Her gaze landed on the framed 4x6 photo on her sister's nightstand. Fallyn's knees buckled and she lowered herself to the bed, her eyes still on that damned photo.

The two little girls, cheeks rosy from the heat of a summer day, stared back at her. Back then they were naive and blameless, Heather's curls tangled in the breeze with Fallyn's as they tipped their heads together. Arms around each other's necks, the girls in the picture seemed happy. The best of friends.

Identical twins, yet the two of them couldn't have been more opposite.

Heather was dressed in a cute sundress and matching sandals, Fallyn was barefoot. Her shorts and favorite ragged t-shirt were dirty and stained. In her eyes was the rebel already taking hold.

How could you leave me, sis?

A tear puddled at the corner of her eye and Fallyn brushed it away, setting the photo back on the nightstand. The doorbell downstairs rang again and her father's voice echoed over the din of the crowd downstairs.

I should go to him. Be by his side.

But Eric Pasche didn't want her comfort.

He wanted his favorite daughter back.

Jordan and her father, Carl, were by his side, sentries ready to do battle for him. They'd loved Heather too. Carl, Eric's long-time friend, and Jordan, personally knew everyone coming through the door. While Fallyn had built her career on fixing problems, this was one problem those two were better at.

Early indications were that Heather had suffered a myocardial infarction, but Fallyn's bullshit meter was pegged. What thirty-year-old woman in good health had a heart attack while sleeping? Sure, Heather had put on a few pounds since being elected to the Senate, but she was hardly overweight. She never smoked, rarely drank, and had never had so much as heartburn.

Maybe the stress got to her. Maybe if I'd been more supportive...if I hadn't moved to New York...

The words whispered through Fallyn's thoughts, an endless loop of guilt tormenting her. Her overactive brain circled back to those three little words. *It's my fault.*

She should have known Heather was stressed. Should have known she was on the verge of having a heart attack. They were twins, for God's sake.

Out on the lawn, the muffled sounds of arguing rose to the second floor. *Damn reporters.*

Part of her wanted to go off on the media for acting like children. A part of her—the fixer in her—wanted to walk out and use her skills to turn them into her allies. Give them the story they were chomping at the bit to run on the six o'clock news.

Heather Pasche: The Senate's 'It Girl.'

A strong proponent for women's healthcare and equal pay, Heather had also campaigned strongly for many of the economic issues American males held dear. She worked tirelessly on the Foreign Relations Subcommittee, and before that, the Ethics Committee, squaring off across the table from a couple of Fallyn's most elite clients.

Heather might have only been thirty, but she was going places, making a name for herself in the world of politics. Some said she'd be the first female president if Hillary didn't beat her to the West Wing.

Now, all that was gone. Heather wasn't going anywhere but into a box in the ground.

Enough.

Fallyn hopped off the bed, ran her hands over her forehead. None of this self-pity accomplished anything.

Work the problem. That's what she'd do. Tend to the details and give her sister the send-off she deserved. Starting with her appearance. Heather would want to be buried in something nice.

She strode to the closet, scanned the modest selection of her sister's suits. Dark blue, gunmetal grey, more blue. One black. Several skirts and a bevy of matching slacks. Two-inch heels in the same monotone colors.

How professional.

How boring.

Blouses offered a bit more color. Pink, purple, red. A dozen different white ones. Several black and blue. Fallyn was fingering a red blouse, holding the sleeve up to the gunmetal gray jacket, when she heard movement behind her.

"Thought I'd check on you," Jordan said, filling the closet doorway. She handed Fallyn a cup of tea and the scent of lemon drifted to her nose. "See if you needed help with anything for tonight. You're staying here, right? That's what your dad said."

The woman had been crying again, her red-rimmed eyes and the dark shadows under them a testament to her loyalty and devotion to Heather. While she might have landed the job with Heather because their fathers were friends, Jordan had proven to be a genuine ally.

"I was deciding on a suit," Fallyn said, kicking off her heels and sipping the tea. It was good. Refreshing. Just what she needed right now. "Maybe you can give me some direction. Which one was Heather's favorite?"

"The gray." Jordan reached down and lined Fallyn's

Louboutins up alongside Heather's more conservative footwear. "She loved to wear the red blouse you were just looking at with it."

Well, at least there was something I had right. "I hate these suits. I want to remember her as the kid she was in that picture." Fallyn pointed to the framed photograph next to the bed.

Jordan studied the photograph. "That was her favorite photo. Maybe you should bury her with it."

Why hadn't she thought of that? "You're right. I should."

A soft silence engulfed them as they worked together to lay out Heather's burial clothes. Jordan attached a flag pin Heather always wore to the suit's lapel. Next came jewelry—a bracelet from Nepal, a pair of earrings from Brazil. Her sister had collected jewelry from every country she'd visited. Hose and shoes, and the outfit was complete.

Downstairs, she heard her father laugh. Carl's laughter joined his.

It seemed disrespectful in a way, and yet, Fallyn knew Heather wouldn't want them moping. "How's your dad, Jordan?" Fallyn asked.

"He's not following the doctor's orders to slow down. He retired from State, but ends up 'consulting' all the time."

A text came in on Fallyn's phone from Caroline. Cavalry is on its way. His name is Tony Gerard. You'll like him.

One guy? That was it? The group of reporters outside would eat him alive.

Fallyn pocketed her cell phone and headed for the safe at the back of the closet. She wanted to finish up here and head downstairs for a front row seat when this Tony character arrived. "I was going to ask you about my sister's safe," she said to Jordan. "The funeral home said to bring the insurance papers and I..."

"Need the combination?" Jordan was always finishing her

sentences. Had she done that with Heather too? "Sorry, I don't have it."

"Surprisingly, that is one thing she shared with me. It's not that. When I was going through the items in the safe earlier looking for the insurance policy, I came across a computer tablet."

Fallyn retrieved it from the safe and held it up. "There's a passcode for the files. I tried a bunch of obvious ones, but none of them worked. Do you know it?"

Jordan stared at the tablet, reached out and touched the edge. "Funny, I never saw her use that. Are you sure it's hers?"

She'd asked her dad about it and he'd been clueless as well. "Who else's would it be? It was in her safe."

"It's just, she wasn't big on technology. A total throwback like my dad, but I could take it and try a few ideas with the passcode tonight after Dad goes to bed."

"Nah, don't worry about it. I'll figure something out."

They went downstairs and found the last of the crowd moving out the door. Carl helped Eric put his coat on. "Going to run your dad home," he said. "You need anything, call us."

Jordan reached to hug her and Fallyn automatically stepped back. "We'll talk tomorrow."

If the brush-off offended Jordan, she didn't show it. She knew Fallyn wasn't the touchy-feely type like Heather had been.

The woman stepped back, nodded. "I'd be glad to order the floral arrangements or line up the caterer if you need help."

While it was tempting, Fallyn needed to stay busy, keep her mind occupied. "I appreciate that. I can handle the flowers, but I'm not sure which caterer to use for the gathering at the church after the interment. Are you able to take care of that?"

Jordan's face lit up. "I'm on it. I'll get the one Heather liked."

No wonder Heather had hired Jordan as her assistant. She

glanced between Carl and Jordan. "You two are welcome to ride with us to the funeral and the cemetery, if you like."

Carl nodded, all business. "Of course. Thank you. Let's go Eric. You've had a rough day."

They said their goodbyes, Fallyn accepting a brief hug from her father before the three of them tackled getting past the reporters. She withdrew, after a moment longer than she would have liked, and saw his face, the harsh lines, the sorrow. And now he had to deal with another crowd.

Those damned reporters. What she didn't need was Dad more upset. Time for a diversion. It was, after all, what she'd built her business on—statements that said a whole lot of nothing, but kept the reporters occupied while people slipped away.

"Hang on, Dad. Let me distract the reporters so you can get to the car." Throwing her shoulders back, she marched out the front door, headed down the sidewalk to give the media what they wanted—and maybe the full Fallyn Pasche brow-beating they deserved—when a big guy in a dark trench coat, wearing mirrored aviators and looking like a one-man army, emerged from the alley and every person on the lawn came to attention.

Well, hello, big boy.

Fallyn's pulse did a funny *thudthud* under her skin as she watched him close in on the reporters. A cameraman made a move toward her dad but the hunk in the aviators beelined, blocking his path and sticking his hand over the man's camera lens.

A female reporter next to him was courteously forced back several steps.

Fallyn returned to the house, where she watched, fascinated.

In under a minute, the hunk had every last one of the media backing away, herding them to the curb, several of them running for their news vans as fast as their footsteps would carry them.

Damn. Who was this guy?

After dealing with the press tearing up Senator Pasche's lawn, Tony rang the bell. Grey had called him less than an hour ago, told him to hot-foot it over to the Senator's place and bust up the collection of reporters turning the woman's death into public fodder.

The door opened and a woman answered.

It might as well have been Heather Pasche standing there. He'd known Heather. Not well, but he'd met her a couple of times when she'd interacted with the chief justice, and Tony, being assigned to the chief's protection detail at the time, had accompanied him.

Now, the good senator, as well as the chief, was gone and that same burn, that reminder of his failure, crawled up his throat like acid.

Don't go there.

He bit down, focused on the woman's high heels, her long legs, any goddamn thing that would take his mind off the chief. Any goddamn thing that would keep the panic, the absolute burning from inside out, at bay.

"Hello," she said, waving him in. "If I thought it was appropriate, I'd kiss you for chasing off those reporters."

"Appropriate?" he shot. "Who cares about that?"

He flashed a smile, a rarity these days, and entered the foyer, glancing at the immaculately tidy living room of the late Senator Heather Pasche.

"I'm Fallyn." She held her hand out. "You must be Tony Gerard. Caroline told me you'd be here."

He shook her hand, a brief clasp before letting go.

Her resemblance to her now deceased sister unnerved him. "Uh, Grey wanted me to let you know Teeg is on his way."

"Teeg?"

"Yeah. He's the Justice Team's techie nerd. Grey said something about a tablet you needed help with."

"Oh, that's great. Thank you."

Tony shrugged. "Don't thank me. I'm the messenger. As far as the press, I'll keep an eye on them, but I gave them the spiel about private property and they backed off. The cops at the corner helped."

"There are cops at the corner?"

"As of ten minutes ago, yeah."

Looking at this woman would never be torture. Her deep green eyes had a depth to them. Intense yet bright. Playful. Her light brown hair had lighter streaks and it accentuated her eyes, bringing out the green. Something told him she knew that. Knew that people, men particularly, would be drawn to them.

And the way she stared at him? The scrutiny. Hell, he could see the gears shifting. Like Grey, the Justice Team's leader, she didn't just look at you, she analyzed, mentally peeling back layers and figuring out how to extract what she needed. *Goddamn headshrinker.*

Last thing he needed now was a psychological exam. What she found inside his head would scare the crap out of her. Send her screaming from the fuckup and wondering why Grey even trusted him.

"So you work with Caroline?" she asked.

Small talk. Great. "Um...Sort of."

Three weeks ago Grey had approached him about full-time employment that entailed...well...whatever the hell they did in search of justice. At the time, it'd been a lifeline. A reason to leave the Supreme Court Police because without the chief, the man who'd been a father figure to Tony, the job was torment. Flat out horrendous. A daily bloodbath into the reminders of his failings.

But, of course, Tony's boss at the Court, fearing the resignation had been a rash decision, one born of grief over the loss of the chief justice—ya think?—wouldn't let him quit. Something Tony couldn't rationalize since they should have strung him up for blowing his assignment. His sole job that morning had been to keep the chief safe. Instead, the man bled out on a bridge.

All that crap about it not being Tony's fault? Who believed that?

Definitely not him. He'd lost control of the situation on the bridge, of the *chief*, and now the man was dead.

Period.

His boss though? He'd flat out refused his resignation. Made the argument that the chief's death was too fresh to make such a radical decision.

Instead, they'd reached a compromise. Tony would take his three weeks banked vacation, go to an island, get some rest, get laid, and at the end of that time, if he still wanted to resign, they'd throw him a great going away party.

Except Tony hated the beach and he hated being idle. The getting laid part he could live with. That was a plan he could get behind, but that first night, sitting alone in his apartment, even picking up the phone to call a woman was too much work. Even if female company could fill the void, she'd eventually have to leave and he'd be alone again.

Boredom and his own looping thoughts terrorized him. Sleeping didn't help. Between the dreams and his hyperactive brain, he'd relived the judge's death a thousand times.

By the third day of his vacation, he'd called Grey and damned near begged him for a temporary assignment until he figured out what the hell to do with his life.

And how to stay sane.

Justice Greystone to the rescue.

"Sort of?" Fallyn teased. "You don't sound too sure about that. You work for Mr. Greystone in what capacity?"

Still probing. But Tony had already diverted his eyes away

from her and her analysis. *Nothing doing, lady*. He walked to the window, checked his peeps on the lawn. All good out there.

A cab pulled up and out hopped Teeg, the Justice Team's wunderkind of hackers.

Saved by Geek Boy.

He strode to the door. "Teeg is here. Mind if I let him in?"

"By all means. I'll get the tablet."

Three minutes later, introductions and the uber-polite can-I-get-you-anything formalities were complete and Teeg plugged the tablet into his computer.

"This'll take me a couple minutes," he said.

Fallyn's gaze came back to Tony. *More studying. Great.*

"So, Mr. Gerard, how long have you worked for Grey?"

Yeah. She wasn't gonna give up. He'd have to deal with her straight away. Tony looked back at her, made direct eye contact. "Not long. For the last five years I've been on a protection detail for the Supreme Court."

"You work for Grey *and* you're a bodyguard at the Court?"

Tony shrugged. He hated that term. But hell, if she'd shut up about his life, he'd let her call him anything she liked. "Yes, ma'am. Consider me a contractor for the Justice Team." He smiled. "Moonlighting. Caroline was worried about your...situation." He went back to Teeg who clicked a file, apparently making progress. "What have you got?"

"Not sure."

He typed in a passcode and the lock screen morphed into a background of colors with a set of file folders lined up along the bottom.

"Neat and orderly," Fallyn said. "Just like Heather. Can I take a look?"

Teeg turned the tablet toward her and she scrolled through a couple of folders, brought up two images of what looked like receipts.

Then she hit a folder with multiple files. She clicked one. A spreadsheet with columns appeared.

"I'm not sure what this is." She angled the tablet back to Teeg. "It looks like dates and times, but this other column is a jumbled mess of letters, numbers, and special characters. Almost like passwords."

"Yeah," Teeg said. "But some have spaces in weird intervals, like a list of names, but the groupings don't make sense."

Tony had seen stuff like this. Classified documents. Hell, based on what Grey had told him, Fallyn probably dealt with shit like this on a daily basis. This was a woman who manipulated sensitive information for a living. Made it go her way.

Spin-doctor.

A job she was damned good at, from what he'd been able to find from his phone on the drive over.

She looked over Teeg's shoulder. "You can't figure it out?"

"I can figure out anything, just not in five minutes. The files are all coded with something I haven't seen before and I don't have a legend. It'll take me some time. Couple days maybe." He looked up at her. "I could take it with me."

"No," Fallyn said. "Absolutely not."

In the weeks since Tony had met Teeg, he'd learned a few things. The first being that Teeg had zero interpersonal skills. A nice kid, but there was a reason he sat huddled behind a computer all day. He simply did not want to deal with the bullshit that came with talking to people. Give him a computer, a keyboard, and some action figures and Teeg was a happy guy. Which was no doubt why Teeg swung back to him with that *help-me* stare.

Hell. Teeg wanted no part of this. Tony went back to Fallyn. "Ma'am—"

"Jesus," she said, "will the two of you stop calling me ma'am? I can't stand that."

Tony nodded. "Of course. Sorry. *Ms. Pasche—*"

She held up her hands. "Fallyn. Please."

"Okay. Fallyn, Teeg is good. The best in DC, but we're not talking about the Romper Room of hacking here. This tablet was locked in your sister's safe and my guess is a United States senator doesn't do that unless the device contains classified information. And classified information is hard to decode."

Fallyn rolled her eyes. "I get that. Believe me, I'm not stupid about classified government documents."

And, whoa, sister. What was up with the attitude? Forgive him for trying to be helpful.

Whatever. He'd cut her some slack. He understood the grief and irritability that came with the loss of a loved one. "Never said you were. Just not sure what you expect him to do in ten minutes. Because, no offense, if he could decode a senator's passcoded files that quickly, I want to move to Neverland and drink beer all day. At least there I'll be safe from terrorists who can hack our government's top secret files in three-point-five seconds."

Fallyn's head snapped up and those sharp eyes nearly took him apart. *Eeee-doggies.* Yeah, he'd been rude. Would probably get his butt chewed out for it, but miracle workers they weren't.

"Fine."

The word fine should have been obliterated from the English language. Fine never meant fine and it sure as fuck didn't mean fine right now.

Teeg swiveled his head to Fallyn then to Tony, eyes wide with panic. Clearly, the kid hated conflict.

Tony let out a mental sigh. If they were gonna get this tablet into Teeg's possession, Tony would have to be the one to do it. A job he didn't much mind because he was stubborn enough to wear Fallyn down, to convince her to let them take the tablet.

Unlike Teeg, Tony wasn't afraid of conflict. He, in fact, thrived on it, hungered for it. Fallyn Pasche, he was quickly figuring out, would be a worthy opponent.

He faced her, met her gaze head on. "Fine what?"

"Fine you should move to Neverland because you are not taking this tablet anywhere."

Nice.

She grinned at him and that grin ignited a fire that got his junior brain—the one in his crotch—ready for all kinds of action.

Hello, Fallyn Pasche.

"Oh, crap," Teeg said.

Tony set his hand on the kid's shoulder, gave it a pat. "Take a break. Go have a smoke or something."

"I don't smoke."

"Then go outside and breathe. Give your lungs a treat so Fallyn and I can talk a minute."

The kid stared up at him with some kind of weird hero worship and Tony snorted again. Total pisser, this kid.

Teeg leaped from his chair and headed for the front door, closing it gently behind him. All the while, Fallyn kept her eyes on Tony, still analyzing.

Chess.

The two of them on opposite sides strategically maneuvering, trying to capture the other's king. And anything else that got in their way.

For him, checkmate meant walking out with that tablet.

Damned if it wasn't twisted, but for the first time in five weeks, he got off on the anticipation. The battle.

Time to get to work.

But Fallyn wouldn't be easy. He saw it in her rigid stance. Add to that the sharp curve of her cheekbones in contrast to her full, sexy lips and he might be done for. All that intensity mixed with feminine softness might just knock him to his knees. Again, something she was more than likely acutely aware of.

A burst of adrenalin roared into his brain and he breathed in. Enjoyed the high. Sick. That's what he was.

Oh.

Well.

"Talk to me," he said.

Her head dipped forward. "Talk to you?"

"Yep."

She laughed. "About what?"

"About why you don't trust us to take this tablet."

Grab your copy of *Protecting Justice.*

WANT MORE OF SEXY THRILLERS?

The Justice Team Series

Stealing Justice

Cheating Justice

Holiday Justice

Exposing Justice

Undercover Justice

Protecting Justice

Missing Justice

Defending Justice

SCHOCK SISTERS MYSTERY SERIES

1st Shock

2nd Strike

3rd Tango

MORE BY ADRIENNE GIORDANO

THE ROSE TRUDEAU MYSTERY SERIES

Into The Fire

HARLEQUIN INTRIGUES

The Prosecutor

The Defender

The Marshal

The Detective

The Rebel

JUSTIFIABLE CAUSE SERIES

The Chase

The Evasion

The Capture

CASINO FORTUNA SERIES

Deadly Odds

JUSTICE SERIES w/MISTY EVANS

Stealing Justice

Cheating Justice

Holiday Justice

Exposing Justice

Undercover Justice

Protecting Justice

Missing Justice

Defending Justice

SCHOCK SISTERS MYSTERY SERIES w/MISTY EVANS

1st Shock

2nd Strike

3rd Tango

STEELE RIDGE SERIES w/KELSEY BROWNING & TRACEY DEVLYN

Steele Ridge: The Beginning

Going Hard (Kelsey Browning)

Living Fast (Adrienne Giordano)

Loving Deep (Tracey Devlyn)

Breaking Free (Adrienne Giordano)

Roaming Wild (Tracey Devlyn)

Stripping Bare (Kelsey Browning)

Enduring Love (Browning, Devlyn, Giordano)

Vowing Love (Adrienne Giordano)

STEELE RIDGE SERIES: The Kingstons w/KELSEY BROWNING & TRACEY DEVLYN

Craving HEAT (Adrienne Giordano)

Tasting FIRE (Kelsey Browning)

Searing NEED (Tracey Devlyn)

Striking EDGE (Kelsey Browning)

Burning ACHE (Adrienne Giordano)

MORE BY MISTY EVANS

SEALs of Shadow Force Series

Fatal Truth

Fatal Honor

Fatal Courage

Fatal Love

Fatal Vision

Fatal Thrill

Risk

SEALS of Shadow Force Series: Spy Division

Man Hunt

Man Killer

Man Down

The SCVC Taskforce Series

Deadly Pursuit

Deadly Deception

Deadly Force

Deadly Intent

Deadly Affair, A SCVC Taskforce novella

Deadly Attraction

Defending Justice

SCHOCK SISTERS MYSTERY SERIES w/Adrienne Giordano

1st Shock

2nd Strike

3rd Tango

The Secret Ingredient Culinary Mystery Series

The Secret Ingredient, A Culinary Romantic Mystery with Bonus Recipes

The Secret Life of Cranberry Sauce, A Secret Ingredient Holiday Novella

ACKNOWLEDGMENTS

As usual, there are people to thank. Adrienne would like to thank Misty for always managing to make her laugh and for being an awesome writing partner. Misty thanks Adrienne for being an awesome research guru who comes up with compelling plots and kick-ass heroines who keep the heroes on their toes.

Special thanks to our go-to guys Milton Grasle, John Leach and Scott Silverii who continually respond to our emails and help us navigate the complicated world of law enforcement. Your generosity continues to amaze!

Thank you also to Anthony Iacullo for sharing your legal experience and for helping us sort through our myriad of research. Look out because you are now officially one of our go-to guys.

Without all of you, we wouldn't be able to do what we love. Thank you.

Exposing Justice

Copyright © 2015 Misty Evans and Adrienne Giordano

Excerpt *Undercover Justice* © 2015 Misty Evans and Adrienne Giordano

ISBN-978-1-942504-05-4

Publisher: ALG Publishing, LLC

Cover Art by Fanderclai Design

Formatting by Beach Path Publishing, LLC

Editing by Gina Bernal & Marcie Gately

ABOUT ADRIENNE

 Adrienne Giordano is a *USA Today* best-selling author of over forty romantic suspense and mystery novels. She is a Jersey girl at heart, but now lives in the Midwest with her ultimate supporter of a husband, sports-obsessed son and Elliot, a snuggle-happy rescue. Having grown up near the ocean, Adrienne enjoys paddleboarding, a nice float in a kayak and lounging on the beach with a good book.

For more information on Adrienne's books, please visit www.AdrienneGiordano.com. Adrienne can also be found on Facebook at http://www.facebook.com/AdrienneGiordanoAuthor, Twitter at http://twitter.com/AdriennGiordano and Goodreads at http://www.goodreads.com/AdrienneGiordano.

Don't miss a new release! Sign up for Adrienne's new release newsletter!

ABOUT MISTY

USA TODAY Bestselling Author Misty Evans has published over seventy-five novels and writes romantic suspense, urban fantasy, and paranormal romance. Under her pen name, Nyx Halliwell, she also writes cozy mysteries.

When not reading or writing, she embraces her inner gypsy and loves music, movies, and hanging out with her husband, twin sons, and three spoiled puppies. She's a crafter at heart and has far too many projects to finish.

Don't want to miss a single adventure? Visit www. mistyevansbooks.com to find out ALL the news!

Check out her humorous pen name Nyx Halliwell for magical mysteries https://www.nyxhalliwell.com .

Made in the USA
Columbia, SC
16 July 2024

38722857R00212